Acclaim for Michelle Huneven's

Jamesland

"Offbeat and vigorously written. . . . Engrossing . . . *Jamesland* is a winning place to while away some time."
—*The New York Times Book Review*

"Generosity, humor and tolerance shine in Huneven's writing."
—*Los Angeles Times Book Review*

"A delicate tale of personalities and longing. . . . The real landscape of *Jamesland* is an interior one, the intersection between the tangible and the not-quite-real."   —*The Oregonian*

"A great L.A. novel. . . . One of the goals of the novel since the beginning of the form has been to realistically capture love, that ever-flitting butterfly, in its contemporary incarnation. Huneven is one of our few writers who can deliver an authentic love story, with characters as unlikely for redemption as possible, as failed and weird and hopeless as ourselves. She somehow nudges them into relationships that change the feeling of everything."   —*LA Weekly*

"*Jamesland* is gold. Michelle Huneven gives as good as any reader can hope to get."   —Amy Bloom

"Michelle Huneven's endearingly comic second novel, *James-land* . . . looks steadily at the convoluted relationship between religion and spirituality. . . . She regards her creations with a benevolently comic eye." —*The Columbus Dispatch*

"*Jamesland* is a blessing of a book. Michelle Huneven proves again that forgiveness has a wisdom of its own, and that real joy can grow in the compost of failure and frailties. Huneven's characters embrace each other in all their brokenhearted striving; they renew our buried hope that we all may be loved as life finds us—imperfect, lost, blameworthy, full of good intentions. The compassion in this book is a rare and welcome gift. Gracefully written, shrewd in its observations, precise in its generosity, *Jamesland* is a wonderful book." —Anne Michaels

MICHELLE HUNEVEN

Jamesland

Michelle Huneven received a Whiting Writers' Award in 2002, and she has also won a GE Younger Writers Award in Fiction and a James Beard Award. She is presently a restaurant reviewer for the *LA Weekly*. Her first novel, *Round Rock*, was named a *New York Times* Notable Book and a *Los Angeles Times* Best Book of the Year. She lives in Altadena, California.

ALSO BY MICHELLE HUNEVEN

Round Rock

Jamesland

MICHELLE HUNEVEN

Jamesland

VINTAGE CONTEMPORARIES

VINTAGE BOOKS

A DIVISION OF RANDOM HOUSE, INC.

NEW YORK

FIRST VINTAGE CONTEMPORARIES EDITION, SEPTEMBER 2004

The Library of Congress has cataloged the Knopf edition as follows:
Huneven, Michelle, [date]
Jamesland : a novel / Michelle Huneven.—1st ed.
p. cm.
1. Hollywood (Los Angeles, Calif.)—Fiction. 2. Parent and adult child—Fiction.
3. Failure (Psychology)—Fiction. 4. Divorced men—Fiction. 5. Women clergy—
Fiction. 6. Mistresses—Fiction.
I. Title.
PS3558.U4662J36 2003
813'.54—dc21
2003040070

Vintage ISBN: 0-375-71313-1

Book design by Dorothy S. Baker

www.vintagebooks.com

Printed in the United States of America
10 9 8 7 6 5 4 3 2

People know that love exists, but they do not know what love is.

—EMANUEL SWEDENBORG

Here is the real core of the religious problem: Help! Help!

—WILLIAM JAMES

PROLOGUE

Alice Black woke to the sound of skidding furniture. "Nick?" she called, certain he'd come back. Their evening had ended badly; she'd wept, begged him to stay, and he'd left angry. Now, as sometimes happened, he'd returned, more than a little drunk, to apologize—and leave again. "Nick?" she said, louder. "Is that you?" The reply was a muffled thump: man meets armchair.

"Hold on, baby." She swung out of bed. "I'll get the light."

In the hall, reaching for the dining room switch, she smelled hills—dry, spicy chaparral—along with a wet-dog stink. She stepped back. Normal night noises drifted in: distant traffic, a mockingbird's complicated song. In the faint, chill glow from some outside light she could make out the rosewood table surrounded by its ladder-back chairs, and the venetian glass vase holding pale, blowsy roses. Beyond the table rose a furry shoulder, a long neck and large, pricked ears.

As the word *deer* came to mind, Alice noted the shiny black nose, wide veins rivering the animal's cheek, a lack of antlers. A doe, then. Crescents of light swung in the animal's moist eyes.

Nick must not have shut the front door.

Alice stepped quietly into the room and the deer sprang straight up—it was almost comical how her skinny, knobbed knees with their coin-sized worn spots lifted into view. She twisted as if to reverse direction, knocked framed pictures off the wall and slammed a shoulder into the wainscoting. Chairs toppled. The deer was snorting, a noise part whistle, part shriek.

Her hooves, like tiny cleft plastic slippers, lost purchase on the waxed hardwood, and she sprawled out on the floor.

Alice's heart boomed.

The doe, panting, slowly began to gather herself, leg by leg. Sticking her rump high in the air, she pushed off from her forelegs, stood, took some tentative, tottery steps before her hooves again shot out from under her and she fell with a sickening thump.

Alice sidled along the wall, to get behind and herd her toward the front door. Then, a human noise, a whimper: Alice's great-aunt stood in the kitchen doorway. Without her glasses, in a white gown, with her white hair floating sideways in a tuft, she looked tiny, shrunken, ancient.

"Oh God, Aunt Kate," Alice whispered, startling the deer into another spasm of scrambling. "Go back to bed. I'll handle this."

With new resolve—*somebody* had to take control of the situation—Alice turned and clapped her hands. "Git! Get a move on!"

Without ever getting fully to her feet, the deer managed to flail and scramble into the front room with Alice close behind.

The front door *was* wide open. The deer stopped just shy of it, though, squatting like a large dog.

"No! Out!" Alice kept clapping, but the deer flinched and stayed put; she appeared to be peeing. A puddle, bright as a mirror, slid over the floor; before Alice could step back, the liquid lapped over her bare toes.

She's in labor! Alice thought, and from some bottom drawer of memory came a lexicon of birthing: dogs *whelp*, horses *foal*, deer *fawn*. A fawn, fawned in her house! She'd have to bottle-feed it, walk it. It could sleep on the rug by her bed. Imagine walking down the street, a spindly spotted fawn trotting alongside.

Alice clapped again, lightly this time, nearly catching the spinal ridge of dark fur between the deer's shoulders. The deer shivered, then sprang from her crouch like a great hinge released. With front legs outstretched, she sailed cleanly through the open door. Hooves hit the porch with loud cracks. Another leap and she'd cleared the porch rail, landing soundlessly on the grass.

Alice ran out. From the far side of a rosebush, the deer looked back at her. The large cupped ears flickered this way and that, a lovely form of radar; the nose glistened, as slick and unreal-looking as patent leather. The doe turned, trotted off a few yards, then looked back again and tilted her head, as if to say, *Hey, won't this chase continue?* Behind her rose the great black hump of Griffith Park, the crumbling eastern end of the Santa Monica mountain range, miles of wilderness clear to the sea.

But what about the saturated floorboards, the scattered dining room? Aunt Kate, carved by age to the dimensions of a child, could never clean it up.

Alice went back inside, pulling the door shut behind her. The bolt clacked into place. "She's gone, Aunt Kate. Go back to bed." She grabbed an armload of towels from the linen cabinet, threw them, still fatly folded, on the wet floor, then walked on them until moisture wicked through to her feet. She carried the whole sodden pile to the Whirlpool on the back porch, added a heaping scoop of detergent and chose the longest, hottest cycle. No telling what bacteria seethed in that terry cloth.

In the dining room she righted toppled chairs into tidy rows and rehung pictures on the wall. Taking a quart of brandy from the sideboard, she drank from the bottle: one, two long glugs. Her chest burned and her eyes watered, but how else would she ever get back to sleep?

Once in bed, though, a dark chasm opened between thoughts, and Alice slid right in.

1   THE HAPPY FARM

1

Alice lived in her great-aunt's large bungalow on Wren
Street in a desirable neighborhood known as Los Feliz. A
hundred and fifty years before, one Corporal José Vicente
Feliz was awarded a Spanish land grant for his role in civilizing
the unruly new pueblo of Los Angeles. Rancho Los Feliz—or the
Happy Farm as it was often called—was a small, wealthy fief-
dom with two thousand acres of mountainous wooded terrain
teeming with game, a thousand more acres in flat arable fields
and pastureland, and several miles of riverbed. Corporal Feliz
enjoyed this windfall for eight short years. His savvy widow,
Doña Verdugo, remarried and held on for decades, establishing
legal title to the land once Mexico gained independence from
Spain. Her heirs were less tenacious; several daughters sold their
holdings at a dollar per acre, and the primary heir, Antonio,
bequeathed his major holding to the family lawyer.

Today, the mountainous area is more or less intact as Griffith Park, but the rest of the Happy Farm went the way of most
Southland ranchos: subdivided again and again into residential
home sites.

In 1919, an Arts and Crafts architect built half a dozen
homes in the lower hills of the district. 432 Wren Street was a
four-bedroom, three-bath bungalow set deep in a double lot; its
selling points included river stone and clinker brick masonry,
teak wainscoting sanded to a skinlike smoothness, cedar-lined
closets, large porches—one of them for sleeping—and a two-car

garage. The kitchen was unusually, gloriously large—the architect's mother talked him into this as well as a potting shed and wood-lath greenhouse. 432 sold to a prosperous young couple from Milwaukee, who raised three children there before selling it in 1946 to Alice Black's great-aunt.

When Aunt Kate made her offer on the house, there was consternation at the bank. Here was a single twenty-five-year-old woman from San Francisco intending to live alone in a family-sized residence at a time when there was an acute housing shortage for returning GIs. Thousands of these GIs, in fact, were living with their wives and young children not two miles from Wren Street in tin-roofed Quonset huts in Griffith Park. Still, if the truth be told, few if any of the families could afford the Wren Street house, and Kate Gordon could; she had both an independent income and a teaching position, so ultimately the bank had no good reason to turn her down.

Kate did not live alone for long. No sooner had she filled the rooms with furniture than she drove up to Palo Alto, sprang her older brother Walter from a private sanitarium and brought him south to live with her.

Some years before, in his mid-twenties, newly married and teaching political philosophy at Berkeley, Walter Gordon lost his ability to think clearly or tend to himself in a responsible manner. The diagnosis was dementia praecox. Though his parents tried caring for him, he exhausted them with his wild talk until, in the end, they had to institutionalize him. By the time Kate signed his release, he'd found an outlet for his most insistent energies in gardening and happily transferred his talents to Wren Street, turning the prosaic lawn and barbered shrubbery into a densely wooded private botanical garden.

Except for short stints back at the sanitarium for "stabilization," or when Kate went traveling, Walter lived with his sister for forty years. He remained tractable and pleasant, so long as he took his medication. He was well into his sixties when he started sinking into what Kate called his "hibernations," dozing for days on end in his Barcalounger and rousing himself only as physical needs dictated. When he stopped getting up to go to the bathroom, Kate had to put him in the VA home. Now eighty, Walter had been fully catatonic for years.

Kate herself retired from teaching at seventy-one, determined to finish a book she'd been writing since college, a novel based on the marriage and family life of her grandfather, the psychologist and philosopher William James. Without a job or brother to structure her days, Kate relaxed her personal habits. She ordered in groceries, lived on toast and tea, spent weeks on end in her bathrobe. The day Alice Black arrived at Wren Street, intending to stay for a semester, her great-aunt was napping at her desk amid perilous stacks of books, manuscript pages and jam-daubed, crumb-encrusted plates.

Alice was twenty-nine years old then, and had just shed both job and lover. (Her boyfriend, who was also her boss at the Riverine Ecology Project, had taken up with the other assistant.) Alice first drove to her parents' home in Lime Cove, a small farm town at the foot of the Sierras, where for two days she lay on her narrow childhood bed, surrounded by boxes of old bank statements, and contemplated her next move.

Before the Riverine Ecology Project, Alice had spent several years as a medical technician in doctors' offices, but she'd had enough of bodily fluids. In college, she'd taken a creative writing class and the instructor, after reading her memoir "The Jewish Farmer's Daughter," had declared hers a talent worth developing—though he just might've been unduly impressed that she was distantly related to Henry James, a fact alluded to in the memoir. Or, since Alice ended up sleeping with him, his praise might have been a come-on by someone keen to sleep with a distant relative of the author of *The Golden Bowl*. (Alice was, in fact, the great-great-granddaughter of Henry's brother William.) At any rate, she had thought often of taking another writing course—*non*fiction—on the off chance that a talent did exist. The time, it seemed, was nigh.

She cleaned out her bank account (three hundred dollars and change), added her paltry household goods and microscope to the clutter in her former bedroom, then drove her nine-year-old Toyota Corolla to Los Angeles.

Throughout her childhood, until she went to college, Alice had spent two months each summer with Aunt Kate at the Wren Street house. Her mother, fearing that Alice might become some coarse-mannered rustic, had prevailed upon this favorite aunt to take the girl in hand. Alice had her own suite in the back of the house, which she continued to use throughout her twenties, when she came to town for a biology conference or rock concert or just a weekend visit with Aunt Kate.

This time, however, Aunt Kate, roused from her nap, welcomed her strangely—"Come in, come in. Where's William?"—as if Alice were Alice Gibbens James, wife to their famous ancestor. This lapse was the first of countless, as Aunt Kate was going without sleep for twenty-five or thirty hours at a time. Deep in these binges, she was manic, incoherent and impossible to reach—back there at the turn of the century with the James family. Even when well rested and articulate, she reflexively steered all subjects back to these relatives, many of whom had the same names. Alices, Henrys and Kates were especially plentiful: William James's wife, sister and daughter-in-law were each an Alice, and a sleep-deprived Aunt Kate might address her niece as any one of them—and Alice Black eventually got the hang of knowing which one.

Once settled in her Wren Street bedroom, she enrolled in a ten-week class called "Getting Started in Creative Nonfiction." The instructor, a woman this time, read and admired "The Jewish Farmer's Daughter" and suggested Alice expand it into a book-length manuscript. After numerous attempts, Alice determined that she'd exhausted her interest with the original eight pages. Her class assignments were also praised (as were everyone else's), but writing them had exposed her to a painful shortfall of ideas, the slipperiness of language and tedious, often fruitless hours at a desk: for all that drudgery, she might as well be back in a lab. Moreover, living with Aunt Kate would temper anybody's literary ambitions. Who's to say that Alice herself wouldn't wind up obsessed to the point of madness, and still be unpublished?

Alice did, however, meet a man in the class, Spiro, a stand-up comedian and by far the best writer there. Coming in one night after a date, they found Aunt Kate on the floor of her study, cold and white with shock. She'd fallen asleep in her chair and slid to the floor, breaking both a hip and a leg.

After surgeries, Aunt Kate was sent to the nearby Beverly Manor Rest Home. With her meals and sleeping regimented, her mental state improved; she could surface and converse with much of her preretirement clarity, although all subjects still led to William James *et familias*. The doctor pronounced this mono-mania mild, harmless and to some extent age-appropriate, and said she could go home as soon as she could walk again.

Alice's writing course ended and she didn't sign up for another. "I thought I wanted to quit biology and write," she told Spiro, "but maybe I only wanted to quit biology." She stayed on at Wren Street ostensibly to assist in her aunt's imminent return. Otherwise Alice's plans for the future were vague. She hoped to move in with Spiro, and maybe go for a master's in field biol-ogy—animal behavior or wildlife management, something far from test tubes. In the meantime, being broke, she took a part-time bartending job at the Fountain, a dark, fusty, intermittently hip and increasingly gay cocktail lounge just around the corner from the Beverly Manor.

Four years later, she was still the lone resident at 432 Wren Street and pouring drinks at the Fountain. (Things hadn't worked with Spiro or his successor, a junior college art teacher, but her yearlong affair with Nick Lawton seemed to be reaching a critical juncture.) And Aunt Kate was still at the Beverly Manor, her bones having not knit sufficiently.

Therefore, when Alice awoke one morning and remem-bered seeing both a deer and her great-aunt in the Wren Street dining room, she dismissed it as a dream.

2

Sore in her lower back and shoulders, Alice padded, blinking, into the kitchen, where the many windows revealed the pink sky of sunrise. She took three aspirin, swallowing them with tap water from her cupped hand, put on the kettle, ground coffee, then sat, arms folded on the cool white enamel tabletop.

Last night, Nick had pried her fingers off his arm. Alice, he'd said. You've got to get on with your life. They'd both had too much to drink. They always drank too much these days, thanks to their situation.

The refrigerator hummed, mourning doves cooed. Alice poured boiling water into the coffee filter, the kettle almost too heavy to hold.

Time to move on, he'd said. But he'd said that before.

Alice went outside to get the paper. The morning was cool and clear. Heavy dew dulled the grass. Sparrows flew bush to bush, diving into the leaves. Spring: maybe that's why she'd dreamt about pregnant deer. She slapped the newspaper against her thigh and scanned the lawns and curtained homes and gleaming cars. Chicken-sized ravens convened noisily in the tall date palm across the street. There *were* deer in this neighborhood. She'd *seen* them. Well, twenty-seven or -eight years ago. So never mind about that.

Coming back into the house through the wide oaken door, with light shooting in behind her, Alice noticed long, dull scratches on the hardwood floor. She dropped to her knees, felt the planks and smelled them too, her nose touching the cool wood. Was that vestigial moisture, a faint uric fishiness? That bit of sticky mud mashed against the baseboard, could it possibly be spoor?

In the dining room, the chairs were arranged with military precision—except for one skidded into a corner. And caught in the seam of another chair's back was a tuft of mouse-brown hair. Had the glass over Uncle Walter's baby portrait always been cracked? If the deer was real . . .

She dashed down the hall. "Aunt Kate?" she shouted, rapping on her aunt's bedroom door. "Are you in there?" She turned the knob and the door popped the way doors do when they haven't been opened since a change in weather. The pink candlewick spread was as neat and perfect as a bakery cake. No unexplained dent in the pillow. No lingering spectral traces.

Alice checked the bathroom, Uncle Walter's old room and Aunt Kate's study, where she dialed the desk phone.

Aunt Kate picked up on the first ring. "Who's this?"

"It's me, Alice Black." Alice gave her full name hoping to avoid being addressed as a historical personage. "Are you okay?"

"Oh, Alice," her aunt said. "You're up early. I'm right in the middle of a paragraph. May I call you back?"

"Yes, but real quick." Alice was relieved that her aunt sounded clear and sharp. "I'm just wondering—did you sleep okay last night?"

"If you mean did I sleep well, why yes, I believe I did."

"You didn't go for a drive last night? Or take a walk?"

"A *walk*?" Soft chuckle. "No, dear. I worked until ten, then went to bed."

"No strange dreams?"

"No, dear."

"Because something peculiar happened last night—"

"I'd love to hear all about it, but Alice dear, can it wait?

May I call you back? I simply can't afford to lose this train of thought."

"Sorry," said Alice. "Bye, then."

She drank coffee and tried to read the newspaper but couldn't concentrate. Had a deer really come into the house? Or was she out of her mind?

Alice returned to the dining room and collected the possible deer hair, placing it in a Baggie. Using a butter knife, she shaved the mud or spoor off the baseboard and put it in another Baggie. Both Baggies went into a shoe box. If worst came to worst, she could send these specimens to a lab for identification.

Maybe she'd just lived too long in this house, which was known for harboring and incubating lunatics. But at age thirty-three, wasn't she out of the woods for adult-onset schizophrenia? Uncle Walter was twenty-five when he showed up to play tennis with his sisters with a lacrosse stick instead of a racquet. He insisted on using the stick even after his youngest sister burst into tears and begged him to stop. Several days later, he arrived at a family dinner wearing a kilt and lurching on crutches although nothing was wrong with his legs. At work, he began haranguing his students with confused, apocalyptic messages and paranoid accusations. All this happened very quickly. One day he was fine, ten days later a complete lunatic. He lost his job, of course. His young wife disappeared a few weeks after the diagnosis, and no one ever heard from her again.

Alice set the shoe box of Baggies on the kitchen counter, poured herself a fresh cup of coffee and reopened the newspaper. She still couldn't concentrate. She needed to talk to someone. She used the kitchen phone, a cheap portable model, and called Lime Cove. "Mom?" she said. "It's Alice."

"Alice, what a surprise," Mary Black said. "You're up early! Everything all right?"

"I'm fine," said Alice. "But this weird thing happened last night—nothing bad—it's just that I woke up and found a deer in the house."

"A live deer?"

"Yes." Alice described chasing it out, and how the deer had trouble on the slick floors.

"Any damage?"

"No, I got it out right away. But it shook me up."

"I would think so," Mary said. "Though I'm not really surprised, not with the way you leave doors wide open for all and sundry to wander in."

"The doors weren't open, Mom." Last year, when her mother came to visit, Alice had left the front door ajar for her; the doorbell was broken, and a knock wouldn't carry to the back of the house where Alice was mopping in anticipation of her arrival. This misguided act of hospitality had already come up several times as proof of a general irresponsibility. "It was the middle of the night. The house was locked."

"Deer don't climb in windows, Alice," Mary said. "Well, maybe you'll be more careful after this. I do worry about you in that big old house . . . Oh look, your father just came in! Hi, darling, want to talk to your long-lost daughter? Alice, here's Dad."

A pause, with almost inaudible whispering, as the phone passed hands. "Allie-Oop! Is this your nickel or mine?"

In less than a minute, he'd said good-bye.

Alice picked up the newspaper, only to put it down and peek inside the shoe box. Sometimes the hair resembled deer hair, and sometimes it seemed more vegetal, like brown grass or a dry tuft of papyrus rays. Sometimes all Alice saw when she lifted the lid was a blank, obliterating fear that her life had veered off course, as she'd always suspected it would, and that she no longer could distinguish what was real from what was not, and thus anything—deer in the dining room, an old lady in two places at once—was possible.

Again, she picked up the phone.

Nick would be at work, but she wasn't supposed to call him (not even there!) except in an emergency. Did marauding deer qualify as such? Or was she just using this as an excuse? She regarded the small, cheap phone as if it were a weapon she didn't know how to use. What about adult-onset schizophrenia—was *that* an emergency?

"Cimmaron, shop," a man said. Nick was in back; could she hold? The voice was replaced by an oboe in a Mozart concerto.

Alice lifted a Baggie. It could be hair. Or very fine, supple pine needles.

"Yeah?" Nick.

"It's me."

Vexation twanged in the ensuing silence.

"Look, I'm sorry for calling. But something really bizarre happened, and I need to talk to someone. After you left last night, a deer came into my house."

"A *what*?"

"A deer. Maybe you didn't close the door all the way, because I heard a noise and—"

"Sounds like a bad dream," he said. "Just a sec, okay? Something I need to deal with. Hold on." And the oboe trilled again, reedy and thin.

Nick ran a company that constructed stage sets for television and motion pictures. His office and warehouse were down by the river, and last July he began stopping in the Fountain late at night. Claiming a barstool near the sink, he nursed shots of bourbon with beers back and, when business allowed it, talked to Alice. He was batching it, he said. His wife was off making a movie in Sumatra, of all places, and their six-year-old son was at tennis camp. His wife, it turned out, was famous—even Alice, who rarely went to movies, had heard of her. Jocelyn Nearing tended to be the one good actress in lousy mainstream blockbusters like *Leatherstocking, Red Ships* and *Jack Knife*. Alice was impressed, but Nick said living with a movie star wasn't all it was cracked up to be, what with the loss of privacy, nosy fans and the retinue of parasites—the agents, managers, personal assistants, coaches, beauty consultants—none of whom, Nick said, could tell the truth if their lives depended on it.

Alice supposed Nick was handsome—the Fountain's patrons certainly thought so. He was forty-six and grizzling up nicely, with white streaks in his beard. But his hair was still black; he'd wrinkled mostly in the laugh lines, which gave the impression—false, actually—of chronic good humor and kindliness. His mother was Portuguese, his father came from Oklahoma, which meant a drop of Choctaw or Cherokee, and somewhere in the mix, Nick acquired the pale green eyes of a weimaraner.

Alice was less compelled by his looks than by the fact that he, too, had been born and raised on a farm in the Central Valley. His father raised 'cots and sorghum south of Porterville while hers ran a dairy forty miles to the north. Nick's was a familiar, surefooted masculinity common among men up there who'd grown up working with other men, brothers, fathers, uncles, hands. His youngest brother, Vernon, they calculated, had probably played football with Alice's oldest brother, Garth.

"Every ten years or so," Nick said, "I run into someone who's heard of Porterville. This decade it's you." He asked her out for a drink after work. They drove in his black '73 Ford pickup to a cowboy dance bar in Burbank. Perhaps he thought she'd like the bar and its shit-kicking house band since it was such a throwback to their old neck of the woods, but Alice had quit such haunts as soon as she left home and now abhorred the all-occasion C&W-pop blend. Hearing it evoked only the isolation of growing up in tiny Lime Cove, California, and the misery of public high school in nearby Exeter, where the apex of female accomplishment was graduating *before* you got pregnant.

Nick came home with her that night to Wren Street. She fried him eggs in bacon fat and made milk gravy from the drippings, a trick cadged from the Okies up where they used to live. They drank beer and shots of bourbon. Alice soon was more than a little drunk. Nick, she was certain, was not going to touch her—why bother when your wife's the exquisite Jocelyn Nearing?—so she was reckless and free with the facts of her stalled-out life. She hadn't been out with a man for a year, she told him. Her last boyfriend, a junior college art teacher, dumped her for a nineteen-year-old girl in his elementary design class. Before that was a comedian she proclaimed the most messed-up person she'd ever known, "ferocious yet incredibly thin-skinned." At any rate, Alice confessed, nothing ever lasted between her and a man.

"You just haven't met the right person yet," Nick said.

When Alice went to clear his plate, he slid an arm up around her hips and pulled her onto his lap. Alice was surprised—as she always was surprised whenever any man touched her (though never surprised when they ceased wanting to). Afterward, she couldn't remember what that first kiss was like because at the time she was too busy wondering if Nick had just volunteered for right personhood and trying to decide how she felt about adultery. (Curiously, she felt nothing at all.)

They had a month before his wife came home, and spent most of it in bed. They ate high-fat breakfasts for every meal, drank at all hours and agreed they had no future, which lent their time together a doomed, erotic poignancy.

Jocelyn Nearing was on the airplane when Nick, en route to pick her up, stopped in at Wren Street and made an announcement. "I'm going to divorce Jocelyn," he told Alice, "and marry you."

When the husband of a movie star decides he wants you instead, what can you say? Alice *almost* said, *Hey, what's with the unilateral decision-making?* But she didn't want to challenge and provoke him, in case he was serious.

He left for the airport, and Alice's mind traveled to dark places: what had she done? Knowing the affair had a definite end had made her bold with her affection and sexual enthusiasm. Almost for sport, she'd set out to make him fall in love with her—never for a moment believing she'd succeed. At any rate, he was in love with her now, and Alice felt some guilt and a keen sense of responsibility. How much did she love him, really? Enough to break up his marriage? Maybe. She *was* deeply flattered. Nobody else had ever wanted to marry her, let alone sacrifice a marriage—and such a marriage—to do so.

Nick left Jocelyn Nearing upon her return from Sumatra, and again two months later. Both times, he went back home within days. Jocelyn was in her forties, Nick explained to Alice, and having problems with her career. Before starring in *The Tea Master,* the movie she'd just finished, she'd sat around the house for seven months having phone fights with her manager and weeping. She was presently in such a fragile state that, until her work picked up or she figured out something else to do with her life, a divorce might be too devastating, a kind of last straw. Nick still intended to leave, he assured Alice, it just couldn't happen as soon as he'd hoped. Also, Thad was small for his age and timid in a way that Nick found disturbing. "I can't see how my leaving at this time could help his sense of self."

In all this fueling and crashing of hope, Alice misplaced her own doubts. She thought of Nick nonstop and waited for him to call, to visit, to divorce his wife, endlessly computing the probability of that actually happening.

When they came, Nick's phone calls and visits reassured her and afterward she'd go about life with renewed interest. She'd clean house, start walking again and flossing her teeth; she'd call friends, get out and about, until gradually, as if a spell were wearing off, she sank back into waiting's still, charged state.

She was lucky to see Nick twice a month now, and they argued and split up almost every time. Last night, Nick said there'd already been rumors in the tabloids about his marriage going south. Someone he and Jocelyn knew was selling information to the press. Jocelyn, he said, simply couldn't handle invasive publicity right now—not to mention a split-up. To be safe, he and Alice absolutely shouldn't see each other for a while.

When things blew over, he told Alice, he'd come looking for her. He couldn't say or even guess when that might be. In the meantime, she should get on with her life.

She'd heard it all before, and he always came back in a week or so. Still, for some reason she'd pitched a fit, wept and pleaded with him to stay. He'd had to pry her hand off his arm.

In Alice's ear, the oboe's thinning cry was subsumed by orchestra, and Nick's smooth bass tones came back on the line.

"Sorry to keep you waiting," he said, then lowered his voice. "I can't talk, I have three trucks out back. And I did shut the door." His voice dropped to a whisper. "But now's not a good time, baby. I'll get back to you as soon as I can."

"Okay," she whispered, but he'd already hung up.

Phone in hand, Alice walked out onto the porch, sat in a wobbly Adirondack chair and resisted the REDIAL key. It had been so easy to call Nick and hear his beautiful voice! What had stopped her from calling him before—or doing it again, right now, in ten minutes, or all day long?

Dew, dark with suspended grime, beaded the porch banister. It was still early, not even eight o'clock! A mockingbird lit on a rock, opened and shut his striped wings. Out in the yard, the flower beds were clogged with weeds, the shrubs and hedges shaggy with new growth. All the mature trees required trimming, pruning or surgery. The elderly gardener Aunt Kate hired after Walter left had stopped coming some months ago; Alice had yet to call and find out why. She kept thinking she'd weed and trim herself, but the only time she set foot in the garden was to cut the flowers—the camellias and roses, iris and hyacinths— that bloomed on and on in spite of her neglect.

Alice sat with the phone in hand for forty-five minutes or an hour, although when she checked her watch, only twelve minutes had passed.

She had to get out of the house, away from the phone. In her bedroom, she stripped off her nightgown and looked at herself in the full-length mirror. Her breasts, as ever, seemed too wide. Without being "big" they took up too much room on her chest; they would be small breasts on a larger woman, but on her they merely seemed misappointed, the wrong set. She was five one, and skinny through no effort on her part, although she had to admit, studying her prominent ribs and soft belly, she looked more underfed than glamorously slender. Nick liked her underexercised look. He hated toned, doggedly worked-out women's bodies. Women, he said, should be soft.

Alice had always looked young for her age—five when she was eight, twelve when she was fifteen—and at thirty-three she was still asked for ID in bars. She'd been called cute more often than pretty and never (except by one smitten wannabe boyfriend) beautiful.

Today, her brown eyes were dull, with inflamed rims and swollen lids from last night's weeping. She hadn't cut her shoulder-length straight brown hair in six or seven months, and even when perfectly clean it separated into strings. All told, she looked exactly as she had at twelve, after a temper tantrum. When would she ever look grown up?

Alice rummaged in the laundry basket for shorts, then slipped on her black platform sneakers, the closest thing she had to decent walking shoes. Once out of the house, she started down the driveway at a slow, stiff pace.

3

Pete Ross overslept. When he came into the living room, his mother was already on her knees at the neatly made sofa bed. Knuckles pressed to her forehead, she was conversing with her second husband, Jesus Christ, from whom she was temporarily and amicably separated.

Some widows take up tennis, or volunteer to be museum docents or to hold crack babies down at County Hospital. After her husband died and Pete finished college and moved up north, his mother became a nun. At forty-one, she'd joined a socially progressive order of Carmelites and went to live in their cloister, a six-unit stucco apartment house in Glendale. Aside from missionary trips to Central and South America, she'd lived there for twenty-two years, until a few months ago, when she was granted a leave to move in with Pete.

They shared a modest one-bedroom apartment in Los Feliz. She'd stay, she promised, until he got back on his feet, with a real job, and the courts—and ex-wife Anne—let him see his son again. In the meantime, she attended mass daily, prayed on a fixed schedule and ran a Catholic charity, a food pantry in Glendale. Pete worked at the Bread Basket himself, as his mother's part-time, barely paid assistant—his toehold in the working world.

Not wishing to interrupt her prayers by clattering around the kitchen, Pete left for his walk without coffee. He headed down Los Feliz Boulevard, where traffic was thick and slow, then across the freeway bridge to where homeless John worked the off-ramp with his WHY LIE I WANT A BEER placard. Pete knew John from the Bread Basket and palmed him a buck. Then, slipping through a wide hole in the hurricane fence, he set out along the river.

An extravagant battlement in the war of man versus nature, the Los Angeles River was built fifty years ago by the Army Corps of Engineers. Essentially a huge concrete chute designed to carry water to the sea as swiftly as possible, it had steep banks crudely paved with sand-colored concrete. (The engineer's tombstone, thought Pete, could read: *He paved a river.*) A recent change in Corps policy—inspired by severe budget cuts—now allowed the river to flow year-round, and in these few miles of riverbed by Griffith Park, where there had always been a natural sand bottom, boulders rolled in, islands formed and nature moved home with enviable virulence.

Healthy great oaks and cottonwoods, greening with new leaves, had taken root on midstream islands. Bamboo thickets, reedy grasses and thrashing willows sprang forth with frenzied life. A breeze snaked up the trough from the ocean, and on its currents coasted gulls, snowy egrets, the occasional grouchy cormorant. Mallards, mergansers and diminutive cinnamon teals, finding safe harbor here, had married and reproduced, now swimming in well-matched sets of two.

Atop the barren banks ran a narrow paved road, preferred by bikers, runners and walkers, that lent good peeks into the modest backyards of Atwater and thus yielded clues to Pete's continuing investigation: *How do people live in this world?* Some yards sported lawns as even and neatly edged as wall-to-wall carpet, others had weedy patches of carrots, peas and lettuce, or tidy raised beds, still others were private dumps or wrecking yards. The downside of the high road was canine, all the snarling and barking dogs—pit bulls, Akitas, Rotts and malamutes, favored pets of the poor and disempowered—hurling themselves against flimsy fencing as pedestrians passed by.

Pete, preferring to walk along the water's edge, took a diagonal path down the steep bank. Braking his bulk, he engaged in a brief meditation on the frailty of knees and then, at the thin lip of concrete shore, inhaled the river's fetid breath. The water was green from algae that grew in long, undulating hanks like the hair of countless drowned women. A great blue heron regarded him from a granite boulder. Shopping carts were lodged nose-down in the stream. Along the banks, busted-up sofas would host teenage beerfests and gang conferences until they were dragged to Sherwood Forest, the homeless encampment in the wooded no-man's-land between river and freeway, right across the water from where Pete now stood. No one was stirring at this early hour except for some husky pups gamboling by the water.

Pete had visited Sherwood Forest just yesterday, hosted by Freddy, whom he also knew from the Bread Basket. With waist-length hair and a thick mustache, Freddy was able-bodied, intelligent, and had some college under his belt, but he loathed work so much that the far margins of society appealed to him far more than the lightest yoke. He'd invited Pete over to see how homey the transient camp had become—"should you ever," he added, "consider the river life."

How do people live in this world? In Sherwood Forest, they strung sheet plastic between eucalyptus trees with lengths of purloined clothesline. They slept on burst and filthy mattresses, variously finessing the dearth of linen with fresh ferns and eucalyptus boughs, plastic shopping sacks or newspaper. In these shaded human nests Pete found a primal, soporific allure. Should he keep sinking through life and wind up here, sleep, at least, could be managed, even sweet.

Freddy had offered Pete an outdated box of grape Hi-C, profoundly speckled bananas and a matzo shard—the very goods Pete had handed him at the Bread Basket earlier that day. They'd sat on bent lawn chairs overlooking the water, munching the unleavened bread while puppies tumbled at their feet and the Samoyed bitch scratched fleas with unflagging concentration. "Pretty swank, eh?" said Freddy. "Enjoy it while you can. The city'll come through soon enough, haul everything away." He previously had lived in a large encampment in Griffith Park called the City of Lost Souls. "Now *that* was a great place to live, till the city 'dozed it." The municipal destruction of homeless dwelling places was de rigueur, Freddy claimed, lest taxpayers glimpse the true joys of unfettered existence and promptly revolt.

Pete kept walking south and, just beyond the Hyperion Bridge, saw six Asians—three elderly couples—straggle to the water's edge. One man set down a greasy box and the others gathered around. Pete observed from a respectful distance as the man tipped out an ivory-colored duck.

The duck stepped on its own flat, pancake-sized feet and toppled sideways. Clearly, the creature had never walked before and must have come straight from some poultry company in Chinatown. Pete used to buy live ducks and quail for Trotwood, his former restaurant, from Supreme Poultry on Broadway, and have them butchered on the spot. But such was not this fellow's fate. Slipping on moss-slicked stones, led by some dim ancestral directive, the bird tumbled into the water with a full-body convulsion of unmistakable joy. *Home!* A man could weep at the sight. Indeed, the spectators laughed and softly clapped and bowed to the ecstatic creature, who now tried to crawl up on a rock, slipping back into the water again and again. His benefactors urged him on, and clapped anew when the duck finally achieved his granite perch. Never mind that his clumped yellowed feathers revealed bare pink skin and no trace of insulating down, or that he was shivering madly. Waving and bowing, they climbed up the bank and departed.

Pete moved in for a closer look. The duck, one foot laid squarely over the other, gazed out upon his new life. He faced not only hypothermia, unleashed dogs and coyotes from the park but also Sherwood Forest's enterprising cooks. On the bright side, should he survive, the duck might swim, meet girl ducks, gorge himself on insects, worms and succulent duckweed. *My friend,* Pete thought, *your karma has definitely changed.*

Walking homeward in a whipping breeze, Pete once again came upon homeless John, who was conversing with a woman by the Hyperion Bridge. The woman, small and slim with too skinny limbs, bounced impatiently on her sneakers. John's body mirrored her shifting; subtle as a dancer, he was actually blocking her path. Pete didn't like the look of it. "Hey there, John," he called.

In the woman's blanching face, Pete saw himself as she did: an ally to her accoster, a bigger, fatter threat.

"Hiya, Pete," John said. "I told Suzy here she can walk on my river anytime."

Suzy took a decisive step away and John slid in front of her as she threw Pete another wild glance.

"First, though, she could show some respect and shake my hand." John's smile bore the blandness of pure evil. "C'mon, Suzy. You too high 'n' mighty to shake an old man's hand?"

Though it might have been amusing to further spike the terror in Suzy's face, there was no sense in letting things get out of control. Pete stepped into John's scent field of urine, woodsmoke and alcohol seepage. Hooking arms with the scrawny wino, Pete neatly turned him aside, downstream. John's resistance was brief. One good reason to weigh 260 pounds is that no near-dead river rat would dream of fighting you.

"God, Pete," John whined. "Just having a little fun."

"You don't need that kind of trouble, my friend. Keep on going, now." Pete gave him another buck, and a southward shove.

Pete himself turned north, partly to keep his bulk between the girl and John, ideally to extend comfort and, possibly, reap her gratitude. Lumbering within earshot, he called, "Hey! Suzy! You okay?" At the sound of his voice, she broke into a run and then slipped through a gap in the fence.

By the time he got there, she was half a block away, scampering down the middle of an Atwater avenue. He considered following, to see where she lived, so that someday, with this morning's gallantry long forgotten, she'd come in from the grocery store, toss her purse on the coffee table, and there he'd be, sprawled on her sofa, skimming *Redbook*. "Well, well, well," he'd say. "What took me so long?"

He did not pursue her, however, as he had not asked for and received his mother's permission to do so, that being the prerequisite for all variations of his daily routine.

After his mother left for work, Pete set the timer on the stove for ten minutes and sat down to meditate. A blocky sofa cushion took some weight off his legs, but within thirty seconds his knees were burning, his heart was pounding like a tribal tomtom and spontaneous combustion seemed imminent. What did he expect? He'd only recently begun his exercise routines, and his blood pressure was still sky high, his heart flabby as cheese. Sitting in silence, he was indeed face-to-face with what *is*—or, rather, with what *he* is: a system near its breaking point. His meditation teacher, Helen Harland, had told him to breathe through such anxiety, but he wasn't confident this anxiety was passable. More likely, his body had been waiting for precisely this attention, as if all it wanted was a spectator for its final, lavish explosion. A full half hour of meditation and he'd doubtless be nothing but an oily sheen on the walls, a few flakes of greasy ash.

As instructed, he noted the rush of air through his nostrils, its pressure on the back of his throat, the swelling of his chest and belly. He thought again of Reverend Harland, her excellent posture, her steadiness, the lakelike quietness of her person. She was the pastor at the Unitarian Universalist Church over by the high school, and she volunteered every Friday at the Bread Basket. In return, Pete and his ever so ecumenical mother attended the Wednesday night community services at Helen's church. There, a few weeks ago, she'd suggested meditation and even offered him one-on-one instruction.

His mother, who'd known Helen longer, said that before entering the ministry, she'd been a prison guard, one of the first women employed in all-male facilities. This made a certain kind of sense, given that she was as tall as he was, six one, six two, and he could easily envision the brown uniform and creaky leather boots, the holstered gun. Helen *was* no-nonsense. At the Bread Basket, even with the hoary street schizophrenics, she was sweetly reasonable up to a point, then just as sweetly firm, and always calm as grass. It wasn't force or shame Helen Harland stunned you with, but stillness.

He'd seen her on the street last week holding hands with a good-looking dark-haired man—the scrawny, lean, athletic sort. Pete had seen the boyfriend before, he couldn't recall where—although Trotwood was a good bet. He saw his former customers everywhere, especially in this yuppie-rich neighborhood, and often had to duck out of sight in order to avoid chronicling, yet again, his restaurant's demise and, by inference, his own.

Pain sang in his knees, and now his lower lumbars burned. Pete noticed his breath only because it seemed to grow shallow, inadequate. He breathed deeper, beginning to gulp air, to panic, and then tried yawning to satisfy the lungs. Alerted to the sudden shortage of oxygen, his belabored heart sped up, squelching like feet through mud. When the timer finally sounded, he rolled off the cushion and, with a cheek pasted to the floor, gasped in gratitude for the awful buzzing. Staggering to his feet—pins spraying through his legs—he vowed to ask his mother to drive him to a store that sold proper meditation cushions.

Pete had to ask his mother for everything: for money, for rides, for permission to do anything beyond his carefully formulated daily program. To be fair, the asking was voluntary; he'd wholeheartedly agreed to it, since otherwise he never could've left Woodview on his own recognizance. The eminent Dr. Freeman, his prescribing psychiatrist, along with his mother and probation officer, had concocted this regime of midlife reparenting, to which Pete could accede or not. Given dwindling, capped-off benefits, the pending end of private hospitalization and the looming of ghastly board-'n'-care homes, plus the fact that if left too long to his own devices, he might still fashion a stiletto from a toothbrush, a noose from a T-shirt, he had agreed to this adult version of Mother May I.

He'd hated prying her out of the convent, of course, especially since his birth had waylaid her plans for twenty-some years the first time around. Luckily, hers was a reasonable order. Apparently, under certain circumstances—a son's crack-up, for example—even a nun could take a family leave.

His next stop was the gym. A gay gym, filled with mirrors, but what did he care? It was the only gym within walking distance of the apartment. Guys gazed raptly at their reflections as they ran treadmills, rode the stationary bikes and pumped iron. And there he was, a slag heap of flesh, monument to the fleeting comfort of food, to whom no one—male, female or mixed—would give the hairy eyeball. Pete pedaled to manic house music for thirty minutes, sweating a cataract. He lifted free weights with sissy poundage and did biceps curls with ten-pound dumbbells, three sets of ten, then triceps extensions with five-pounders. He still couldn't lift a weight without thinking of the one that had broken through his ex-wife's computer screen—the crackle, the exquisite gratification, the utter irremediability. Oh, the look on her face! (And the terror in their son's.) Leg curls he performed on the machines, twenty for hamstrings, fifty for quads. As for squats, the bare bar was all he could manage, and even then he had to elevate his heels. A set of ten lunges got him quivering like a great unmolded gelatin. His gut had grown so large in the last six months that it sabotaged his sit-ups, requiring him to spread his knees so wide his balls popped from his shorts for the amused perusal of passersby. For weeks he'd obliviously left pools of sweat on the inclined board until the owner of the gym presented him with a stack of towels and asked ever so politely if Pete might possibly mop up after himself.

The workouts had sparked some improvement, although not so as anybody else could notice. For Pete, the bottom was rising. At least not every oncoming car, or height above twenty feet, or electrical cord and length of nylon rope, presented itself as the solution to all his problems.

4

I told you not to walk along the river," Rosalie said over her shift drink. "Gangs and bums have free rein down there." A tall plump woman in her early sixties, Rosalie wore her dyed black hair in a slumping beehive and made short work of a gin gimlet. "A woman got drowned there a few years back."

"Yeah, but she jumped." Alice was counting the cash in the register's drawer. "I remember, because in her suicide note she said she was lonely."

"Anyhoo, it's not safe." Rosalie pushed her empty glass toward Alice. "And by the way, 'the Voice' called." This is what people at the Fountain called Nick, because of his unmistakable baritone. "He'll call back." Grunting, Rosalie climbed off her stool. "I'm heading out. It's all your'n, killer."

Afternoons were slow, mostly a long-standing, geriatric set of regulars who came in for a snort and drifted off before the after-work contingent started trickling in. This group was mostly gay, with maybe a few old hets at the bar. Alice turned up the sound system then, Jo Stafford, and Fats Waller with his chipper, exultant piano blues. *Give me love, give me love, baby / You got me under your thumb.* The namesake fountain, three tiers of sediment-encrusted fake marble, gushed eternally, lending the bar's recycled air the stale dampness of theme park waterways. After dark, traffic picked up and Alice was grateful for the distraction of pouring drinks and hauling liquor from the storeroom, washing and toweling dry so many glasses that she forgot for minutes at a stretch that Nick had neither called back nor turned up.

At promptly nine o'clock, Monty, the gay therapist from across the street, sat down at the bar. Every night after his last client, he stopped in for a single beer and checked out the men. By that hour, the Fountain had become what Rosalie called a "sweater bar," with an older gay crowd. Monty was small and dark with acne scars and a scraggly goatee, but had no trouble picking up men, an ability he attributed to good listening skills. On nights when he didn't find anyone to chat up, he talked to Alice. As a therapist, he'd specialized in counseling male-to-female transsexuals and Alice never tired of hearing about their transitions, the cross-dressing and hormone therapies and surgeries and coalescing new identities. All of which reminded her how far she'd come from Lime Cove.

Monty, in turn, encouraged Alice's confidences and seemed to relish making snap diagnoses of her friends and family. With alarming certainty, he pronounced Alice's father a narcissist, virtually a textbook case; and her ex-boyfriend Spiro, he said, had a narcissistic wound that was well on its way to becoming full blown, definitive. In fact, Monty declared, narcissism was so rampant in Alice's life, that she should read up on it, starting with something by the psychological theorist Heinz Kohut. At the library, Alice dutifully thumbed through one of Kohut's books, stopping at random to read a case history about a man who wanted to be an artist; he had considerable talent and easily completed his commercial assignments, but he could not generate any work of his own. Alice thought then that Monty had sent her to read about herself. She'd had no trouble working in the lab or writing for her extension class or showing up for jobs, but was still impossibly distant from her true vocation, whatever that might be. Shamed and afraid, she'd slid Heinz Kohut back on the shelf.

"On me." Alice set an Amstel Light before Monty. "I have a question for you." A friend, she explained, had woken up in the middle of the night only to find a coyote inside her house. Then, shooing the coyote out, she saw her brother in the same room. She's pretty sure about the coyote being real, but her brother lives in the Bay Area. "So now she's all freaked out," Alice said, "because she can't tell what was real and what wasn't. Do you think she's schizophrenic?"

"I doubt it." Monty chuckled. "Not unless these episodes occur all the time, and in broad daylight. It just sounds like your friend has some unfinished business with her brother. And she might want to think about what coyotes signify to her."

"So you don't think it's adult-onset schizophrenia?"

"No." Monty poured beer into his glass. "This could be a wake-up call, though, and she should pay attention. It could indicate—"

A group of customers approached the bar, and Alice held up a finger to Monty—*Hold that thought*—but by the time she finished making drinks and taking money, he was exercising his excellent listening skills on a tall blond in a yellow T-shirt. More customers pressed forward, all wanting blended margaritas, and someone pulled the white Steinway upright away from the wall and started belting out torch songs. When Alice next glanced up, Monty and the yellow T-shirt were heading out the door.

Norm, the owner, relieved her at eleven. The parking lot was still half full, the night sky a luminous cobalt, the moon the thinnest fingernail. Alone in her car, Alice realized that Nick hadn't called back as Rosalie said he would—her punishment for calling him at work. What's more, for the first time in her life, she dreaded going home. The Wren Street house had never before frightened her, not even when she was four and her mother first abandoned her there.

Mary Black was seven and a half months pregnant when she and Alice drove down from Lime Cove, ostensibly to visit Mary's mythic favorite aunt. And indeed, Aunt Kate's yard was all flowers and secret paths, lunch was small, crustless tea sandwiches, and her playmate a frisky dachshund. Mary said, "Don't you love it here, Alice?" and she did. Max was just her size, as were the sandwiches, and Aunt Kate was kind even when Alice's ham fell out of her sandwich onto the floor. "Wouldn't you like to stay here with Max?" her mother asked. Yes, Alice had nodded, she very much wanted to stay with Max. And so her mother left. Aunt Kate would later tell how, two days later, Alice came to the breakfast table and announced with chilling adult gravity, "I've made a terrible mistake. I have to go home right now."

Alice did not remember this; instead she recalled a stretch of strangeness in the large, childless house with its dark walls and wood and Oriental carpets, and her skittish, muttering great-uncle. Then, the beautiful housekeeper, Haydee, was there in the mornings, and she let Alice dry the silverware, sweep her own patch of kitchen floor and come along to the market. Aunt Kate emerged at lunch, and in the afternoons took Alice to the zoo or to department store tearooms and, as Alice grew older, museums, libraries and public gardens. They hiked in Griffith Park and rented saddle horses in Toluca Lake, Aunt Kate ever intrepid and tireless. In Santa Monica, she taught Alice how to bodysurf while Uncle Walter stood on the beach exhorting the waves. Evenings, they went to movies or community theater, or read together in the living room.

Alice's girl cousins in San Francisco claimed that Aunt Kate had her heart broken once and would never marry, that Walter was as close as she'd ever get and that Alice was almost like their child. One cousin, during her particularly nasty adolescence, insisted that Alice really *was* the child of this unmentionable union—but was forced to apologize after a nearly hysterical Alice related this theory to her mother. Much as she disliked her role as Aunt Kate's surrogate daughter, which suggested how disposable she was to her own family, Alice never balked at the summer visits and in fact looked forward to her secret places under bushes, the comfortable reading chairs, the surfeit of adult attention.

Alice was nine when Haydee married and moved away. The

new housekeeper came only once a week. In the cool hours while Aunt Kate wrote, Alice read or played with children in the neighborhood or helped her great-uncle in the yard. Uncle Walter had her water the roses and pull snails off strawberries. He gardened from dawn till dusk, then watched television until bedtime, whispering unintelligible commentary. At dinner, he occasionally posed questions: "Alice, do you know when the earth will fall into the sun?" "Alice, can you tell me the difference between nuclear fission and nuclear fusion?" "Kate dear, do you suppose the devil has bones or merely cartilage, like a shark?" Once, wild-eyed, he clutched the table, jolting china and silver, and asked, "Are we going over a cliff?"

Alice visited him at the VA home a month ago, at Aunt Kate's request. Locked in a catatonic curl, he'd grown tiny. The rungs of his spine arched out of his hospital gown like cogs on a gear. His hands were clamped together with such force that bones would have to be broken in order to separate them. His eyes were open and vacant; a direct beam of light could not constrict the pupils. Uncle Walter seemed in no way human, yet Alice knew that the distance between them was the sheerest membrane, a tiny pinch of fate.

Nick's black truck, bustled with toolboxes, was parked a few doors down from the house on Wren Street. Nick himself sat in the cab. Alice pulled into her driveway, walked back and climbed in beside him. "Hey," she said.

His baseball cap was pulled low and she couldn't see his eyes. He handed her a bottle of beer from a six-pack at his feet, took another himself. The white streaks in his beard glowed in the mercury-vapor streetlight.

"Why didn't you wait in the house?" she asked.

"I was thinking that I should give this back to you." He held up the house key she'd given him, already removed from his key chain.

She absorbed a slap of fear. "I don't want that."

"It's not really fair," he said. "I have access to your house, but you don't have access to mine."

An excellent point, Alice thought, but one that was hers, not his, to make. "I'm okay with that."

"I'm not," he said, again holding the key out to her.

Since she wouldn't take it, he placed it on the dashboard and they drank beer in silence until she reached over and gently raised the bill of his cap to see his eyes. His lips twitched and he pulled the bill down. "So what's this about a deer?"

His coldness made her speak quickly. "After you left last night, I woke up and found this deer in the dining room, knocking over chairs . . ." Nick, now facing her, had reared back. "What?" she said.

"You were pretty wrought up last night. And you do sleep-walk."

Last summer, back when they actually spent nights together, she'd dreamt that a dozen guests were in the living room, waiting to be fed. Feeling tremendous pressure to set the table and serve them, she was arranging silverware on what turned out to be the foot of the bed when Nick woke her up.

"This was completely different," Alice said. "A thousand times more real. Setting the table, I knew that was a dream. This, I honestly can't tell—"

Nick slid over and embraced her, as if to stanch her words. The buttons on his denim jacket dug into her cheek. "I love you, Alice," he murmured, "but this is getting to you."

She pulled away. "*What's* getting to me?"

He pointed from her chest to his. "Us."

"A *deer* has nothing to do with *us*," she snapped. "It just wandered into my house. It did. Come on, I'll show you. I have a box with deer hair—"

"No, no." He embraced her again, patting her back. "I don't need proof."

"Don't pat!" She struggled out of the hug. "I hate men who pat."

He let go. "Sorry."

They sat on opposite ends of the bench seat and gazed out at the gentle uphill curve of the street, its high curbs and old-fashioned streetlamps.

Nick spoke in his lowest voice. "My problem is, I love two women, and all I do is drive both of them crazy."

"*What?*" He'd never actually *said* he loved Jocelyn.

"I love you, Alice, far more than you know. But I love Jocelyn too, in a very different way. I thought I could leave her, but our ties run deeper and stronger than I ever imagined . . ."

Ahh, the My-Wife-and-I-Have-Deep-Roots speech.

"It's not even a question of love," he said. "We just have so much history together. I don't expect you to understand . . ."

Alice could sucker-punch him with I've-Been-Wasting-Precious-Childbearing-Years-Waiting-for-You, although this could provoke the Pressuring-Me-Won't-Further-Your-Cause soliloquy. When had soap opera hacks taken charge of all these conversations?

". . . feel such terrible guilt," he was saying. "You've lost so much weight, Alice. And so much of your spark. It's horrifying. I rarely see the happy, exuberant woman I fell in love with."

"Nick!" she yelped. "For crying out loud! I've never been happy! I've never been exuberant!"

He shook his head: no joking matter. "And you were so frantic last night, so upset this morning. It scares me, seeing you like this."

She looked up the street to the ruffled silhouettes of old trees and high hedges in her yard. Deer, Alice thought, would naturally be drawn to such a place.

"We've *got* to stop seeing each other." Nick faced her. "I mean it."

She was suddenly, desperately tired of this conversation, which she only wanted to be over. In an hour or a week, he'd call and say he had to see her; they'd have sex, then break up again. "Okay. Whatever you want, Nick." She held out her hand. "Good-bye."

He looked at her hand.

"Good-bye, Nick." Unable to stop herself, she added, "And good luck."

"Cut it out, Alice."

What was she supposed to do? Weep? Plead? Explode? She'd done all that last night, and to what avail?

She plucked her key off the dashboard. "You're right. Enough is enough. This has got to stop or we'll bore each other to death." In one fluid motion, she opened the door and sprang out of the truck. His expression, when she looked back in at him, was dark and dangerous. She waved through the open window. "See ya."

She strode away, up the sidewalk. As expected, his truck didn't start. Any moment now she'd hear the thud of his feet, and she steeled herself for the abrupt, possibly rough grab of her shoulder and his whispered, low-decibel fury. Nick liked leaving to be his idea. She turned up the driveway, past the front rose bed, the deodar cedar, the banks of iris, then slowed a little so he could catch up. On the porch steps, she allowed herself one surreptitious glance at the street. The truck slid away like a large black fish.

5

In the morning, Alice had a fever and a raw, swollen throat. She got up, made a pot of coffee and went back to bed without drinking any. The soreness crept down her throat, spread to her chest and tightened. She called in sick to the Fountain. Her voice was hoarse and for once Norman expressed no doubt that she was ill.

She brought the answering machine into the bedroom to screen calls. Nick sometimes phoned within twenty-four hours. "It's me," he'd say, and together they'd cross a long, vibrating silence. Meanwhile, her mother called; "Just checking to see if your doors are locked." Her ex-friend Rachel wanted to return a book. "I'll leave it on your porch if you prefer." They'd had a falling-out when Rachel had refused to hear another word about Nick. "I can't engage in your little obsession," she'd said. "It's too toxic." Alice, who'd suffered through all the details of Rachel's love life, felt unfairly rebuked and ceased returning her calls.

The bed faced a large window. The camellias and hydrangeas Uncle Walter once kept trimmed to the sills were now much taller; from her bed, Alice could see only humps of dark green foliage and a band of sky. The window hadn't been washed in years—never in her custodial tenure—and when the sun hit it midmorning, the dusty glass blared with light. Alice rose to pull down the green roll-up shade. In motion, her body felt strangely heavy, unfamiliar, as if she were a different shape altogether—a battered wooden cabinet. She had to sit down and rest in the window seat. The old shades were crackled and creased; with light shining through them in veiny, riverlike patterns, they resembled some luminous, maddening map.

It was almost a relief to be sick, truly sick, too weak to do anything. Back in bed, she drifted in and out of sleep, lingering in a borderline state where Nick seemed comfortably nearby, in the living room, say, or kitchen. When she surfaced enough to recall how he'd returned the key, professed love for his wife and, most wounding, called her skinny, sparkless and unebullient— that is, as dull as she felt—Alice was consumed by ringing panic and weak fury. How did she get this way? That's what she should've asked him. Who kept feeding her false hope? Who said, Hold on, have faith, I'll be there? Who brought up marriage in the first place?

She'd never say any of this, of course. It was part of their pact, that she would take the big chance, commit to him, wait through anything and still be there—and she also would be all right no matter how things turned out. She'd assured him of this, but now realized she'd exaggerated her own capacity for endurance. Some hypothetical woman, perhaps one of those crisp, shrugging Frenchwomen, could've weathered the endless equivocations with *je ne sais quoi;* indeed, such a woman might have expected nothing more. But Alice, caught up in the terrible details and plot twists of their situation, had allowed her whole life to dwindle to this single impoverishing focus.

At three in the afternoon, Rosalie phoned at the end of her shift to ask if Alice needed chicken soup or anything, and she picked up the phone to say no thanks, that if she got hungry there was plenty to eat. The freezer was full of pork chops, sausage patties, biscuits in tubes—Nick's Okie breakfast food. Besides, Alice didn't want her coming over. Rosalie was always trying to get inside the house, which fascinated her. "You live on a lordly estate," she'd say. "You lead a lordly life."

Alice hung up and slid back into a feverish doze, and sometimes it wasn't Nick who was nearby but the deer, circling the house, trying to peer inside.

The sun finally moved past the window and the room settled into a long and deepening dusk. She'd normally be at the Fountain now, boredom pounding like a headache, as she'd grown impervious, lately, to the small talk. Why so glum? her customers asked. Aren't we Little Miss Droopy Drawers today? Cat got your tongue? Monty suggested she exercise, get out and get those endorphins moving—yes, he was a wellspring of suggestion, even for her nameless friend whose unfinished business was with a coyote, and a brother. And what of her own brothers, Alice thought, Garth, Billy and Doug? It had been years since she'd seen any of them. They lived miles away, deep in their marriages and families; even Doug, five years her junior, was married. How had they managed matrimony and children when she hadn't come any closer than a provisional proposal from a still married man?

Anyway, her unfinished business lay elsewhere. No weighty symbolic psychological secret there. She knew which obligations she hadn't met.

The agreement had been simple, no contract required. She could live rent-free at Wren Street if she kept up the place and helped with Aunt Kate. The whole extended family agreed to this, since Alice's presence in the house relieved the others of countless dutiful trips to Los Angeles. She would probably inherit the house anyway, the cousins said. She was always Kate's favorite; Alice's mom had made sure of that, sending her to spend every summer there, thus securing her fortune. Oh, there was some grumbling, as the old house was now worth a true fortune, but nobody else showed up to take the situation in hand, although Alice wouldn't blame them if they did. Look at the yard. And the roof was thinning, the rain gutters were clogged, the toilets ran constantly. Whenever Alice washed dishes, water with unidentifiable black flecks surged into the tub in Uncle Walter's old bath. A fund existed to take care of such problems, and all she had to do was make the calls.

And then there was Aunt Kate. For years Alice had taken Aunt Kate out of the home at least once a week, often two or three times, to plays or movies and restaurants. Like the old days, only now Alice did the driving. All that petered out when Nick showed up.

For a while, Aunt Kate had hinted about new releases or a good thick steak, wondering what plays the kids were putting on over at Oxy.

Nothing good, Alice had said. Neil Simon, her aunt's least favorite playwright. The deplored *Fantasticks*.

But Aunt Kate read the newspaper and had friends and must have known. *Twelfth Night. The School for Wives. The Mikado.*

Alice didn't need to dream about a deer to know that she owed Aunt Kate years of attention.

And then, last year, Alice and her mother decided to collect Aunt Kate's writings, have them edited and printed in a limited edition for her eightieth birthday. *Katherine Gordon: Selected Writing.* Alice had promised to start collecting pages. So far she didn't have page one.

Night passed into day and Alice dozed and woke replaying the last conversation with Nick, which blurred into the near-disastrous run along the river, the dirt-burnished madman with his insinuating grin, intimidating her like some evil mud king. He seemed to know her, to imply that they had an agreement she'd forgotten and betrayed. Deep in her drifting, he held her a hostage wife in some filthy lean-to hidden in the oleander and plumbago along the freeway.

But he'd been superseded by a larger lunatic, who in routing her accoster provided a brief crack in Alice's fate, and she'd somehow had the sense to run. Because no sooner was the first nut deflected than the big one raced after her, bawling her false name into the wind like this was some overheated Greek tragedy.

When had crazies become so horrifying? Wasn't there a time when the mentally ill were more benign? Look at Uncle Walter, gentleman lunatic, and his harmless, helpless friends. Working out in the yard day after day, Walter came to know all the local wanderers. The one childhood Thanksgiving Alice was at her Aunt Kate's, two of his friends were seated at the table: a long bearded character named Bud and a loud plump grand-motherly type named Viv. They talked and laughed, mostly among themselves, saying the same things over and over again, including exclamations over nine-year-old Alice's beauty. Viv also told a story about Bud proposing to her. "And I told him," she brayed, "I wouldn't marry him until he cut off his beard. I said, 'Why, Bud, you look like you live in a Christmas tree. You need to cut that thing off.' And he said he'd rather die. Didn't ya, Bud? You'd rather die!"

Tramps, Alice's father called them. "How was dinner with your aunt and the tramps?" he'd asked over the phone.

The skin over Alice's chest became tender to the touch. When she rolled over, pain sprayed across her back. Taking the phone into her bed, she called the Beverly Manor. "Aunt Kate? It's me, Alice Black . . ."

"Oh, Alice dear. How are you?"

"I'm sick, Aunt Kate. I've got a flu or something, so I prob-ably can't come see you for a few days."

"Not if you're contagious. God knows, they drop dead of bug bites around here."

"Yes, but when I'm better, I'd like for us to go out, to the movies or a play."

A curious silence.

"Aunt Kate?"

"I've been thinking, dear, that you've been sick quite often lately. I find that worrisome. We have to be careful in this family. Somatic complaints have been known to run away with us."

Most previous illnesses had been inventions, Alice not wanting to stray from Nick's attentions. "I have a bad cold, Aunt Kate, that's all."

"That's the problem, dear. The somatisms become real. Never underestimate the mind. Illness, for us, is a complicated issue. Harry and William used their bad backs as a way to get to Europe. With them, it was almost competitive—a case of dueling dorsals."

What next, Henry James's constipation?

"Illness is a Pandora's box, Alice. William's youthful malingering—the European cures, all those hot baths and medical quackery—drained him of vigor to the point where he was dangerously depressed and suicidal for years. I don't want the same thing happening to you. And you know what finally pulled him out of his slump?"

"Getting a job at Harvard," Alice said flatly. "Teaching physiology."

"Exactly! Apparently I repeat myself. But one's life's work is crucial. Teaching freed William from the tyranny of self and set him on his path."

"I'm sure it did." Alice closed her eyes. "I'm sorry, Aunt Kate. I can't talk anymore. I really don't feel well. I'll call you later."

She hung up and began to cry. She truly didn't have the energy to deal with the exemplary Jameses, the perfect, genius Jameses. How often had Alice, in good faith, gone to visit her aunt, only to be addressed as Alice Gibbens, the wife; Alice James, the sister; Alice Runnells, the daughter-in-law? Most often, it was the famous sister, the diarist, lifelong invalid and possible lesbian who died of breast cancer in her forties. She, Alice Black, had been grilled countless times about the arcane treatments for her neurasthenia, her alleged girlfriend, the progression of her fatal tumor. Who could blame her for preferring to wait at home in case her boyfriend called?

Remembering Nick's resolve to stay with his wife, she wept anew, then again for her aunt's defection, again for Nick's. Back and forth, loss to loss. Alice cried until her head was so packed and pressurized, and her chest so sore, that she could barely breathe.

Sunday afternoon, Alice finally forced herself out of bed to heat a can of tomato soup. By dusk there was a loosening in her chest, and she began to cough—hard enough, several times, that she blacked out. Then, coming to after one spell, she felt a new, throbbing pain in her lower back, and a tender rib. *Pneumonia.* The word sounded gloriously optimistic, as utopian as a colony in upstate New York. The austere and lovely community of Pneumonia.

Monday she was still coughing, but miraculously stronger. Tuesday, she got up as usual and drank coffee. A second cup in hand, she walked outside. It was eight in the morning, cool and clear, the last day in March. In her aunt's blue chenille bathrobe and blue furry mules, Alice scuffed slowly down the long drive-way. Popsicle cellophanes, fast food wrappers and all the hand-outs tucked into the front fence had blown around the yard. Bending gingerly, like an ancient woman, she gathered flyers for Thai food, carpet cleaning, yardwork. Another, fluorescent yel-low flyer was from the church around the corner, an announce-ment of a neighborhood interfaith worship service. It might not have snagged Alice's attention but for the drawing at the bottom of the page: Buddha, on a lotus throne, talking to half a dozen tiny deer.

The deer were drawn with a steady line of unvarying thick-ness. Small as they were, Alice could see they had large, intelli-gent, almond-shaped eyes outlined, it seemed, in kohl. Their ears were proportionately as large as rabbits' and their faces, each in profile, bore lively inward smiles. She carried the flyer inside and gazed at it before folding it into a small square and placing it in the shoe box with the putative deer hair and spoor.

6

From her folding chair by the podium, Helen Harland faced twenty-four people in the Family Center of Morton Unitarian Universalist Church. To her right, five tiny Ecuadorians, a woman and four men, were assiduously exercising drums, guitars and panpipes, all of which were small, ill made and, very possibly, toys. The intonation and rhythm were elastic, and she soon felt mildly drunk. Seeing Pete Ross sitting sideways, his big face slack with irony, she giggled and then feared she couldn't stop.

A tall, beige-haired congregant called Francine had come to Helen's office that morning, enthused about these musicians, and offered their services. It would not cost the church a dime, she said, if Helen took up a collection for their cause—saving the rain forest. Francine openly, even gaily, confessed to finding them at the large Episcopal church in Pasadena, as if challenging Helen to have feelings about such errancy. Francine was, of course, free to attend any church she liked, and in fact Helen partly wished she would choose another. But it was also true that, given the general discontent at Morton, Helen wasn't entirely thrilled at the prospect of one of her highest-pledging members slipping over to the Church of the Divinely Dressed.

She hadn't wanted Ecuadorian or any other musicians, but how could one balk when a congregant in good standing actually volunteered to do something? She could've said no, that she did not care for Ecuadorian bands, having heard them all over France last summer, whistling and chuffing to the wee hours in the plaza of every small town until even the briefest scrap of their music evoked only nights of lost sleep. She could also have said that she'd made a solemn promise upon becoming a Unitarian Universalist minister that she would avoid at all costs any service that could double as a skit on *Saturday Night Live*. If Helen had learned anything in her sixteen months at Morton, however, it was to pick her battles. She was not going to lock horns over a panpipe band, least of all with the queenly Francine, who, despite her Episcopalian flirtation, could still be classified as a supporter.

The band's rattling, pounding and whistling continued unabated, interminable. When the song did wind down, it sounded exactly like an LP dragging to a standstill. Applause was scant. As Helen rose to proceed with the service, Francine called out from her seat, "One more?" and the music started up again, the next song indistinguishable from the last.

The entire program was supposed to last an hour, yet twenty minutes had elapsed and Helen had yet to say the opening prayer. Things *would* have to swerve out of control the night her own meditation teacher was going to speak.

This year, her second at Morton, Helen presented the notion of these services to the board as a form of community outreach—something everybody at Morton claimed to want and that Helen had been hired, in part, to facilitate. Her other outreach projects had been met with stubborn indifference: nobody at Morton had the time to bag groceries for the hungry or tutor the underprivileged. But when she suggested an interfaith lecture and discussion series—and more or less promised to do all the work—the board unanimously endorsed it.

Helen had motives, of course: to draw in new members, build up her own constituency and slowly, inexorably dilute Morton's powers that be, namely an executive committee of elderly white men who'd hired her, a woman fresh out of seminary, because they thought—correctly, it would seem—they could push her around. Which they had, her entire first year.

Her sermons, they said, were too religious or, as one man

said, too "woo-woo." Helen talked too much about God and indulged in "navel-gazing." In board meetings, she went "overboard" on goal-setting, mission statements and consensus-building. According to the church president, she was also "too Methodist."

Thank God that Unitarian Universalist ministers had summers off, since Helen otherwise might have resigned, or bludgeoned someone. She went to France with her boyfriend, Lewis, for most of August, and spent the rest of the time at his house in the orange groves east of Ventura on a ranch that served as a work farm for recovering alcoholics. Lewis was one of the administrators, and while he worked she broke up her theological and literary studies with self-help books about anger and, on Lewis's suggestion, Machiavelli, which proved to be the most useful of all. *It is better to be feared than loved . . .*

Now, well into her second year, Helen had expunged much of the woo-woo from her sermons, and stopped asking anybody to volunteer for anything. Around Thanksgiving, she'd launched these midweek services, whose attendance was running better than she'd hoped. Tonight, the two dozen present included two previous guest speakers who'd returned of their own accord, a Rumi scholar and a former state senator. The gay couple from last week was back. And Beth Ross was here with her son, Pete, for the fifth or sixth week in a row.

Beth, a tall and lean woman with short gray hair and a severe expression, was a nun who ran the Bread Basket; Helen had tried to interest church members in volunteering there, if only to learn how a food pantry was run so they might open one at Morton; but so far the only dependable volunteer was Helen herself. Beth, in turn, had allowed her to pin up flyers for the midweek services on the Bread Basket bulletin board. After half a dozen flyers, Beth had asked, "What is this, Helen, some kind of religious sampler?"

"More or less," she'd said. "I'm trying to present options, I guess, for spiritual development."

Beth studied the flyer announcing a cantor's "Singing Prayers" lecture. "You think a taste-test approach works?"

"We'll see."

"But you can't just concoct religion from a little of this, a little of that."

"I agree, of course," Helen said. "But I minister to a tough-minded crowd, a lot of them atheists or agnostics. And yet they come to church—*my* church." Helen patted her chest. "They clearly have religious needs, and it's my job to address them. But if I say 'Jesus' or 'God,' they see homeschooling survivalists stockpiling paper towels and semiautomatics. Yet people need a vocabulary to express themselves religiously, even to experience the world religiously. So *that's* what I hope to provide—a vocabulary to contain and express their religious experience. And all with no God, no Jesus, no holy smoke!"

Beth smiled. "You have your work cut out for you."

"As do you." Helen nodded at the Bread Basket's waiting room. On a bench along the wall, three older black men were chatting. A skinny blond teenager, newborn in arms, tried to distract the wailing toddler at her knee with a filthy stuffed animal. Nearby, a small brown-haired schizophrenic woman chanted, "Fuck off, fuck off, fuck off."

Beth touched her arm. "My son is certainly one of the religiously disenchanted. Maybe I'll bring him by one Wednesday night."

"You have a *son*?" Helen blurted. A nun with a son?

"And a grandson!" She seemed to be enjoying Helen's surprise. "I didn't take orders until I was forty-one. After my husband died, and Pete moved up north."

"And now he's close by?"

"Actually, we're in an apartment together up on Griffith Park Boulevard. He hit a rough patch and needs some help getting back on his feet. You'll meet him. He'll be working here."

Pete turned out to be in his forties, large, dusky and vaguely derelict. Within days of turning up, he'd taken an outdated

donated Macintosh and computerized the food pantry's opera-
tions. There was no doubt about his intelligence, but he was shy
and abrupt and weeks passed before he did anything but
mumble and look away when Helen greeted him.

For some reason—Silverlake's large gay population, perhaps—she at first assumed his difficulties were AIDS-related.
After observing him for a few weeks, however, she wasn't so
sure, and thought he might instead be kicking an addiction—
alcohol or cocaine, most likely. At his mother's suggestion, Pete
started coming to Helen for meditation instruction, and these
brief encounters only made her less certain what, exactly, his
problems were, though he clearly had some. He had no manners
and was a manifold complex of tics and shudders. Physically,
he'd let himself go. His potbelly was reaching gross proportions.
His posture was terrible, his clothes clean yet rumpled. In half a
dozen visits to her office, he never once sat down and instead
paced, asked three or four questions, then fled. Despite his
middle age, he was always as disgusted as a teenager. On
Wednesday nights, he barked a laugh at any false note, be it a
sentimental prayer or faulty theology. Smart and pitiless, he let
nothing get by him. Helen soon found herself directing her
remarks to him, and gauging her success by how well she kept
his derision at bay. He reminded her of prisoners and mental
patients she'd worked with: all that excess mental energy and no
place to put it.

It was Pete's interest in meditation that had inspired her to
invite Perry to speak at this service—although if and when Perry
would get his chance remained to be seen. The panpipe band
careened on, and Pete had twisted so far around on his chair
that he virtually had his back to them. Beside him, Beth sat
stiffly upright, as if to counter her son's bad manners.

Ten more minutes elapsed before the next honks of closure,
and again Francine beat Helen to the punch. "One more song at
the end, okay?" she called. The musicians gathered their instruments and, with much banging, went to a couch at the far end of
the room.

Helen raced through the opening prayer, sent the collection plate around and then invited the assembled to light a candle for a joy or a concern.

Using the gunlike device, one man lit a candle for a friend diagnosed with pancreatic cancer. Bernice Hall lit a candle thanking Helen for holding these services. Carol Ewers, at thirty-five one of Morton's youngest congregants, announced, "Blake and I are going to have a baby," before igniting the wick. "This is for our child."

"Awwww." Pete's drawl, lavish with sarcasm, drew a shocked communal gasp. Beth grabbed his upper arm, just where you'd grab a naughty five-year-old, and whispered sharply. Pete's anger flashed—then, just as quickly, died. He ducked his head in instant, convincing contrition.

Helen swiftly embraced Carol. Since no more candlelighters came forward—who else would brave Pete's contempt?—she introduced the speaker. "Perry Newton has been my meditation teacher for seven years. He studied Buddhism in the Tibetan Nyingma lineage and was one of the first Westerners to complete the traditional three-year, three-month retreat."

Sixtyish, a short, bald and blue-eyed Irishman, Perry thanked Helen and the panpipers, who ignored him. "Twenty years ago, I was a chemical engineer with Union Carbide in India," he began. He was on vacation with his wife in the northern hill country when they visited a monastery near Dharmsala. For a few rupees, they obtained an audience with the lama, who took one look at Perry and said, "I've been waiting many years for you to arrive."

"You can imagine what that does to a person." Perry laughed. "Oh, the ego doth bloom. And bloom."

Only after Perry finished his *second* three-year, three-month retreat did anyone explain that the lama gave the same greeting to every affluent Westerner. "But it was too late," Perry said with a chortle. "I was already a monk."

He then described meditation. "We all do it for moments here and there—waiting for a memory to surface, or trying to remember a word or a dream, or listening for we-know-not-what. The *practice* of meditation enlarges these moments so we can inhabit them and sit in the stillness. The great Catholic philosopher Pascal once said that all the world's ills can be traced to man's inability to sit alone in a room."

Next, he led the group in a five-minute meditation. As Helen dimmed the lights, people uncrossed their legs, sat tall and folded their hands in their laps. The room grew quiet. A chair creaked. From the back, a murmur came from the band. Outside, something large hopped in the ivy. As a minister, Helen yearned for moments like this, to sit silently with others and attend to the great, mysterious pulse of breath.

The murmuring at the back of the room grew louder, and the hollow knock of an instrument case opened Helen's eyes. All five musicians were on their feet. Two of the men were in a shoving standoff and, as the others quickly gathered the equipment, flesh smacked flesh. Helen rose, as did some of the men in the audience, but the other musicians managed to shove the battlers and their instruments outside.

Perry had remained perfectly still, unperturbed, hands in his lap, eyes open. Following his lead, the audience settled down, and Helen tried to quiet her own fury. Finally, the clang of a prayer bowl ended the meditation on a long, pulsing note, and Perry asked people to describe their experiences.

"I fell right asleep!" said an older man.

"After ten seconds, I thought I was going to explode," said pregnant Carol Ewers.

"Exactly! Excellent," said Perry. "These are the two most common hindrances to beginning practitioners. Sleepiness and anxiety." He then asked for questions, and to Helen's surprise and gratification there were quite a few. How often should you meditate? (Daily; since consistency was the meditator's most useful tool.) Had he ever had visions? (Oh—a laugh—he'd seen a little of everything on the pillow.) Was he enlightened? (He had no idea!) When the service had run fifteen minutes past its closing time, Helen stood and nodded to Perry.

"One last question?" he said.

A young woman way in the back raised her hand. "Can you tell me the significance of deer in Buddhism?"

"What's that again?" he said.

The woman was slight, her brown hair pulled back into a ponytail, her face wan, slightly elfin and sweet. "On the flyer for this service, the Buddha is surrounded by deer."

Perry glanced at Helen, who'd never seen the woman before.

"Oh," Helen said. "I did use a drawing of the Buddha talking to deer."

"Of course." Perry bowed. "The first talk the Buddha gave was to five friends who lived in a deer park near Benares. That's when he laid out all the basic teachings of Buddhism—the dharma, as it's called. The Four Noble Truths, the Eightfold Path. I don't have time to go into it now. But symbolically, deer in Buddhism represent listening to the dharma. Does that answer your question?"

The young woman shrugged. "I guess."

"Is there anything else you want to know?"

"That's okay." She looked away.

Perry's answer was so clearly disappointing that Helen made a mental note to find the young woman after the service. She then gave a brief benediction and invited everyone to stay for refreshments.

Francine rushed up before Helen could leave the podium. "I'm absolutely mortified. They promised three songs!"

By the time Helen reassured Francine that the band had provided ample entertainment, the woman who'd asked the question about Buddhism had disappeared.

7

Rosalie lingered at the bar, fidgeting, after Alice came on shift.

"How's it going with the Voice?"

"We broke up."

"So that's why you were sick, eh?"

"No." Alice gathered empty glasses off the bar.

"How long will it last this time?"

"This could be it," Alice said.

"For your sake, I hope it is."

Tears sprang to Alice's eyes, and she turned away. Illness had oversensitized her. She probably shouldn't have come back to work so soon.

As the afternoon wore on, the roar of the blender frightened her. The bass on the sound system contradicted her heartbeat. Cigarette smoke abraded her raw throat.

Monty came in at nine. "How's our friend with the coyote?"

"I don't know," Alice said. "Still mulling it over, I guess."

"She might want to talk to a professional. A counselor or minister."

Alice shook her head. "She's not religious."

"Send her to me. I'm working with a low client load and could use the income. Any chance she could pay full scale?"

"Absolutely not," said Alice.

"Well, darn," Monty said. "But we could work something out."

For the rest of the week, Alice refrained from chatting up lingerers, was often home in bed by eleven and slept fitfully until noon. Coffee had acquired a strange metallic taste, so she drank red zinger tea, highly sweetened, a hummingbird's drink. Messages collected on her machine: Aunt Kate asking for Santayana's *Persons and Places;* a former college roommate ("It's Cara Oliviera! I got a job with the L.A. Zoo! Pachyderms! Call me!"); her mother ("Any more night visitors?"). She ate only Jell-O with red seedless grapes, the dark, trembling substance cool on her throat and childishly sweet, like something well-intentioned aliens might feed their abductees.

She woke around three in the morning—deer time—to enjoy dry, painful hacking, then started worrying about lung cancer and Legionnaires' disease; for four years she'd been working in a bar with secondhand smoke and chemical evaporates from the fountain—and God knows what spores incubated in the bar's antique air filters. What if she *was* dying? When people are told their disease is terminal, she'd heard, the most common response is not terror but relief. In this dullish dusk of her own illness and loss, relief made perfect sense.

Sometimes when she coughed, a mockingbird outside the window sang back, as if they were conducting a conversation. In this bird's song Alice identified the neighborhood noises of a three-tone car alarm, the short piercing bleats of a microwave timer, the caw of ravens who nested in the palms, and swore, too, she heard Aunt Kate's inflection as she had called Uncle Walter in to dinner, her tone rising on the last syllable. Wall-*ter?* Wall-*ter?* But Walter had been gone from Wren Street for seven or eight years. Did mockingbirds live that long? Or did they pass on noises, parent to child, as a senseless, persistent inheritance?

On Monday, Alice woke at eleven. Every inch of her spine was sore, her scalp was unusually tender, and her teeth rang painfully against the lip of a glass. She debated going in to work—after today, she had two days off—then called in sick. Norm was annoyed. If she wanted to keep her job, he said, she had to bring a note from her doctor.

"I love you too," Alice said, then hung up. She took her red zinger to the front porch. The St. Augustine lawn had grown as thick and dense as a mattress. In the deadwood thicket of an ailing mock orange, the mockingbird loosed a medley of cricket noises and alarm-clock buzzers. A woman holding a sheaf of fluorescent pink paper was coming up the driveway. By the time Alice recognized her as the minister from that peculiar service, it was too late to escape.

Going there was such a mistake. She'd expected a chapel, a plush, crepuscular hall of worship, not a sour-smelling cinder-block room lit by fluorescent tubes. The audience was made up of older people and, she recognized with a jolt, the fat weirdo who'd come after her at the river. Then the musicians got into a brawl right behind her seat, their punches spraying her with alcohol-scented sweat and saliva while an old white guru type described meditation as the same thing she'd been doing for days, listening to the breath, which at that point, for her, was like listening to a drain unclog. When Alice had asked her off-the-wall question about the deer, she'd sounded as pathetic as the rest of them. The guru's answer meant exactly nothing to her. So the Buddha preached his first sermon to deer: what was she supposed to make of that?

The minister was now mounting the steps to the porch, extending a pink sheet of paper. "It's *you*!" she said. Her brown eyes were lit and expectant, as if Alice was supposed to *do* something.

But what? Convert on the spot? Bark like a dog? Sprout wings? Oh, take the flyer. She did.

"I saw you at last week's service," the minister said. "I'm so sorry about those god-awful pipers."

"They were all right," Alice said. "A little out of tune, maybe."

"Man alive, I about died. I thought they'd never stop. And

that fight!" The minister hid her face behind the flyers. "It's only my second year of ministry, and I've already had a fistfight!"

"It wasn't your fault," said Alice. "Nobody could blame you for that."

"I wish my executive committee took such a generous point of view." The woman extended her hand. "I'm Helen, by the way. Helen Harland. I'd wanted to talk to you, but you slipped out before I could."

She was tall, six one or two, and big-boned, with heavy, mink-brown hair. Though good-looking, she played it down with khakis, a powder-blue blouse and white cardigan with pearl buttons. Helen dressed, in fact, the way Alice's mother wished *she* would dress: tidy, feminine yet sexually blank. Only Helen might've shopped at JC Penney, while Alice's mother would never go lower than Macy's.

"You asked a very mysterious question," Helen said.

"Pretty stupid."

"Not at all. Did Perry help?"

"I don't know what would." Alice was about to take a sip of tea, but didn't want to be rude. "Would you like some red zinger?"

"Love it," Helen said. "I've been all over the darn neighborhood."

"Have a seat. I'll go get it." Nothing gained by showing off her bad housekeeping to a minister.

However irreligious Alice considered herself, she automatically ascribed special spiritual powers to ministers. She assumed they could look at a person and see things that person didn't know about herself—if she was a good person, say, or owned by darkness.

Alice wished there were cookies to go with the tea. In novels, she recalled, people were always giving ministers something to eat.

And wasn't it odd: Monty told her to talk to a minister, and here was one sitting on her porch.

Helen, having settled into an Adirondack, reached up for her glass. "Cheers!" Down the street, a Weed Eater buzzed like an amplified mosquito. "Your garden's so lovely," she said.

This was not true. Weeds choked the beds. The roses hadn't been pruned, and shriveled, blackened hips hung alongside new bronze growth. The myoporum hedge had shoots twenty to twenty-five feet tall, and the house would soon be completely hidden from the street. "I can't keep up with it," Alice said. "And my gardener's vanished."

"I like a yard all wild and grown up. I've always loved this place, how far back it is, how private, all these trees. I always wondered who lived here."

"Well, me," Alice said.

"Lucky you!"

Alice knew girls like Helen in high school and college, energetic, athletic girls with dazzling smiles and a kind way with everybody, girls annually voted Most Friendly. Helen might be Miss Congeniality, the outsized and ecstatic version.

Alice feigned interest in the flyer. A Sister Elizabeth was speaking next Wednesday. "A Nun's Spiritual Journey." The illustration showed the Virgin of Guadalupe with her heart lifted out, an image seen all over Los Angeles on trucks, the walls of grocery stores, on air scenters swinging from rearview mirrors. Alice never saw it without remembering how Spiro said it looked like a vagina—the wavery ovoid outline, the sheathing robes and flames, the sliced-open chest. "Cool illustration," she said.

"It is good, isn't it? I got it off an old Mexican religious tract." Helen said. "I have more fun designing these little handouts than I do writing my sermons."

"I liked last week's picture too," said Alice. "With the deer."

"That's right!" said Helen. "You asked about it! I'm dying to know why."

"I'm looking into what deer, uh, symbolize."

"For what? Are you a writer? A student?"

"No, no." Alice picked at the loose paint on the chair arm. "A deer came in my house the other night, or I dreamed it did, and this guy I know who's a shrink said that I might want to learn what they symbolize—"

"Hold on." Helen held up her hand like a traffic cop. "A deer came into your house? I'm sorry, but you're going too fast. And please move your hand away from your mouth so I can hear you. Please, start at the beginning, and *take your time.*"

When was the last time anyone faced Alice with such alert, obvious interest? Even Nick's long stare-downs had a tentative, skittish quality, as if he'd bolt at the slightest provocation.

Now that she had a willing ear, Alice's story of the deer unwound like a ball of string rolling down a street. This was the first time she'd been able to tell it all the way through, without interruption, and nothing she said seemed to invite dismay or contradiction. Helen nodded and sometimes narrowed her eyes as if listening to a familiar piano sonata or poem. Yes, she appeared to be saying: yes, to the thrashing deer; yes, to Aunt Kate's impossible presence; yes, to the fluid in the entryway.

Encouraged, Alice gave all but the most lunatic details— she left out the fight with her married boyfriend, her raising-the-fawn fantasy, that the deer had seemed to desire pursuit. Hypnosis, she'd heard, was like this: perfect recall, with no self-incrimination. "My shrink friend," she added, "said I should look into deer symbolism. Then I got your flyer, and it was such a coincidence that I had to check it out."

"And Perry's answer, about the deer park . . . was it helpful?"

"He was nice. But I don't think I need to learn all about Buddhism."

"Did he say that? I thought he said deer symbolize listening."

Was Helen implying she wasn't a good listener? "I listen," she said.

The minister regarded her mildly. "Of course. But maybe the deer symbolize a new *way* of listening. A more spiritual way, perhaps."

Right, and Alice knew exactly what Helen had in mind— open your heart to Jesus Christ, and blah blah blah.

"At any rate," Helen went on, "I appreciate your talking so freely to me."

Embarrassed, Alice took several sips of tea and scratched her ear, though it wasn't itchy. A mourning dove sang the same note over and over again. A dog barked down the street. She would like to be alone now.

"Tell me." Helen, shifting positions, tucked her brown hair behind her ears. "Have you ever seen deer around here before?"

"Not for years," Alice said. "Once, when I was five or six, I came out to get the paper for my aunt and saw a whole herd walking down the street. They stopped to graze on that lawn over there." Alice pointed to a steep shingled roof across the street. "Eight or nine—bucks, does and yearlings. I watched until Aunt Kate called me in. When I told her about it, she laughed and said I'd been dreaming, but later the neighbors said they'd also seen them, and then she believed me."

"And there you have it," Helen said.

"Have what?"

"Proof you can trust your own perceptions! When you think you've seen a deer, you probably have."

"But what about seeing my aunt? She definitely wasn't there. She can barely walk."

"Okay. But just suppose for a second that she *was* there, and she had something to tell you. Any idea what it might be?"

Alice's skin prickled. *Cease and desist with the married men.* Except that Aunt Kate didn't know about Nick. Or the other married *men,* for that matter. The plural was accurate.

"Sure," Alice said. "She'd tell me to call the gardener, for starters."

Helen smiled, obviously waiting for a more serious reply.

"But she wasn't saying anything," Alice said. "She just

needed help. Which she does. I should see her more, take her out. I used to, all the time, but I got lazy."

"Or you needed a break. Caregivers often get burnt out."

I wasn't burnt out. I was obsessed with a married man. "Maybe," Alice said.

"So what else, about deer in general? What comes to mind about them?"

"I don't know." This woman was relentless! Alice picked at the flaking paint. "*The Yearling. Bambi.* But I don't want to turn this into more than it is. Maybe it doesn't mean anything."

"Maybe it doesn't! But you're the only one who can decide that, you know."

"Also, I was coming down with the flu and the next day was sicker than I've ever been. That could've caused a weird dream."

Helen's face clouded with concern. "I thought you looked a bit wan. Let's see." She slid a palm over Alice's forehead. It was such a natural maternal gesture that Alice's eyes filled with tears. "You're warm, all right. Can I get you anything? Aspirin, juice? Do you want to go to the doctor?"

"No, but thanks," said Alice. "I need sleep, is all."

"You're really going through something, aren't you?" Helen felt Alice's forehead again, then stroked the side of her head. This caused an involuntary sob—for which Alice hated herself. "I'm a little emotional," she allowed.

Helen laughed softly. "I can see that!"

"I'm all right." Alice wiped her eyes. "I just need to go back to bed."

Helen promptly picked up her flyers. "I hate to leave you like this." She stood. "But come on Wednesday night. We can talk afterwards."

"Wednesday night?" Alice said.

"The midweek service." Helen lifted the pink sheets for her to see.

Oh right, the nun's story. Alice had always been curious about why any woman would so willingly constrict her life, but she had no intention of going back to that damp, sour room of misfits.

"I'm not really a churchgoer," she said, scrubbing tears away with her palm. "I only came last week to ask about the deer."

"I wouldn't call these services church per se. They're more of a discussion series. Or variety show." Helen gave a short laugh. "A religious variety show. The variety show of religious experience!"

Alice glanced at her sharply. "Why did you say that?"

"'The variety show of religious experience'? Oh, because that last service was such a circus, and I'm making a little joke. There's a book—"

"I know the book," Alice said. "My great-great-grand-father wrote it."

"*The Varieties of Religious Experience*? William James is your great-great-grandfather? You're kidding! It's my favorite book ever. Oh! I hope you didn't mind my little pun . . ." She sat back down in the chair next to Alice.

"I don't care. Actually, I've never even read it."

"Never? Oh my God, let me lend you a copy."

"That's okay. I have one." A first edition, in fact, given to her by Aunt Kate, who had three more firsts and several other handsome editions. *Varieties*, in fact, took up half a shelf in the study, but Alice had never read beyond the opening remarks.

"I was just this morning talking about William James!" Helen said. "One of my best friends is doing postdoc research on him—I can't wait to say I met you! He's collecting James's *posthumous* contributions to psychical research. Did you know that to this day, James appears to more psychics than anyone except Elvis?"

"No." Alice was only mildly surprised. According to Aunt Kate, her famous ancestor had always appealed to nuts.

Helen glanced at her watch, then loosed another laserlike beam of concern at Alice, whose eyes promptly refilled with tears. "Sure you're okay?"

Just go away, Alice thought. She nodded.

"So much to talk about! And I do hate leaving you like this!" Helen checked around, as if for someone else who might help out with Alice, then turned back. "I have to meet my boyfriend in half an hour and get rid of these flyers first, but why don't you come to lunch with us?"

Alice didn't think this boyfriend, whoever he was, would appreciate a surprise guest. And there was no way she'd meet a stranger with her eyes all puffy and red. "No, no. Thank you, though," she whispered.

Helen dug in her sweater pocket, producing first a Kleenex, which she gave to Alice, then a pen and business card. She scribbled on the card and handed it to her. "My home number's on the back. Call me later today and tell me how you're doing. Promise? If I'm not home, leave a message on the machine. Otherwise I'll worry. May I have your number, too?"

Alice hesitated, but didn't want to hurt Helen's feelings, so she duly recited it.

"I know!" Helen plucked her card from Alice's hand. "Here's more deer symbolism for you. I know you're not religious, but do you have a Bible?"

"There's probably one in the house."

"Good, then you might want to look up Psalm Forty-two. I think it's Forty-two. I did a whole paper on it, you'd think I'd remember. Here." She wrote on the card and handed it back. "Sure you're all right?"

"I'll be fine."

8

Helen Harland distributed her remaining flyers with renewed enthusiasm. This was her least favorite, most humbling and grueling chore in her spiritual practice. She had to shove the leaflets into fences and door cracks, as it was illegal to put them in mailboxes. She'd been yelled off of properties, accused of proselytizing and littering. Of course she'd also met many neighbors; for every flyer crumpled in her face, there was a lively chat, a homemade muffin, a new face at the mid-week service.

Since last November, when she'd started leafleting, Helen had wondered about the dark, vaguely Japanese Craftsman bungalow on Wren Street and its large, unkempt yard. Tall pomegranate bushes and trained cypress met over the driveway; beyond this portal, the climate seemed to change, sliding back in time to an old style of gardening, idiosyncratic, with distinctive areas—roses, drifts of flowers, a hill of cactus and succulents, benches tucked in private spots, the whole of it held together by a clever network of stepping-stone paths. Every week Helen passed a battered Toyota to leave a leaflet rolled in the brass handle of the massive oak front door.

That the sole resident of the dark house was Alice, the same young woman who'd shown up at the service and then turned out to be related to William James, seemed a remarkable and energizing convergence, one that suggested, to Helen, she was exactly where she ought to be, after all—in L.A., at Morton, even handing out flyers.

Alice was wearing the same faded sweatshirt and jeans she'd had on the other night. Her feet were bare, her light brown hair straight and fine. At first Helen thought she was around her daughter Rosemary's age, twenty-two; but after a few minutes, she saw beyond the teenage clothing and childlike winsomeness and guessed early thirties. Alice had a harrowed look, perhaps from lack of sleep, or illness, or some kind of spiritual distress—the famous Jamesian despair, perhaps. If so, she might find solace in reading her ancestor's brilliant work. Helen would've been more adamant in recommending this had Alice not seemed testy and defensive, too frightened, clearly, to take any such advice.

Helen stuck a flyer behind a screen door and wondered if anybody else was monitoring Alice Black's frail emotional state. The echoing house and wild yard suggested otherwise, so until it was clear that someone else was at least aware of the situation, Helen gladly would keep a friendly, watchful eye on her. William James had helped Helen through her own spiritual difficulties, and here was an opportunity to return the favor.

She'd first read William James in a required course called "Backgrounds of Contemporary Theology." James came late in the semester, after a long wallow in the mausoleum of white male Christian thought—Calvin, Schleiermacher, Strauss, Feuerbach, Harnack—after which James's humor, intelligence, open mind and lively prose were profound pleasures.

Helen wrote her final paper on the closing chapters of *The Varieties of Religious Experience* and how James's own religious beliefs anticipated such strains of contemporary theology as process theology, panentheism, the Unitarians' interconnected web and interdependency of being. Her professor found the paper brilliant, and Helen resolved to expand it into her doctoral dissertation. Over successive semesters she read more deeply in the James oeuvre—*The Will to Believe, Pragmatism, A Pluralistic Universe,* his first book, *Principles of Psychology*—

and took comfort in the fact that he was a late bloomer. He was forty-eight when he published *Principles*, the manuscript delivered twelve years late to the publishers.

For her dissertation adviser, Helen chose an older woman, a respected, widely published church historian. When Helen described her idea, the adviser's expression became half smile, half cringe.

"I don't mean to discourage you," she said, "I adore James myself, and every semester I have several students utterly enthralled by him—especially, uh, women of a certain age. There's something seductive in all that charm and picturesque language, I imagine. But you should know that more academic papers, dissertations and books have been written about William James than any other American philosopher." She let this sink in. "Still, if you want to add to this deluge, well, I won't stand in your way."

This conversation shamed Helen into abandoning her plan, not because she thought less of James or his work, but because of her own deluded assumptions. She thought she'd discovered his contemporary relevance only to find out that she was yet another starstruck reader who'd fallen like a wallflower for the most popular guy in the pantheon.

The Vanities of Religious Experience.

Helen wrote her dissertation on Buddhism in America from 1950 to 1970, and in the years it took to finish her degree she spotted many of the James fans her dissertation adviser described: middle-aged women toting their dog-eared, underlined copies of *Varieties* like talismans. And then there was her good friend Foster Allbright, who wrote his dissertation on James and Alfred North Whitehead (later revised into a book entitled *The Multitudinous God*). Foster was the one now doing postdoc work in Claremont on James's alleged involvement in psychical activity, where, even as an apparition, he was hogging the limelight—or the twilight, as the case may be.

She arrived home to find Lewis making coffee in the parsonage's small kitchen. "Hi, Hell's Bells," he said, and gave her a good squeeze and a few friendly kisses. He had a wiry body and a reassuringly tight grip.

She nosed his ear, and his curly dark graying hair. "You'll never guess who I met today." She sat on a folding chair at the kitchen table and watched Lewis pour water into the coffee-maker. "The great-great-granddaughter of William James."

"No kidding. And what's she like?"

"Depressed, of course!" Helen cried. "What would you expect?"

"Is she fanning the flames, keeping the legacy alive?"

"Hardly. She's never even read *The Varieties of Religious Experience*."

"Even I've read *The Varieties*."

"You've read everything."

"And flattery will get you everywhere." Lewis, sitting, grabbed her leg and lifted it onto his lap, then slipped off her loafer and sock to massage her foot.

They'd met three years ago, when she was doing her clinical pastoral fieldwork at a detox center in Ventura County. He worked at a nearby halfway house, where her detoxed clients often were sent. Although he mainly worked with drunks, Lewis had a Ph.D. in comparative literature and was fluent in French and Russian. He taught a class or two every semester at a nearby Jesuit college or a junior college in Ventura. Helen, he said, was the first woman he could read with, and many of their dates that first year were spent reading side by side, Helen cramming for her orals and Lewis preparing a course in the contemporary French novel.

She offered up her other foot. "Are you hungry? I found a good Peruvian place in Glendale."

"After coffee." Lewis peered at the coffeemaker. "You

know, *The Varieties* had a huge influence on the founder of Alcoholics Anonymous. A lot of James's ideas helped him formulate the Twelve Steps. James came up with the idea that a relationship with a higher power, however you conceive of it, is the basis of self-regeneration."

"I didn't know that," Helen said.

"Yeah, and he showed that people can have all different kinds of spiritual awakenings, not just the blinding-light, God-of-the-preachers kind. Like the gradual, educational variety of religious experience. So there's hope for everyone, even without lightning bolts from Jehovah."

She wiggled her toes into his ribs. "And how would you classify your spiritual awakening?"

"Mine? The remedial, slow-learner variety."

"I find that hard to believe, Dr. Fletcher."

"Although maybe it was the caffeine-induced, ninety-nine-nights-of-insomnia variety. Though to tell the truth, if I've had any kind of spiritual awakening, it was so gradual as to be imperceptible." He pulled on each of her toes, making the knuckles pop. "And you? Oh I know. You had that dunk in the pleroma."

"Yeah, my 'glimpse,'" Helen said. A few years ago, while meditating, everything seemed to fall away, and for about forty minutes she grasped emptiness and the illusory nature of existence—except she hadn't found emptiness particularly empty. "That's what Perry called it, anyway. A glimpse. The glimpsing variety of religious experience."

"I hear a sermon in the making," Lewis said.

"Yeah, but for Morton we'd need the *Masterpiece Theatre* variety."

He lifted her foot off his lap and stood. "Cuppa joe?"

"No thanks." Helen got the hint: he didn't want her to start in on Morton, and she didn't blame him. He'd heard it all before, dozens of times, and had given his support and advice whenever she asked for it. For the last year, his advice was unwavering: Fuck 'em, just quit. She'd had to explain, over and over, that walking out of a three-year contract would damage her chances of getting another job in the denomination. So what? was Lewis's response. He wanted her to be a chaplain at his drunk farm, but she hadn't spent six years at seminary racking up forty thousand dollars in school loans to minister to the newly dried-out at some remote all-male facility. No, she wanted a congregation of all kinds of people, of all ages, especially children: a growing, healthy, active-in-the-community church.

"So how was the drive down?" she asked.

"Gorgeous." Lewis, coffee in hand, began pacing from one side of the kitchen to the other. "Snow on the Santa Susanas. No traffic."

Helen was used to Lewis's pacing, a habit that indicated neither boredom nor impatience, only energy turned pedestrian. It began, he said, after he stopped drinking six or seven years ago, when the movement helped him relax. Now, every time he drank coffee, morning or night, he paced. Ever since they were first getting to know each other, Lewis put in a good stint of pacing right before bed—he'd be drinking decaf, roaming back and forth in his small kitchen, talking and gesticulating happily to a seated Helen. This was so often a prelude to their lovemaking that Helen's desire, thus trained, now stirred. "How big a hurry," she said, reaching for his hand, "is lunch?"

9

Alice cut the yellow freesia and violet, yellow-throated iris that flaunted her neglect by reappearing every year. She wrapped the stems in a wet paper towel and aluminum foil and, holding them offhand, like a distracted suitor, walked the nine blocks to the Beverly Manor Rest Home. "Hey, Dora," she said to a terribly ancient woman in a wheelchair just inside the glass doors.

"Please help," Dora said. "I need twenty-five cents for the bus. I'm going home and starting over again." She deposited Alice's coin in a red plastic coin purse. Other residents liked to snatch Dora's purse and steal her quarters for the snack machine. Luckily, Dora had no short-term memory and was only briefly, if ever, upset by the thefts.

Alice walked past the line of wheelchairs. "Hi, Bibi," she said to a round-shouldered, big-armed woman working an acrostic. "Hi, Mrs. Spawler," to the near skeleton tied to her chair. "Hello, hello," to other near skeletons she didn't know. "Angie, are you okay?" Tiny Angie, too, was tied to her chair—a new development since Alice's last visit—and she didn't respond at all.

Aunt Kate lived behind the courtyard in a separate building, where residents ate in a common dining hall and required less care than those out front. She had a private room and bath, and her windows, were she ever to open the curtains, would give a view onto a hillside of yucca and eucalyptus. Except for the chrome hospital bed, all the furnishings had come from Wren

Street: a green velvet overstuffed reading chair and ottoman; the rattan desk she'd shipped back from India, her favorite Chinese carpet, midnight blue with bug-eyed orange and white koi, which was far too large and hence was partially rolled up against one wall. Her yellowed chintz curtains' vine-ivy pattern gave the room a dense, green insularity. Two small mahogany bookcases were filled with the complete works of William and Henry James as well as letter collections, biographies and critical studies of the family. A cabinet contained countless files dated from 1962 to 1992, the year Aunt Kate retired, all of which held versions of Chapter One.

Alice's aunt was at her desk, books open all around her. Her hair was white and waved back, her blue eyes fogged by cataracts.

"Aunt Kate?" said Alice.

She peered over her reading glasses. "Who's there?"

"It's me, Alice."

"Ah, Alice," she said, rotating in her chair. Her aunt always had been an elegant, stern, almost mannish woman, and still had a commanding presence—even at her most confused, which Alice saw immediately was her condition today. "I've been meaning to ask you, Alice. Every time you had a child, William absconded. Was that something the two of you agreed upon?"

Alice had been mistaken, she knew, for William's wife, Alice Gibbens. "I'm not that Alice," she said, wanting to add, *And not that fat.*

"Because it almost looks as if he were jealous of the infants." She nodded to William's portrait in its sterling frame, a bearded, balding profile that emphasized the impressive forehead and outstanding cranial capacity. "He did refer to little Harry's birth as 'our domestic catastrophe,' which like all jokes must've contained a dollop of truth." She gave Alice a deep look. "But maybe you wanted him out of your hair. William was so lovable—but with his sickliness and melancholy, his deep need for attention, it must have been easier to get him out of the house, at least until the babies had settled in. Am I correct?"

"I'm not that Alice," Alice said more loudly. "I'm Alice Black."

"Alice Black? Billy's wife?"

"I'm nobody's wife. I'm your grandniece."

Aunt Kate touched her hair as if to set things straight, the panic flickering in her cloudy eyes. "Of course. Sorry, dear, I'm all muddied up. Are those flowers for me?"

"They're from Wren Street." Alice took a blue ceramic vase from the closet. So many visits began like this. The doctors said Aunt Kate's problem wasn't Alzheimer's but incipient senility. It was common, apparently, for older people to confuse generations—to mistake their grown children for their own parents, for example—but usually only the generations they'd known personally. Thanks to her studies, Aunt Kate had gone a little further back. She'd never met her grandfather William, who'd been dead eleven years by the time she was born; and although she had met her grandmother Alice only as an infant, she claimed to remember her ("Cross, and as large as an armoire").

Alice sometimes considered playing along. *Oh, of course I ordered him out of the house. The babies' charms were lost on him; he preferred people with whom he could converse.* But her desire to be recognized by her aunt overrode these impulses. Once Aunt Kate was in the correct decade, she could be sharp and sane as she'd ever been.

The older woman rose unsteadily from her chair. "So long as you're here, dear, would you mind helping me to the rest room?"

While her aunt was in the bathroom, Alice glanced at the page in the typewriter, a snatch of dialogue she'd never seen before.

"My darling, this melancholy is not a medical condition, but a philosophical one: 'tis nothing but the bitter manufacture of my own ruminations. I need to read and reflect without interruption. Europe affords me this."

"Then go," Alice said frigidly. "Mother and your aunt are far more useful to an infant than you, William, have ever been."

"No. Rather than have you so short and distant with me, I shall remain and exude my poisonous gloom, and a week hence you will be handing me off to an arctic expedition . . ."

Maybe her aunt was finally moving beyond Chapter One. She wrote by accretion, typing the same page over and over again until it was perfect, so Alice checked the wastebasket and found a page almost identical to the one in the typewriter. She folded and slid it into her back pocket, and when the toilet flushed, she helped her aunt back to her desk.

"I had the strangest dream, Aunt Kate." She was crouched on the floor, unwrapping the flowers, and placing them in the blue vase. "I dreamt you were at Wren Street, and maybe trying to tell me something." Alice crumpled the paper towel and foil into a ball, then tossed it into the wastebasket. "*Is* there something you want to say to me?"

"What an intriguing question," said Aunt Kate. "I'll have to give it some thought." She pointed to a far corner of her desk. "Put those flowers right here, where I can see them as I work. Lovely. They remind me of Walter."

Alice took her aunt for a slow turn around the courtyard with her walker, then they sat on a bench in the weak spring sunlight until Aunt Kate announced she was ready for a nap. Alice left her at the door to her room.

"I'm still thinking about your question, dear," Aunt Kate said, "and I may indeed have something to tell you. I'll let you know."

As she undressed for bed that night, Alice found Helen's card, inscribed with *Ps. 42*, in her pants pocket and took it into the study, where two Bibles were shelved above the many editions of *The Varieties of Religious Experience*. She pulled out a hand-sized red-letter edition of the King James Version with gilded page edges, then remembered, although from what archive of trivia she could not say, that Psalms were smack in the middle of the book.

> As the hart panteth after the water brooks,
> so panteth my soul after thee, O God.
> My soul thirsteth for God, for the living God:
> when shall I come and appear before God?

Harts, she knew, were deer, but the archaic language irritated her—*panteth, thirsteth*, she couldn't even say these words. And what other kind of brooks were there?

When she was growing up, Alice's religious training had come largely from her father, Meyer, who in his frequent rants on the subject insisted that religion was superstition and that belief in a God was infantile wish fulfillment, a form of regressive dependency, while the social religious urge was a vestigial form of tribalism whose sole function was to cause trouble for others. Deep trouble. Witness, he'd say, the Holocaust.

Mary, Alice's mother, occasionally suggested in measured tones that religion might, at times, enhance a person's life. She'd cite her great-grandfather James, who asserted that people who *choose* to believe in God and an afterlife often lead calmer, happier and more productive lives.

"The same can be said of people on tranquilizers," Meyer would reply.

When Alice was six, her mother had taken her and her brothers to a large Episcopalian church in Visalia. While Mary attended the service, the children went to Sunday school, colored in pictures of Jesus and sang easy hymns. After several Sundays, when Alice's father asked what they did in class, she told him about a coloring project in which Jesus fed the multitudes, even though there were no fires, grills, pots or pans in any picture. The bread was in loaves, you could pull it apart and eat it in chunks, she said, but did people back then have to eat their fish raw?

Meyer slammed his hand on the table, much to her alarm. "I'm a Jew!" he shouted. "I will not have my daughter pondering the miracles."

"I thought you hated Judaism," her mother said calmly.

"I hate Christianity more," he said. "If they keep feeding her this crap, how will she ever stand on her own two feet?"

After some discussion, her parents decided that when the kids were old enough, and further along in their education, they could choose whatever religion drew them—or none at all. In the meantime, they should remain free from it all.

In the sixth grade, when everyone else in her class was bused to various churches for twice-monthly religious education, Alice remained alone in the classroom and contemplated her options. Her teacher Miss Myrtle, before going into the faculty room to smoke and read a fat novel, would give her a heavy coffee-table book on world religions. Alice soon had her favorite pages, turning first to a full-page photograph of the hundred-foot Jain statue of Bahubali, whose head was anointed every twelve years with gallons of saffron-colored sauces; set rather too high up on his torso was a well-defined, proportionately small penis which Alice studied intently. In another photograph, black men in white dress shirts and belted trousers stood waist deep in a wide glassy river and sang as they baptized a friend; their obvious joy, plus the naughtiness of getting wet in good clothes, was deeply appealing to her. She was also fond of the section on Zoroastrians because they had so many angels, and because they left their dead to be eaten by birds of prey, which seemed far less frightening than being sealed in a box to rot for all eternity.

For years Alice hoped that the right religion would send out an invisible tendril to make itself known and draw her home. Looking at her high school friends, she sometimes was relieved not to be a dreary Lutheran or guilt-suffused Catholic, and she had no interest in her father's Jewishness, which he himself referred to as "a thankless legacy." The older she got, the clearer it became that any deep-felt religious choice was unlikely, that the pleasures of faith and blind devotion were lost to her, as she'd already heard the bad news: religion, no matter its trappings, was nothing more than a man-made construct devised to obscure the insignificance of human existence and then used to gain power over others.

Nick's suspicion of organized religion was one of their bonds. His wife had been going to churches, wanting Thad to have some religious education and also looking for God-knows-what herself. "As if," he added, "she's going to find consolation for Hollywood's ageism in singing hymns." This gave Alice hope that Jocelyn, once born again, would divorce him for religious incompatibility.

She closed the Bible, marking her place with Helen's card. Even if deer had trotted into every verse, it couldn't have meant a thing to her, so overwrought, overdevotional and thus repellent was the language of Psalms.

Helen phoned at eight o'clock the next morning, waking her up. "How are you? I felt so bad about leaving you there alone yesterday. I didn't wake you, did I?"

"No, no," said Alice.

"You sure? I never know when it's okay to call people," Helen said. "Anyway, I was thinking about your deer and wondering if you still wanted to talk about it?"

"I guess. Why, what were you thinking?"

"Well, sometimes an experience like this is part of a larger, more systemic process."

Alice felt a queasy flush of fear. "What kind of process?"

"A general shift in the way a person sees the world."

"Oh." That didn't sound so dire. And Helen's professional, diagnostical tone, like a doctor's, had a reassuring authority.

"So, other than being sick, have you had any other strange physical feelings or cravings?"

"Well," Alice said, "I only want to eat Jell-O."

Helen laughed, as if at a joke. "Does your back hurt?"

Another fast flush of fear. "It does hurt. How did you know?"

"Back pain often goes with the territory," said Helen. "Seeing any lights? Or have any sensitivity to light?"

"Yes, when I was sick! The sun bothered me. So much I had to pull the shades."

"Okay. And any significant upsets recently? A death? A job loss? A breakup?"

Alice, feeling spooked, wished Helen would go more slowly. She'd just woken up, after all, and hadn't even had her morning tea. "I did break up with my boyfriend," she said. "The night the deer came."

"Well, no wonder! I'm so, so sorry. I wish you'd said something!"

Alice found herself stifling a sob.

Helen changed the subject, a mercy. "Did you have a chance to look up that psalm?"

"I did." Alice swung her feet to the floor and started walking to the kitchen. "But, you know? I'm not into all that God stuff."

"Do you have to be?"

"I mean, I'm not into it at *all*." Moving from room to room somehow gave her courage. "I think I've given you the wrong impression. I only came to that service because of the deer thing. I'm not a church person, and I don't like having religion, especially Christianity, crammed down my throat."

"I hope you don't think I'm trying to cram anything down your throat," Helen said mildly. "Heavens, I'm not a Christian myself."

"You're a minister, aren't you?"

"Yes. But I don't identify as a Christian. Oh, I come out of a

Judeo-Christian tradition. But I don't accept Jesus Christ as my own personal savior, or take the Bible as the word of God."

This went against everything Alice knew about clergy. "And they let you be a minister?"

"Why not?" Helen laughed again. "And who's 'they'?"

Alice was confused. "If you're not Christian, what do you believe in?"

"Plenty! You'd be surprised," Helen said. "Come hear me preach sometime. Or not, since you don't go to church. But I can give you some printouts of my sermons, if you're interested."

"Okay." She didn't want to sound entirely hostile. And she wouldn't mind looking at a sermon. She'd never heard one before.

"You know," Helen said quietly, "I only suggested that psalm for its deer symbolism, 'As the deer longs for flowing streams . . .'?"

"My Bible said 'hart.' As the hart longs—"

"Different translation," said Helen. "At any rate, in this context, the deer's an image for spiritual longing."

"Really?" The notion of spiritual longing produced another quickening of fear. Was it possible this is what she was feeling? Alice opened the refrigerator and took out the gallon jar of tea. Surely she'd know if she had longings, spiritual or otherwise. Monty's transsexuals knew about their true, hidden sexes, often from toddlerhood; until very recently the majority of transsexuals, he said, were to some degree hermaphroditic. You'd think if she had spiritual longings, she might've thought about God or prayer or Jesus with something other than complete indifference at least once in the last decade.

"I wasn't trying to evangelize," Helen continued in her calm, low voice. "Not at all. I enjoyed our talk so much yesterday and find you very interesting . . ."

Yeah, Alice thought, *because my great-great-grandfather's William James.*

". . . and you were so kind to give me tea, and to be so open and honest with what you're going through. Deep calls to deep, I guess."

In spite of herself, Alice registered how nice it was to be seen as deep—and by a minister. "Yeah?"

"Which actually brings me to another reason I'm calling," Helen said, then hesitated. "I don't even know if I should say this. I'd hate to impose myself on you . . . but what the hell. The thing is, I don't have much of a support system here in L.A. I haven't done a great job of meeting people outside my congregation. So I was wondering . . . Actually, what I wanted to ask—unless you absolutely don't want to have anything to do with ministers—is if you had any interest in being friends?"

"Friends? Like—?"

"Get to know each other. Have some meals, spend some time together. Talk. What have you."

Helen had already caught Alice off guard by waking her up and cross-examining her, and now this. Could people *decide* just like that to be friends or not? Still, she could hardly refuse, especially since Helen clearly was feeling friendless. A social fib was acceptable here; a placeholder while the truth was determined over time. "I'd like that," she said.

"Oh good," said Helen. "I'll give you a call later on in the week."

Alice hung up and took her tea out to the front porch. She was flattered that an ordained minister would consider being *her* friend. Yet Helen really wasn't the kind of person she was drawn to: too sincere, too hokey, too much about "support systems."

Alice sat in the chair Helen had occupied yesterday. It *was* different to have someone actively *want* her for a friend. Alice was usually the more interested party. Her childhood in Lime Cove had been a long solitary stretch with occasional playmates supplied by whatever family occupied the rental next door. When she began making friends in school, Alice had been surprised by how deeply she felt about them; the strength of her devotion unnerved her, as did the jealousies friendships inspired, and the sheer gratitude that flooded her whenever someone accepted her. Patty Cutler, Natalie Hernandez, Bobby Hofflemeyer—how she adored and pestered them, her ardor always a little keen, her enthusiasms apt to embarrass everyone concerned. She'd had to learn to calm down, to ape indifference, to be cool even as she clamored and yearned within. Even so, she wasn't always successful. Her most recent best friend, Rachel, once had said to her, "You want something that I can't give."

And frankly, Helen Harland's unabashed desire for human connection seemed just as uncool, unwieldy and embarrassing as her own.

That night, a loud thump jarred Alice from a sound sleep. She assumed, of course, that the deer was back. She didn't get out of bed. So far, nothing but trouble had come from the deer's first visit. She had lost her lover, her job was hanging on by a thread and she'd entered into an agreement she neither understood nor desired with a tall, wild-eyed minister. For all she cared, let a whole herd of deer stampede through the house.

10

When he first moved to Los Feliz, Pete was embarking on a new prescription of antidepressants and taking both a powerful antianxiety medication and a mind-numbing antipsychotic to ease the transition. Altogether, the mix caused him to tremble and flinch at thin air. He couldn't watch television, or even imagine sleeping. Whenever he sat or lay down, his feet wagged and flapped on their own like flippers governed by some ancient aquatic instinct. At times his hunger was obscene. More than once he consumed whatever paltry supplies had accumulated in the kitchen cupboards, eating bowl after bowl of shredded wheat, then chili straight from the can, entire loaves of bread and boxes of crackers, chewing without pause, now a ruminant. Would he, personally, have to recapitulate phylogeny once more as a full-grown adult? For a month his only respite from crazed eating was taking long walks along the river and up into Griffith Park, where he roamed the trails from Fern Dell to Captain's Roost or Dante's View, soaking through shirt after shirt.

When the new SRIs began to kick in, Freeman, his psychiatrist, weaned him off the antipsychotic, then the Xanax. Pete, then, could sit down for one, two, three minutes at a time. He caught glimpses of a world beyond his own blaring, haywire system, and began working a couple of hours a day at the Bread Basket. Afterward, he'd walk the three miles home, sometimes stopping at the small branch library on Hillhurst to skim art and architecture books—printed words still squirmed on the page like so many upturned insects—and to surreptitiously observe mothers and offspring in the children's section. This or that six-year-old boy could put him in a cold sweat: he hadn't seen his own son in almost two years, so any olive-skinned boy with thick brown hair and green eyes could be Garrett in the flesh.

Pete soon colonized a remote niche called the Local History Corner—the bequest of an amateur neighborhood historian, now deceased—that was made nearly private by floor-to-ceiling bookshelves and chin-high wood and glass museum cases. He'd sit at one of the two battered oak carrels in a spindly, old-fashioned office chair that threatened to pitch him off whenever he leaned back past a certain angle. In the halogen glare, he began paging through the local histories (most vanity-pressed), agricultural records, field guides, theosophical texts. He jimmied the lock of a display case with a paper clip and peered into the fragile old picture albums, handwritten diaries and a child's autograph book bookmarked to a page that read, *Dearest Bernadette, I will never forget our ostrich ride! Your Friend, Thomas Mann.* He spent an entire afternoon going through a stenciled wooden box full of handwritten recipes, copying ninety-year-old instructions for gingerbread, sauerbraten and potted rabbit.

Nobody bothered him in the Local History Corner. People peered in, saw a jumbo ragamuffin gnawing on pencils in a shamble of books and decided to browse elsewhere.

On Wednesday morning, Pete showered quickly at the gym and hoofed it to Glendale for his requisite part-time employment.

The Bread Basket was located in two adjoining storefronts a block off Glendale's main drag. One storefront served as a reception area and waiting room, the other, a food pantry separated from the waiting room by a half door. Private offices, storerooms and a room of free donated clothing were in the back. All the walls were an institutional pale green. On hot days, an enormous and thundering swamp cooler blew damp, barely chilled air over the waiting clients while a gruesome half-life-sized plaster crucifix reminded everyone that human life, even for God, is grim.

Helen showed up with a haul of canned goods. Pete hadn't expected her today, and bumbled when helping her bring in the boxes from her car, spilling several cans, snagging his shirt on a door handle, then saying *shit* in front of her. When another delivery arrived, she helped him unload pink boxes of day-old baked goods sent from Pattyann, his long-ago pastry chef, who now had her own thriving bakery. He opened a box, selected a croissant and, breaking it apart, handed half to Helen. "Day-old and they're still the best croissants in town."

"I've already had my Grape-Nuts," Helen said. "And wouldn't know a good croissant from a bad one."

"Taste it," he said.

She complied, concentrating as she chewed. "Oh my God!" she said. "It's like essence of buttered toast."

"Exactly," he said. "They're made with natural yeasts."

"How can you tell?"

"I can tell," he said. "And the baker used to work for me."

She scrutinized him with a new interest. He became acutely aware that his shirt was untucked and tight across his belly, that his jeans sagged, that he'd bitten his fingernails. "You had a bakery?" she asked.

"A restaurant. Trotwood?" he said. "On Beverly?"

She shook her head. "Sorry, don't know it. And you owned it?"

"Till I couldn't pay the lease."

More frank scrutiny. "I'll just bet you're a good cook."

He patted his paunch. "You noticed."

"No." Dismay upped her voice half an octave. "That's not what I meant!"

Her color was high. He laughed and kicked at a box of canned goods. "By the way, I have a meditation question." He tore into another croissant, again offering her half. "When I meditate, whenever I try to focus on my breath? I hyperventilate. What should I do?"

"Nothing. Breathe through it."

"How can I breathe through it when I'm hyperventilating?"

"In a month, you won't remember this difficulty," she said. "I promise."

"Yeah? And then what happens?"

"Any number of new difficulties."

"So when does the good stuff come?"

"That depends on what you mean by 'good stuff.'"

"The stuff you meditate for."

"And what do you meditate for?"

Chewing, he nudged the box at his feet. He swallowed. "A whole new personality."

She smiled. "*That* could take a while," she said. "In the meantime, though, it'll improve your relationship to your present personality."

"Now that's what I call a booby prize!"

They ate their croissants. A volunteer peered around the corner giving Pete a *Where are you?* look, but he didn't care. He'd spend the whole day drifting in the reverend's placid presence, the lovely Lake of Helen.

Seeing that he was being summoned, she fished car keys from her pocket. "If you have more meditation questions, come see me at the church."

He pawed the floor, stuffed a half croissant she'd refused into his mouth.

She moved toward the exit. "Your mother's speaking at the service tonight, remember?"

"I'll be there." Crumbs sprayed from his lips. *Charming.* He stepped ahead of her to open the door. "I still cook for my mom," he managed to say. "Maybe you'll come to dinner some night."

. . .

Pete's responsibility, fifteen hours a week, was to call up food orders for the clients. Four months ago there was a paper-based filing system, but having computerized the process, he only had to punch in an identifying number, and ideally, the correct food list printed out, which the client carried over to the pantry window. Volunteers then bagged up the usual pinched and bruised fruit, past-dated baked items, dented canned foods plus, this week, a treasure trove of Passover chow: gefilte fish, egg noodles, matzo, beet-dyed horseradish, maroon borscht.

Midmorning, an eighteen-year-old black woman with three babies grew shrill when trying to swap a box of matzo meal for something, *anything,* else at the pantry desk. "No exchanges allowed," said the new elderly volunteer working the pantry window. "Use it to bread your fried chicken."

Homeless and otherwise impoverished men and women and children shuffled in and out and the new pantry volunteer couldn't keep up. The waiting room filled. Children fidgeted and fussed, then cried with extravagant abandon.

Pete was relieved when Shirley pushed through the front door. A six-foot-two homeless transvestite with the dubious habit of imitating black American speech patterns, she'd been given thirty days at County for public indecency, but apparently had served only a few. She looked dangerously cheerful—potentially manic—in a yellow Chanel knockoff suit and matching heels with large white daisies on them. She strode through the waiting area as if the dirty green linoleum were a Milanese runway.

"Shee-it," said Burgess, a heavyset black man with a bad leg in a brace, who slouched with two other homeless men against the wall.

"Lookin' good, Shirl," Pete called. "Welcome back."

"Thanks, baby," she said. "I won't be needin' no food today. I only come by to say hi to my friends here and to tell y'all my good news." She turned to Burgess's group. "Boys," she said, "you be happy to hear: I'm getting me a new car. A 1983 Cadillac Fleetwood Brougham."

Burgess rotated his heavy head. "I believe you mean a Cadillac Fleetwood Blow-'em," he growled, "since that's what you gon' do to git it."

The men on either side of him whooped and slapped their knees.

"Y'all jus' jealous." Shirley gazed at them haughtily. "And I ain't in no mood. See if I haul yo' sorry asses to the track in my new car. Now you, Petey baby"—she pivoted toward him—"I drive you anywhere you wanna go."

Slowly bags were filled and names checked off, clients wandering out with their food. By two-thirty Pete had locked the door and printed out the day's journal: 217 people fed, 88 of them children.

He stepped into his mother's tidy office. She would stay on until five, arranging food deliveries, scheduling volunteers, writing reports to her superiors. "Want anything in particular for dinner?" he asked.

"You know? I'd love some lamb."

In return for alienating her affections and breaking up her marriage to the Resurrection Kid, he cooked the hell out of dinner every night. She stayed trim as a broom. He'd swelled.

He kissed her dry cheek and set off. Half a block from the Bread Basket, snug against the brick wall in an alley, sat a redorange box of matzo meal.

At the Mayfair supermarket, Pete bought fresh asparagus, butter lettuce and lamb shanks. He had to keep it simple, since his mom's digestion was a little dodgy.

The late afternoon had turned warm and smoggy, and he considered stopping in at the Fountain for a cold beer. But part of his agreement was no intoxicants, no mind-altering substances—he who rarely drank a second glass of wine, he, the ever-designated driver. Two years ago, however, he'd tried to make a pint of Jim Beam compensate for a shortage of Seconal caps—a grave miscalculation. He not only survived but totaled the Alfa and also lost his license in exchange for six months of outpatient rehab and AA meetings. Recalling this, he suddenly knew where he'd seen the minister's beau before: at an AA meeting in Woodview. Pete barked a laugh in broad daylight. That the pacific Helen Harland boffed a drunk seemed hopeful and inspiring. Did that mean other has-beens might reap such fruit?

In the apartment's narrow pink-tiled kitchen, he floured and browned the shanks, made a mirepoix of carrots, celery and shallots, added a cup of boiling veal stock and set everything to braise on low. Mom arrived home at five-twenty, and he met her with a chaste cocktail of cranberry juice, club soda and lime. "Have a highball, Ma." Haydn blazed softly on the stereo.

She kicked off the orthopedics. "You're a thoughtful man, Pete."

"I'm trying."

"I know you are."

She read a murder mystery as he put dinner on the table. Lamb shanks like caveman clubs. Asparagus steamed, no butter. "You nervous about speaking tonight?" he asked.

"You're one tough audience, dear."

The usual suspects had crammed into the church rumpus room. Mom spoke well, starting with how, widowed and suffering from the proverbial empty nest, she'd joined a convent known for its social justice work. She concentrated on the years in El Salvador with radical Jesuits who'd founded a school and a clinic and rebuffed a large American textile factory. When a priest and two nuns were killed in a nearby town, Rome sent her group back to the States, much against their will. Oh, her story was glorious, exemplary *and* selectively edited. She left out the introductory material. At age seventeen, when all she'd wanted to do was enter the convent, she'd met Gabrielo Rosales at a school carnival. He wanted to be a priest. They felt such kinship that she was pregnant within the month. Certainly Mom didn't confide to Wednesday's faithful that her punishment for flunking

God's first test was marriage and a child—Pete himself—and a twenty-four-year wait before Our Little Sisters of the Blazing Cross received her into their shrinking ranks.

Pete sometimes grokked, of course, that his own devout self-loathing was born in *her* disappointment and rage at having had him, at his very being—deadly emotions that he'd assimilated and internalized, possibly even prenatally. The shrinks agreed—hell, they'd helped him to formulate it—and even Mom concurred. It was true, she admitted, that Pete had not been welcomed warmly into this world. And the result? As Freeman, his psychiatrist, scrawled so succinctly on his chart: *personality incompatible with life.*

How odd, then, that she was his last, best hope. She came out of the convent to mother him, this time willingly, with affection and patience. She wished to accomplish now what she'd failed at, thanks to youth and devastating guilt, the first time around: that is, to utter the great *Yes* that most mothers instinctively grant upon conception, as even Mary did when informed of her otherworldly pregnancy. *Yes, Yes,* to whatever had taken hold in the womb, child or deity, five-fingered or web-toed. The fundamental *Yes,* the basic undergirding upon which any life-embracing personality was built.

It might already be too late. His shrinks had been blunt about the risks. Forging a strong connection to life might be age-specific, like eyesight: if a blind person doesn't see by a certain age, the equipment for decoding visual input withers. Likewise, Pete might lack the receptors needed to absorb this overdue maternal love.

Yet he did want to live. Most of the time, at least. To do so, he'd had to start all over, first by relearning the trick of acting within reasonable bounds, a skill abandoned once he went to work on his estranged wife's apartment. Up to the moments before the computer screen gave way, he could've left undetected; but then Anne and Garrett had walked in on him, and there was no stopping himself. But damn, to finally fracture that brittle glass membrane, to capitulate to violence and break into the wide-open geography of impulse, had been such an extraordinary release after months and months of civilized acrimony. Now, after two years of ranging as he pleased, emotionally unkempt, rude as a hermit, he was back to the basics. *How do people live in this world?*

It had been agreed: Mom was to scold him, nudge him, signal the limits, train him as a mother bird or coyote or human would so he didn't end up in tarp-walled rooms above the river, sleeping on ferny beds and brushing his teeth with river scum.

But surveying those assembled in this moldering rec room, Pete despised the cheerful, oblivious life-lovers even as he envied their immersion in his mother's story, the tilt of their faces toward her voice, their expressions unquestioning and near-sighted as a cow's. Yet his very hatred was hopeful. Hadn't St. Paul despised and tortured Christians until the moment he became one? Dr. Freeman liked to say that new personalities formed continuously, like eggs on an umbilical rope, and while the predominant one reigned and struggled to maintain control, there could be a coup at any time. Somewhere in his truant, disaffected psyche might not there be a Pollyanna skipping rope, chirping rhymes, rising in prominence?

Pete joined in the applause following his mother's talk.

11

H elen Harland was on the sofa at two in the afternoon on Thursday—Maundy Thursday, in fact, *and* the first night of Passover, not that Unitarians observed either one, although they paid some lip service to the latter. (She'd been invited to three seders by congregants, but having declined the first invitation was happily obliged to refuse all subsequent offers.) Beth Ross had asked her to the Catholic service in Glendale, where "the new young priest really goes all out," and in an ecumenical moment Helen had considered going; but it would've taken more than Catholic pomp to get her off the couch today.

Since coming to Morton, Helen had wasted more time on the sofa than during her six years in the seminary and prisons combined. And this wasn't even a comfortable sofa, but boxy and sprung, in scratchy brown Herculon, a hair shirt of a davenport—donated to the parsonage along with a pink Formica coffee table by a congregant eager to save himself the dump fee.

Helen had started the day in high spirits: forty-two people had shown up for last night's service—to hear a nun, no less. By eleven, however, Frank Rosen, the chairman of the ministerial relations committee, called to relay a complaint. Betty Clip, chair of the membership committee, had objected that Helen was setting out the membership book on Wednesday nights.

This was a large bound volume of blank pages where people indicated their intention to join the church by scribbling their names and addresses. Since Helen became Morton's minister, she'd invited visitors of any sort—including Wednesday service attendees—to write in the book as well; in turn, she'd phone, invite them all to new membership classes and send them the church newsletter free for six weeks.

According to Frank, the membership committee liked to see and talk to the people who signed it in order to connect the names with faces. Since she'd started putting it out on Wednesdays, there were suddenly too many strangers around.

"Wasn't I hired to bring new blood into this church?" Helen asked.

Not some forms of new blood, Frank eventually admitted. Not, for example, the two men, first seen at a Wednesday service, who now also came on Sundays and held hands in the sanctuary. In front of the children.

Working in prisons while attending seminary, Helen cultivated detachment by letting prisoners' remarks come and go without reacting to them; this was part of her spiritual discipline. She'd worked at all the large, difficult penitentiaries—the great madhouse at Atascadero, the women's facility at Stockton, San Quentin's death row—and had reached a point where insults, wolf whistles and outbursts of rage drifted right past her. But nothing any homicidal sociopath had to offer could compare to some of the potshots she'd fielded at Morton. Detachment, she now realized, was a lot easier with a big old magnum on your hip.

So Helen had taken to the sofa, to cool off before phoning Betty Clip. Lying there, she fought the urge to call Lewis and tell him about this incredible new example of bitchiness. He, of course, would consider Betty's complaint neither new nor incredible, but simply further proof that Helen was casting her pearls before Morton's swine and would be better off elsewhere. *How much evidence*, he'd say, *is it going to take?*

The wind was kicking up outside and the red paisley sheet she'd tacked up over the louvered windows ballooned into the room like a lung. Outside, a plastic trash can rumbled like thunder down the street. Helen reached for her address book. Alice Black had agreed to be her friend, so why not get things rolling? After many rings, Alice answered, short of breath.

"Hey, it's Helen. From the church."

"Oh . . . hi." Her disappointment was unmistakable. Whose voice had she raced to hear? "Sorry I didn't come last night."

"I didn't expect you! But you missed a great speaker."

"Really . . ." She was still catching her breath.

"Are you better?" Helen tried to sound upbeat. "Back at work?"

"I went in today," said Alice, "but I've been sick so much, they hired someone else. And now I have to split my shifts with him."

"Can you get by on that?"

"I couldn't get by before."

"This doesn't sound good."

"It's not. Except that maybe it'll force me to find a real job."

"Well, I have an idea," said Helen. "Why don't you come over for dinner? We'll have our own Last Supper and seder combined. Or our first supper, as the case may be. Very informal. I'll feed you something delicious. And I'm kidding about the religious stuff. No Last Supper *or* seder, promise."

"I know," Alice said. "All right."

Seven o'clock, they agreed. Alice would bring Jell-O.

Helen then managed a brief, neck-cramping nap and, after a few delicious moments planning Betty Clip's funeral service—with the Gay Men's Chorus and readings by Auden, Whitman and Merrill—she returned to her office, where the part-time secretary handed her a sheaf of pink messages, including one from Pete Ross *re: meditation.* She tried calling, but there was no answer. She did talk to the church electrician, then arranged for the two pianos to be tuned. When she could put it off no longer, she dialed the Clips' number. "Betty," she said, "I have an idea. How about if the membership committee hosts a hospitality table on Wednesday nights? That way, you can all get a good look at everyone who signs the book."

"Oh, Helen," Betty said in her trembling, old woman's voice. "It takes so much work to get a host for the Sunday table. You have no idea how many phone calls I make as it is."

"I'd be happy to help out with calling," said Helen.

Betty Clip breathed loudly for a few moments. "You know, Helen," she said, having summoned a firmer voice, "until you came, people didn't sign the membership book until they'd actually *joined* the church."

"I thought we agreed to expand its usefulness."

"The book is a registry of members. That's all the membership committee wants it to be."

Helen was also a member of the committee. A de facto ex officio and very active member. God knows she'd attended every endless meeting where business mingled with coupon swapping and long digressions into the pros and cons of cataract surgery. "I don't remember this being discussed, Betty," she said. "Have I missed a meeting?"

"No, Helen." Betty spoke with exaggerated patience, as to a stubborn child. "Still, we all agree. It's our book to use as we see fit, and we wish you would respect that."

"I assure you, Betty, I respect all the work your committee does and I was merely using the book to help us bring in new members."

"That's not what it's for," Betty said.

Helen let the words hang there and listened to Betty breathe. "I'll tell you what," she finally said. "I won't ask any more visitors to sign the book until we discuss this at the next committee meeting."

This provoked a martyr's sigh, all resignation and contempt. "As you wish, Helen. Obviously I can't stop you."

. . .

Helen knew a free-floating gay community minister who worked with various congregations to address their homo-phobia and welcome homosexuals into their churches. She'd planned to bring him in next year, after Morton had gotten used to her modernizing ways; but the need, clearly, had presented itself, so she made the call and scheduled his visit in May, *after* the yearly fund-raising drive.

Locking the office, she drove to a chain bookstore in Glendale, where she bought a large bound book with a marbleized cover and two hundred blank pages, paying for it out of the minister's discretionary fund.

The afternoon had turned glorious, with bursts of cold wind and a ruddy light that made every living thing appear viru-lently healthy. Bubbly, flat-bottomed clouds had sailed in like a fleet, filling the sky as far as the eye could see. Helen dropped her new membership book at home and decided to walk to the market.

At the Mayfair's meat counter stood Pete Ross. "Hey, Pete," she said.

"Hey, Rev." He flung a packaged chop back into the refrig-erated case. "Busted with the tortured baby beef."

Before becoming one, Helen assumed that ministers were generally regarded with heightened esteem, even awe, which was how she'd always viewed them. Since she'd been ordained, however, it seemed more likely that people saw her as a one-woman vice squad. "I don't care if you eat veal," she said.

"I'm not *that* into it," he said. "But Mom's eating up at the convent tonight, and I can't decide what I want. I've been stand-ing here so long the butcher thinks I'm hitting on him." He gazed into the meat case. "That veal does look good, but it's nine dollars."

"Oh, treat yourself," said Helen. The butcher *was* giving Pete sharp, nervous looks. "I tried calling you earlier," she said. "You weren't home."

"That's because I've been standing here for the last five hours."

Helen slung a whole bagged chicken into her cart, knowing full well what she needed. She made the same meal each time she had company: roast chicken, rice and a green salad.

Pete took a decisive step away from the meat. "Maybe I'll have an omelette," he said. "I haven't had an egg in six months. I should take advantage when the old gal's out of the house."

"I think you should get that chop," said Helen.

"Naw," said Pete, "now I want evil eggs."

Eggs and lettuce were in the same direction, so they wound up shopping together. As they went to check out, Pete pointed to a large black-and-white photograph hanging above the manager's station: the former Disney Studios, which used to sit on this very lot. Model As and Ts drove in the street. Only a few homes dotted the hills. Helen recognized the high school's stately brick towers. "Look, Morton!" she exclaimed, pointing to a slice of mansard roof. "It still has the cross!"

In the checkout line, Pete embodied the mannerisms of a hyperactive child, squinting at strangers, leaning against the chrome railings, muttering under his breath. Behind him, a couple in their forties exchanged tight, smug smiles. It was smugness, not cruelty, Helen decided, that was the opposite of compassion.

Outside, the wind surged and swallows flew in wide, swooping arcs. Pete, scuffing along the pavement, swerved over to walk between Helen and the street, then offered to take her groceries. "That's all right," she said, and restrained herself from telling him to stop dragging his feet. Pete moved as if he were on massive doses of Thorazine—and for all she knew, he *was*—but it was hardly her place to correct him, however much he invited it. Which he did. Several times in the last few months,

Helen had caught herself wanting to say, *Why don't you tuck in your shirt?* Or, *You'd be so great-looking if you lost forty pounds.* During worship services, when he sighed or har-rumphed or turned his entire body to face the side windows, she'd been tempted to unpack the schoolmarm's heavy artillery: *You—yeah, you in the back pew—can't you behave yourself for five lousy minutes?* That he evoked such motherly scolding was not surprising; he was, after all, in his mid-forties and still living with his mom.

Helen also suspected that much of his churlishness was an act, behind which he could hide. And she sensed something solid in him, some entrenched strength he held closely, showing it to no one.

The sun slipped in and out of the clouds. The wild air sparkled with dust and carried the smell of mown lawns and newly dug dirt and an occasional burst of sage from Griffith Park. Pete paused at a court of half-timbered cottages with whimsical peaked and shingled roofs. "These were the original Disney offices," he said.

Each lawn was intensely green, each hedge fastidiously shaped, ficus in sharp clean boxes, hydrangeas in perfect spheres. "It does looks like the seven dwarfs live here," she said.

"Walt himself lived right around the corner."

"How do you know all this?"

"Library," said Pete. "They have a local history thing." Turning, he pointed behind them to hills full of cliff-hanging houses and trees. "All that was Tom Mix's ranch, called Mixville. Hard to imagine cows in them thar hills."

"No kidding," Helen said, and they started walking again. "Hey—maybe you'd give a talk on the history of the neighbor-hood."

"And maybe I won't."

" 'The Spirituality of Place,' we'd call it. You know, how history enhances and deepens your experience of the place you live."

"It does?"

Helen knocked his arm with her elbow. "Just give it some thought, okay?"

He scowled, swinging his grocery bag against his leg like an eight-year-old. "Don't hold your breath."

"Speaking of breath," she said, "how's the meditation coming?"

"I'll be honest. I can sit for twelve minutes."

"Twelve minutes is excellent."

"I can't imagine how you can sit for thirty."

"Forty-five, actually," Helen said. "But at first all I did was bawl myself out whenever my mind wandered. I finally realized, if anybody else talked to me the way I talked to myself, I'd leave the room. When I stopped being such a nag, I could sit longer."

"All I hear is how hard and fast my heart's beating," said Pete. "That's a lecture we could call 'Prelude to a Heart Attack.' And then I can't breathe *at all*."

"Which is normal and good," Helen said. "Keep sitting and soon you'll not only breathe more deeply, you'll be able to slow down your heartbeat at will."

A skeptical snort. "I look forward to that."

They climbed a low hill to a four-way stop and waited while cars took turns through the intersection, everyone polite and watchful before hitting the gas. Then, as they stepped into the crosswalk, a maroon Crown Victoria driven by a white-haired man surged forward, forcing them back to the curb. "Wouldn't you know it," Helen said, squinting at the receding car. "A member of my church."

"You do have a lot of grayheads," said Pete.

"That's right! I completely forgot! You were in church Sunday!"

"It was that or mass," said Pete. "I cut a deal with my mother superior."

"So what did you think?" Helen waltzed sideways so she could see his face. "I know you have an opinion."

He ducked his head but couldn't hide the emotions passing over his face. It was, Helen noted, like watching a baby's face, a guileless, unedited, involuntary working-through of every shade of thought. "It was okay," he said.

"I can take it," she said. "The truth, *s'il vous plaît*."

"I think," he said slowly, "you should find yourself a real big stick and go in swinging. Instead of practically apologizing every step of the way."

"When did I apologize?"

"Each time you said 'the overarching spirit that I choose to call God.'"

"Oh, that," said Helen. "I have to do that. If I say plain old 'God,' they freak out and think I've gone Baptist on them."

"Then I'm confused," said Pete. "I thought it was a church."

"It is," Helen said without checking the bitterness. "It's the original church of Christ with no Christ, where the blind don't see, the lame don't leap and the dead stay right where they're supposed to be—dead."

"Ah," said Pete, "my kind of church."

"Then why are you complaining?"

"I'm not," said Pete. "You could hit 'em a little harder, is all."

"I'll think about it," said Helen.

They continued up the street, past the back of the high school where people walked and jogged around a dirt track. In the grassy, oblong center, dogs leapt to catch Frisbees that swerved crazily in the wind. "You have to understand," Helen said. "The older people in my congregation came of age between the world wars. They're dyed-in-the-wool secular humanists who believe goodness and mercy and justice come *exclusively* from humans."

"That doesn't sound so wrong to me," said Pete. "A bit optimistic, maybe."

"Sure, but if you deny the divine, you risk deifying the human ego. Any concept of an other—let alone a higher—power becomes untenable. For my group, it's unthinkable."

"It's weird they still want to go to church."

"I know!" Helen shifted her groceries to her other hand. "But come Sunday they like to see their friends and hear the music. They like their bazaars and rummage sales, potlucks and cocktail hours. They just don't like religion."

"I can dig it," said Pete.

"Me too, in some ways. Some of my parishioners have had truly hideous experiences—terrorized by fire and brimstone as kids, tortured in Catholic school. This one man grew up in a utopian community where they practiced psychoanalysis and channeled the spirits of Abraham Lincoln and George Washington—a real lunatic fringe of the psychoanalytical movement. For a cult, it was fairly benign, but that guy's had enough hocus-pocus to last a lifetime.

"Then I have ex–Jehovah's Witnesses ostracized by their own families, which has wreaked far more damage than Abe Lincoln's ghost. I could write a book on the variety of religious trauma at Morton alone."

"They should try having a nun for a mother," said Pete.

"That's traumatic?"

"What do you think?"

Helen thought for a moment. "There is an inherent contradiction—"

"No shit," said Pete.

Against a brick retaining wall, a teenage girl and boy were kissing vigorously. As Helen and Pete passed them, the girl's long, loose black hair lifted like a flag in the wind, giving off the smell of ripe fruit, peaches or cherries.

Morton's slate-blue mansard roof came into view, and Helen shifted her groceries to her other hand. Loath to relinquish the company, she turned to Pete. "I'm having a friend over for dinner. Nothing fancy. If you'd like to join us—"

He stopped to execute a virtuosic set of snorts and shrugs, unmistakable pain passing over his face. "You don't need me coming to dinner."

12

Alice boiled water for the Jell-O and nursed second thoughts. What if Nick came by when she was gone? But she'd been caught off guard when Helen called, couldn't say no, and now could only hope that she didn't want to talk about William James. If so, Alice would only disappoint. She hadn't read more than three pages of his writing, and knew only anecdotal—and no doubt fictionalized—biographical snippets from Aunt Kate. Also, if Helen considered the deer incident a vision of some sort, and Alice, therefore, a fledgling mystic— well, Alice could only disappoint there, too. She had no interest in visions and saw no cachet in having them; nothing like a little mental illness in the family to deromanticize such goings-on. A single disoriented deer in the dining room had been upsetting enough. Poor mystics—how did they bear it!

She dumped mauve powdered Jell-O into a glass bowl and poured in boiling water to make a deep purple ink. This was alchemy enough for her.

She didn't have to be at Helen's until seven, and it was only four. She went outside, picked some purple hyacinth and yellow daffodils, and then, once she added grapes to the thickening Jell-O, headed for the Beverly Manor.

"Are you Jewish?" Aunt Kate said by way of a greeting.

"Hi, Aunt Kate," Alice said. "Technically, no."

"Didn't Mary marry a Jew?"

"Mom? Yeah, but it goes through the maternal line and, as you know, Mom's a total WASP. I don't consider myself un-Jewish, though."

"What I'm wondering is, should I wish you Happy Passover?"

Alice couldn't say what exactly Passover was, except that the Jews passed either into or out of the wilderness. "Naw," she said. "I'm not that Jewish."

"Sigmund Freud was Jewish." Aunt Kate frowned at her typewriter. "And I wonder if that colored William's opinion of him. I'd hate to think so, but a general, unexamined anti-Semitism was common back then. Mostly, William considered Freud's emphasis on sexuality distasteful—even Freud knew that. When he heard that William was coming to hear him speak, he switched his lectures around so William wouldn't have to hear anything of a sexual nature. Which seems so respectful."

"It does." Alice drew Monday's flowers out of the vase and jammed them into the wastebasket. "I didn't realize they'd ever actually met."

"Yes, it was when Jung and Freud came to America. I have a photo from the conference. William's in the front row, clutching his hat and jacket like he ran up at the last minute. Everyone else looks so formal." She rummaged through a stack of books on her desk, then gave up. "After the talk, William and Freud walked together to the train station, an encounter you'd think would've changed history, the two fathers of psychology, tête-à-tête. But William had a terrible attack of angina and had to stop. Freud later told people that he was very brave about the pain." She thought for a moment. "Otherwise, not a great meeting of the minds. William did admire Freud's concept of the uncon-scious. Only William saw the unconscious as a vast under-ground sea that occasionally sent the individual a shot of energy. But he didn't presume to know its contents. He found Freud's dream analysis outlandish and silly—such as all tables and balustrades and credenzas representing female sexual organs! How could Freud know, let alone say, a thing like that? Wasn't he ever embarrassed?"

"I thought Freud was discredited," said Alice. "I thought nobody paid attention to him anymore."

"Oh, he's still very important. He completely changed the way we see ourselves; the id, the ego, the superego. We take his unconscious for granted."

Yeah, Alice thought, *so long as it stays unconscious,* and replaced the vase on the corner of her aunt's desk.

"Thank you, dear. Perfect." Aunt Kate stared at the flowers until her blue eyes seemed as violet as the hyacinths. "Now Alice," she said in a crisp, unexpected voice, "you gave me quite a start the other day when you asked what kind of grisly old skeletons I had in the closet."

"That's not exactly—"

"I don't know if somebody's been telling tales, or it's your natural perspicacity, but there *is* a matter I've always intended to discuss with you; I was holding off until you were married, but you appear to be taking after me in that regard, and at thirty, you're sufficiently mature."

"Thirty-three, actually."

Aunt Kate's eyes dimmed, as if this fact saddened her. "At any rate, it's high time I brought it up. So come here, dear." She held out both hands, which Alice came and clasped. "I assume you've heard about Colin Crowley?"

The name rang no bell. "No."

"He was a friend of Walter's at Harvard. I met him when he came out to lecture at Cal, a lovely man and a brilliant law historian. Although you've probably heard otherwise." She released Alice's hands.

"I've heard nothing," Alice said, and then an inkling came. "This wasn't the man your parents sent away?"

"So you do know about him."

"Not really. Only the family story."

"Which is?"

"That you were engaged, then someone saw him with another woman and your parents sent him away."

Aunt Kate made a small French puff of disgust. "He was married, dear."

"I never heard that." Alice was careful to keep her response neutral.

"They were separated when I met him, but his wife was Catholic and wouldn't give him a divorce. And when she found out about me, she threatened to sue. Alienation of affections. Enticement. All those old chattel laws were still on the books back then. Criminal conversation."

"*Criminal* conversation?"

"Sexual intercourse," Aunt Kate said crisply. "Don't be outraged, dear."

"I'm not outraged." But she did have to sit down on the foot of the bed. *Of course he was married—how did I never guess?* "So he went back to her?"

"He had no choice, between her lawyers and my father . . ." Aunt Kate smiled and briefly closed her eyes. "And I moved down here."

"Why didn't you tell me this sooner?" cried Alice.

"Why? What difference would that've made?"

A red koi swam in the indigo sea of the old Chinese carpet. *Because, well, what a relief not to be the only enticer. The only criminal conversationalist.*

"Is there anything more you want to know?" said Aunt Kate.

"I don't know," Alice said. "I have to think."

"I hope you don't think ill of me."

"Of course I don't. I think it's great. Or, not great, but interesting." Alice was flailing. "I just need to assimilate it."

"Assimilate away," Aunt Kate said, and turned to her typewriter. "You know, Colin was the only friend of Walter's who didn't abandon him after he grew ill. I've been thinking about that." She ran her fingers over the typewriter keys. "Poor Walter. In the end, I, too, had to abandon him."

"That's not true, Aunt Kate. Uncle Walter had to be hospitalized." Alice stood and clumsily hugged her great-aunt's shoulders.

"No. I just got too old and too damn crazy to help him."

This acknowledgment of diminished capacities was, for Alice, even more frightening than Kate's time-traveling. Being insane could conceivably be bearable if you never knew you were, but realizing you were out of your mind? What else to do but fill your pockets with rocks and head for the river? Remembering how Helen had comforted her a few days ago, Alice stroked her aunt's head. What fine, silken white hair! Alice couldn't recall ever having touched it before. "Uncle Walter's all right," she said. "I'll go check on him again if you'd like."

"You must give him my love." Her voice quavered, then regained its briskness. "Old age is not for the timid, Alice. You get shot full of fissures. And memory takes on a life of its own."

With an hour to go before she was due at the minister's, Alice sat in the Wren Street kitchen—its many windows opened like transoms—and waited for the time to pass. Noises drifted in from the darkening world, traffic, children yelling, car doors slamming. At intervals, wind grabbed the whole house, then released it.

She was glad, now, to be going to the parsonage. Helen had been right: Aunt Kate did have something to say, something that felt like the first piece of something larger. Alice felt poised, as if this greater knowledge were close by, glinting like a dark lake glimpsed though the woods.

The mockingbird trilled, and then called Alice's long-gone uncle for dinner.

13

He warned her. Yet she'd insisted, leading him through the cactus garden past waxy, spinous green paddles and squat red-bristled barrels to her door.

How does Helen Harland live in this world? She tacked Indian bedspreads over the windows and breathed the sweet stale must of burned incense. She lounged on a sofa whose savagely clawed arm extruded plump cauliflowers of stuffing, and worked at a card table desk with one capless leg shimmed with Niebuhr's *The Nature and Destiny of Man.* Her Macintosh SE was more ancient even than his relic at the Bread Basket, and its printer required the obsolete paper with holey edges. Cardboard boxes served as her files. Like a college student or prisoner, she'd tacked posters, prints, photos and postcards willy-nilly on the walls and strewn candles, toys and small statuary across sills and shelves.

"In here, Pete," Helen called, already in the next room.

The pictures and gewgaws, Pete noted on closer inspection, were all religious—and peculiar. A paint-by-numbers of St. Francis with animals was a study in gradated blobs of color. A framed Russian icon had crossed eyes. A collection of five small crucifixes was especially gory. On a milk crate draped with bandannas sat a gaudy porcelain Buddha, laughing, obese and big-breasted. Votives, fresh fruit and chipped Hummel angels clustered at his feet.

"Isn't he jolly?" Helen had backtracked. "And I love this." She pointed to a print of Jesus, crudely drawn, standing in stylized waves while a squadron of angels flew overhead. "It's from the ninth century," she said. "He's been baptized, and the angels are bringing him towels!"

Indeed, each of them held a neatly folded cloth. "What do your, uh, church members think of all these pictures and things?"

"I have no idea," Helen said gaily. "I never asked!"

This worried him; too eccentric.

"I know, I know," she said as if reading his mind. "My boyfriend says I've fetishized my environment to a hostile degree."

The mention of the boyfriend caused Pete a quick plummet, which reversed course when she touched his arm. "I've got to start cooking," she said. "Come keep me company."

He followed her into a small kitchen with yellow tile, a dripping tap and an apartment-sized gas stove above which she'd nailed a dozen cake and aspic molds, all Paschal lambs, in copper, tin and Tupperware, some cartoonish, others almost scientific in their detail. "It's like you find religion funny," he said.

"Don't you?"

He couldn't answer.

He might be seriously in love.

He rolled up his sleeves, laved his hands and more or less co-opted the dinner prep: mashing garlic with salt into a paste to rub on the chicken; rolling lemons until soft, pricking them until they oozed, tucking them into the bird's cavity. Helen brought him whatever he requested, or some approximation; he pounded garlic with the butt of a knife, trussed the chicken with dental floss, sent the readied bird into the oven in a pie pan, dried lettuce first by swinging it in a clean pillowcase outside the back door, then toweling it leaf by leaf as she described the other guest. "She's descended from one of my favorite writers— William James? I swear, you can see the same sparkle in this woman's eyes. Same broad forehead, too."

So what if Helen Harland's kitchen was dismally equipped?

Here they were, working together, side by side, in a simulacrum of domesticity. "What's for dessert?" he said, growing giddy.

"I forgot all about dessert," she said.

"We should have something for dessert," he said, then froze. *We?*

She failed to notice his presumption, or else ignored it. "I don't know if I have anything, but you're free to look. See what you can find."

He rummaged in her cupboards. Helen Harland lived on canned soup and tuna fish, Grape-Nuts and herb tea. But he did find cocoa, cornstarch, sugar cubes; add nonfat milk, a few of his eggs—and voilà! Poor Parson's Pudding.

She brought him a dented aluminum saucepan. He turned it over, tapped its bottom. "Is there a heavier one?" he asked. "Milk might scorch in this."

"Sorry," she said, flinging an old-fashioned flowered cloth over the table.

He made do, kept the flame low, stirred constantly.

Helen set the table with mismatched stainless steel so light and flimsy you could probably bend it just by thinking the word *curlicue*. She added funny ceramic monks whose bald heads held shallow tea candles. "Pete," she said, "have you ever seen deer around here?"

"In the park," he said. Now she was beside him, reaching in the cupboard for green plastic tumblers. "Dozens of them. Why?"

"Just wondering." Helen set the tumblers on the table and came toward him. "Hey."

She had grasped his left wrist. Slowly, she turned it, revealing the underside, the white welting of scar tissue. With her other hand, she lifted his right wrist and found matching ridges. "My God, Pete," she said, grasping both his arms. "What's all this about?"

He shivered and wanted to pull his arms away, but not to lose her touch. Heat flooded his skin and he opened his mouth to speak without the least idea of what to say . . . and then, miracle of miracles: the doorbell chimed. "Avon calling," he cried in triumphal relief. "Saved by the beauteous bell."

She squeezed his wrists—with impatience, irritation or affection?—and let go.

Embarrassment, white-to-blinding, sickened him. Why had he rolled up his sleeves? She'd pull away for sure, from pity if not pure disgust, and at the very least would consign him to a remote stratum of acquaintanceship reserved for the marginal and dicey. The handle-with-care crowd. The hold-at-arm's-lengthers.

Pete stirred, the circular motion and the scrape of spoon on metal a comfort.

He hardly remembered the actual scar-producing incident. He'd never intended to go so far. Self-damage at first had been only a daydream, romantic, vengeful and deeply satisfying to contemplate. He'd show them. But it got away from him; like inviting the devil to checkers, he'd conjured a more ferocious entertainment than anticipated or sought.

He recalled not knowing which way to cut, so tried it both ways, drawing bloody crosses on each wrist, the razor breaking through the skin with the faintest pop. How did he make it to the emergency room? Something to do with his probation officer.

He remembered clearly his queasy surfacing into consciousness, finding himself wide awake and strangely sedated: in fact paralyzed—stunned, he'd learn, by the loss of blood, Thorazine and whatever else they'd shot into him. The young ER intern, a generic surfer boy, had lifted and turned Pete's slashed arms much the way Helen just had. Severed tendons had sprouted from the wrist like thin, limp stalks of rhubarb. "Watch this," the intern told a nurse, then touched a gloved finger to one dangling length. The tendon snapped back like a sensitive form of tide-pool life. "Let me," said the nurse. Taking turns, they made his tendons snap and coil, exclaiming as if he could not see or hear them, or feel the tugging at his wrists. No, he saw them perfectly, but could make no move or sound to put an end to their game.

"Pete?" Helen called. "Meet Alice. Alice, Pete."

He turned. The face before him was familiar, in both its features and dismay. "Why, Suzy! How ya doin'?" Her all-black outfit and evident displeasure brought out his folksy side. "Didn't I see you at the church a while back?" She scowled, but he couldn't stop. "Been down to the river lately?" He turned to Helen. "I rescued her from a potentially ugly situation—not that she ever thanked me."

"My name is Alice," she said coolly, studying the lamb-shaped molds. "I wasn't going to give your disgusting friend my real name."

"You two know each other?" Helen sounded hopeful.

"No." In unison.

"Well then, what would you like to drink, Alice? Wine, Coke, water?"

"Wine, please."

This one reminded Pete of the heroin girls at Woodview—the same diffidence, the same sexy lassitude, the same automatic, reflexive rejection of his olden stoutish self, which in turn prompted a knee-jerk inventory of his many faults: great gut, advanced age, lousy haircut, sloppy clothes, breasts like the Buddha in the living room. Clearly she'd expected to have the reverend all to herself. Tough break, then, to have this gorilla at her tea party.

The chocolate mixture was thickening. Pete focused on its wide, belching bubbles, wondering why he'd stayed and when he might leave, the discomfort drifting off him like unfortunate cooking smells. If he had any guts at all, he would up and exit *ahorita*.

Helen poured Coke for him and wine for the girl, a cheap supermarket white zin left over, she said, from some church function. "I hope it's still okay."

"It's fine," said Alice. "Good, in fact."

A snort erupted—from him it would seem. Helen shot a sharpened sideways glance. The girl guest turned as pink as her swill. Certainly he couldn't explain how bizarre it was to find himself, Pete Ross, in the same room with white zinfandel, let alone with anyone who would not only drink white zinfandel but also praise it, however insincerely. Helen's now direct stare bore into him and he ducked his head in contrition. At contrition, he was an adept.

"I'm going to toss the salad now," Helen said. Sweet and final.

Glistening greens were set out in a blue plastic bowl, rice in another dented saucepan. Helen pulled the chicken from the oven, transferred it onto a Melmac platter and called Pete to carve. He was grateful for the activity and flattered by its husbandly reek. "This isn't really a carving knife," he said. "More like a hacking knife."

"I know, I know." With the same gunlike device she used at church services, Helen lit one candle, giving the little monk a halo, or miraculous hair. "The kitchen was furnished when I moved in. Mostly junk left over from church jumble sales and potlucks. Like six melon ballers and not one decent knife." She concentrated on lighting the next candle. "I did own a fully equipped house once, with china and silver and linens and adult furniture, but I cashed out when I went to seminary. My garage sale lasted for weeks," she said. "Having people paw through your things really weakens the will to ownership. Since then I've had almost an antipathy to stuff. Except stuff like this." She tapped the little monk's cheek with her lighting device, then switched off the overhead light and sat down. The room grew luminous and burnished, like an old oil painting. "Alice, you're across from me. And you're between us, Pete."

He obediently brought the chicken, which was more in clumps than in slices, and sat where ordered.

"I'll say a little grace"—Helen glanced at the real guest—"if you don't mind." She did not consult him, so obvious was it that he'd allow her anything.

"I don't mind," said the girl.

It was hard to think of her as Alice and not Suzy. Whatever her name, the scrawny thing was lying. One unaccountable side effect of going nuts was an ace, if involuntary, bullshit detector. Like it or not, he was a living, breathing lie-catcher. This one disliked prayer, plain as day.

"God," Helen rang out in a disturbingly loud voice, "we give thanks for new friends and good food. We recall the Last Supper . . ."

He could hardly listen; his legs had begun to jump, his knees bumping the underside of the table.

". . . and Passover, and celebrate the freedom and the faith found in their stories."

He pushed his thighs to hold them down.

"May we each know such freedom, and find such faith, and may we also be filled with loving-kindness toward ourselves and others," said Helen. "So be it."

"Praise the Lord." Pete, relieved by the prayer's brevity, reached for food. "Jell-O! I haven't had Jell-O since jail." Oh Lord. Shut up, shut up, shut up.

Alice poured herself more wine, quite a bit more. Did they have a guzzler on their hands?

The food was delicious, if he did say so himself, the chicken lemony, with sticky, deeply golden skin, the basmati nutty and buttery.

Helen loosed more light and brightness from her eyes. "I'm so glad you both came," she said, reducing them—the pink-wine drinker and himself—to mumblers. Mortification burned on the poor girl guest like a rash. He knew, as she knew, that he shouldn't be there.

"This food is good," the poor thing managed to say.

Alice, he thought to himself. *Her name is Alice.*

"Pete made most of it," Helen said. "He used to have his own restaurant. What was it called again?"

"Doesn't matter," he mumbled. "Been closed for years." The oven had heated up the kitchen, and he was sweating. He could smell himself, soap going rank. When was he last a dinner guest? Long before Anne moved out, so more than two years, a drenching darkness ago. How do you cut meat, drink water, appear to be listening? The women were talking, but he couldn't catch the topic for all the trepidation churning within. Helen had to ask him three times to pass the salad.

"I talked to Pete about it," she said to Alice. "He says there are deer in the park."

Alice looked at him. "Yeah? Are they tame?"

"They're used to people," he said. "I don't know if you could pet one."

"Maybe that's all it was, then," said Alice. "A deer from the park. I wasn't sure there were any left."

Had Pete missed something? He looked from woman to woman.

"A deer wandered into Alice's house the other night," Helen said, and then, to Alice: "It's okay if I tell him, isn't it?"

"I don't care."

"There are deer around," said Pete. "Herds. They're almost pests."

"That's a relief, then," Alice said. "Thanks. That's good to know."

Helen smiled at him. He'd done okay. The real guest had engaged him in conversation, and expressed gratitude for his response. He, Pete Ross, had supplied the necessary erudition! He scooped another wedge of Jell-O and held it close to the candle, where it gleamed and shivered, shiny and dark as obsidian. "Did you know," he said, inspired to impart more knowledge, "that gelatin was made with both meat and fruit until the

sixteenth century, so it was savory *and* sweet? Meat *and* strawberries. Pigs' feet *and* peaches—"

"How disgusting," said Alice.

"I don't know," Helen said. "I find food history so interesting."

Pete addressed her, then. "To get the gelatin, they boiled
huge cauldrons full of bones, knuckles, hooves, horns and
antlers for hours."

"Antlers?" said Helen.

"Oh, sure," said Pete. "Hartshorn. It's a natural gelatin.
Also a smelling salt. An aphrodisiac, too. Or so I hear."

"Antlers," Helen said again, but to Alice. "Maybe that's
why you're eating Jell-O."

"But there aren't deer antlers in Jell-O," Alice said.

"Still—the deer comes, gelatin comes from antlers, you
crave Jell-O . . ."

"It was cool on my sore throat. Besides, I didn't know gelatin was ever made from antlers. That's too far-fetched."

"Yes, but I'm fond of the far-fetched," said Helen. "And
you never know what's stored in the collective unconscious."

Another snort, again from his mouth. "Sorry," he said, and
turned to Alice. "I've heard her preach, is all. She *is* far-fetched."
He meant it lightly—he was ribbing Helen, or trying to, for
God's sake—but both women looked at him blankly. "In a good
way. I mean, I don't have anything against far-fetchedness . . ."
Perhaps a muzzle would help.

Candles flickered in the little monks' hollow tonsured
heads. Forks rang on plates. "By the way, Helen," Alice said quietly, "you were right about my aunt. She did have something to
tell me."

"No kidding!" This perked the good reverend right up.
"Can you say?"

Alice glanced at him and reached for the wine bottle. "I'll
tell you later."

"Hey." He pushed back from the table. "If you gals want to

get down with the girl talk, I'll leave. I shouldn't have barged in to begin with—"

"I invited you, for heaven's sake," Helen said. "Please stay."

"I wouldn't want to obstruct a conversation," said Pete.

"Oh, it's nothing," said Alice. "I have this great-aunt, who's been practically a second mother to me. And today she said that before I was born she met—"

"You mean someone had a life before you were born?" Pete, propelled by the urge to provide humor, sat forward. The remark, when forming in his mind, had seemed quite funny—but once spoken, it resounded with sarcasm and mockery.

"Of course she had a life. I never said she didn't." Alice now spoke just to Helen. "I'd heard she had her heart broken once, but I never thought—"

"Thought what? That she could be somebody's piece of ass?" Still straining for laughs, again purely rude, and now crude as well. God help him.

Alice took a big swig of wine.

Helen looked on, calm as a mirror.

"I was just surprised," Alice said quietly. "She never told me . . ."

One more parry, he decided, and they'd be slapping their thighs and peeing their pants. "Why should she tell you anything? So you can blab it to us?"

Alice's mouth guppied.

Could someone just shoot him?

Helen leaned forward with a thoughtful look on her face. "You know, Pete, people can learn a lot about themselves by looking at their relatives. Especially when they're willing to see what's really there, and not just who they imagine them—or need them—to be."

"Thank you, Reverend. That's quite profound." Didn't she know he wasn't dense or stupid or cruel, but simply, and unforgivably, unfunny?

"Really . . ." Helen regarded him with her relentless calm. "I'd think you of all people would be interested in these things.

Pete's mother"—she turned to Alice—"is another remarkable woman."

Was there a cure for involuntary snorting?

"You don't think your mother's remarkable?" Helen asked him.

"I'm not saying she isn't." Pete stood, bumping the table. A wing of wine leapt from Alice's glass. "But all this mother talk reminds me. I better get back so the old gal won't worry. Thanks for the chow."

"You're not leaving?" Helen said.

Pete spoke to Alice. "I told her not to invite me."

"You haven't even had dessert," Helen said. "At least stay for pudding."

"Nope." He pushed in his chair. "I'll go so you two can yak to your hearts' content." Would he never shut up and haul his lard ass out of this sweltering kitchen? Or would he first have to melt into a puddle of pure humiliation? "I'm leaving," he assured Alice, pulling his groceries from the refrigerator.

Helen walked him to the door. "Hey," she said, coming up so close that he had the mad thought she might kiss him. "What happened in there?"

A wild pain oscillated through him like a high-pitched wail. He would've sacrificed a hand to touch her face. He said, "Pete Ross came to dinner."

14

Alice dumped out her wine and wondered when she, too, could slip away. She'd come to see Helen only to find herself paired with a weirdo. Even before he ran after her at the river, hollering and stumbling like a frantic, oversized schoolboy, she'd seen him around town, shirttails flapping, head bowed in conversation with himself. Is that what Helen took her for—another local lunatic? Was Thursday charity night at the parsonage, dinner for the strays—a street mutterer, an hallucinator of deer?

Helen came back into the kitchen. "Poor Pete." She opened the refrigerator. "But what a good cook. He made this out of thin air. It's still warm!" She tipped a saucepan toward Alice. Chocolate pudding bulged, its dark skin cracking. "Let's eat all of it," she said.

Alice, being fond of chocolate, sat back down. "He sure is smitten with you."

"That's just transference. Happens with ministers just like it does with shrinks. It's nothing serious."

"Does he know it's nothing serious?"

Helen laughed, spooning pudding into bowls. "He'll figure it out." She licked a spattered knuckle. "This much chocolate will keep me awake till next week—but maybe I'll finish my Easter sermon. Oh, I know. Chamomile tea'll counter the caffeine." Helen picked up a kettle, turned. "Now, tell me about your aunt."

That beam of attention again—so intense, and aimed exclusively at her! A person was obliged to meet such interest with the truth, or as much truth as could be managed. "I always knew Aunt Kate's heart had been broken, and today I found out why. The guy was married!" Helen's attention neither flared nor relaxed; clearly she expected a better punch line. "I mean, I can't wrap my mind around it. My aunt Kate and a married man?"

"Yes, it's not easy to find out someone you love and admire is just a plain old human being."

"No!" cried Alice. "That's not it! I never thought she was perfect, or that she's *sinned*. I just wish I'd known sooner. I mean, it explains so much . . ." Helen's expectancy was undimmed. "I mean, it's so weird—the first guy I slept with was married, when I was fifteen."

"Ahh! And so young!" said Helen. "How old was this man?"

"Joe? I don't know. Twenty-eight or -nine. But isn't it weird, I mean a coincidence, about my aunt and . . ." Alice broke off, cowed by her failure to communicate the impact of Aunt Kate's revelation.

"Was he a family friend?" Helen said. "I mean, your fellow."

"Kind of—a neighbor. I worked for him my sophomore year of high school. His wife had just had a baby, so I was hired to do her chores—feed chickens, build racks for the bees, take him lunch in the vineyards."

"And he seduced you."

"Oh God no. It was all my idea." Alice took a spoonful of pudding and let it dissolve on her tongue. Poor scrawny Joe Gemminy, with his straw hats, his dusty skin, his eyes green as lime candies. His sweat had a sharp goatlike musk she'd liked, at first. "His wife was so involved with the baby. And he was so lonely I felt sorry for him, so one day I just grabbed him."

"Yes, but he was the adult," Helen said. "He should've shown restraint."

"Oh, he tried!" Alice said with a laugh. After the first time she and Joe had sex, he'd sat in the dirt sobbing, his skinny chest heaving. "I'm a child molester," he kept saying. "I should be shot." Two days later, of course, his remorse had ebbed and he was game for another go-round.

The kettle whistled, so Helen got up and made tea. "How did it end? Did his wife ever find out?"

"No. I came here to visit Aunt Kate, and mooned about for a couple of months. But when I got home in August, he'd already moved in with someone else." Alice toyed with the monk candleholders, making them face each other. "But I always wondered why didn't I go for cute John Hall in the tenth grade? Why did I go for someone's creepy old husband? And Joe was just the first in a series . . . so when Aunt Kate told me about her guy, it was like, *Oh! It must run in the family.*"

Helen gave Alice a keen look. "The man you just broke up with—was he?"

"No! Not him."

"Is this upsetting you?" Helen said. "You look wan."

"I still don't feel well. It hits at night. I probably should go."

"Have some tea first, to warm you up." Helen poured the tea into green plastic thermal mugs with the *Morton UU Church* logo. "And you know, Alice, it can happen to the best of us."

"What?" She glanced at the minister's bright eyes. "You mean you . . . ?"

"You can't be single for as long as I have and not skirmish with a husband or two. But talk about pain! Whoa, Nellie!" Helen slapped the table.

"Yeah. Poor Aunt Kate," Alice said. "It's hard to imagine her going through it. And I thought I had a monopoly on that brand of misery in our family."

"Yeah, but that's so often not the case. I thought I was the first person in my family even to *think* of being a minister. Come to find out my father studied for the ministry in college, took all

his Greek and Hebrew, *then* found he couldn't speak in public—
he'd freeze up every time. His failure was so humiliating that he
never even told my mother. So imagine his surprise when, in my
middle age, I start pursuing *his* old dream."

"And you don't think it's coincidence?"

"I did at first. But then, in seminary, my church-history
professor had us do genograms—these family trees of traits
and patterns. We had to write what each ancestor did for a
living, and who was fat, who drank, who gambled, who told
the stories, who was rich, who was sick—all for as far back as
we could. Turns out, I was far from the first minister in the
family, and not even the first prison guard! One great-uncle
was on a firing squad—talk about a dirty little family secret.
All the unrealized ambitions, yearnings, secret lives—all that
repressed, unspoken stuff—seems to resurface in succeed-
ing generations. I saw I was just a remix of inherited traits,
another squiggle in big powerful patterns. It was quite humbling," Helen concluded, altogether too cheerfully. "And very
freeing."

Being a remix of your ancestors' traits hardly sounded freeing to Alice, who had always felt burdened by the expectations
and scrutiny engendered by her Jamesian ancestry alone. "At
least your ancestors programmed you into professions. All I've
inherited is a thing for married men. And the family depression.
And maybe adult-onset schizophrenia."

"Your ancestors *were* famous, virtuosic depressives," Helen
said. "What was it the father—Henry James Sr.—called his two-
year breakdown . . . a vastation? I love that word. *Vastation.*
Can't you just see three hundred and sixty degrees of dusty, arid
emptiness?"

"I never thought about it." Alice hadn't meant to steer the
conversation to family mythology. "And I'm not all James, you
know. I had fifteen other great-great-grandparents. Who knows
what they put in the mix."

"It's funny this came up tonight," Helen said, "because

lately I've been wondering how much of my life I have to spend fulfilling my father's discarded ambitions."

"Really?" To Alice, Helen's vocation was the most interesting thing about her. "Don't you like being a minister?

"This fucking church would kill anyone's enthusiasm!" Helen gave a short, flat laugh. "Oh—you're not shocked, are you? Because I need friends I can say 'fucking' in front of. And to answer your question, no, I don't like being a minister, not at Morton. It's like having a hundred disapproving parents."

"God, and a single call from my measly pair has me fetal on the couch for days!"

"I know! I've never done so much couch time in my life!" Helen now ate pudding straight from the pan. "The one thing that keeps me going are my Wednesday night services. More people come each week. This great old L.A. novelist, a congressman. And last night, a famous actress. She said it was her first public foray in years where nobody bothered her. I didn't say it's because Unitarian Universalists only go to art films and probably didn't recognize her."

"Who was she?" said Alice. "Can you say?"

"Sure, except I'd never heard of her. I only go to art films myself!"

Alice wished Helen wouldn't laugh quite so heartily at her own jokes.

"Pete knew who she was, though," she said. "Red-brown hair? Tall. Allison something?"

Alice's heart began to seize and release.

"Carolyn? She lives in the neighborhood." Helen peered at Alice. "You look downright peaked. You wanted to leave half an hour ago and I just keep jawing."

"I am a little tired." Alice stood up. "I had fun, though. Thanks."

Helen walked her to the door. "This is an interesting, difficult time for you, Alice, and you don't have to go through it alone. Call anytime, even the middle of the night. I don't care if you wake me."

"That's so nice." Alice would never phone anyone late at night, not unless it was Nick.

"Let's get together soon. We could watch a deer video—like *Bambi,* or *The Yearling.*"

"Okay. Great." And Alice finally was out on the windy streets, alone.

15

Pete, on his morning constitutional, paused to salute the bronze statue of Colonel Griffith J. Griffith at the park entrance on Riverside Drive.

Until moving to the neighborhood, Pete had assumed that Griffith Park had been given to the city by the pioneering film-maker D. W. Griffith with proceeds, say, from *The Birth of a Nation*. The actual benefactor—at least according to this bronze portrait—bore an uncanny likeness to Chester A. Arthur; slack-mouthed, buck-toothed, of benign demeanor, he resembled nothing so much as a large bespectacled beaver.

In the local history section, Pete had pulled out a biography, a clumsily bound, blurry carbon copy of a 1952 doctoral disser-tation by one Evelyn Pendergast: "The Misanthropist Philan-thropist: The Turbulent Life and Times of Colonel Griffith J. Griffith." In the smeared and arcane academic prose, Pete learned that the teenage Griffith J. Griffith had escaped abject poverty in Wales by coming to America, where with an immi-grant's vigor he received an education and got rich quick. In the early 1880s he bought the four-thousand-acre Rancho Los Feliz and shortly presented more than three thousand of the acres to the city of Los Angeles, with the stipulation that they become a park for the people. Riding waves of goodwill generated by his gift, he married a high-society girl named Tina Mesmer and became wealthier yet.

Despite his success and lavish benefactions, Colonel Grif-fith was disliked by acquaintances, associates and family alike, who described him as condescending, long-winded, boring, a braggart, eccentric, imperious, grandiose and grotesque. Griffith himself admitted in print, "I had the wrong personality." Who would guess it from his buck-toothed, blandly grinning effigy in the park? Also, unlike the revisionist statue, the colonel had been fat, fat like Pete, and just as mental. And even more felonious.

Griffith's unfortunate personality had deteriorated as he aged. Fifteen years into his marriage, he became convinced the pope was poisoning him in cumulatively toxic doses. At restaurants, banquets and private dinners, Griffith made his wife, herself a devout Catholic, exchange plates of food with him.

One day, in a luxury beachside hotel in Santa Monica, he aimed a gun at poor Tina, forced her to her knees, made her swear on her prayer book, then asked questions he'd scribbled on the back of a menu. Had she poisoned a recently deceased friend? Was she poisoning him? Had she been faithful to him? Griffith didn't make it all the way through his list before he pulled the trigger. Tina ducked but took the bullet through her eye, then managed to throw herself out an open window. She landed on a rooftop patio below. Imagine that—a woman with a geysering head wound dropping onto your terrace!

At the trial, Griffith's lawyer pleaded alcoholic insanity— the first such plea in history—and brought in a parade of experts. The prosecutor, who would soon become governor of California, put Tina Griffith on the stand and slowly lifted her waist-length black veil, whereupon the jury found her husband guilty of assault with a deadly weapon. The judge handed down the maximum sentence, two years. Thus the self-aggrandizing paranoid park-giver went to prison, where he eschewed special treatment, worked in the laundry room, sewed grain sacks and gathered his wits. He emerged still wildly rich, sober, a shade more humble—depending on whom you consulted—and devoted the rest of his life to prison reform and protecting Griffith Park from the city's exploitative whims.

Only eighty years after his death had Griffith's notoriety

faded sufficiently for a public monument to be erected in his honor. (Compared to shooting your wife in the head, trashing an ex-wife's apartment seemed downright neighborly!) That there could even *be* a statue of such a pompous psycho blowhard gave Pete thousands of acres of hope.

And he needed to feel hope as he strode uphill hemorrhaging sweat, his lacerating pace intended to outstrip the humiliation of last night's dinner. The problem was—*still* was—that he'd cross one line and then keep on going, seemingly forever. Last night, he'd bullied the poor girl, and Helen had allowed it. Mom would've put a quick stop to it; but she wasn't there, and the deeply quiet Helen Harland didn't take on the task. Nope, Pete was not fit company for man nor skinny-hip girl, let alone his own adorable minister, whom he'd face in a few short hours at the Bread Basket. And on top of all that, Mom wasn't exactly thrilled that he'd accepted the invitation in the first place; without her consent, it violated their permission-for-everything agreement.

Pete pushed himself up a park road that had long been closed to vehicles. Tufts of bunchgrass burst through cracked asphalt. Two years ago, at the age of forty-four, Pete had exited his role as husband and family man with one final, extravagant gesture, and since then he'd seen too much—his wife's apartment in shambles by his own hand, terror in his son's eyes, a county jail cell, Carrie Dupray's springy breasts, his own wrist tendons snapping like rubber bands—to rejoin his peers in their midlife primes, with their sport-utility vehicles and Encino ranch houses, their late-in-life children and tax-deferred Keoghs. If Pete returned to an independent, nonprobationary existence— and it sometimes seemed as if, however haltingly, he might be doing exactly that—it would not be to yuppie fatherhood or the forty percent tax bracket, but to far more modest outposts such as the banks of a fake river, a dingy Catholic charity, the company of a deconstructed cleric and a deer-obsessed waif.

. . .

Whom he encountered an hour or so later at the farmer's market on Brand Boulevard, where she was eyeing head lettuce. He said, with characteristic charm, "Don't buy that shit."

"I like iceberg," she said. "I hate those hedge clippings everybody else eats."

"Fine, but don't buy it from these sleazeballs."

She had already put down the lettuce and was moving away from the stall, if only to draw him to a place where the vendors couldn't hear him. Pete didn't care who heard him, although maybe he should.

"Those guys load up at the produce mart. You want to buy from growers."

"And how am I supposed to know who's a grower and who's not?"

"Look at the boxes. If they're from all over, they're not from one farm. Look—Temecula and *Oxnard* and *Clovis*, for Christ's sake."

"Do you have to make a scene?"

"Seems so," he said, mildly pleased with himself, and motioned her down to a tidy stand run by Asian women, where the greens were bundled like bouquets and heads of lettuce were stacked in a plump, veiny-green pyramid.

For the second day in a row, Pete was shopping with a woman. This one was even skinnier than his mother, as small, in fact, as teenage Carrie. She knew how to pick a good orange, though—by weight. She'd grown up, she told him, in the citrus groves up north. As they moved from stand to stand, he lectured—or hectored—her on potato types, strawberry production, the ideal size of okra pods. Back at her car, and clearly against her better judgment, she offered him a ride.

He should have refused. His huge mountain of flesh and his bags of food in her toy-sized dented Japanese import? A fucking circus skit. He grunted directions to the Bread Basket. "Hey, your friend should be here today," he said.

"I don't have any friends," Alice said.

"Your friend the minister," said Pete.

"She's not really my friend," she said. "I just met her."

"Come say hello, anyway," he said, having by then resolved to make the good reverend a gift and thus atone for his charmlessness of the previous evening by delivering up deer-girl herself, who was not, to his mind, the best candidate for ministerial friendship, though certainly a better bet than his sorry, oversized carcass. At least this creature had a notable ancestor.

Pete Ross, per se, had no ancestors at all. He was a fiction, an assimilation fantasy dreamed up by one Gabrielo Rosales, who by changing his name to Gabe Ross had erased the Mexican part and thus allowed his son, Pedro, to slide unhindered into American youth culture. Pete completed this transformation by refusing to learn Spanish and eschewing all things Mexican, wincing at and mocking his father's lingering accent. As an adult, while not judgmental of others' ethnicity, Pete welled with pure hatred for his own easily darkened skin and overlarge brown eyes. He never mentioned his south-of-the-borderness to his wife, and hadn't needed to, because by the time Anne came on the scene his Irish-American mother had taken the veil and was running bootleg medicine in Central America and his unmistakably Latino father was dead.

Gabe Ross had died at age thirty-nine, having gone to the doctor with a small bladder problem and emerged with a prognosis of four to six months. Reality, as it unfurled, would split this cleanly down the middle: twenty weeks.

Pete, still in college then, had lived on with his mother in their South Pasadena home. She didn't want him to leave. He turned twenty-one, twenty-two, twenty-four, in her house, staying on after Cal State gave him a B.A. in anthropology, until the Culinary Institute up in Napa offered him a scholarship. When he went north against her wishes, she promptly dove into the convent. That showed him.

Pete proceeded to make his fortune in the kitchens of fine restaurants, first in San Francisco and then, during the eighties food boom, in Los Angeles. He rose, inexorably, from prep to line to executive chef, and after several executive chefdoms became chef-owner of Trotwood and, eventually, its doomed offspring, Peggotty, which reversed his impressive trajectory and spiraled him downward through debt, bankruptcy, unemployment and disability.

Yet here he was, after a three-year ruin, back in food service of a sort, doling out beat-up canned goods and stale cookies to the hungry.

He pulled himself out of Alice's tin can, dragging his groceries behind him. He ushered her through the men and women waiting for the Bread Basket to open, unlocked the front glass door and let her in. "A few more minutes," he told the people waiting.

The Reverend Helen Harland was already wielding her clipboard behind the pantry's half door.

"Look what the dog dragged in," Pete said.

"Alice!" Helen said. "I just tried to call you! We're desperate for a bagger."

"I can't!" Panic made her voice warble. "I have food . . . perishables."

"If you give me your key, I'll stick 'em in the back fridge with mine," Pete said. "You want some coffee? Sorry, no white zinfandel."

The girl was trapped, her head swiveling. He took the car keys from her hand.

"It'll be fun," Helen said, and before the poor thing could object she'd opened the bottom half of the pantry door and drawn her inside.

Pete stored groceries and started a pot of coffee in the storeroom, then switched on the computer, all the while feeling a good hundred pounds lighter. Helen didn't hate him! She'd smiled at him! Perhaps he had not degraded himself fatally and could still paddle back into her wide, deep heart.

At the stroke of ten, he threw open the plate-glass door.

Today's volunteers—aside from Helen—were elderly women golfers who relinquished their Friday morning tee times to perform good works. They signed the clients in, Pete printed out the food orders, Helen handed out sacks of toiletries and her sulky new lieutenant filled bags from the pantry shelves.

At noon Shirley arrived in a shiny red blouse, short black gabardine skirt and red high heels. She looked like a secretary, an impression driven home by the tapered red plastic pen stuck in her bun; trailing an inch of beaded chain, it had clearly been yanked from some public writing station. "I'm back in the breadline, Petesy baby," she sang while signing in.

"Shirley," Helen called, "I've got something for you." Over the pantry's Dutch door, she handed Shirley a bulging Nordstrom shopping bag. "I went through my closet and wanted you to have first choice."

"Thank you, Rev. We big girls gotta stick together," she said, taking the bag. "You just can't find the larger sizes no more. Oh, now, will you look at this." She pulled out a white slip. "I say. And this . . ." She held a pink nightgown against her angular flat body. "Hey, Burgie," she called. "Whaddya think of this?"

"Not much," growled Burgess, sitting against the wall.

She turned to Pete. "I ain't so ugly, am I, baby?"

"No ma'am," he said with complete honesty. He did admire Shirley's nerve—despite looking like the Caucasian man she in fact was, she nonetheless embodied black femininity. To have such a clear sense of self, and one that went against all appearances! Pete also admired her grooming, her style and *range;* always clean and tidy, she somehow produced an endless number of outfits—quite a coup for a homeless cross-dresser. When wearing the genteel shirtwaists and pearls of San Marino matrons, she grew prim and chilly; in a vintage rayon floral housedress, she became sultry and languid. She'd once shown up in an aqua sari embroidered with gold and tiny mirrors, sweeping through the place like a great aqua heron.

His mother left before noon to take the groceries home and attend the Good Friday services—a theatrical young priest she liked was going to reenact the whole Crucifixion—but Pete stayed until the Bread Basket was locked up. Helen then drove him over to the church in her sensible Ford Taurus station wagon, its backseat littered with papers, water bottles, sweaters and books. She wanted to go in, she said, "to check out the competition." Though Pete didn't care for or about such theatrics, and might've waited for his mother outside, he couldn't pass up an opportunity to loll in the presence of his own favorite clergyperson.

The sanctuary was dark and they stood inside the doors, letting their eyes adjust before finding a seat. "Oh my God." Helen grabbed Pete's arm. The young priest, in a short white sarong, was mounted on a large cross, its wood as thick as railroad ties. His arms were flung out, his head was down, his eyes closed. Red-black liquid oozed from spikes in his hands and feet, the thorns on his brow, the gash in his side. *This is the wood of the cross*, another priest droned from the pulpit, *on which hung the savior of the world*. Meanwhile, the congregation was filing up to kiss the priest's foot.

After the initial impact, which Pete had to admit was pretty effective, you could see that the guy's feet rested on a small platform and his arms sat on narrow shelves, and that he might also be *sitting* on a little seat. The whole cross sat at a slight backward tilt, so gravity eased his ordeal. Being up there couldn't have been comfortable, but it wasn't impossible. The young priest, Pete noted, had a well-muscled build and a good tan; a famous skateboarder and pickup basketball player, he was also very popular with the parish youth.

"Talk about hitting people with a big stick . . ." Helen whispered.

At Pete's snort, heads turned.

After each congregant knelt to kiss the priest's foot, a teenage girl wiped the skin with a sanitizing cloth.

"Look," Helen whispered. "Imagine trying *that* with my congregation!"

They slipped into the last pew. Helen perused the missal, then cupped her mouth close to his ear. "Don't you love how in this context *passion* is synonymous with *suffering*?"

"Isn't it always?" he said.

Stained glass windows, backlit, glowed in deep reds, blues and browns as the older priests droned on. In front of Pete, a woman's stomach rumbled. A baby's squeal broke out like a bolt of light. When everyone was seated again, the room went completely dark and a priest asked them all to rise. They stood in the thick darkness, seeing and hearing nothing. In the deep gloom of the nave, two candle flames appeared. The Crucifixion was gone. The faces of the candle-bearers belonged to a boy and a girl, both adolescent, and between them a priest carried the golden ciborium. Many years ago, Pete had done this job, candlelighter for communion.

Neither he nor his ordained companion made any move toward the rail. "I haven't been to confession in ten years," he whispered. As if she cared. Why did he feel the need to explain himself?

"I'm going now," Helen said. "This just reminds me I've got an Easter service to finish." She clasped his shoulder, flooring him. "See you soon."

Pete met his mother, as planned, at the side of the church. Together they drove to Doc Freeman's office in Encino for the twice-monthly psychiatric check-in. She brought up the errant dinner right away.

"It was with a minister, for chrissakes," Pete said.

"A woman minister," said Mom.

Freeman's bushy eyebrows leapt an inch. "Tell me about her, Pete."

"She's my meditation teacher," he said, not without pride. "And more Mom's friend than mine. She was just ministering to the socially impaired. Treating me like someone who might actually use silverware, make small talk."

"And how'd it go?" Freeman said.

Pete grinned broadly. "A spectacular failure."

"How so?"

"I was rude to the other guest."

"Also a woman," his mother interjected.

"And why the rudeness?"

Pete shrugged. "Preemptive strike."

"I see," Freeman said, and sent Pete out of the room to roam the halls.

Was he in trouble? He hadn't thought roasted chicken and chocolate pudding that dire a transgression. But Mom had caught the sexual currents and was overplaying them as much as he was underplaying them. He sincerely hoped Freeman wasn't pissed off, since pissing him off was not a good idea. Freeman was the first of countless talk curers he'd tolerated or—okay— gotten attached to, who knows why. Talk about an egomaniacal gasbag! Yet Pete admired the doc's unflagging self-esteem. Their first session, Pete had asked why he charged two hundred bucks an hour. "I'm good," Freeman said, "and I'll save your fuckin' life." Which, not to put too fine a point on it, he had.

But you couldn't piss him off and get away with it. A year or so ago, Pete devoured the contents of a medicine cabinet, drank most of a pint of whiskey and went driving, his big pink hands luminous on the wheel. He'd drift off and come around and those brilliant big hands would still be steering, at least until he woke up in the ambulance, a bag of clear liquid swinging over his head.

At the hospital, the residents pumped his stomach and put him under suicide watch while trying to transfer him elsewhere, into anybody else's care. (Nobody likes a would-be suicide, especially the police, who treat you like a common murderer.) They called Dr. Freeman, who refused to refer Pete anywhere, who in fact claimed that Mr. Ross was not his patient. The residents then called all the local nut wards and got the same reply: "No, we're sorry, we cannot admit Mr. Ross." The omniscient, omnipotent Freeman, it seemed, had sent an all-points bulletin throughout the San Fernando Valley to the effect that Peter Ross was extremely dangerous and would require a twenty-four-hour-a-day suicide watch. Nobody had the staff for such extravagance, or could guarantee such constant attention, or wanted a sure death on their hands. No room at the inn for Pete. He had them call Freeman again. "I'm sorry," the receptionist droned. "Mr. Ross is no longer a patient of Dr. Freeman."

Pete's mother had eventually located a ward beyond Freeman's immediate bailiwick, in Glendale, and he was admitted for sixty to ninety days, during which time he was obsessed with one thing and one thing only: getting Dr. Freeman to take him back. "Mr. Ross, Dr. Freeman is no longer your doctor," the receptionist said in her maddening singsong. "No, Dr. Freeman will not reconsider you as a patient." Pete knew this receptionist, a dark-skinned, dark-haired young woman from Gujarat he'd seen twice a week for a year; they'd discussed the finer points of *dosas* and *bhel puri*, how to make the crispest *pakora*, and now she spoke to him as to a stranger, which made him want to howl, to pound the nuthouse walls, to rip the pay phone off its mounts and hurl it down the corridor. But one peep, a single yelp of frustration, and the orderlies would strap him down faster than you can say *oops!* This knowledge Pete had acquired firsthand. They strap you down with four-point restraints, shoot you full of Thorazine, and for the next twenty-four hours, hardly even a glance in your direction. You pee and shit in your own clothes; truly, it is cruel and unusual punishment, if not as unusual as it should be. Thus no peep from Pete, no matter how maddening the Gujarati lass.

Instead he wrote Freeman letters, then lengthier letters. He left messages on Freeman's voice mail after business hours, then lengthier messages. Pete regaled his new hospital-appointed therapist ceaselessly—and, he saw now, thoughtlessly—with grief and longing for his previous shrink. Nobody could stand in for Freeman, or even come close. "A lot of psychotherapists speak of their clients," he'd told Pete at their first session. "But let's be clear. You are not my *client*. You are my *patient*." Pete understood this to mean that he was ill and that this man was his doctor, whose job it was to make him better, even well. Nobody else had spelled out the roles so clearly, or shouldered such responsibility.

More phone calls, more scribbled outpourings. Pete concentrated so intently on recapturing his doctor's good graces that he forgot about his other plan, for self-annihilation. And finally, Freeman appeared on the Glendale ward. Pete, certain he was hallucinating, could neither speak nor move. It turned out Freeman had a patient at that hospital—one he recognized as such, that is—a fragile pillhead housewife too depressed or medicated to respond to Pete's interrogations about the doctor's next scheduled visit. He practiced what he would say, given a second sighting, and when Freeman did reappear, Pete stopped him in the hall and said, with miraculous calmness, "I want to see you again. I want another chance."

Dr. Freeman, always in a hurry, barely glanced at him. "It's possible."

The ensuing negotiations were endless. Dr. Freeman would not see him until he was released and off the Xanax and any other narcotics or hypnotics whatsoever. At last, a substance-free Pete was summoned to the office, bashful as a boy, baking with embarrassment, his heart squeaking like a guinea pig.

"If you're on your way to jump off a bridge or buy a gun, call me and I'll send an ambulance," Freeman informed him. "But if you *ever* take another swipe at yourself without calling first, that's it. Over. *Finis.* You'll see neither hide nor hair of me again. And try to remember this, Mr. Ross: If you kill yourself, you're killing the wrong person."

Who, Pete wondered, was the right person?

Dinner at the parsonage was hardly a suicidal swipe, but going there sans permission had violated the terms by which he'd agreed to live. And what would mother and psychiatrist make of his transgression?

"Mr. Ross?" Dr. Freeman motioned him inside. "Please."

His mother's face bore stoic displeasure.

"Your mother and I," Freeman said, "agree that you can start socializing, providing that you clear it with her first. And your assignment is to have excellent manners, regardless of what anybody else is doing. The manners of a gentleman. You know what those manners are, Mr. Ross?" Freeman peered over his glasses.

Pete met the doctor's eyes.

"Are we agreed, then?"

How few millimeters could he move his head and still signify assent?

16

After escaping from the Bread Basket, Alice headed west into Los Feliz and drove north through a neighborhood where homes were grand and architecturally random—a Frank Lloyd Wright, say, between a Georgian and a Cape Cod saltbox. In a grassy meridian, the naked branches of coral trees ignited at their tips with long scarlet petals. Magnolias formed a bronzed-green canopy, the waxy white flowers large as stop signs.

Beyond the shuttered Greek Theater, the road entered Griffith Park, then narrowed and climbed to the quaint, dark tunnel, its semicircular opening a giant mouse hole. Alice drove for another mile past the observatory and parked in a turnout marked by a battered, gang-tagged trash can. Buckling on a fanny pack, she headed up a steep, crumbling trail.

Dust glinted in the hot sun. The gusting breeze was cool. Alice followed a streambed still trickling from the last rains. Wild cucumbers, spiny as sea urchins, hung from vines, a cruel fruit; mountain lilac bloomed in blue-violet shafts. Climbing quickly, she emerged from the brush onto a bald promontory, where across the ravine she could see a series of large new hillside homes, including Nick Lawton and Jocelyn Nearing's six-thousand-square-foot Spanish six-bedroom, with its red tile roof and ham-pink stucco. She pulled a pair of binoculars from her fanny pack.

Before the no-talking-about-Nick rule went into effect, Alice admitted coming here to her friend Rachel, who informed

her that it was stalking, and there were now laws against it in
California and Alice could be arrested, fined and even jailed for
such behavior. Alice doubted this truly constituted stalking—she
wasn't bothering anybody, and whoever wanted to could see as
much of Nick's home as she did. Plus, any stranger could call
him, or knock on his door, which he had forbidden her to do.
"It's hard enough having your marriage disintegrate," he said,
"without your wife finding out there's someone else."

Alice found the sight of Nick's house reassuring, proof that
he wasn't a figment of her imagination. She'd once seen Jocelyn
Nearing watering plants on the deck, her chestnut hair in a low
ponytail; her sloppiness with the hose suggested she was annoyed, possibly angry, due, Alice hoped, to marital discord.
Another time, she saw Nick's son, Thad, eating a sandwich
alone at the picnic table; he patted his lips with his napkin after
each bite with heartbreaking correctness. But today, the only
sign of life was a shadow of repetitive movement behind glass
doors. A housekeeper vacuuming.

The enormous houses shimmered, the windows and shiny
surfaces shooting out painful shards of light. Alice started back
down the trail.

Up ahead, bushes started to shake. A rogue gust of wind,
she thought, or frolicsome squirrels. Twigs and sticks snapped,
branches thrashed. Something big was in there. She expected, of
course, a deer. But what stepped from these shrubs were two
tall, plump women remarkably ill dressed for hiking; skintight
short skirts, tropical-colored sandals with chunky heels. Both
women had short bleached hair and dark complexions. Were
they Arabs? Maybe Spaniards or Gypsies? They glanced at Alice
as if she were no more notable than a bush, then moved nimbly
down the trail in a tumble of color, a strong rose perfume drifting in their wake. They ducked to avoid a low-hanging oak
bough and rounded a bend out of sight. On reaching the same
bough, Alice did not duck since it was a foot and a half above
her head. How tall could they have been? Six eight? Six ten?

Wouldn't that make them giants? They were certainly the tallest women Alice had ever seen. Or maybe she'd just imagined the women ducking—or imagined them, period. Alice started running down the trail, but when she reached the next clearing, they were nowhere in sight.

They couldn't have gotten *that* far ahead. They must have gone back into the bushes, or taken another trail. They couldn't have just disappeared.

Maybe they were surgically altered men, two of Monty's transgendered clients cruising in the park. Or cross-dressers like Shirley, the Ebonics-spouting white guy at the Bread Basket. But these women had not seemed remotely mannish; they were hugely, flagrantly female.

Back at her car, Alice saw a man digging in the garbage can, tossing his finds into a black plastic sack. She locked her doors and drove up. "Excuse me," she said, rolling her window halfway down. Startled, the man turned. He was younger than she expected, and looked remarkably like her boyfriend Kurt, from college. "Excuse me," she said again. "Did you see two women come off the trail?"

He pointed to his ear and stepped closer. She saw then that he *was* Kurt. He'd left her after two years for an old girlfriend, whom he married within a month. Alice had heard since that they'd divorced and he was drinking heavily—and now she waited in fear for recognition to spike in his eyes.

"Come again?" he said.

"Did you see two women around here? Very tall, short skirts?"

"No ma'am." His bag of cans, when he moved, made a noise like muted chimes. "You have any change to spare?"

Alice dug in the bottom of her purse. She almost spoke his name but didn't want to embarrass him.

He accepted her few coins in filthy cupped hands. "God bless. Have a good day."

The oval floaters in Alice's eyes, those usually ignorable,

drifting dead cells, were ringed in a blue-white light. Her back ached. A dull tone reverberated in her head. She considered scouting the trail for sandal tracks, or finding out if that man really *was* Kurt. Because if she'd just imagined two big women and an old boyfriend, then the worst was happening, and she was having "episodes" in broad daylight.

17

Helen emerged from the church into the unabashed and shambling material world, a clear, cold afternoon alive with traffic. She stopped at the Wok Inn #3 on her way home and ate the tepid, oily wonton soup and stir-fried vegetables out of cartons at her kitchen table while paging through a catalog of New Age products that came, unsolicited, in the mail: yoga props, pot-metal Buddhas, Celtic crosses, aromatherapy "scent essences" called Druid Dew. She was filling out an order blank—the name was so misbegotten, Druid Dew was a must-have!—when the phone rang, Alice Black calling. "I was so glad you pitched in today," Helen said. "You were a big help, and it made being there so much more fun."

"I had a good time, too." She sounded muted.

"You okay?" Helen asked. "What's up?"

"You told me to call if anything else weird happened."

"Absolutely." Helen took the phone to the couch. "So what happened?"

Alice described two giant women, and a homeless man who might or might not have been an old boyfriend. "And now I'm not sure any of them really existed."

"Let's take the most extreme possibility," Helen said. "Say these people don't exist in any real way. Suppose they *are* figments of your imagination. Is there any reason why these particular figments might appear at this time?"

"Not that I know of."

"Let's try something, Alice. Imagine those women are in the room with you. Can you do that?"

A noncommittal hum.

"Now imagine asking them why they're there. What would they say?"

"I can't do that," Alice said in a very low voice. "I can't talk to imaginary people."

"Even if you know they're imaginary? And it's just an exercise?"

"I don't want to start. My uncle used to argue with the devil."

"Yes, but this is actually a technique. It's called active imagination—"

"I understand," said Alice, "I'm just not interested. I don't want to open a can of worms. I just want the weird stuff to stop."

"I know you do," Helen said quietly. "But it might not, not right away. I don't mean to frighten you, but you're going through a difficult, important shift, and you can either see it as an opportunity and work with it or fight it every step of the way. I know it's scary to look at these things head-on, but the alternative—not facing up to them—is far scarier, believe me."

This time, Alice was quiet for so long that Helen had to ask, "You still there?"

"I'm just incredibly tired," she said. "I have to go to bed."

Helen let her go, then wandered through the small rooms of the parsonage contemplating the familiarity of Alice's stoniness and petulance.

Back when Helen was in seminary and still working in the prisons, her daughter felt neglected. There'd been fights, with Helen trying to explain her need to pursue a spiritual path. "I hate your spirituality," Rosemary shouted. She decided to live with her father, Helen's first husband, who was a jazz musician and heroin addict and sometime methadone user. When he wasn't on tour or on a tear, he lived in a ranch house in Altadena with his mother and assorted relatives. Once she'd moved out there, Rosemary began phoning Helen, much as Alice had to-night, to describe her problems—and resist any solution. The household was in constant turmoil. Her father came and went, sometimes in withdrawal, sometimes clean, inevitably using again. An uncle was arrested on traffic warrants. A cousin was pregnant at thirteen. People wore Rosemary's clothes, used her toiletries, took money from her purse. Her litany of complaints was various but endless. Helen would say, "You know, honey, you can come home anytime," and Rosemary would counter, "I can't, I can't leave Grandma."

Rosemary stayed for six years and moved just last June to Northridge with her boyfriend, a rock-and-roll musician fond of alcohol and narcotics. Now Rosemary's litanies concerned him, and the pressures of attending junior college. Helen listened and continued to offer advice, largely because her daughter seemed to gain some strength in rejecting it.

Alice Black, Helen suspected, might derive a similar benefit from scorning her counsel.

In the morning she began typing her handwritten fifteen-page Easter sermon into her computer, starting with the title, "Neither Here nor There." The topic was transitions. Helen opened with an allusion to Passover, using a quotation she'd copied off a seder pamphlet—her congregation found Judaic myth far less objectionable than Christian myth.

> *The Israelites, coming out of Egypt, came from bondage*
> *to freedom, from sorrow to gladness, and from mourning*
> *to festival day, and from darkness to light . . .*

She saw this sermon as one more in a loose, ongoing series attempting to address Morton's collective, unarticulated grief for the loss of their former minister. Nobody, of course, admitted to this. It had come time for Link to retire, they said; nobody begrudged him that. And Link was not *dead*, after all; many

Morton members still saw him socially. In the meantime, their unacknowledged feelings of loss found expression with regard to their new minister in misdirected anger, resentment and relentless criticism.

If we look at this sentence, we see that the little word "to" carries within it the entire journey, the actual process, all the mechanics of a great change . . .

Her first illustration of transition was the caterpillar's metamorphosis from larva to pupa, cribbed from Nabokov:

There comes a point in her transformation when, to shed the last of her larval skin, our little creature must let go of the branch she hangs from. For that briefest of moments, she is neither caterpillar nor chrysalis but purely in between. She is attached to nothing, in free fall, and a state of pure possibility. But then, with an amazing little flip, she reattaches herself in a whole new way—with a brand-new little hook at the end of her tail.

Helen had won the annual preaching award given at her seminary—a hundred-dollar gift certificate to Cokesbury bookstores—and, coming to Morton, would've wagered any amount that church administration would be her Achilles' heel. But what her homiletics instructors and seminary colleagues had perceived as lyricism, depth and mature spirituality in her sermons was judged scattershot, abstract and excessively religious by her new listeners. After she'd mentioned Jesus several Sundays in a row, the ministerial relations committee cried, "Too much Christianity!"

She'd laughed—her, Christian? She'd never espoused any Christian doctrine, not even the two her denomination was named for: the unitary nature of God and universal salvation.

But she'd backed off. Preaching was, after all, a dialogue between minister and congregants and not a solo rant. Yet how to conduct this dialogue without a common vocabulary? She'd taken, then, a secret crash course in homiletics, locking herself in the church library to consult the many thick notebooks of sermons delivered by her all-but-beatified predecessor. Reverend Link wrote well, with a friendly confiding tone and a straightforward humanism. It was he, in the early seventies, who'd had the steel cross removed from Morton's roof—and split the congregation in two. It had been a strong, growing church then, the membership having all but doubled with the merger of Unitarians and Universalists in the mid-sixties. Long-range building plans were in place for a new sanctuary and classrooms; temporary modular units housed the increased activities while construction funds were raised. After Link removed the cross—and the subsequent outcry—the more religiously conservative departed Morton to form a fellowship in Glendale. Though only a scant third of the congregation, they were also the wealthiest and accounted for half of the operating budget. After their departure, Morton never again attained its former numbers or prosperity, and the flimsy modular units never had been replaced.

Reverend Link stayed on another twenty years, preaching four Sundays a month. Helen had checked again yesterday to see how he handled the religious freight at Easter. "Spring Fever," "Spring Flings," "Bunnies, Beans and Bonnets" were paeans to concupiscence that reflected his approval of sex, especially joyous, spontaneous sex. "How Easter Got Its Name" (from a Saxon fertility goddess); "Easter in Chichicastenango" (a travelogue of arcane Easter rites Link had observed in Guatemala) and "Where Was Mary on Saturday?" (observing the Jewish Sabbath—the point being that original Christians were mostly Jews) all allowed Christian content when insulated by Freud, Alan Watts and baseball lore. Many of Link's sermon illustrations came from movies, public television and magazines—*Harper's, The New Yorker, The Nation*—familiar to his congregation. Reliably, he fed his parishioners' own ideas back to them in a cogent form, making them feel good about what they already thought.

Helen, hoping to make her own theology as palatable, had begun practicing what her colleagues referred to as "translating," and what Pete objected to as "apologizing": using unobjectionable, non-Christian language to express spiritual concepts. As a subtle, compensatory form of mischief, she often drew sermon topics from the Common Lectionary, the handbook of weekly Bible lessons used by Catholic and some Protestant clergy. This week's Gospel reading was John 20, where Mary Magdalene finds the tomb empty. *Another mythic metaphor for transition is the empty tomb of Jesus* . . . Easter was one of two annual occasions—Christmas being the other—when Helen could allude to the New Testament without undue repercussions; normally she buried the Bible lessons so deep in her sermons that no one, excepting a most attentive Christian minister, was likely to spot the lectionary's influence.

> *Between Jesus's death and resurrection lies the empty tomb. In the tomb, we find only Jesus's linen shroud and the napkin that covered his face, bits left behind like discarded skins or insect casings—which remind us that death itself is a transition, and possibly not as unfamiliar a process as we fear.*
>
> *After all, we go through life leaving behind the things we've outgrown—clothes, friends, habits and ideas that once saw us through, houses, pets, jobs, marriages, sometimes whole lives.*
>
> *The image of the tomb also reminds us that transitions contain an emptiness: a hollow, heart-stopping instant between what we were and what we're about to become.*

Helen stood and paced. She went to the bathroom, peed, brushed her hair, checked her face. Why, at forty-five, with drooping eyelids, crow's-feet and deepening puppet lines around her mouth, was she still getting acne? Was that fair? She tweezed a few eyebrow hairs—and two stray wiry black whiskers new to her jaw. Barefoot, she went outside for the mail. Retrieving a thick stack of envelopes and magazines, she sat in the sun on her front stoop and ripped open a packet from her denomination's Boston office.

Distracted by a movement across the street, she looked up to see Pete Ross, his head down, moving at a good clip with a slightly sideways stance, as if he were shouldering through a series of doors, or else was intent on not casting one glance her way. Helen, smiling, watched him barrel out of sight.

Inside the packet were this year's evaluation forms, one a self-evaluation, the other for an ad hoc church committee to complete. Last year, she'd been criticized for the Christian content of her sermons, and her "incessant call for volunteers." Also, she was working too hard, and needed to take better care of herself and use her vacation days. Pastoral skills and listening were cited as her strengths, and on a scale of one to five she had received a surprising four. *She is just getting to know us*, the committee wrote, *and we have confidence that given time, we will reach a better understanding of each other*. The report bore none of the anger and intractability—the Grief for the Lost Link, she called it—she faced on a daily basis.

Indeed, at the last church service of the year, the members presented her with a thousand dollars to spend on "something nice, even frivolous"—though the woman who'd raised the money suggested that she buy curtains to replace the Indian bedspreads she'd tacked up over the parsonage windows. Instead Helen spent the money on her trip to Europe.

She looked up to see Pete again, traveling in the opposite direction but in the same barrier-smashing stance, now on her side of the street. Oh dear. In college, she and her girlfriends referred to such coyly casual cruising as a drive-by, though in Pete's case you'd have to call it a walk-by. This was exactly the sort of beautiful folly without which the human race might not continue, but Helen could not countenance it from a congregant, and now that he was attending Sunday services, that's what Pete had become. Best then to call him on it before things got out of hand. "Hey," she called. "Pete!"

He stopped as if she'd thrown a switch, swinging his head around and grimacing hugely as she walked down to him. "What's up?" she said.

He squinted in the direction he'd been heading, a deep ruddiness blooming in his dusky cheeks. "Just takin' a walk."

"Nice day for it," she said. "I saw you go by before."

A split-rail fence with a charmingly hewn wooden gate stood between them. Pete shook the gate, making its hardware clatter. "Another twenty passes and I might've got up the nerve to stop," he said. His hair was still damp from his morning ablutions and slicked back, giving him a wide-eyed, vulnerable look; his untucked shirt was clean, starched, a glaring white.

"Was there any particular reason you wanted to see me?"

"None that I could come up with." He gave the gate another shake. "Nothing that would justify interrupting you."

"Oh please. I was just reading mail and avoiding my Easter sermon."

"So how's that coming?"

"You'll like it. I'm going to hit 'em with a big ol' crucifix."

"Yeah, but will you make 'em kiss it?"

"Wouldn't that be something!" Helen laughed. "You want a cup of tea?"

"Naw, I should be getting back. But I was wondering . . ." Under the bottom rail of the fence, sand from the cactus garden had spilled onto the sidewalk, and he began kicking it back into the yard.

Sand sprayed over Helen's bare feet. She waited.

"So tell me," he said. "What *is* your beef with God?"

"I don't have a beef with God."

"Come on, everybody does."

"Oh, Pete," she said gently. "It's been a very long time since I had any notion or concept of a God I could have a beef with."

He pried a gray splinter off the silvery fence rail. Underneath, the wood was a rusty orange color.

"And what's your beef?" she said.

He frowned, ground sand underfoot. "The usual," he said. "The Holocaust. The Inquisition. Hiroshima. And Mom always liked Him better."

18

Easter morning, Alice brought a potted lily to the Beverly Manor. Aunt Kate was working at her desk. "Do you mind, Alice dear, if I finish this page?"

"Go ahead." Alice set the plant on the nightstand and picked up a magazine, beneath which were typewritten pages. Slyly, she slid them inside the magazine and began to read.

It would do humanity a disservice, William claimed, for him to reproduce. "Natural selection will take its course," he rued. "One peek at my dubious dorsals, my dire temperament, my queasy philosophical vocation and the females of my species flee—laughing uproariously!"

So Alice never worried that he'd wed.

And besides, William said, he could find none as fair as his own sister; none as well spoken or beauteous, as gentle or wise. "We shall move on together, Alice," William vowed, "knowing that we possess the devotion and sympathy of the other."

As a child, Alice took it for granted that novel writing was the apex of human endeavors. When Aunt Kate entered her study, the house grew reverentially quiet. Uncle Walter would not watch television or use the power mower or the clackety Rainbird sprinklers; Alice would not jump rope in the backyard; they tiptoed and whispered and directed all visitors back down the drive. On rare and heady occasions, her aunt called her into the study and read aloud to her, passages which sounded, at age eight, ten, eleven, intelligent and profound.

At a family party in Wren Street when Alice was ten, sixteen-year-old Hal found some discarded pages in the trash and, after gathering the other cousins in the garage, read them with a bad English accent. Alice, outraged, reported this to her parents. Her mother laughed—laughed!—and said, "That Hal, he's a devil!"

Even now, she couldn't tell if the writing was good or not; it seemed a bit overwrought and nineteenth-century, but wasn't that appropriate to the subject?

Then, one wintry Thursday night, their papa came home from the Radical Club; he strode directly to the library, cold billowing from his woolens. "Tonight," the patriarch announced to wife, daughter and eldest son, "I have met the future Mrs. William James."

This news caused much merriment, and for the next week, William and his sister cracked wise on the subject. "Papa's prerequisites for a female are certainly stringent," Alice declared, reading from one of their father's self-published tracts. " 'Woman,' he says, is 'man's patient and unrepining drudge, a beast of burden, a toilsome ox, a dejected ass.' "

William laughed. "Perhaps she is a delectable drudge. And one hopes, however dejected, that she is a comely little ass."

Aunt Kate was hunched over the typewriter reading what she'd just written. She worked in cavelike darkness, as if sunlight and concentration were incompatible. But she worked, and worked, and worked. She'd spent decades on the first chapter, without receiving the least encouragement, as far as Alice knew, from any publisher or even friend. It was possible that only Alice had read a word in over twenty years, since the night of Aunt Kate's one reading.

She had belonged to a group that met once a month for a gourmet meal and cultural entertainment, its members giving slide shows, reading poetry or playing musical instruments. Alice went along once, when she was twelve and Aunt Kate was the featured speaker at a grand house in Los Feliz, where twenty-odd men and women were served poached salmon, tomato aspic and ice cream topped with crème de menthe. Afterward, in an ornately draped living room, a woman banged out a Chopin polonaise, then Aunt Kate came up to read the first chapter of her book.

She was in her mid-fifties at the time, already white-haired and farsighted. She held the manuscript low, at arm's length, as if looking down her nose at both her writing and her audience. Both the prose and her crisp elocution were quite impressive—when she actually read. But after every few sentences, she'd stop to talk about where she got the idea, the underlying historical facts and all the choice period details she couldn't include. After an hour, with many pages yet to go, when she paused to take a sip of water, the audience burst into applause and the hostess sprang from her seat to extend congratulations. Aunt Kate naturally took this as premature effusion and made several attempts to continue. "Ah, but Kate," the hostess said. "No need to wear yourself out when we are so sufficiently pleased." Although she spoke with longing of publication, Aunt Kate never again shared her writing. When Alice asked to read something, she invariably replied, "Wouldn't you rather read it all of a piece?"

The next Thursday, William accompanied his father to the Radical Club to meet the beastly burden. He wore the violet and crimson cravat Henry had sent from Paris, a blue shirt, his charcoal Norfolk jacket.

And overnight, the siblings' pact was discarded, as if never spoken, as if a contingency clause had existed all along.

The usurper—her name was Alice too—

"Thank you for waiting, Alice dear. That's a lovely lily."
Aunt Kate swiveled around in her chair. They both studied the
plant. The top blooms were open; the lower, flushed with green,
were swollen, about to burst.

"Is it okay if I borrow this magazine?" Alice said.

"Of course, dear."

She rolled it up, the pages still inside, and shoved it in her
purse. "I was wondering, Aunt Kate—do you know that church
on Harrison?"

"The Unitarian church? Why yes. I went there for a while,
years ago."

"I never knew that."

"A friend took me. She was terribly fond of the minister—
too fond." She paused. "What's his name? He was so smart and
funny, and literate. A forceful speaker, marvelously nondog-
matic! William would've approved."

"So you went to church?"

"Not for very long. This same minister took to coming by
the house a bit too regularly. He claimed to be making his
rounds, but I didn't care for it."

"That's so funny." Alice swung her feet off the bed. "Because I know the new minister."

"Oh, so what's his name finally retired?"

"Recently, I think," said Alice. "The new minister's pretty
new."

"A word of warning, dear. Ministers aren't always what
they pretend to be. They're men like all other men."

"Not this one, Aunt Kate. This one's a woman."

"Do tell. I've never met a woman minister. It makes sense,
though, since we always outnumber men in the pews. Is she
good?"

"I've never heard her preach. But she holds these talks on
Wednesday night, lectures on spiritual subjects. This week it's a
woman from the Jung Institute talking about Gnostics. We
could go, if you're interested."

"I've always been interested in Jung. One of my big regrets is never trying Jungian analysis." Aunt Kate stopped, frowning. "I wish I could remember that darn minister's name. Memory becomes mercurial when you get older. Stops delivering on command."

As if this *were a surprising new development!* "It'll come to you," Alice said, standing. "Feel like a little walk?"

They went out to the courtyard. Alice wanted to ask more about the married boyfriend, but there were too many people and no moment seemed right. Wheelchairs clustered by the central fountain. On their favorite bench, an older man in a skimpy green hospital gown sprawled, smoking, his long skinny legs poking straight out, pale as ice.

Aunt Kate hummed, then squeezed Alice's arm. "Link," she said, memory clouding her eyes. "Reverend Link. The Unitarian." She squeezed again. "Now, Alice, weren't you and William married by a Unitarian minister?"

To keep herself in Norm's good graces, Alice agreed to work on Easter Sunday. She opened the bar at three in the afternoon and for an hour had not one customer. She busied herself scrubbing the sinks and bar top, then read another page of her great-aunt's writing.

William did not marry right away; but spent two years in agonized equivocation. His sister Alice slyly fed and fanned his doubts.

Any marriage the melancholic William made, Alice agreed, would not be normal or natural, but difficult, tragical. Any wife of his must repudiate the usual connubial satisfactions: William was not robust, nor financially ambitious; his temperament was inconsistent, his swings from inert lethargy to prodigious occupation were unpredictable, verily dizzying.

William so strenuously warned Alice Gibbens of his defects that she broke off the courtship.

The sacred sibling pact was thereby reinstated. "It shall be you and I," William told his sister, "once again each other's solace and delight, champion and passionate beloved."

The great doom thus averted, Alice James underwent a period of almost giddy renewal; she went visiting, she took a teaching post at a women's correspondence college, she sewed for charity.

Unbeknownst to her—for he was surely now aware of his duplicity—William's relationship with the other Alice was soon revived. Once the engagement was announced, the wedding quickly followed.

This betrayal, so unexpected and profound, took the twice-duped sister of William James to the portals of madness.

Duped. Once, then twice. Perhaps this was another family trait knit in the female lines—to be chronically dupable. Alice shoved the novel pages back into her handbag.

She didn't mind working on the holiday. None of Easter's symbols and accoutrements, be they jelly beans, bunnies, white gloves, Crucifixion or Resurrection, spoke to her. It was just another holiday when she was invited to one household or the other, usually with the caveat "If you have no place else to go."

Nick, of course, would be with his family.

The last Easter Alice could remember enjoying was more than ten years ago, in Fresno during college when her boyfriend—Kurt, as a matter of fact—gave her a small, leathery, buff-colored egg that came with Xeroxed instructions. Accordingly, Alice put the egg in a towel-lined box under a bare lightbulb, and a few weeks later a small black reptile poked its nose out. Big-eyed, moist and two-thirds head, the creature was undeniably babylike, and Alice, with a rush of maternal pleasure, adored it on sight. The baby, promptly named Ana, grew into an iguana twenty-six inches from nose to tail tip and roamed freely through the house Alice shared with three other women. Coming home, they had to open the door slowly because Ana might be right there behind it, waiting for them. Or on the wall, camouflaged by the ugly floral wallpaper. When called, she would scutter across the wall, tail swishing, long thin nails rasping. Alice forever had scratches on her arms from Ana climbing onto her shoulders, but she also liked to curl up on Alice's lap. Alice had Ana for almost a year, long after Kurt left and married his former girlfriend. Then someone accidentally left the back door open and she disappeared. Alice still missed Ana, and having pets, and often thought of buying another egg or rescuing a dog from the pound. But if Nick did leave his wife, he and Alice planned to go to Europe or Asia for a year or so, until the uproar passed.

Alone, Alice began to cry. She cried because Nick had abandoned her, and also for beautiful iridescent Ana. Scaly, needle-teethed, yellow-bellied, earless, cold to the touch, Ana proved that a person could love virtually anything at all. And she made Alice question the fundamental principle of animal behaviorism, that everything has to do with the reproduction of the species. More basic and universal, Alice thought, was the desire for attention—to be noticed, heeded, singled out, tended.

The Fountain's door finally opened at ten after four, when several male couples came in. She blew her nose on a cocktail napkin, made drinks and, idle again, decided to drain the fountain. Over the years, she'd scooped all sorts of things from those lime-encrusted tiers: rags, rubber ducks, a small mechanical swimming shark, condoms in a rainbow of hues and textures; the occasional hypodermic or crack ampule still shocked her. Today, low tide revealed cigarette butts, a checkbook cover, a letter rinsed of words.

While the fountain refilled, she wiped down the bottles of fancy Scotch whiskeys until a gruff female voice interrupted. "Can't a girl get a drink in this place?"

Helen Harland sat at the bar.

"Helen!" Alice's first response was pleasure, although disappointment trotted close behind. Why couldn't it be Nick? "To what do I owe this honor?"

"I'm lookin' for a good, stiff highball."

"I don't know, Reverend. Is that kosher?"

Helen laughed her loud laugh. In her cable-knit cardigan and bouncy curls, she looked like a big, pretty, congenitally cheerful kindergarten teacher.

"What'll it be?"

"Rum," said Helen. "With lots of Coke. Diet Coke, if you have it."

Alice poured dark premium rum in a bucket glass, dropped in a lime wedge and wrote down a comp. "On me," she said. "Happy Easter."

"Thanks. And cheers! One more time I got Him out of the tomb and into the ether. It's a dirty job, but somebody had to do it . . ."

"I thought you didn't believe in all that," Alice said.

"I don't?" Helen squeezed the lime, dropped it back into her drink and swizzled vigorously. "I do love the Resurrection, though, how, every year, up he goes." The swizzle stick, trailing drops, described a series of upward arcs. "I'm slaphappy. Easter always takes it out of me. Largest attendance of the year. And everybody in their Easter best—you could smell the mothballs! Next year, I'm burning incense, no matter how many people sneeze. But it's over, thank God, and now I'm dodging a postpartum slide. Lewis couldn't make it down this weekend—you know, holidays in rehab—so here I am, trolling for company. This drink is *very* strong! But delicious. I already feel smashed. Doesn't take much." She opened her purse and took out some paper, stapled and folded in half. "For you, my Easter sermon. I wrote a lot of it after we talked the other night."

"Uh-oh," Alice said, sticking the pages in her purse.

"Why 'uh-oh'? You inspired me, and it was a hit. The sanctuary was standing room only. Pete was there—second Sunday in a row—and only sneered, oh, three or five times. And that movie star—whatever she's called—she brought her son for the egg hunt. And I spotted a dozen other people from the midweek services." Helen took a drink, grimaced. "Maybe Morton can amount to something after all."

The day's first four drinkers stood up together and pulled on their jackets. One man tossed Alice a small bag of candy. "Happy Easter, doll," he said. That left two men drinking quietly in a wooden booth.

Alice poured jelly beans onto the bar before Helen. "Now I feel guilty I didn't come hear you today."

"I don't care!" said Helen. "Really, I'd much rather see you when we can talk. Although if you ever did show up, I wouldn't bar the door."

"Actually, I might come on Wednesday with my aunt."

"I'd love it, but don't do it for my sake. I don't want you as a congregant, I need you as a friend." Helen smiled up at her. "But speaking of your aunt, how is she? Any more news about her married fellow?"

"No, but guess what? She used to go to your church. She knew the minister before you—Link?"

"Ah, the ever revered Reverend Link."

"Aunt Kate didn't come out and say so, but he sounds like sort of a lech."

"Oh, absolutely." Helen selected three pink beans from the pastel spill. "Reverend Link was a very bad boy. But charming. And the congregation *adored* him. He may have been a bad and lazy boy, but he was *their* bad and lazy boy. Then I come in all serious and gung ho—not to mention that I actually do some work—and they have no idea what to make of me."

"You're not that serious," Alice said. "I mean, you're always laughing."

"Yes, but I take my work seriously, and expect Morton's members to do so as well. That makes 'em nervous. They're used to Link, who didn't go to one committee meeting in his last ten years. You should've seen the looks when I started showing up! Hah!" Helen hit the bar top with her hand, sending jelly beans jumping. "Reverend Link didn't even have office hours; people needed appointments to see him. So here I am, at the church six days a week, in my office, with my door open. I take phone calls and walk-in visitors, and make home and hospital calls—and not just to attractive members of the opposite sex, either. So they say I'm coming on too strong."

"You'd think they'd like all that attention."

"Ah, but I've wrecked their little social club. They'd like me more if I preached a dry secular sermon every week, then vanished till the next Sunday." Helen took another swallow of her drink, and this time her wince relaxed into a wry smile. "God, Alice. Give me three sips of rum and I'll talk your ear off."

"It's interesting," Alice said, thinking that one sermon a week sounded like a dream job; you could have the rest of your life to do whatever you wanted. "You're the first minister I've ever known."

"I might not be such a great example. But tell me, what else did your aunt say about Link?"

"Nothing much. You can ask her more on Wednesday. You'll like her. And ask her anything about William James. She knows *everything,* except she's not always completely lucid."

"Me neither!" Helen gave another hearty laugh.

The last two drinkers stood and left. Alice called Norm to report the place was empty, and he said he'd be right in to close down. Alice put Miles Davis on the sound system, poured herself a weak screwdriver in a paper cup—Helen's drink was still three-quarters full—and took a seat around the elbow from Helen.

"So how are *you* doing?" said Helen. "Any more odd activity?"

"Not really," said Alice. "Though I am really aware of birds singing. I know it's spring and they're going at it. But Thursday night, after we talked, I couldn't sleep and just listened as a mockingbird sang for hours. After a while, I *got* what he was saying. Not that I could put it into words."

"Knowing the language of birds," Helen said, "is considered one of the great mystical gifts. "

Alice twisted a lock of her fine brown hair. She didn't want to understand bird chirps or see things that didn't exist. Bar, fountain, faucet—these tangibles were good enough for her. Solid, stalwart trees and ordinary sparrows. A reliable blue sky, with or without clouds. And humans made of skin and bone, in credible sizes. "What if a person doesn't want mystical gifts?"

"I'm not sure there's much choice," Helen said. "Unless it's to work with or against such gifts—and against seems the surer road to madness."

"And if one did decide to work *with*, how would one go about it?"

Helen gave Alice's forearm a friendly tap and popped another pastel bean. "One would *start*, Alice, by changing one's pronouns. One would start by saying *I*."

19

Without regular hours at the Fountain, Alice drifted through the house, lifting pillows to inhale any vestigial scent of Nick, or daydreamed and dozed on the couch, willing time to pass. She was roused by a phone call, but it was a hang-up. Another came in the late afternoon. Nick, of course. If she was psychic about anything, it was about him. In bed, she'd sometimes had a cruel thought—that he was cowardly for not leaving his wife, weak, or duplicitous—and he would flinch as if she'd spoken aloud. She'd never had such rapport with anybody, and he'd felt the same about her. "We're two of a kind," he'd said. "Two peas in a pod." So how could he let her go?

It was all she could do not to phone. *Nick, Nick, let's not give up!* But in the last year, she'd read everything she could get her hands on about women having affairs with married men, and in a book entitled *What Every Other Woman Should Know*, the author insisted that all affairs are essentially about the MM's (married man's) PR (primary relationship), and therefore the only chance the OW (Other Woman) has is to remove herself from the triangle and see what happens.

So, now the OW was out of the triangle and the MM was back in his PR, where, he'd told Alice at least a hundred times, he hadn't been happy for five minutes in the last ten years.

She simply had to let him stew—and hope he'd come back. But who's to say he wouldn't ditch his marriage and bypass Alice altogether, find himself a true farm girl, a genuine, rosy-cheeked, unruined, honky-tonkin' dairy queen?

Alice lay on the couch in the dim living room. Hang-up
number three came at seven-thirty.

Tuesday morning, she walked into Hair Today and asked for a
cut and color, didn't matter who did the work. She traded her
T-shirt for a slippery brown gown and, waiting in a pink Nauga-
hyde chair, pulled Helen's sermon from her purse. Helen had
circled several paragraphs on the third page and scribbled *I
wrote this after we spoke!* in the margin.

> *The most difficult and most important task in a transition
> is to stay conscious. The Buddhists talk about maintain-
> ing detachment in the bardo, in the storm of human sen-
> sations—they're all illusions, we're told. But they don't
> seem illusory—not when they look like our mother's face
> or the torturer's grin, and smell like fresh baked bread, a
> lover's perfume or something rotten in the walls.*
>
> *Our job is to maintain mindfulness in chaos. To stay
> awake and not get drawn in while old arguments replay,
> indignities are heaped, insults compound.*
>
> *All transitions are practice for the last great
> transition.*
>
> *Let me say that again: All transitions are practice for
> the last great transition we all face.*
>
> *It behooves us to pay attention.*

Chuck, with orange hair and all visible parts tattooed with
Maori glyphs, invited Alice to his station. He started with color,
going first to the whitened outer reaches of peroxide, then rins-
ing in a pale palomino. For the cut, Alice asked him to go short
as a boy's.

Still reeking of transformative chemicals, Alice drove to the
Salvation Army thrift store in Glendale to look for clothes that
weren't black. Spiro had made fun of what he called her eco-
warrior look—the jeans and logo'd T-shirts, the hiking boots

and Birkenstocks—and advised her to go with black jeans and
T-shirts and Doc Martens, a slinky black slip dress for clubs, a
black leather jacket over all.

The store's air was still and stale and two small boys raced
up and down the aisles. Alice quickly selected a blue gingham
blouse, a soft, pilling sweater in baby blue and a pair of generic
khakis. She modeled the ensemble in her bedroom mirror at
home. Neo-dowdy, this new style—not unlike Helen, whom she
suddenly remembered to call.

"I liked the part in your sermon about transitions being
practice for death," she said.

"I'm glad somebody did," Helen said. "A couple of oldsters
found it morbid. Oh, I have something else for you, too. I found
a copy of *The Yearling* in the church library. Did you ever read
it, or did you just see the movie?"

"Uh . . . I don't know."

"Let's rent the video, then. I'd watch it again. How's Friday?"

"Fine," Alice said. "Except you'll probably see me tonight,
too. With Aunt Kate."

"And what does that have to do with getting together on
Friday?"

Alice paused. "I wouldn't want to make a pest of myself."

Aunt Kate was in the bathroom, so Alice sat at the desk and read
the page laid out beside the typewriter.

Alice James refused to see the newlyweds when they came
to call. The other Alice's euphonic tones drifted through
the walls. "This speaks of a jealousy so distasteful, I have
difficulty speaking of it!"

Alice James, on her small sofa, pulled a fine paisley
tightly around her shoulders. The marauder was nothing
to be jealous of—Alice Gibbens was a smallish bovine;
short, stocky, mannishly robust; endowed with a grand

resonant moo and a martyr's iron will. In short, a near replicate of their own mother.

And the turbulence in Alice James's chest was not jealousy but the violent, unendurable throes of injustice: her brother's breach of contract, the alienation of his affections, the enticement of him to another's side— crimes for which there would never be either recompense or sympathy.

The bathroom door opened, and Aunt Kate emerged with her walker. "Goodness," she said, reaching for Alice's hair. "You were born with hair this color." She then glanced at the manuscript on the desk. "You haven't been nosing about, have you?" She sounded almost hopeful this was so.

Alice couldn't tell what the right answer might be. "Of course not," she said. "I'm waiting to read it all of a piece."

Aunt Kate gave her a shrewd look. Together they walked down the rest home's corridors and out to the car. Alice collapsed the walker, drove the half a dozen blocks to Morton and pulled into the parking lot. "Aunt Kate—how did you know I was born blond?" she asked. "You never saw me as a baby."

"Of course I saw you, dear."

"I thought we met when I was four."

"I saw you before that," Aunt Kate said. "I remember your flaxen hair."

Now, as many times before, Alice wondered if there'd been an intrafamily switch. Once, when she was ten, she even asked her mother, who laughed and accused her of adoption fantasies. "Do we make you so miserable you're hoping for another family?" she asked, her jocularity forced, unconvincing. "I'm your mother and I've got the photos to prove it. When I was pregnant with you, I was as big as a bus!" Alice had seen these snapshots, dates printed on their deckled edges; but those were the dates the film was developed, and it was impossible to say for sure which child incubated under that sailor-style tent dress.

. . .

Morton's Family Center was lit by candles and firelight. A Palestrina mass surged and ebbed from a boom box beside a portable podium. The usual taupe metal folding chairs formed a semicircle within the sunken conversation pit. Incense veiled the sour air.

Guiding Aunt Kate, Alice spotted Jocelyn Nearing in the otherwise empty second row of chairs on the left side of the pit, and so maneuvered the walker toward seats with a good view of the famous high cheekbones and thick, gold-streaked chestnut hair, the wide, plumped lips. Collagen-enhanced lips, Alice happened to know. And Botox-enhanced eyes.

Jocelyn Nearing pinned her hair in a loose flattering twist that would've seemed merely messy on a plainer woman. She wore a white shirt and a soft sweater the color of espresso. Thin gold hoops in her ears caught the flickering candlelight, as did blond strands in her hair. Even her skin had a fine-grained sparkle. She was by far the loveliest creature in the room, if not an altogether different species, her strong, long neck and regal posture anomalous among the drab older people and overweight moms, the gay guys in jeans, not to mention the furious fatness of Pete, who at that very moment twisted around and glared as if Alice had pelted him with a marble. She gave him a blank, unfriendly look and turned away.

Didn't it bother Jocelyn Nearing to sit in this dank, moldy bunker?

Jocelyn bowed her head, and Alice realized that Helen was at the podium, saying a prayer—*We give great thanks for being together here tonight.* She asked for a moment of silence, in which the fire hissed and spat, then invited people to light candles *for a joy or concern.*

"This is very much like a church service," Aunt Kate whispered to Alice.

A tall wrought-iron rack held a dozen thick ivory-colored

candles. Using a gunlike device, people lit them for a friend undergoing chemotherapy, a granddaughter in a swimming championship, a husband retiring. Then Jocelyn stepped forward. "This candle symbolizes my commitment to this group, to being here regularly. Each time I'm here, it's like coming home." Her voice was melodic, lilting, slightly clipped. "I also want to light a candle for Helen, who makes these evenings happen."

"A very handsome woman," Aunt Kate whispered. "Wonderful bearing."

After Jocelyn returned to her seat, Helen announced that the scheduled speaker was ill. "She'll join us in a month. Meanwhile, I feel as Jocelyn does, that this group is becoming a community, a community of seekers and of friends, so I thought I'd talk a little about community tonight—spiritual community in particular—and then open it up for discussion."

"Sorry," Alice whispered back.

"It's fine, dear," Aunt Kate said, patting her knee. "I'm enjoying this."

Alice could look straight ahead, as if listening raptly to Helen, and still study Jocelyn Nearing's profile. Except for one sighting at the neighborhood bookstore, and another through binoculars from Griffith Park, she'd never seen Nick's wife in person. She'd seen her films, of course, had rented the videos.

Jocelyn listened to Helen with a faint, sweet smile that broke into her famous wide smile when the whole room burst into laughter: Helen had said something funny, but Alice had missed it.

Nick used to say that his wife had no sense of humor. She was far too sensitive to joke with, and he rarely made her laugh. Unlike Alice. Alice was a great laugher, he said, and her quiet, soul-filled laughter is what he fell in love with. He lived, he had said, to make Alice laugh.

All the same, he'd chosen Jocelyn. And why wouldn't he? Anyone seeing the two of them side by side would do the same.

Especially now. Look at Jocelyn with her movie star's gorgeous, generous laugh, and Alice, glum as mud.

"This minister *is* delightful," whispered Aunt Kate. "Very, very bright."

Alice didn't seem to be drawing oxygen, and her hands sweated. She felt dissociated, as if she'd drunk too much coffee. The ammoniac smell of her hair intensified in the warm room. This undertaking, she saw, was pure, selfish folly. Dyeing her hair, bringing her fragile old aunt as a blind so she could spy on her lover's wife—how low could you go?

Alice should never have come; she had no interest in joining anything, least of all a church. Whereas Jocelyn went on jags, joining up with this book circle or that master class, as Alice knew well; because on the nights of Jocelyn's meetings, Nick visited Wren Street.

He could be at her house now. Alice was suddenly certain of it. He'd wait on the porch, but not for very long. If it wasn't for Aunt Kate, she would've left.

Again the room burst into noisy laughter. What could Helen have said that was so funny?

When the service finally concluded, two older women converged on Aunt Kate, one of them, an ancient pink-haired specimen, had been a teaching colleague of Aunt Kate's at the academy, while the other knew her from the long-ago gourmet group. "We're all three still alive," this woman said. "Isn't that something?"

Alice excused herself and went to the refreshment table, where Pete was arranging cookies from a paper sack on a plate. "Heya Blondie," he said, offering her one.

"Oh hi." Having not eaten since breakfast, she bit right into it. Still warm. "Yum. You make these?"

"Yeah. Toll House, right off the package—a tad more salt. How'd you like your pal's talk?"

"It was okay." Alice reached for another cookie. "For my aunt," she said just as Jocelyn Nearing broke away from a small group of men and looked right at her. In slow motion, like a woman in a feminine hygiene commercial, strands of hair floating, a smile breaking across her face, she wafted straight toward Alice. Then the room went white, as if swallowed by a cloud.

"Is that you, Peter?" Jocelyn's voice pulsed soft to loud. "Peter Ross? Remember me—Jocelyn?—from Trotwood? I thought I recognized you!"

Alice blinked, and a small area cleared in which she saw Pete's hand slide into Jocelyn's.

"Sorry. I didn't mean to interrupt, but I know Peter from years ago. From his restaurant." This, Alice realized, was directed at her. "He is absolutely my favorite chef, ever."

Alice, nodding, realized her mouth was still full of cookie.

"I'm Jocelyn."

"Alice," she whispered, swallowing madly and allowing her own hand to slip into Jocelyn's. "I, uh, admire your work."

"Why thank you. Such a cold, cold hand!" Jocelyn sandwiched Alice's hand between both of hers. "And what do you do?" Jocelyn's wedding band was thick, hammered, and a very yellow gold.

"Research biologist."

"I swear"—she squeezed Alice's hand and released it—"this church has the most interesting people. Everyone I meet does something incredible. And Helen! What a great talk she gave, don't you think?"

Alice, in concert with Pete, muttered, flushed, pawed at the ground.

"She's so profound," Jocelyn went on. "Do you two come every Sunday?"

"No," said Pete.

Alice's throat kept closing, and her skin flushed hot and cold at the same time.

"I went to the Easter service, and from here on out it's every Sunday and Wednesday for me," Jocelyn said. "I'd hate to miss a thing that woman has to say." She touched Pete's arm and his face paled. "Tell me, what happened to Trotwood? And where have you been?"

Alice barely heard Pete's muttered answers. *Investors,* he said. *Landlord. Unemployment.*

"I can't believe it's really you, Peter," Jocelyn said. "It's amazing. Unfortunately, I have to leave right now, but I'm dying to talk more. Will you be here Sunday? Good." Again, she clasped Pete's hand. "So nice to meet you, Alice."

Another handshake, the smooth, warm skin and frank, decisive grip. Then the brown sweater, glinting hair and large expensive handbag receded. Alice's heartbeat slowed, her vision cleared. Pete was gone. Around her, people were folding chairs. Her aunt, she saw, was talking with Helen, and Alice moved toward them.

Pete, hauling three chairs, brushed by. "Biology?" he said. "Since when?"

"Since forever. *Peter.*"

After the service, Helen had slipped Alice an old hardback of *The Yearling,* and she read a few chapters in bed that night. Nothing seemed familiar to her, not that she could concentrate on the dense prose while comparing the actual physical fact of Jocelyn Nearing to Nick's litany of disillusionment and exasperation.

Ever since her first feature film, he claimed, she'd surrounded herself with hirelings who insisted that she was the most talented and best-looking actress in the business. They still said so, but she was forty-two now and so infrequently cast, she was unable to reconcile this discrepancy. Nick said he never knew, coming home, if he would face her inflated ego or rampant, frantic insecurities. It was hard enough being married, he said, without having to contend with the vicious lookism, ageism, fickleness and misogyny of Hollywood.

But he never said how gracious Jocelyn was, how warm and

utterly pleasant. Or how convincing her enthusiasms could be; through the scrim of her admiration, Helen seemed brilliant and Pete even passably human.

Of course, Alice had never intended to meet the woman, let alone clasp her hand, or speak to her—and was assuring herself that this was so when the phone rang. The clock's red digital numbers read 10:37. Only one person would call so late: Nick, having heard that his wife had just met her. He would guess it was no accident. She considered not answering, then lifted the receiver and whispered "Hi."

"I hope I'm not waking you," Helen said. "I was so happy to see you tonight. And I loved meeting Aunt Kate."

Alice kicked the covers, wishing for Nick after all. "She liked you too."

"The reason I'm calling," said Helen, "is that I just got off the phone with a friend of mine . . . Are you still looking for work?"

"I haven't even started. Why?"

"Can you type?"

"Around fifty words a minute."

"Remember I told you about my friend Foster who's doing psychical research on William James?"

"Not interested," Alice said.

"Wait! It could be fun. You know, James appears frequently to psychics."

"Yeah, almost as frequently as Elvis."

"I already told you. Sorry. Anyway, Foster needs a typist. He's been doing all these interviews and needs to have the tapes transcribed. He got very excited when I told him about you."

"Why, what did you say?"

"That you were a descendant, a scientist, and psychically labile."

Labile. Liplike. Alice knew the word from biology. Susceptible. Psychically susceptible. Is that what she was?

"The pay's fifteen an hour, twenty hours, more or less, a week."

"Not bad."

"At least take down his number. Do you have a pen?"

As much as Alice did not want to follow Aunt Katherine and squander her life on their famous ancestor—least of all from this wacky angle—fifteen bucks an hour was significantly more than the Fountain paid, including her tips.

20

Friday night, minutes before Helen was due with the *Year-ling* video, she telephoned. "Shall I invite Pete?" she said. "It'd be so good for him."

Alice was standing in the kitchen. "Can we not?" She'd planned on a movie, then the two of them talking. "I was looking forward to just you."

"That's fine. We can do that," said Helen, "if that's what you prefer."

"Yeah, and I'm not so sure I want Pete to know where I live."

"Oh, Pete's a good egg. But if you're uncomfortable, I won't bring him."

"You don't mind?"

"No. But I have to confess I already invited him. I can uninvite him, though. Or we could watch the video at my house instead."

Alice had already cleaned house; she'd bought popcorn and, recalling Helen's fondness for chocolate, double fudge and chocolate mint ice cream.

"Sorry," Helen said. "I didn't mean to put you on the spot."

"No, no, if you really think he's okay, he can come." Alice watched dusk gathering in the windows. "Aren't you afraid of encouraging his big crush on you?"

"If he has one it'll pass, believe me. Once he gets to know the real me."

. . .

"This isn't at all like the book," Alice said ten minutes into the video. Pete was sprawled in Uncle Walter's chair—he'd headed straight for it, as if the headrest were needlepointed *Nuts Sit Here*. She and Helen were on the couch, a blue bowl of popcorn between them. "In the book," she explained, "Pa's a tiny, sickly runt, and Ma's a big fat battle-ax. Gary Cooper? Jane Wyman? I don't think so."

"And that kid," said Pete. "What a little fag!"

Helen barely glanced his way. "What makes you say that, Pete?"

"Look! So pale and sensitive and *so* in love with Dad. What a girl."

"What's wrong with being a girl?" Alice said.

"I think the child who inspired the story *was* a girl," said Helen.

"Well," Pete said, "the sex change didn't take."

"And this," Alice said, "from a man with boobs."

Helen's eyes widened, but Pete grinned. Alice liked him for that. The boy in the movie, Jody, did seem both cloying and cringing, like some tyrannical adult's vision of a perfect child.

"The woman at the video store knew the man who played Jody," Helen said. "He's an aircraft engineer, lives in Burbank. And he never made another movie. Apparently he didn't enjoy the process."

"Can you blame him?" said Pete. "How'd you like to wear stupid outfits, skip like a fairy and talk like a pompous hick?"

The women exchanged an identical look of studied blankness and turned back to the film, where to swelling music boy and deer raced through woods and meadows. Sometimes whole herds of deer ran with them; deer swerved and coursed through the forest like a river.

"I do wish he wouldn't run with that little skip," said Alice.

"He can't help it. That's how fags run."

"Good God, Pete," Helen snapped.

"What?" Pete said. "I'm probably the least homophobic person you know. In fact, I'm jealous of fags. They have strong personal identities and know exactly who and what they are—they're fags. They also have more fun than the rest of us combined." He gestured at the towheaded boy leaping alongside the deer. "Case in point."

"Yeah, that's right," Alice said. "You should see the guys at the Fountain, vamping and belting out torch songs, completely uninhibited. I envy that."

"But Pete," Helen said, "you're hardly lacking in personal identity."

"Really?" said Pete. He surveyed his hands and lap. "How come I have no idea who I am? Why, whenever I try to look at myself, do I see *absolutely nothing*?"

"People meditate for years to experience that," said Helen.

"Yeah?" Pete thumped the arms of Uncle Walter's chair. "I'll be damned."

"Stop it," said Alice. Pete's thumping raised clouds of dust, a fine, dark, airborne grit whose stale smell she'd begun to notice a few months after Aunt Kate moved out. It was the smell of old varnish and rusty screens, of a house neglected. She stood. "Anyone for ice cream?"

Both guests followed her to the kitchen, but Pete dawdled in front of the dining room hutch. "What kind of sterling is that?" he said, pointing at the tea set. "May I look?"

Alice waved at the hutch. "There's silverware in the drawers, too."

Helen helped her scoop out the ice cream. "This is fun," she said. "I'm so relaxed I've forgotten what I do for a living. Don't tell me, either."

"Speaking of jobs," Alice said, "I called your friend Foster. I'm going out there on Tuesday."

"You'll love him. Foster's *very* dry."

"Don't get your hopes up. We're just going to talk."

"Hey," Pete said from the doorway. "This is Georg Jensen silver, and Limoges porcelain. What are you doing with this stuff?"

"It's my Aunt Kate's. From her mom, I think."

He prowled around the kitchen next, tapping the hanging pots and pans, peeking in cupboards at the California pottery, examining the antique gas stove Aunt Kate had sent back from France. He swung the oven doors, making them creak and twang, then touched the copper legs, the green-tiled backsplash and enameled knobs. He turned on a burner and a vigorous, thick ring of fire sprang up. "Whoa!" he said, incredulous, and turned to Alice. "You little shit."

Back in the living room, they ate ice cream and watched in silence as drought and rain and money problems besieged the hapless family.

"This is the longest, slowest film," Alice said.

"I saw it on the last day of school for years," said Helen. "A double feature in the school auditorium with *To Kill a Mockingbird*. We called it *The Yearlong*."

Alice herself was beginning to recall something about the movie—nothing specific about the plot or the characters, but a turn, a darkening, some stain of betrayal. "Something awful happens, doesn't it?"

"Yes indeedy," said Pete.

The little deer became unmanageable. He ate all the family's crops, and no fence could hold him. He had to be shot or else the family would starve. Ma couldn't shoot straight, and Pa had rheumatism. The boy had to pull the trigger.

"Now I remember," Alice said to Helen. "It's a morality tale. Not only does the thing you love the most die, you have to kill it."

"Ahh. And I wonder—what does that correspond to in your life?"

Alice thought for a moment. "Just about everything."

. . .

Morton's sanctuary was a bit like a barn—not the pews, of course, or the stained glass windows, but the open-post construction and wooden beams were very barnlike, as were the wide double doors and the way light streamed down from the clerestories in dust-flecked shafts. Alice, early, slid into an empty pew near the back.

Parishioners trickled in, older men in sport jackets, their wives in suits or blazers, with brightly colored scarves. The youngest adults appeared to be in their forties, men in beards with their big-bottomed, dirndled wives, their children in cargo pants and outsized sport shoes. In the sanctuary's unkind light, dumpiness ruled and everyone looked like caricatures of themselves. Why would Jocelyn Nearing ever come here? These were not her people.

Pete squeezed into the pew. "Greetings, O woman who runs with the deer."

"Shut up."

He laughed and segued into squirming, flinching and contagious knee-jumping. If he didn't settle down, Alice thought, she'd pop out of her own skin.

The organist, gray-haired and red-faced, crashed into a dozen loud minor chords; in his harsh, melodramatic style, the Bach prelude sounded like a monster-movie soundtrack.

Pete, with a flinch more violent than usual, pinched her upper arm against the pew. "Jesus, Pete," she said, and, shoving him off, saw Jocelyn Nearing in the aisle. With *Thad*. From her one sighting, through binoculars, and from Nick's descriptions, she'd expected a wan, timorous child. But this boy was alert and charmingly small for six, his longish brown hair sun-streaked, his complexion at once ruddy and golden. His white dress shirt and blue jeans were manly in miniature. When Jocelyn spoke to him, he answered with animation, his lips red and expressive.

Pete picked up a hymnal and commenced speed-reading as the organist crashed recklessly about, finally landing on a major chord with such obliterating force that sound throbbed through the room long after his hands left the keys.

Helen stepped to the pulpit wearing full-length ivory robes and a long multicolored shawl in which were woven a cross, a Star of David, Islam's crescent moon and star, a mandala wedged like a pie. She waited for the organ's reverberations to fade away, then said, "*Wow*," but it didn't sound like praise.

Jocelyn, Alice was surprised to see, was wearing the same soft brown sweater she'd had on on Wednesday.

"Welcome to Morton Neighborhood Church," Helen told the congregation, "on this chilly and crystal-clear spring morning. I trust we're all wide awake now"—an eyebrow raised to the organist—"and that's good, because today we kick off our annual pledge drive and we need everyone bright-eyed and bushy-tailed. First, however, I'd like to extend a special welcome to our first-time visitors."

Pete elbowed her.

"Stop it." Alice, afraid she'd be singled out, ducked her head.

"I urge all visitors to stick around for coffee after the service. Stop by our welcome table, if you haven't already, and fill out a name tag, give us your address, and we'll send you our newsletter for six weeks to acquaint you with the many programs, activities and social opportunities we enjoy here at Morton."

Jocelyn slipped her arm around Thad's shoulder.

"As ever," Helen continued, "I urge *everyone* to wear his or her name tag, so our visitors and new members can get to know you." She lifted a hymnal. "Our opening hymn is number 192 . . ."

Alice and Pete rose. Alice didn't sing—too skeptical and shy, and she couldn't carry a tune anyway. Pete, surprisingly, sang firmly, in tune and without excessive irony. *Hail the glorious golden city / Pictured by the seers of old . . .*

Announcements followed: a progressive dinner, a talk on Kosovo, petitions for gun control and doctor-assisted suicide.

Helen called for the offertory, and as wooden collection plates were passed, Alice dug out eighty cents from the bottom of her purse.

"Hey, big spender," Pete whispered. "You'll make the rest of us look bad!"

She spoke into his shaggy hair. "Bug off."

He cackled quietly.

When the bowls finished circulating, children were called to sit on the risers below the pulpit. Helen sat among them and read a story about a poor little boy who shared his tiny allowance with a beggar. Thad sat on the edge of the group and glanced often at his mother, showing no interest in the illustrations when Helen held them up. The beggar, of course, turned out to be a prince in disguise, and gave the poor boy's family a large new home and many farm animals. After the story, the children were released for Sunday school, and Jocelyn left with Thad.

Now Alice had to sit through the rest of the service for nothing. *Serves me right,* she thought. At least she hadn't dragged Aunt Kate along this time.

Helen turned over the pulpit to an older man who suggested that people pledge two percent of their earnings to the church. To Alice, this meant around three hundred dollars, and she hadn't spent that much on anything—except for rent, back when she actually paid rent—since she bought her car six years ago. Here was another reason never to join a church: she couldn't afford it.

Helen finally reclaimed the pulpit and, seizing its sides, gave her congregation a good long once-over. Pete downshifted to a lower-level fidgeting but apparently couldn't breathe without a small, audible sigh on each exhalation.

"What use is a church?" Helen called out dramatically. "What use is this building, this organ, these hymnals? What use is gathering here each Sunday?" She opened her arms to indicate the whole room. "What use is *this* church? What do you, personally, get from it? What does it give to your family? To your community? To the larger world?" She dropped her hands. "Today, when you're asked to make a financial commitment to Morton, it's appropriate to take a good, hard look at what you get for your investment."

Oh boy. Alice had thought that only TV evangelists dunned people for money, but here was Helen stumping away like the best of 'em.

But she didn't mention money again. She talked instead about the Jewish temple, the synagogues in the Jewish Diaspora, the households of faith in early Christianity, temples in Asia. Alice drifted. This was church? She'd imagined more mystery and moral instruction, not to mention a more serious and veiled approach to the holy, and certainly not this rambling history lesson.

Then Jocelyn slipped into a pew a few rows ahead of Alice, and things got interesting again.

Nick never spoke of his marriage, except for his excoriation of Hollywood and his routine complaints about his wife's transformed character, and when Alice asked about other aspects of their life together—what they talked about, where they lived before, why they had only one child—he'd claim, "I'm not interested in my past, only in *our* future." Alice never dared to ask Nick if he and Jocelyn still made love, but now studied Jocelyn's luminous skin, intentionally messy hair and miraculous smile, and drew the obvious conclusion. Nick had told her from the get-go: Don't ask questions you don't want to know the answer to.

Alice did know that they rarely ate together, and that Jocelyn insisted on a diet low in fat, high in fiber, and would no sooner eat a pork chop than a pig's eye—except at fancy restaurants, where Nick said she could eat him under the table. Even then, Jocelyn ate little red meat or poultry, only steamed or poached fish, and only fish with snow-white flesh: sea bass, halibut, turbot. For breakfast, she downed several handfuls of vitamins and herbs, and drank a spirulina concoction spiked with human growth hormone—dietary supplements that ran over a thousand dollars a month. None of her wishful-thinking male fans, Nick said, knew that having breakfast with Jocelyn Nearing meant watching her down a glass of gray-green slime, then gag. She also had facials and manicures every Thursday, and had her hair colored every three to four weeks at three hundred dollars a pop. At fifteen times a year that would be . . .

Pete's elbow interrupted her arithmetic.

She pushed back. "*What?*"

A nod toward Helen.

"James tells us that the truth of an idea is determined by the goodness that idea manifests in our lives. The cash value, as it were, of a concept."

Alice recrossed her legs and accidentally kicked the pew in front of her. How do you get from the history of world churches to William James? And who even cared, when it was so obvious—given Jocelyn's inarguable and breathtaking existence—that Nick Lawton would never, ever file for divorce.

"Coffee?" Pete asked.

They were in the receiving line to shake Helen's hand. "Sure," Alice said, mostly to get rid of him. She wouldn't even be in the damn line if he hadn't nudged her into it. "Now, we thank the speaker," he'd said as they filed from the pew. Alice would've bolted to the coffee line too, but Helen had already seen her, and lit up with obvious pleasure. So Alice dutifully waited.

Helen hugged her. "You don't know how happy I was to see you out there," she whispered. "You didn't have to come, but I'm thrilled you did."

"I liked it," Alice said. "Good sermon."

"Far from my best. But thanks."

In the pergola, under a grid of beams supporting crinkled new wisteria leaves, congregants greeted one another, signed petitions and bought tickets for upcoming church events. Children presided over a display of asymmetrical cookies, brownies and ominously dark bricks of banana bread. Alice, still waiting for Pete to bring her coffee, feigned interest in the Unitarian best-sellers—*The Jefferson Bible, Walden, Everything I Needed to Know I Learned in Kindergarten*—displayed on a wheeled bookcase. She'd leave, but didn't want to hurt his feelings. Glancing up, she saw Jocelyn intercept him by the baked goods. He splashed coffee on his white sneakers and said something that made Jocelyn smile, then toss her head back to laugh, one hand on her long, beautiful neck. Pete spotted Alice, raised a Styrofoam cup and started moving toward her, Jocelyn in tow.

"Alice, good to see you," she said, offering that hand. "How are you? Peter and I are talking restaurants. Where do you like to go?"

"I ate at L'Odéon once." Alice had been to only a handful of good restaurants, all courtesy of her former friend Rachel's expense account.

"If you like French food, you must adore Peter's cooking."

"I've only had his chocolate pudding."

"You should cook for your friends!" Jocelyn seized his arm. "Don't let him sandbag you, Alice. He's one of the very best there is."

Pete kicked at the concrete underfoot.

Jocelyn checked her watch. "I've got to run and get Thad from Sunday school. But please, Peter, think about what I said."

Alice waited until she disappeared inside the building. "What—she just stands around telling you what a good cook you are?"

"Mostly," said Pete. "And that she wants to open a restaurant."

"*Her?* Why?"

"Oh, Hollywood. They make more money than they know what to do with, and sooner or later, after they've bought all the cars and vacation homes and art and stock and trekking holidays, they just have to open a restaurant. And it's always the *same* restaurant: small neighborhood jewel box, exquisite food, million-dollar wine cellar, friends only . . ." He snorted.

"What's wrong with that?"

"In the first place, nobody has enough friends to keep a restaurant like that open. And nobody imagines the hundred-hour workweeks and constant employee turnover." Pete stared into his cup and frowned. "Or the opinionated, know-nothing investors, and the sleazy rich cretins you need to ass-kiss. Restaurants make lousy hobbies. You have to be obsessed and driven and completely out of your mind to own one."

"But you had—"

"Two, yes. But Alice," Pete said almost tenderly, "I've been totally nuts my entire fucking life."

alone reproduce them under laboratory conditions. Ahhh . . ."
He passed Alice an unidentified magazine folded open to its classified ads. "Here's an example of our query."

> For a book on the posthumous appearances and communications of William James, I would appreciate hearing from anyone who has had any kind of contact or communication with him, including but not limited to mediumistic contact, automatic writings, dreams, channeling, Ouija board messages.

Foster had placed the query, he said, in every magazine and journal dedicated to such matters, along with a more staid version in academic journals that might attract James scholars. To date he'd received over three hundred replies, of which he had processed only a fraction. Alice would help him sort through them, responding with a personalized letter and a standardized questionnaire. When the completed questionnaires came back, she would enter the data into a computer.

"I already have forty or fifty questionnaires and twenty-odd phone interviews. So you see, I can keep you as busy as you want to be," Foster said, and, reaching into a duffel on the floor, pulled out three tapes in plastic cases. "You'll deal, first of all, with data from mediums. This, mind you, is gathered under the strictest protocols." Foster selected two tapes and handed them to Alice. "Other material, such as this interview, is largely anecdotal." Alice took the third tape. "You'll see for yourself that much of the data is absurd, even incomprehensible." He lounged back in his chair. "I hope you don't find it annoying or offensive, seeing as how he's your great-grandfather."

"Great-*great*-grandfather. Have you yourself ever . . . *communicated* with him?"

"I've had *alleged* contact with him through mediums, as you'll hear soon enough. Although, of course, it might not be him, precisely." Foster grinned. "One British medium claims that James operates a school over there on the other side where

21

S he drove out to Claremont on Tuesday morning, intending to talk to Foster Allbright about his job offer. But from the moment she walked into his office he assumed she'd already accepted and was so pleased and grateful that she didn't have the heart to disabuse him.

"A good transcriber is hard to find," he said, beaming. "Let alone one with your background."

"I've never transcribed a thing," she said, hoping to temper his enthusiasm.

"At any rate, it's good to have another scientist on board." Foster, a faded former redhead, had prematurely adopted the bookish-grandfather look with his shabby fawn-colored sport jacket and steel-framed bifocals. After her initial panic—for taking a job she didn't want—Alice found his unfounded trust touching, and hoped she wouldn't disappoint him.

"William James wasn't dead a week when the first message came in from a fellow in Boston named Ayers. And they haven't stopped coming since."

"What was the message?"

"Good question, and . . ." Foster chuckled. "I forget. Probably just 'Hullo, it's fine over here.'" He rummaged through papers on a side table. "Nothing earth-shattering, at any rate. I probably don't need to warn you that psychical activity is rarely gratifying—or coherent, for that matter. The phenomena don't take kindly to scientific investigation." More rummaging. "It's difficult enough to glimpse the flickerings of the spirit world, let he trains spirits in his techniques for communication with the living. These trainees, in turn, are sent out under his auspices to work with mediums. This would account for the large number of communicants who claim to be William James. They're part of a franchise."

"Sort of like Santas?" Alice said.

Foster laughed. "Exactly. Although another medium suggests it's more like Fred Astaire dancing schools—that James lends his name for quality assurance."

"Do you really believe he or his, uh, recruits actually communicate?"

Foster's right eyebrow lifted impressively. "Let's say I keep an open mind." He pointed to the tapes in Alice's hand. "So you have a good sighting by a woman in the Adirondacks—you'll enjoy that, I think—and two sessions with the medium I work with. Her name is Patricia Hodges. When she goes into a trance, she'll speak in a male voice with a thick Mexican accent. It's still Patricia talking, but you'll have to take my word for it. The voice claims to be Gustavo, who's what we call a control. A control is someone who relays messages to and from the spirit world, a go-between. So the medium goes into a trance and summons the control. He then communicates with the dead. In this case, we have Gustavo contacting an entity identified as William James—that is when Gustavo stops talking about himself!" Foster stood. "This will all make a lot more sense before long. Come, I'll show you where you'll work."

He took her one floor up in the cinderblock building and unlocked the door to a narrow beige room with two gray metal desks. "You share with a grad student named Dewey Hupfeld. And wait till you meet his Merle—she's terrific. Forgive me, but I couldn't resist putting you here, you know, given that William James and John Dewey were such good friends."

And Madame Merle, oh, blah blah blah, thought Alice.

On the back desk sat a computer and a cassette player with

a set of headphones plugged in. Beside the desk, a narrow window looked out to the skin-pink limbs of a eucalyptus tree, a rocky field and, not a mile away, the San Bernardino Mountains. When Foster left, Alice put in a tape and fitted the headphones over her ears.

"Hello? Hello? Testing?" Foster's voice. This, he announced, was a telephone interview with a woman named Maureen McGonigle. He began with biographical questions. Mrs. McGonigle, it seemed, was fifty-four, mother of two grown children and a grandmother of three. She lived in Boston. She'd had the usual childhood diseases and now took thyroid pills. She was a nonpracticing Catholic who believed in God, and was not a professional, an amateur or even a dabbler in any field of paranormal experience. No epilepsy, depression, bipolar disorder; no alcoholism or substance abuse. Her sister-in-law, a therapist, had spotted Foster's query in *Mindsong: A Journal of Psychology and Spirituality* and sent it on to her. Finally, Foster asked if she would please describe what happened on June 9 and 10, 1991, in Keene Valley, New York.

My husband and I had come from Boston that day, and I was very tired. My sister-in-law had fixed a nice dinner, but when everybody else went to have coffee in the living room, I excused myself and went upstairs to lie down.

We always have the same bedroom at the cottage, in the back of the house on the second floor. I fell right asleep and woke up sometime later because I was cold. It wasn't very late, my husband hadn't come to bed yet. Reaching for the quilt at the end of the bed, I saw a man standing by the bedpost. He had a beard and a high, high forehead. I noticed his eyes, which were blue. He seemed very amused by something. I remember thinking, Those are "laughing eyes." I was startled but not at all frightened. He had his hand over his heart, though, as if I'd given him a start.

He was dressed oddly, in a bright yellow shirt, a blue vest, a short, shimmery green tie. I assumed he was a visitor looking for the bathroom so I pointed down the hall, pulled up the quilt and went back to sleep. I woke up again when my husband came in. I asked him, "Who was that nice man in the yellow shirt?"

He had no idea who I meant. The next morning, I asked my brother and sister-in-law and they didn't know what I was talking about. The men went hiking then, and I went to town with my sister-in-law. We stopped in at the Keene Valley Library, and there on the wall was a photograph of the man I'd seen. It was William James standing with a group of other men at Putnam Camp. I would've recognized him anywhere.

Coincidentally, my husband had a mild heart attack on his hike that day, and I've since found out that James also developed heart trouble on that same trail.

Allbright: Have you ever seen that photograph or any image of William James before?

McGonigle: Not that I remember.

A: Did you know he was a frequent visitor to the Adirondacks?

M: No.

A: Have you read any of his books?

M: No.

A: How would you yourself categorize this experience: as seeing a ghost, or a spirit, or . . . ?

M: An angel! He was trying to warn me about my husband.

A: Have you ever seen another such apparition?

M: As a little girl, I saw an old woman in my aunt's flower garden whom I later recognized as my grandmother's grandmother.

A: Do these sightings differ in any way from dreams?

M: Yes. I always know when I'm dreaming. But these encounters seemed so real, it didn't occur to me to question them until afterwards.

Alice stopped the tape. Helen must've asked Foster to give her material about people who didn't know the difference between ghosts and reality. But if this was supposed to make her feel better, Helen had miscalculated. That other people had hallucinations and found perception unreliable was not reassuring, but terrifying.

When she noticed the tapping on the door—her earphones were still on—Alice had no idea how long it had been going on. "Come in," she called.

The young man who entered had a short summer haircut, fair skin and scrubbed, generic good looks—the exact sort you'd expect to see at a seminary. She lifted her chin in greeting and he gave her such a hopeful look that she yanked off the earphones and rose to meet him properly.

"I didn't mean to interrupt." He reddened as she drew near. "Alice, right?" They shook hands. "Dewey Hupfeld." Early to mid-twenties, she thought. His straight white teeth were either the product of great genes or a master orthodontist. His skin was unblemished, his blue eyes clear. Alice would not have been surprised to see milk drip from behind his ears. "Foster told me all about you," he said.

"Uh-oh," she said. "And what did he say?"

"You're a biologist, a friend of Helen's, and descended from William James."

"That about sums it up," Alice said. "You know Helen?"

"I've met her at Foster's get-togethers. But William James is one of my all-time favorite writers. I just used him in a paper."

"Don't tell me you're a James scholar too?"

"No, no. My paper was on the theology of animals. I only cited him."

"I had no idea ol' Billy Jim wrote about animals."

"Billy Jim?" Dewey's genuine puzzlement made her feel

mean. "Oh, I get it. That's cute!" He smiled. "And yeah, he said that animals used for scientific research sacrifice their lives for a higher good that they can't possibly understand. Of course he went on to say that we humans are like those dogs on vivisection tables—that we're just as ignorant of the greater purpose of our lives."

"I like that," Alice said. "God: the great vivisectionist in the sky."

"Oh, I don't think that's what he meant."

"No?" Alice was teasing, but Dewey didn't smile. "So what *is* the theology of animals? And how do you know they have one?"

"Actually, I'm writing about how religious views of animals have changed with the theory of evolution, the industrial revolution and scientific materialism. Like, are animals just stuff, or do they have consciousness, thoughts and souls?"

"Do you think they have souls?"

"Absolutely. Anyone with a pet knows they do. A few years ago, even the pope announced that animals can go to heaven."

"How nice of him," Alice said. "But does that mean animals have always gone to heaven, or only now, since the pope decreed it?"

Dewey thought for a moment. "Oh, always, I would think."

Alice had never met anyone so unironic. As perplexed as he was by some of the things she said, Dewey wasn't the least offended, as if it never occurred to him that anybody would ever be other than perfectly kind. And she used to be kind, a real pushover, but she had set out to change that much as she'd resolved to lose her virginity, with the full intent to shed herself of a liability.

Before leaving for his class, Dewey showed her his cupboard of office supplies, which she was welcome to use; and she was free to read any of his books, a small library of Christian history and theology. She couldn't help but notice he was quite tall and broad-shouldered, athletic. As if on cue, he pulled open a desk drawer to reveal a stash of protein bars. "If you get a little slumpy, just help yourself." He grabbed his knapsack, waved and was out the door. "Gotta run."

Alice returned to the thin voices piped into her ears: Foster cross-examining Mrs. McGonigle with such irritating thoroughness that he clearly suspected this older, matter-of-fact Boston housewife was trying to pull one over on him.

After finishing the tape, she was loath to start another. The office was cold. This year, spring and warm weather were too slow in coming, and in her new view, a low cloud cover sealed off the sun, and the grainy gray light sapped color from the world, making the eucalyptus limbs white as bone. Alice felt far from everything and everyone she knew, in exile from her own life, out here among kind, if humorless, religious folk. Her family had no idea where she was. Nick could never ever find her. In another sense, she knew exactly where she'd landed—the one place she'd avoided all her life, while dreading its inevitability. Along with mad and maddening Aunt Kate, she'd come smack to the heart of Jamesland. To finally encounter the benign specifics of this long-dreaded place—a small stark office, scratchy piped-in voices, the bashful office mate and his preposterous goodwill—was almost a relief.

22

On the flats of the park, down by the freeway, the sycamores' furry new leaves shaded Pete from the morning sun like so many green hands. In one glade a transient slumbered on a picnic table, his face slicked with heavy dew as a curious coyote sniffed his toes. According to Freddy of Sherwood Forest, only half a dozen years ago the park had spawned a vast homeless encampment, a spontaneous outbreak of tents and lean-tos and large-appliance-box bedrooms called the City of Lost Souls. Showers were devised, portable toilets donated, and playground equipment for the children; leaders were elected to mediate disputes and coordinate the distribution of food, fresh water, clothing and toys which flowed in from churches and schools. A feature article in the *Times* described the camp as a model of human resourcefulness, and the accompanying photographs showed muddy children frolicking with a scrawny dog and families sitting around campfires with laundry flapping like white shadows behind them. Less than a week after the article appeared, however, the City of Angels sent its bulldozers into the City of Lost Souls, the homeless scattering and moving on.

Two decades of tax cuts had left the park with a single ranger and a skeletal maintenance crew. The former quietly allowed a couple dozen men to live in the hills—Pete knew several of them from the Bread Basket—providing they built no fires and donated a few hours every week to picking up trash, whacking weeds or maintaining trails. Freddy had tried this life, but found even these small expectations too burdensome.

Pete imagined rising from a hard dirt bed, rambling down to cadge a cup of pisswater coffee from the driving-range concession stand, and then later in the day spearing up Doritos bags and used condoms or shoring up a switchback on the trail to Dante's Peak, and thus he found a moment's peace from the two conundrums otherwise occupying his mind: on the one hand was Helen Harland and what she did or did not feel for him; on the other was Jocelyn Nearing's half-baked restaurant plan niggling like a foxtail in his sweater cuffs. The chances of becoming Jocelyn's chef he rated slightly higher and wished for far less than becoming Helen's husband. Mr. Helen Harland, spouse with an edge? Could he suffer finance committee meetings in his living room? Calls at midnight when consciences could not sleep, or death had done some work? He could feign nothing, not politeness, cheer, goodwill or indifference. In lieu of small talk, he could always snort and blurt and sneer—and oh how he'd sulk when male congregants hugged the missus, assuming he did not beat them to a pulp instead.

Better a residency in some City of Lost Souls than to risk the rage that had eaten away his marriage like some disfiguring acid.

Back when Trotwood was flourishing, a mere hint of anger used to stop Anne short, but a year of sofa-loafing, weight gain and self-pity had sapped his credibility. Then he could bellow and wail till the neighbors started yelling through the door— *Anne, Anne, is everything all right in there?*—without her getting the least bit ruffled, her cruel passivity only raising his volume and frenzy levels. *Whose side are you on? Go fuck yourself.*

Pete, walloped by the memory of his behavior, came to a standstill. He kicked the grass at his feet, sent divots flying through the air like small toupees until the smell of torn grass and dirt recalled him to his senses. Around him, in the dark oaks, small, leathery, prickled leaves clattered softly. A whiff of the pony rides rode in on the breeze. How could he think of either husbanding or cooking, the twin engines of failure that propelled him into emergency rooms, nut wards, statutory embraces?

But he could not regret the latter, and smiled, as ever, at the thought of young Carrie. He'd met her at the ATM machine a block from his halfway house. She was visiting from Lancaster for the summer, staying with her sister, hoping to find a job; he was withdrawing money for his donut circuit, a path charted through east Glendale from Winchell's to Doug's Donuts to Mister Donut, one maple bar and a raised glazed at each. She accompanied him that day—she ate chocolate-dipped chocolate cakes, one per stop—and for three months they were virtually inseparable. Pete felt no remorse for that, although perhaps he should. The very thought of her yellow-blond hair and skinny limbs got him walking again, and grinning. Why she chose his awful lumpen self was such a beautiful mystery. He and she'd had nothing—blissfully nothing—between them but fucking. In the late afternoon in her older sister's loft in industrial Burbank, witnessed only by the sibling's deeply awful art school paintings, portraits in murky impasto. When he graduated into freedom, Carrie came to his rented room on the fourth floor via a piss-soaked elevator in the Glendale Flatiron, a shabby downtown residential hotel otherwise occupied by geriatric alcoholics. For two months they had a great run of sex, with interludes of sleep, soap operas, junk food (she lived on Slim Jims and PayDay candy bars) and smoking. In the fall, she went home to high school in Lancaster, and shortly it was back to the nuthouse for Pete. His psychotherapist—not the illustrious Freeman but some assigned hospital staffer—blurted, "Just out of curiosity, what on earth did you and a seventeen-year-old girl talk about?"

"Sex," Pete shrugged. "Cigarettes."

It was hard not to romanticize those times when, assuming himself good as gone, with all the clasps of culture and nurture fallen away, he was carried—or rode—upon a muscular invisible tide. Nothing, he understood, mattered. This wasn't mere nihilism. His usual angle of perceiving the world had slipped, and from his new, wide-open vantage point, it was utterly clear that being sick or well, rich or poor, saint or murderer, even alive or dead, was not in the least bit important and in fact, that all such human conditions, whether pitiful or exalted, amounted to nothing more than the briefest puckering in the vast fabric. How could he explain that this insight was not tragic, and in truth offered the greatest freedom imaginable? Within it, he moved as was his wont; compelled by no statute or convention, summoned by no job, called by no human attachment except, perhaps, the sleepy glance of a naked girl as she reached to turn off the bedside light.

23

On her second day of work, Alice arrived to find a gray-and-white Australian shepherd curled up on her desk. The dog froze, as if by being perfectly still it might remain invisible. Only one pale blue eye flickered as Alice approached.

"I see you," she said softly, "up there on my desk."

With a scramble and sudden airborne flurry, the dog was down, wagging, smiling, apologetic.

"Come here," Alice said, and offered a palm for the dog to sniff. Her name, she saw, was woven into her collar: Merle, and she had a docked tail and a beautiful salt-and-pepper cape with a jaunty chevron of white on her back.

Dewey pushed the door open with his shoulder, balancing a cardboard tray of coffee and muffins. "She wasn't on your desk, was she? It used to be her spot."

"I'm sorry to dispossess her."

Dewey held out the tray. "I bought extra in case you were here."

Merle was a year old, crazed as a puppy and extremely intelligent. Dewey had trained her to sit, stay, roll over and speak. She could bark once, twice or three times on command. He took a Hula-Hoop from behind the bookcase and, out in the hall, held it up for Merle to leap through, the wisps of her ears flying. When she hit the waxed concrete floor, she skidded, legs outstretched, another ten feet.

"I did a lot of research about breeds and breeders," Dewey said. "She comes from up around San Jose."

"Seeing her," Alice said, "nobody would dispute that dogs have souls."

The next tape she transcribed was a session with Foster's medium, Patricia Hodges. As promised, the woman went into a trance and spoke with a man's thick Mexican Spanish accent.

Man: Who have we got here? Foster?

Foster: Yeah, Gustavo. How are you?

Gustavo: Gustavo is very well for someone in a skin. So itchy and restricting. Gustavo goes stupid the second he's in.

F: In the medium?

G: He only has half his own sense and cleverness when he's in the medium, yes. You would never know it, but disincarnate, Gustavo is a highly educated entity.

F: We'll have to take your word on that, Gustavo. Can you find Dr. James for us, please?

G: Wouldn't your friends like to hear a little about Gustavo?

F: We all know quite a bit about you.

G: But did I say how I was forced to flee to America? No? My brothers and I walked across the Sonora desert to Mexicali, where we found a coyote; we gave him a shameful amount of money and he led us through the hills for two nights. No water, no food. We hid under bushes during the day. We finally got to America, and a minute later, as we were about to cross a hayfield, my brother lifted a strand of barbed wire for me, and when I put my head through, a rattlesnake bit me right on the nose! (*Laughs loudly*) I died, of course. (*Laughs again*)

Foster: Very interesting, Gustavo. Will you please get Dr. James now?

Gustavo: He's right here, with his skunky gray beard. He has little tufts of hair growing off his ears like . . . how do you say . . . a wizard! He has quite the pate, very shiny and pink. *Muchos sesos.* But his heart does not beat, it . . . it squelches. Gustavo diagnoses valve problems. Sloppy, inefficient valves. No wonder he's dead . . .

At this point, Foster stopped in to see how she was faring.

"William James hasn't said very much. Or anything, for that matter."

"In some sessions he's more talky than others," Foster said. "He's always saying how difficult it is for the dead to contact the living. Apparently, pathways between the spirit and material world are neither wide nor easily traversed—and then we have Gustavo and Patricia to deal with. In his lifetime, James said there has to be an active will to communicate and an active will to receive that communication. Ideally, working with a medium is a conscious, systematic attempt to bring these two wills together, but I'd say that Patricia and / or Gustavo are at best ambivalent about their roles."

"I can see that," Alice said.

As she transcribed further tapes, Alice was always glad to hear Patricia's real voice; she sounded like a friendly, reasonable, down-to-earth woman. But once she went into a trance and spoke as Gustavo, it was creepy, to tell the truth. And tiresome. At every sitting so far, Gustavo would tell his own story before even attempting to contact William James. Alice imagined her great-great-grandfather in his Norfolk jacket, pacing in frustration on the edge of some foggy divide as his messenger, a logorrheic megalomaniac with limited English, first clogged the tenuous connection and then, when he finally relayed a Jamesian message, jumbled it.

Alice transcribed Gustavo's story each time he told it, since Foster wanted to check for inconsistencies, and there were countless. Sometimes Gustavo claimed to have been a doctor, other times a medical student, a medic, a male nurse, and not once did he reveal a knowledge of medicine that exceeded Patricia's.

Controls were traditionally lively characters, Foster said, and mediums often quiet, unassuming women. "Such a polar split indicates that controls are probably subpersonalities of the medium, and not spirits of the dead. Gustavo's jockeying for attention could be an unconscious ploy on Patricia's part, a way of asserting herself. After all, we don't go to see her—she's useful to us only as a messenger. And I have yet to dig up one scrap of evidence corroborating Gustavo's previous existence on earth."

Between classes, Dewey sometimes took Merle for a walk, and Alice often went with them, never tiring of Merle's flying leaps. "Leave Merle with me," she'd said whenever Dewey headed off again, and the dog soon adopted the cool spot under Alice's desk.

Dewey was the son of a dentist in Arcadia. He'd grown up in Presbyterian church youth groups, sung in the choir and, as early as the tenth grade, set his sights on the ministry, serving as youth pastor and a church camp counselor. In college, on the advice of his own minister, he majored in business. "Churches run on a corporate model now, so it was helpful. And I knew I'd get my Greek and Bible studies in seminary."

But then seminary was not what Dewey had anticipated. "I didn't expect to hear that the virgin birth was borrowed from mystery religions, and that most of what Jesus says in the Bible was made up and inserted after he died. Plus, if you referred to God as 'He' in a paper, your grade automatically dropped a full point, like from an A to a B. I had a hard time."

After that first year, he transferred to a more conservative school in Pasadena, but it was too late. God as the great camp counselor in the sky no longer seemed plausible, so Dewey dropped out and went to work for his cousin, a landscaper. His girlfriend of seven years broke up with him because, she said, he'd changed too much. "That's when I got Merle, and she was my reconversion experience," Dewey explained. "There had to be a God for there to be a Merle."

Alice told Norm that she had a new job, but would still pull a few shifts if he needed help. He called her in on a Thursday afternoon.

Rosalie gave her a brief hug and said, "The Voice was in at noon."

"*What?*"

"Your boyfriend was here for a liquid lunch, and his friends practically had to carry him out."

"At noon?" Since Alice hadn't been working her usual hours, he must have come hoping to find her on another shift. "Did he ask about me?"

"Not so's I could tell," Rosalie said. "He wasn't exactly making himself clear. Like I said, his friends had to haul him out of here."

Nick had done this before, showing up on the margins of her life as if testing his welcome. Her spirits rose, buoyed by hope.

"You're chipper tonight," Monty said at nine o'clock sharp. "What's up?"

"New job," she said, then described it. "Do you think William James actually makes contact with these people?"

"I think they wish he would," said Monty. "But to me this smacks of group hysteria, like UFO sightings. And James was so much more than just a dabbler in psychical research. He was a scientist and clinician—America's first clinical psychologist, in fact, and he's considered the father of cognitive psychology."

Alice wrung out a bar towel and kept glancing at the door.

"For a depressive old coot, he sure kept busy. Or maybe that's why he kept busy."

The hours flew by. She hummed along to Fats Waller and Judy Garland. Nick might not show up tonight, or this week, but clearly he'd begun his roundabout journey back to her, this time, she hoped, for good.

II JAMESLAND

24

The pledge drive was a flop. After two weeks of canvassing, the take fell short of even last year's budget—and twenty thousand dollars shy of this year's goal. Last-minute appeals would help, but building repair, salaried musicians and a religious education director were dead in the water.

The same day she received this report, Helen was given a copy of her evaluation. Her overall performance score for the year was a middling three, down a point from last year.

> *Reverend Harland has become more confident in her second year at Morton. Her pastoral care of members continues to be impressive. She has a tendency to champion programs and causes which lack churchwide support . . . Midweek services have engendered only minor interest. Several committees report that she overrides their decisions . . .*

Helen detected a familiar self-defeating stinginess in both the pledge-drive results and her evaluation. The congregants were, after all, denying themselves decent music on Sunday, safer, more comfortable buildings and a growing church. The money was there. These were well-off professionals: teachers, scientists, lawyers, architects, doctors. Then again Helen knew that the poor, not the prosperous, are traditionally the most generous.

Reverend Harland's preaching has improved . . . We can only trust her ministry will, over time, grow more attuned to Morton's needs.

She spent the rest of the day on her sermon, then attended committee meetings until nine-thirty that night, all with steadfast good cheer, as if she'd received no mingy evaluation, no fuck-you on the pledge drive. But then she couldn't sleep.

Rising early, she walked through the neighborhood and across the L.A. River to a small Episcopalian church in Atwater, arriving in time for the eight o'clock communion service. She knelt, took the wafer on her tongue as men and women had been doing for two thousand years, and briefly was dissolved into a body far greater and more everlasting than her lonesome, besieged self.

The speaker at that night's midweek service was Ivo Meberian, a bald five-foot-four-inch Iranian Jew who'd escaped through the mountains into Turkey during the revolution and then emigrated to Glendale, where in a cloud of cologne, with great charm, persuasiveness and many cups of strong Mumtaz tea, he sold rugs in a minimall. Helen had met him at the takeout window of Hari's Kabobs; he'd struck up a conversation as they waited. Short men with a yen for tall women had been a fact of her life—and an unceasing irritation—since she'd shot up five inches during the seventh grade.

So she conversed without paying much attention until her shoulder-high companion, on hearing she was a minister, mentioned antique prayer rugs. Ivo, quick to register her interest, explained that many rugs were spiritual in design, that the central image in medallion rugs, for example, the sun gate, represented the center of the universe, the opening to the world beyond.

Helen stopped by his shop some days later, where he unrolled rug after rug, explaining the symbology of each. While he accomplished neither sale nor amorous conquest, Ivo was nevertheless gratified as she asked him to speak at a Wednesday night service at her church. This was five months ago, and since then he'd been planning his program with a touching assiduousness, reading widely and making several trips to his family's large rug market and warehouse in San Diego to find classic examples. The night of his talk, Ivo arrived at Morton an hour early with a good portion of his store's inventory in tow. Helen worked up a sweat helping him lug them inside the Family Center.

"It is a common misconception," Ivo soon told the assembled, "that Islam forbids all pictorial representation. At least it is a gross exaggeration." He spoke seriously and slowly, with a heavy accent. "For many centuries, figurative rugs were abundant, but in the sixteenth century there was a crackdown in Persia and imagery having any reference to the mosque was forbidden. So what we have on this prayer rug is an abstracted reference to the niche, which orients the worshipper to the Holy City." He unfurled rugs, as needed. "Here's a highly stylized mosque lamp. This rarer basin shape represents cleanliness before God."

The borders found on most Oriental carpets, he went on to say, contained symbols to ward off evil and protect those within the design. "I present you now with this interesting photograph," Ivo said, and held up a book open to a photograph of Freud's office at 19 Berggasse in Vienna: "You will notice what I believe to be nice Kazak draped over the famous couch; thus his patients, as they talked to him, were always circumscribed from evil."

Several weeks ago, Helen had called and asked Ivo to discuss rugs with deer imagery, and although this request initially threw him, he brought a stunning carpet from his own home with a repeating pattern of tigers and lions killing deer and wild ox. "The pun is a popular technique in carpet design," he now said. "The word *dam*, for example, has several meanings: the fleeting pleasures of this world; a snare, or temptation; and it is also the word for horned animals. Thus when the tiger and the lion kill deer in this Sufi rug, you see the mystical Sufi's struggle to kill his craving for worldly delights."

Ivo squinted at his notes.

"Deer, in fact, figure in the oldest known carpets, which were discovered in Scythian burial grounds in southern Siberia dating back to the fourth or fifth century B.C. The border design is a repeating pattern of *cervus dama*, or fallow deer." He glanced at Helen, who smiled and nodded.

After his talk, Ivo handed out coupons for a ten percent discount off of any item in his store. *Oh dear,* Helen thought, *now the grouches have something else to squawk about— speakers using the podium to drum up business.* But she'd underestimated the attraction of a bargain, and during the question-and-answer period, one congregant asked if he also sold wall-to-wall, and another if the ten percent applied to rug cleaning and repair.

Afterward, Helen approached Alice. "So, what did you think of Ivo?"

"Who knew a seedy rug merchant could be so interesting?" Alice, in her choppy short hair, looked like a little boy fresh from a nap. "Sweet of him to do that deer research." She poked Helen's upper arm. "I wonder who put him up to it."

"Did anything resonate for you?"

"I keep getting the message that I have to kill what I want the most."

"And that would be—?"

"Uh, I'll tell you later." Alice nodded. Ivo, his dark eyes huge and glossy with love, was headed straight for them. "Let's have breakfast tomorrow."

"Sure!" The invitation, a first from Alice, seemed a small success, and arrangements were swiftly made. The Cheese Chest at nine o'clock.

. . .

Lewis was lying on the sofa when Helen came home—a surprise. "You're a sight for sore eyes," she said, and wondered why he hadn't come to the service.

"This'll be quick. I have to leave first thing in the a.m." He struggled to his feet, clutching his lower back. "We've got to get you some decent furniture, baby. This lousy bed of nails would take all the fun out of being depressed." He kissed her more than nicely. "How'd it go tonight?"

"Ivo was brilliant!" she said. "*And* I hate my church!"

Lewis laughed and led her to the couch. "Want me to hurt somebody for you?"

"Sorry. You always get the brunt of it."

"Well, I have a surprise for you. Two, actually." He reached over the sofa's arm and brought up a crumpled sack. "Forgive the wrapping job."

Helen drew out a carved, painted wooden hand. Larger than life-sized, its slim fingers were slightly cupped, the palm punctured with a splintery hole.

"I love it!" Helen said. "You always give me exactly what I want!"

"It gets better," he said. "I won a cruise." A six-day, five-night eco-cruise around Baja that was donated to the drunk farm's raffle by an ex-resident. "It's a fancy, high-dollar gig. No gambling. Health food—vegan if you want it. Yakking naturalists, portholes, polished brass, lap robes. All I have to pay is the tax. Which I'll have to borrow from the bank, but what the hell."

"When do we go?"

"That's the rub. It has to be on or before June fifteenth."

Then it was impossible. "My church year isn't over till then."

"I thought you'd saved up a big chunk of vacation time."

"I can't take it now, not with everything so up in the air."

Lewis's face tightened.

"I'll see what I can do," she added. Not a good surprise after all—simply more pressure.

He left at five the next morning and Helen couldn't get back to sleep: the bad evaluation rankled, and the sluggish pledge drive. Lewis said both were perfectly in character with Morton and the problem wasn't with the church, not anymore, but with Helen's inability to accept things as they were. "You keep thinking they're going to change, and they keep telling you they're not. When will you get the message?" She *knew* he was right, but couldn't adopt that enlightened perspective, not quite yet. Finally she rose, dressed and, carrying the beautifully carved hand of Christ, walked over to her office.

She prayed here, on her knees, most mornings, often before dawn and always before the secretary arrived. Today she began with ten prostrations. During her internship—also the year of her most intensive training with Perry—she'd done ten thousand prostrations. Up and down, face to the ground, thirty times a day, thousands of giving-overs. The base of her palms had thickened; rough dark spots appeared on her knees; her forehead was tender to the touch. In the last five hundred prostrations, she became oversensitized and constantly felt dilated, exposed. Walking down the street teetered on unbearable: the greens in trees, the friendliness of dogs, the expressiveness of the human face—all of it asked far too much. The fragility of being alive sickened her, and she described her state to Perry as a nausea of the heart. The keenness of these sensations eventually receded to a dull ache, which Perry identified as compassion. So today, she went flat again and again, in hopes of rekindling some trace of it.

The church offices were housed in one of the dilapidated modular units, but Helen's office was better furnished than any room in the parsonage. The wantonly comfortable feather-filled couch and chairs and the large mahogany coffee table had been selected by Reverend Link himself. He'd taken his desk, also church property, and when the interim minister pointed this out, some heavy, battered oaken thing, lugged from a congregant's garage, appeared to fill the void. Behind it, sliding glass doors opened onto a private courtyard filled with Link's famous roses. Helen had read about them in his sermons; he liked the big red teas and grandifloras—Lavaglut, Ingrid Bergman, Chrysler Imperial—and pruned them, cured them of disease and infestations, entered them in rose shows and county fairs. All coffee grounds from church functions went into their soil. He brought them seaweed once a year and urinated on their roots as needed.

Helen had tried to administer the bushes; she deadheaded, scattered pricey organic rose food over the soil, read a book about rose pruning and followed the instructions. Emulating the mystical theologian and rose enthusiast Howard Thurman, she even tried talking to the bushes on a daily basis. But like Morton's other constituents, the roses missed their old master. The enormous blowsy flowers bloomed ever more mauve or magenta than crimson, and wilted even as they opened, their mildewed and yellowed leaves littering the ground.

Eventually she relinquished their care to the church gardener, who pruned radically and applied chemical fertilizer. Though the plants did marginally better, Helen didn't care if they died.

The office she'd had painted a dark, warm taupe, then filled the floor-to-ceiling bookshelves with her hardback library and favorite art; carved wooden crosses from Russia, a ceremonial doll from West Africa with human teeth, stone animal effigies from Honduras, a pot-metal Shiva, a plaster St. Sebastian pierced with rusty nails. She placed the new stigmatized hand on the coffee table beside the bejeweled blue plaster elephant, Ganesha, the Hindu god of new endeavors, a previous gift from Lewis.

After her prostrations, she lit a dozen candles and a stick of incense, did yoga stretches for her spine, then set a timer and meditated for forty-five minutes. When the timer beeped, she rose to her knees and prayed for detachment, self-containment, a release from anger—the usual—until a light tap on the door brought her to her feet.

The woman wore pink sweats, a Yankees baseball cap and dark glasses, so several seconds elapsed before Helen recognized Jocelyn Nearing. "I was running past," she said, her nostrils red. "I thought I'd see if you were in. Is this a bad time?"

"No, it's perfect. Come in." Helen, self-conscious for all the candles and incense, reached for her snuffer. "Just doing my morning thing."

"I love it," said Jocelyn, heading for the Honduran carvings. "May I look?"

"Feel free." Helen put out candles. At close range, Jocelyn's head seemed large, and oddly proportioned on her slight, narrow body. Unless you knew, you'd never guess she was one of the country's most beautiful women.

Jocelyn moved to San Sebastian, touching the rusted nails, and Helen felt her usual need to explain the collection to a first-time viewer. "After college, I spent two months in India," she said. "I was in a little shop in Benares that sold religious statuary. The very talkative and charming owner said, 'I know you Westerners think we're polytheists and worship hundreds of gods, but we know that these statues aren't gods. They're just tools to *get* to God.'" Helen pointed to her Shiva. "That was the first tool in my collection."

"He's lovely." Jocelyn straightened the many-limbed statue and spoke over her shoulder. "I've wanted to tell you I'm so happy I found your church. And you, Helen. You always say exactly what I need to hear."

"I'm happy you found us."

Jocelyn turned. "And there's something I've been meaning to ask you."

"Feel free. Why don't you have a seat?" She waited until Jocelyn settled on the sofa. "What's up?"

"Remember how you talked about mindfulness on Easter?" She picked the wooden hand off the coffee table. "I'd like to know more about that."

"Oh, okay," Helen said. "Mindfulness is first of all just being mindful. It's also a distinct state of mind cultivated through meditation that's sometimes called 'bare attention,' a kind of pure awareness that stays steady in the midst of distractions—far easier said than done!" Helen laughed. "I can get you started with the basic techniques."

"I'd love that," said Jocelyn.

"Although several people have expressed an interest, so I'm thinking of starting a meditation group. Would that appeal to you?"

Jocelyn turned the wooden hand over, as if to see if the puncture went all the way through. "Yes, of course. But to tell the truth, I was actually asking more for my husband than myself. He's been so agitated and unhappy lately, and that kind of calmness and clarity sounded like just what he needs."

"In that case," Helen said carefully, "I should probably talk to him."

"I could just pass along the instructions."

Helen paused. "You could. But mindfulness isn't easy under the best of circumstances. And learning about it secondhand from someone unfamiliar with the practice probably isn't the best approach. I'd be very happy to talk to him. And he's welcome to join the group, if that happens."

"He'd never go," Jocelyn said. "Not to you, and certainly not to any group. He's very private. He thinks people should solve their own problems." She cupped her knee with the wooden hand. "He doesn't believe in asking for help."

"And you?" Helen asked gently. "Do you ever ask for help?"

"As we speak!"

A phone rang down the hall. Outside, a truck pinged as it backed up. Helen said, "What's going on, Jocelyn?"

She returned the wooden hand to the coffee table. "A lot of the time Nick is fine. But Tuesday night, we went to my manager's house for dinner and he was so gloomy and testy. And drank everything in sight. As soon as we were out the door, he threw up. My manager poked her head out to ask if everything was all right, and I'm standing there thinking, *No! Nothing's all right. I'm old, I'm ugly, my career's over and my husband's drinking again.*"

"He's an alcoholic?"

"No. Well, I don't know. He was when we got married, but I put a stop to it."

"Wow!" Helen said with a light laugh. "How'd you manage that?"

"I told him I'd leave if he ever drank again." Jocelyn looked away and held a forefinger to her lips. "So much for my credibility."

"May I ask you a question?" Helen waited for her nod. "Have you ever heard of Al-Anon?"

"Funny you bring that up. My therapist sent me to a meeting a couple of months ago. I read about it in the tabloids a week later."

"That's bad," Helen said. "I'm really sorry."

"People get paid for those tips. Soon as I go, somebody calls the tabloids, tells them my marriage is shot and makes a couple hundred bucks." She shrugged. "Five years ago you could've made thousands—even my gossip value's shot."

Helen upended a stick of incense into its sand bed. "You might want to give Al-Anon another try. I'd be happy to go with you. I know some good little meetings in Glendale. God knows I could use a meeting myself."

"You? But you're so . . . together!"

"Me? Please! I'm hardwired for coaddiction. I come from a long line of drunks, God love 'em. My mother and grandfather . . . and my first husband was a heroin addict. I told my second husband I'd marry him only after he stayed sober for a year. He did, I married him and a week later he was pie-eyed. He blamed me—for setting the time limit!" She slapped her desk. "I can laugh about it now, but I was in *shreds* at the time. Al-Anon put me back together. They told me to take the focus off of the drinker and put it on myself. Get my own life together so I could function and be happy with or without him. When he finally did get sober and wanted to come back, I said no. A man who'd spent the last year in bars, jails and hospitals, who was unemployed, with huge debts and a serious liver condition, wasn't so appealing anymore. I had my own life by then. And he didn't stay sober anyway, of course."

"I'm *trying* to have my own life," Jocelyn said. "That's why I'm coming to church. And why I may open a restaurant."

"You mean and quit acting?"

"How can I quit if I don't have a job?" She looked at her lap. "I've been thinking about a restaurant for a long time. I found the perfect space in March. And when I ran into Peter Ross at your church, it seemed like a sign." She looked up at Helen. "This great chef, not working, set right in my path."

Helen looked at her. "He's that good?"

"The best. If he'd cook, I'd sign a lease in a second."

Helen glanced at her watch. "What are you doing right now? I have to meet my friend Alice for breakfast, and I'm wondering if you'd like to join us." Alice's self-absorption could stand some aeration, she thought, and Jocelyn might appreciate being included in something so casual and ordinary. And the mutual befriending of newcomers was a classic strategy for growing a congregation. "You know Alice, from church? Short, bleached-blond hair?

"Peter's little friend? Oh yes, *yes*." She did indeed seem pleased. "I like her, but she's so shy. Don't you think she'd mind my barging in?"

"No, no. The more the merrier."

25

Habitually now, after cataloging Jocelyn's attributes—the shiny rust-and honey-colored hair, the famous, radiant, impossibly wide smile, the unflagging grace and graciousness—Alice set them beside Nick's physical and temperamental darkness and soon the logic of the Nearing-Lawton marriage became so obvious that it was laughable: the clichéd union of sunny goddess and saturnine, nocturnal prince. Alice's own position in this equation was, by definition, weak: she'd be the mortal girl, briefly beloved in a fleeting, bittersweet dalliance, whose desperate, intensifying demands would eventually provoke her metamorphosis into a shrub, a sparrow or dim, remote constellation.

The back of Jocelyn's head could hardly engage a person's interest for an entire Sunday service, so Alice found herself listening to the sermons in which Helen talked about ideas and history and told odd stories. While she hadn't thought so at first, Alice had come to suspect that Helen was a good preacher. The sermons always started out steady and sure, but she kept pulling in more images and ideas until it suddenly seemed as if she'd gone too far, leapt over a cliff, with various subjects flying pell-mell through the air after her. Convinced that Helen was disgracing herself, Alice initially was mortified for her. But every time Helen had pulled something surprising and clever from the mix, made sense of the disparate parts—or most of them—and swung back around to the original topic, a kamikaze technique Alice was learning to appreciate.

Last Sunday's sermon was simply entitled "Friendship," which Helen claimed was not only the only human relationship based on equality but also uniquely voluntary. She quoted Tacitus—*Friendship seeks or creates equals*—and spoke of Emerson and Margaret Fuller's friendship, which was so intense that Fuller mistook it for romantic love and embarrassed them both. She discussed Simone Weil's assertion that a true friend shared in the other's sorrow and happiness but never ever had to *please* the other, which Alice found especially confusing—if you didn't please people, why would they ever want to be friends with you? Helen illustrated this and other points with examples from her own life. Contrary to Alice's first impression, Helen's friendships seemed legion. Of course many of them had failed the equality test: some friendships were transient, she said, while others were permanent, and you could never be sure ahead of time which was which, since the closest, most intense ones sometimes burned themselves out while steady, slow-to-deepen acquaintanceships could end up the most long-lasting and satisfying.

Foster, delighted by her speed and accuracy, had trusted Alice with a shoe box full of tapes and almost a hundred completed questionnaires. She could work from home, he said, but Alice liked having an office. With Merle there and Dewey coming and going, she was hardly ever alone.

Dewey reminded her of her brother Doug; they were close to the same age, both athletic and sweet, with a similar innocent denseness. Dewey liked to talk about his former girlfriends—the one who'd left him when he'd lost his faith, and Cynthia, who was here at the seminary. He pointed her out to Alice in the cafeteria, a serious, pretty young woman with long straight blond hair who dressed in sweatshirts and jeans as if to downplay her attractiveness. Dewey still didn't know what went wrong. "She was taking these women's studies classes," he said. "She got so irritated with me."

Alice spoke to him as she might to Doug. "You have nothing to worry about, Dewey. You're great-looking. And incredibly nice, and you have the best dog." Alice's praise seemed to baffle him. Was she joking? Did she really think he was great-looking? "Dewey," she'd cry like a bossy older sister, "you're a babe! A catch! You have classic WASP good looks. Anybody would be thrilled to be your girlfriend."

He brought her PowerBars and donuts and coffee, whatever he'd picked up for himself. He gave her a snapshot of Merle in a magnet-backed Plexiglas holder to stick on her refrigerator at home.

"What about you?" he asked. "Do you have a boyfriend?"

"I'm betwixt and between," she said. "I'm still recovering from the last one. And not in the market for the next." She liked the sound of this, and wished it were truer.

"Well, you're nice too," Dewey said. "And pretty. You could be on MTV."

"Yeah, well, thanks," she said dryly. Her thrift store clothes and tufty bleached hair, already dark at the roots, certainly distinguished her from the seminarians.

Dewey came from a conservative moneyed family; he had spent weekends at a cabin in Big Bear and vacations at rented condominiums in Vail and Oahu, yet for all his sophistication he might have been raised on a farm. He'd gone to college in Riverside, only sixty miles east of L.A., and except for a few days at the beach and church conferences at Brentwood Pres he'd never ventured west. The closest he'd come to Alice's neighborhood was a field trip to the zoo in elementary school. Still, maybe such a sheltered upbringing had its advantages. Dewey seemed so hopeful and good—so uncynical and unironic—that Alice quite liked him even as she wondered how he possibly could be, at twenty-six, so unbesmirched.

Foster promised the material on the tapes would become more interesting, but whatever halting messages Gustavo deigned to retrieve from the grand ancestor tended to be fragmented and nonsensical. Alice kept waiting, if not to be amazed, at least for something more than "Hurry the place." Or "Listing hopper multi welsh."

"Still enjoying it?" Foster asked. "Not too kooky?"

"I'm used to kooky. My aunt, you know . . ." She'd told him, by then, about her great-aunt's novel and lifelong fascination with the James family.

"I'd love to meet this Aunt Kate. Tell me, does she consider herself 'in contact' with our boy? If so, should I send her a questionnaire?"

"I'll take her one," said Alice. "But you might get more than you bargained for—like hundreds of pages. This is her subject, after all."

"And mine!" said Foster. "I'd love it. Now tell me, Alice, do you have any interest in meeting the medium?"

"I'd love to put a face on those voices. But Foster . . ." She leaned forward confidentially. "What if Patricia's making this stuff up? What if it's all delusion?"

He clasped his hands behind his head, a classically philosophical stance. "That's probably the case. But why and how do these delusions occur so often, across such a wide swath of society? What does it mean?"

Alice, having no answers, went back to work.

Foster: Gustavo, how are you?

Gustavo: Crammed in tight.

Foster (*laughs*): Well, we appreciate it. Will you get Dr. James please?

Gustavo: He's right here. And so vain; you should see his green cashmere vest and his stripety blue necktie. Casual, but eye-catching.

F: Does he have anything for us today?

G: Dr. James is fussing as usual. He is so afraid Gustavo will not get the essential references across—though you don't see *him* squeezing into the medium, now do you?

F: No, we don't.

Dewey came in, emptied his knapsack of books on his desk and invited Alice to go to the cafeteria with him. "I should at least take you to lunch for watching Merle all these times."

"At the very least." She seemed compelled to tease him.

"We *could* have dinner if you want, but, well, it's lunchtime now and I thought—"

"Dewey," she cried. "I'm joking. Lunch is fine. And I'd watch Merle for nothing, even pay for the privilege." To see Dewey's face pass from blank incomprehension to the hot pink flush of understanding was, she thought, weirdly gratifying.

He bought them each a tuna sandwich, a prewrapped chunk of frosted carrot cake and lemonade, which they arranged on a table not far from his ex and her friends. To avenge her sweet, spurned office mate, Alice laughed readily at everything he said and made a show of regarding him as the most fascinating creature on earth. Cynthia, she noted, observed everything.

When they went back outside, Merle was perched on the roof of a green Camry, her eyes half closed, her chest lifted, the hairs on her ears trembling in a light breeze, her nose quivering as if she were receiving signals. Dewey was standing so close to Alice that he grazed her at the shoulder, arm and hip, provoking an unexpected surge of emotion. How long had it been since she'd been so near to another human?

"Some people say dogs exist in a continuous meditative state," Dewey said, then he gave a short whistle. Merle flew through the air.

Upstairs, he opened the office door and, as Alice headed for her desk, grabbed her upper arm. He grabbed it lightly, but at the same spot her mother used to seize in anger, so her first thought was, *What did I do wrong?* Turning, though, she saw that he meant to kiss her. Oh dear. So the shoulder-grazing was no accident. Didn't he know that she was too jaded, hard-hearted, *ruined*? He was trembling, poor boy. Yet so deter-mined. And dead serious. Kissing, clearly, was not something Dewey Hupfeld did lightly. Her heart went out to him. If she'd guessed his intentions, she might've deflected him. He hadn't seemed like the kind to go for an older woman; rather, she thought, he'd have to go young, very young, to find a taker for such sincerity and innocence. But here she was, caught off guard and loath to humiliate or even disappoint him. Her lunchtime behavior was meant to be perceived as flirtatious, but only by Cynthia, and how could she ever have guessed that this sweet, handsome young man would have a drib of sexual interest in her?

Dewey by now had her in his arms. His body, she had to admit, was that of a full-grown male, tall enough that he was bending over her. Oh, what the hell, if only for the sheer sexual thrill, she'd accept the kiss. And stood on tiptoes to do so. Even knowing how seriously he'd take it, she kissed him and then, since the first was altogether too quick, allowed another longer, deeper kiss. She was bad, she knew. Hell-bound.

They kept kissing. This was the first man other than Nick she'd kissed in over a year, and the enormity of this step was mitigated by not only a certain relief but also a certain vengefulness, a sense of evening the score. Nick, after all, had no doubt routinely kissed Jocelyn.

That night, she took Aunt Kate to the midweek service and, on the way, finally described her new job. "It's all about his posthumous activity in the spirit realm."

"Yes, he's been very active," Aunt Kate said, gazing at her niece's profile. "Since when did you take such an interest in William?"

"It's not that I'm so interested in him," Alice said carefully. "But the job came up, the pay was good—and my boss liked that I was a descendant."

"I'm sure he did." A touch of frost.

Alice wondered if her aunt was, if not exactly jealous, a bit proprietary. "My boss would really like to meet you," she added.

"I'm sure he would."

"And he wonders if you'll fill out one of the question-naires."

"I'd have to see it first."

"Of course."

Whether Aunt Kate was upset or merely thoughtful, Alice still felt a pang of remorse. "I hope you don't mind that I took this job. I'm not trying to horn in on your territory."

"Don't be ridiculous. I've always hoped you'd take an inter-est in your legacy."

At Morton Alice sat there brooding. If, as the speaker said, deer depicted in rugs were symbols of worldly cravings, and worldly cravings had to be given up, what about her craven behavior with Dewey? How dare she lead him on for her own sexual entertainment? On the other hand, maybe the attachment she had to forgo was with Nick, and all the drama and treachery of adultery. Maybe Dewey was the new, appropriate happiness. He *was* single. Willing and available. Physically beautiful, if a little boring. Some of her college girlfriends had settled for men who weren't very interesting. Could Dewey Hupfeld be her chance, finally, at what everyone else already had?

In the morning, Alice dropped off a questionnaire for Aunt Kate then dashed around the corner to the Cheese Chest, a gourmet cheese shop and sandwich bar. The service was slow; the food overpriced and the espresso machine so loud that it stopped all conversation, but its proximity to Aunt Kate and the Fountain (right down the street) had made the Cheese Chest an inevitable fixture in Alice's life. Today, pushing through the door, she spot-ted Nick's Yankees cap, then Jocelyn Nearing's face beneath it and also, at the same table, Helen, who was standing up and waving. They were here, obviously, to confront her about Nick, with Helen serving as a mediator. Alice froze in the open door, but now Jocelyn was waving as well, with the whole breakfast crowd turning to see who the incredible Jocelyn Nearing was beckoning. Alice had no choice but to wend her way to their table.

Jocelyn clasped her hand. "I hope you don't mind my tagging along."

"No." The word came out as a warble. "But I can't stay. I have to go to work."

"Sit for one second," Helen said, pulling out a chair. "Tell Foster I insisted. Blame everything on me."

"Yes, please do stay," said Jocelyn.

Alice sat on the very edge of the chair.

"How *is* work?" said Helen. "Learning anything new about your illustrious ancestor?"

"Not really."

"Alice is descended from William James," Helen said to Jocelyn.

"Helen!" Alice cried in dismay. If Jocelyn went home and told Nick she'd just had coffee with a girl named Alice who was related to William James, he'd know it was her and think that she was meddling and stalking. And she *had been*, though she wasn't today. But isn't there a rule that when you finally get caught, it's for the one thing you didn't actually do?

"Am I not supposed to mention that?" said Helen. "I'm sorry, I didn't realize it was a sensitive issue."

"No, no, it doesn't matter." Alice wanted the subject to disappear.

"Who's William James?" said Jocelyn. "I don't even know."

"You know Henry James, the writer?" Helen said.

"Of course. I did *The Heiress* at the Pasadena Playhouse a few years ago."

"William was his brother, a philosopher and psychologist. He also did psychical research while he was alive, and now that he's dead, he supposedly makes contact with all sorts of mediums. My friend Foster is doing the first systematic study of these contacts, and Alice is his assistant."

"How fascinating," Jocelyn said to Alice.

"To be honest, it's pretty boring," said Alice. "Now I really have to go."

"Real quick, though, Alice," Jocelyn said. "I'd like to ask you a favor."

Alice gazed at the pale poreless skin, the lively brown eyes, and awaited the inevitable. *Would you please stop sleeping with my husband?*

"I'm seriously thinking of opening a restaurant," Jocelyn said, "but only if Peter will be the chef."

After a long pause, Alice realized a response was expected. "Yeah?"

"Yes. And I was wondering if you'd help me talk him into it."

"Me?" Alice, confused, turned to Helen. "Does she mean your Pete?"

"*My* Pete?"

"Isn't he *your* Pete, Alice?" Jocelyn said.

"Fat Pete? From church? Are you kidding?" Is that how Jocelyn saw her—girlfriend to a nutcase? *Hey, lady, I'm not with that loser. I'm with your husband!*

"Guess he's your Pete, Jocelyn," said Helen. "Your chef, at least."

"I'll take him! I want him," she said. "And I don't think of him as fat, though I suppose he is, a little. Back when I knew him he was so good-looking, and I still see that, I guess."

"Oh, I see it too," said Helen. "More so since he's lost a few pounds."

"God," said Alice, "how fat did he used to be?"

Nobody answered her.

"Actually," she added, "Pete's got his heart set on the reverend here."

"Not true!" Helen rang out. "We're friends—he knows I'm with Lewis."

The espresso machine roared, and was followed by a soft trilling. "Oh!" Jocelyn produced a small red cell phone from her pocket. "The babysitter," she said, hitting a button and turning away to talk. A moment later she was on her feet. "I completely forgot the nanny had a doctor's appointment. Take my latte, Alice—if you want." She took out her wallet, but Helen waved it away.

"We'll do this again soon," Helen said.

"I'd love to." Jocelyn slipped off, smiling and waving.

Helen turned to Alice. "Can't you stay for another minute?"

"I don't really have to leave. Jocelyn just makes me nervous."

"Really? I find her so down-to-earth."

"All famous people make me nervous. I don't know how to act around them. I wish you'd warned me—"

"It was all very spur-of-the-moment," Helen said. "She seemed pretty depressed, and I thought we might cheer her up."

"Her? What's she got to be depressed about?"

"I think being in the public eye like that must put her under enormous pressure. She needs normal people around her."

"And that includes Pete?"

"Come on, now. Pete's a good guy, completely trustworthy in his own way. You always know where you stand with him."

"I suppose," Alice said. "He just takes up so much space. It's *exhausting* to be around him."

"He likes you."

"He likes *you*. I'm just the beard."

"Not true," said Helen. "He even worries about you."

"About me? Why?"

"He's afraid you're unhappy."

"I am unhappy! What's the big fuss? That's like worrying that I have a big toe, or hair. I've always been unhappy!"

Alice had meant to be funny, but Helen sounded concerned. "Tell me, Alice, are you really bored with your new job?"

"It's not that bad." She shrugged. "Most of the so-called communications we get are like ham radio signals or something typed by a cat. Everyone got all excited at one sitting when the medium said 'The spotted dog is outside,' because one of the women there had a pointer and when she called home it *was* outside. That's about as exciting as it gets." Afraid of seeming ungrateful, she added, "But I love Foster, and the money's a big help."

"I've read that the dead can be incredibly banal," said Helen. "They want you to put their picture back on the piano, or wash the windows, or take Grandma's beaver coat out of storage."

"Great," Alice said. "After years of transcribing incoherent gibberish, we end up with a laundry list! Get those damn rugs cleaned. Flush out the gutters. Prune those trees."

"I'm sorry, though, I thought the job would be fun."

"Oh, I'm having fun," Alice said, and felt her face form a grin. "In fact, I've started seeing someone out there. A guy."

Helen gave her a sidelong glance. "Not Foster?"

Foster? Fifty-something Foster with his beige clothes, fading hair and distant paternalism? Could you get any further from sexy? Besides, Foster had been married forever. "No! Dewey—Dewey Hupfeld," Alice said, then felt a twang of betrayal: that Helen assumed she'd go for the *married* man.

"I know Dewey," Helen said. "Since when?"

She gave a small laugh. "It just started. Why, don't you approve?"

"What's not to approve? Dewey's great. I can't quite see the two of you together, though."

"Neither can I!" said Alice. "That's why there's hope. Everyone *I've* gone after has been a disaster. Dewey came after me. And who knows? Maybe a junior Jesus-freak jock's *just* the man for me."

"I'm not sure it works that way." Helen shrugged. "But stranger things have happened."

"I do feel like the evil defiler of youth."

"Dewey should be so lucky."

"And you have to admit, he does have the best dog."

"I haven't met the dog," Helen said, and the waitress came with lattes and took their order for bagels.

"I'm at my wit's end, myself," Helen said, and described the dire state of her church finances, the mediocre evaluation. "It's so frustrating. It's like there's a great church only inches away from Morton, and I still can't get there."

"I know the feeling," Alice said. "Is there anything I can do to help?"

"There is: this. Hanging out with me. Yakking. Helping me forget that I'm a minister for two minutes at a stretch. I was hoping we could do something tomorrow night, a movie maybe. Though with a new boyfriend, you're probably not free on a Friday night."

"I am free," said Alice, since she and Dewey had plans for Saturday.

"Is it time for *Bambi*?"

"More tragic deer? I guess."

"May I invite Pete?"

"Why ask? You already have, right?"

"No, but if he's going to work for Jocelyn, he needs all the socialization he can get."

Alice studied her face, which seemed to grow brighter under the scrutiny. "Sure you don't have a crush on him?"

"Can't say as I do," she said. "Why don't you ask Dewey to come too?"

"Are you kidding? It's way too soon to take him out in public. And besides, Pete would eat him alive."

She went home and wandered through the house, rinsed out the coffeepot and thought about watering the yard. She was still in some postadrenaline jangle from the nonconfrontation with Jocelyn, but no red light pulsed on the answering machine. She went to the bathroom to wash her hands and check the mirror. She'd slept funny on a clump of hair, and though she'd wet it earlier, it was sticking straight out again. To think she'd had coffee with Jocelyn Nearing with her hair sticking out. She rubbed in molding gel, which was no help. Short hair was every bit as hopeless as long, and she already needed another cut-and-dye job. She was washing gel off her hands when the phone rang.

"Miss Spiritual Deer person? Pete Ross here."

"Oh, *Pete*. Helen and I were just talking about you."

"That's why I'm calling. If I'm ever going to design another menu, I ought to be cooking—and for someone other than Mom, who gets heartburn from Cream of Wheat. Now, your preacher friend just invited me to this private screening of *Bambi,* so what would you think about me cooking dinner beforehand?"

"Where? Here?"

"You've got that stove and Limoges, and all that amazing Georg Jensen."

"I'd have to wash it all before you could use it."

"I'll do that."

She was curious about Pete's cooking. "This would be just the three of us?"

"You, me and her holiness."

"Not what's her name, the actress?"

"No. I don't want to get her hopes up—or dash 'em, for that matter. I need a few dry runs, with willing guinea pigs."

"Okay," Alice said. "Just don't let her holiness invite anyone else."

26

I f it's all right with you, Ma, I'll have dinner and watch a
video with the gals tomorrow night," he announced over halibut and peas, feeling way too much like he was sixteen and
having to divulge his plans in order to get the car, which had
been difficult enough even before his plans involved the opposite
sex and excruciating to the point of impossibility once it did.

"Which gals are we talking about?" Beth said.

"You know, the reverend and her little friend."

"And how long have you been planning this get-together?"

"Helen phoned this morning."

"Is Helen still seeing her boyfriend?"

"I suppose so. Why do you ask?" But he knew why: to
nudge him into acknowledging that Helen's focus—at least her
amorous focus—was elsewhere. He scowled and kicked at a
dark spot on the linoleum. Mom, damn her, had a point.

In the morning he was afoot early, moving toward Glendale and
deciding as he went what to cook and where to shop and how
much he could get done before the Bread Basket and then afterward. So fuck the gym.

After months of making subtle, low-salt meals, Pete craved
big clarion blasts of flavor. Jocelyn had been talking about
Mediterranean cuisine—Sicily and northern Africa—which
made Pete think perhaps a lamb tagine, only where could he

ever find salt-preserved lemons? Of course there was always lamb tagine with prunes or fresh grilled figs, but it was early for figs . . .

Pete concocted menus as he crossed Riverside Drive. Wending through a maze of public tennis courts, he admired the resonant *pock! pock! pock! pock!* of a strong volley, then took a packed-dirt ramp under a bower of blooming blue plumbago. The ramp led to the only walking bridge over the Los Angeles River. It first spanned the I-5 freeway, and, over those eight lanes of traffic, was completely encased in rusted steel mesh. No suicidal leaps allowed, nor pelting of cars with anything larger than a corn kernel. Over the river, however, the narrow bridge had only a chest-high, grafittoed steel railing, so without much ado a person could topple him- or herself into the shallow black drink some thirty feet below. A number of folk had done just that, but far more shopping carts had made the plunge. In fact, giving the occasional Kmart or Costco cart a heave-ho had become something of a neighborhood sport. One orange plastic number rested below, and fifty feet downriver, carried there by winter runoff, sat an earlier piece of mischief, the chrome basket having strained out stones and muck enough to form a trapezoidal island on which tufts of optic grass and tiny yellow daisies flourished.

Pete didn't even know what was being sold in restaurants anymore. As he was fading from the scene three years ago, mediocre Tuscan was ubiquitous. In fact, Pete's former landlord, after evicting Trotwood, opened a crappy trattoria all his own. The landlord knew nothing about restaurants and less about food, but he knew success when he saw it, and if Pete Ross could enjoy it, surely he could too. So he'd doubled Trotwood's lease when it came up for renewal, thus easing out Pete, who'd tried to hang on, but the good times were a-changing—the boom was going bust, the market collapsing, the bottomless expense account fast becoming a thing of the past. Peggotty closed before it really opened, and Trotwood's clientele had been dwindling even before the raise in rent. By 1995 all anybody seemed to want—or be able to afford—was a bowl of pasta and a booze-oozing slab of tiramisù. If Peggotty had done even a modest business and Trotwood's lease hadn't doubled, Pete might today be gainfully employed; some chefs who'd started up around the same time were still in the swim, although many, many others also bellied up in the recession or were reduced to boiling novelty pastas in this ho-hum café or grilling flavor-free steaks at that hotel chophouse.

After his twin closures, Pete worked for two years at a high-end French place in Pasadena, until the owner decided to conceptually downsize to Provençal rustic: veal daube, overdone roast lamb with flageolets, steamed mussels, stuff any blind, drunken sous-chef could cook by the trough. "I can't afford you," the owner said, so Pete moved on to the downtown Sheraton, where his menu opened to critical acclaim. But the hotel guests wanted ground sirloin and mashies, not matsutake mushroom salad and line-caught, pan-seared *loup de mer* floated in tomato water. When the food and beverage supervisor insisted on a Caesar salad sans anchovy and raw egg, plain grilled fish, a New York steak and crème brûlée, Pete blew up and knocked some pans off their hooks, creating far more noise than damage, which he knew but his boss did not. Within moments he was fired, and word spread fast. Lost his restaurants. Fired twice since. A worse-than-usual chef temper; cracked, in fact. Meanwhile, restaurants were folding left and right.

Anne told him to take a few months off to relax and contemplate his next move. Relax he did, sinking and sinking, he and Garrett and the nanny cooped up in the house all day while Anne earned the living. She'd gotten herself a top-dollar PR job, making more than any two of his salaries combined. Who knew what she was capable of once she wasn't boostering his career? Months passed with Pete on the couch, and with them went Anne's patience. Disapproval hardened her face, narrowed her eyes. As Pete couldn't seem to help himself, she rewrote his résumé, printed it on heavy granite-gray stock, wrote cover letters by the half dozen which he signed, folded and stamped under her scrutiny and then—on slow, endless walks through the neighborhood with Garrett—mailed in various trash bins and dumpsters.

The more efficient Anne became, the greater his lethargy and the darker his mood. No longer could he picture their Clifford May–look-alike ranch home in Encino Hills, its glistening lawn and artfully pruned oaks and slate-lipped swimming pool with a valley view. Instead he remembered a series of small dim rooms closing in on him: the incredible shrinking house. Had he gone to Freeman then, Pete would've learned he had an illness—one caused by life reconfiguring brain chemistry—but an illness nonetheless, and treatable. At the time, however, both he and Anne assumed his descent was a question of his character, which the challenges of unemployment and fatherhood had exposed as contemptibly weak and selfish.

If Pete had not gone back to work to support the wife and son he loved, how could he promise Jocelyn Nearing, whom he knew only mildly and might not even like, anything at all? And who could say if Paxil and working out, meditation and feeding the poor, attending church and taking endless walks, would keep him operative? Much depended on unmanifested self-improvement. Haircut. Civility. Cooperativeness. Willingness to proceed.

At the farmer's market Pete purchased lettuces; red oak leaf and arugula and, recalling Alice's pedestrian preference, a pale green brain of iceberg. He found squat Brandywine tomatoes, heavy as gourds; beets in red, gold and the striped chioggia variety; a hairy, phallic knob of fresh horseradish. He bought mint and tiny sheaves of chives, and was tempted by bales of fresh chickpeas still in lanternlike pods on dusty stems, but had no sous-chefs to shuck 'em, and doubted that the pleasantly disagreeable Alice Black would volunteer. He also bought ripe Santa Rosa plums and organic Meyer lemons and en route to the Bread Basket, lugging his purchases, stopped in at a little Armenian grocery for couscous, canned chickpeas, squares of puff pastry, twelve tiny frozen quail and three different kinds of olives.

He was checking out at the counter when a woman came in with two dusky, dark-eyed boys close to Garrett's age. They nudged and elbowed each other, infecting the narrow, jam-packed aisles with untamed energy. Pete would not have been surprised if cans began tumbling from shelves and the sheet glass cracked.

Stunned by a loss he hardly ever dared formulate, he pushed himself outside, limped drunkenly to a cinderblock wall and dropped his white plastic sacks to the ground, where they gathered around his feet like a clutch of small, attentive, bottom-heavy ghosts.

"I am not on steady ground." He had arrived at the Bread Basket—sleepwalked, apparently—and gone straight to Helen in the pantry. Sitting on crates of canned goods, he clamped hands on his jumping knees.

"But there is no steady ground," she said, as if this devastating fact mattered not a whit. "Everything shifts and changes. It's the one incontestable fact of life."

"Well, I hate it."

"I know. The trick is to give up fighting, sit back and enjoy the ride."

"I'd need a Dramamine IV. Everything stops me cold, makes me sick or scares me shitless. Every damn thing. I'm not up to it."

She thought this over. "How's the meditation going?"

"I sat for fifteen minutes this morning."

"Bravo!"

"But what's that growing roar I hear?" he said. "Physiology?"

"Oh, I don't know . . . the storm of inner thoughts? And it's not all that rare, Pete. Nobody can sit still, or haven't you noticed? It's been said that all of the world's problems can be traced to man's inability to sit alone in a room."

"Yes, but I never used to be so nervous. It's got to be partly, or mostly, my meds. I don't see you flailing and snapping like a hot pan of beans."

"I have my flailings," Helen said. "And you've got to ease up on yourself. You're doing fine. You've got a better grasp of things than most."

"How can you say that? Even my brilliant genius psychiatrist says my personality is incompatible with life—way-way-way oversensitive."

"I'm not so sure that puts you at odds with life. I mean, what's more sensitive than the universe itself, where every action causes an equal and opposite reaction?"

Pete was stopped by this line of reasoning and, taking it in, approved. Imagine if he was the universe manifest—or the universe a vast, macro version of himself.

Or maybe that wasn't so good.

"As Alice's great-great-grandfather says, we are not external creations but internal parts of God."

"Ha!" he said. So what part of God was he? A molecule of spleen? An ever-pulsing heart cell? He gazed hard at the rough, pale green stucco wall, frowning and thinking, until the wall sank into a mist that shivered into a faintly prismatic radiance and slowly dissolved into nothing at all, the increasingly familiar, sea-sickening nothing into which he'd stumbled often enough when the bottom fell out, a couple of times during meditation and in the rare strange moments of stillness when his mind went blank, as he faced a clean sheet of paper or the wide-open mouth of a frying pan.

Hours later, in the yellow air of late afternoon, Pete arrived at the house on Wren Street with a box of sharp knives, three pounds of boneless lamb leg, two sacks of groceries and a grinding mind. "Helen's bringing the rest," he told Alice. "I wanted to get the lamb on. Here." As if this semisurly creature would care, he handed over a menu scrawled on the back of a Bread Basket registration form. But she read it, her lips moving.

Beet and horseradish salad on greens
Eggplant salad
Hummus
Quail b'stilla
Lamb tagine with dried figs
Plum tart with lemon sorbet
Chocolate truffles

"I love beets," she said, and Pete regarded her with new approval. He had a theory that the world could be divided into beet lovers and haters, with very few equivocators. Anybody who hated beets, he found, he did not care to know.

"Do you think this will be enough?" she asked, handing back the list. "Shouldn't there be a third dessert?"

"Somebody has to keep you girls on a diet."

He pored through her cabinets, pulling out pans and plates and the chest of sterling, indulging his penchant for fine tableware. He cut up the lamb, jimmied spices and set the mess to cook on a low, slow light, then began to pan-braise the quail with shaved leek whites, minced carrot and a trace of brandy as Alice sliced plums and wrapped beets in tinfoil with twigs of fresh thyme. Beyond passing tools and her practical questions—"Trim the roots?"—they barely talked. Two shyboots, he guessed. He readied both a sweet and a savory pastry while she chopped bittersweet chocolate, then onions. Helen walked in to find her weeping at the cutting board.

"It was nothing I said or did," Pete declared.

As they unloaded more groceries, he tried to keep his panic down. He decided to skip the hummus. With Helen there, he felt giddy. He turned to Alice. "Where's the new squeeze I've been hearing about?"

Alice gave Helen a dirty look. "I thought ministers didn't gossip."

"You never said it was a secret, Alice. I thought it was good news."

"Oh." Alice wiped her eyes with her forearm. "That remains to be seen."

"So?" Pete asked. "Why isn't he here?"

"I'm not ready to show him off," Alice said. "And you won't like him."

"What makes you say that?" Pete's outrage was not entirely false.

"He's nice. I mean, *really* nice."

"You're right. I'd hate him."

"Hey, what's wrong with nice?" said Helen.

Pete crumpled a shopping bag and his heart sank like a cinderblock. So Helen liked nice. Which he surely was not. Earlier, at the Bread Basket, she'd admired his great soul immensely, but now a gulf had reopened with one mild, slightly pointed question. She was his minister, distanced and didactic, and all her talk of how wide-awake and cosmically connected he was seemed, in retrospect, mere consolatory spew.

A small, quick pain above his ear broke this brooding spell, and he looked down to see a plum pit spinning by his shoe. Alice, it seemed, had beaned him, knocked him back to the here and now. He rubbed his head and returned to work. The women set the table, then washed his first sinkful of pots and pans before he chased them from the kitchen. "Go watch your dismal deer show," he said.

"We want you to watch it with us." This, playfully plaintive, from Alice.

"I've seen it," said Pete. "Believe me."

He did join them during lulls, as the lamb slow-cooked by the braising quail and the beets and eggplant baked shoulder to shoulder in the oven. A young and timid Bambi explored the forest. "Another faggy voice."

"Don't start," said Alice. "Please don't start."

On his way back to the kitchen, Pete straightened out the table settings. Salad fork on the *outside*. Water goblets over the *knife*. Then he boned the cooked quail, bundled it in small pastry purses and set them in the oven, assembled salads and plum tart, checked the lamb. Not much more to go. He returned to see Bambi slip and slide on the frozen lake.

"That's how the deer was in my house," Alice said. "Only so much more frantic and loud."

"The artists studied actual deer to make this film," said Helen. "They obviously got some things right."

"They sure got the voice wrong," said Pete.

"For someone who never goes to the movies, Helen," Alice said, "you sure know a lot about them."

"I read the video boxes, is all."

Winter deepened and the cold, hungry deer peeled bark from trees. Pete approved of nothing in this movie: not the anthropomorphism and cuteness of the animals, not the songs, not the long collaged sequences of colors and shapes, nor any of the attempts at authenticity and incursions of grim realism—nor did he remember any of these things from his several childhood viewings. Only one thing did he recall with clarity: a small, thin voice calling *Mother* in a silent world.

He retreated to the warm kitchen—now scented by cinnamon, onion, chilies and the deep musk of lamb—and hand-rolled a dozen chocolate truffles.

They called to him when the mom went missing. "It's happening," Alice called, "the awful, awful thing. If you want to see." He took his time transferring the quail-filled pouches to a cooling rack, then rained powdered sugar over them. He reached the living room as the shaggy, big-chested stag showed up to give Bambi the news that "your mother won't be with you anymore."

"How do kids survive this?" Alice cried. "It's worse than *The Yearling*."

A split second later, the film was a frenzy of kissing birds and snuggling skunks: Disney's version of mating season. Pete's

jaw went agape. "Mom's blown away," he said. "So now everyone fucks their brains out."

"Not exactly," Helen said.

"Pete's right," said Alice. "And see? Bambi mates for life
with the first girl he ever met. This is what American kids cut
their teeth on."

"No shit," Pete said. *No shit.* Back to the kitchen he went,
where he dunked a whole b'stilla in his mouth, inhaling powdered sugar and cinnamon, biting down through fragile, butter-
drenched pastry layers to the extremely hot morsel of stewed
quail. To staunch the burn, he scooped up a cool fingerful of
oily, garlicked eggplant, then went for another that was almost
to his mouth when Helen walked into the kitchen.

"Are you okay?"

"Mmmm."

"Helen," Alice yelled, "you're missing the forest fire."

"I'm dandy," said Pete. Was he blushing, or just blistered by
b'stilla? "By the time your movie's over, we'll be ready to eat."

They started with salads, beet and eggplant. The gals uttered
nothing but praise. Pete noted to up the horseradish in the beets,
temper the garlic in the eggplant. Next came the two-bite quail
packets. "It explodes in your mouth!" Alice exclaimed. "It's the
most amazing thing I've ever had. I want to go someplace dark
and quiet and *think* about what I've just eaten."

This might have been the best thing anybody had ever said
about his cooking. Pete dared not even peek in her direction.

"I can see why Jocelyn's so determined," Helen said.

He'd always found praise as jolting as derision, and more
difficult to answer. When the lamb was served, he cast about for
another subject before the compliments resumed. "So, Alice, tell
me about Mr. Nice Guy."

"You aren't really interested," she said. "You just want to
cast slurs."

"I'm completely riveted," he said. "If it weren't for living vicariously, I'd have no life at all. And for God's sake, Alice, I cast slurs on everybody. I'm an equal opportunity slur-caster. You can't take anything I say personally. You know it says far more about me than anybody else."

"Can you believe him?" Alice turned to Helen. "He thinks if he takes responsibility for it, he can say anything he wants."

"I can't?" said Pete.

"A little self-editing never hurt anybody," said Helen.

"Are you ever *not* a minister?" Pete scowled and fought off several more impulses to speak. "So come on, Alice," he said finally. "What's his name?"

"Dewey . . . see?"

"See what?" said Pete.

"You were already going to say something."

"I was not!"

"His name's Dewey," prompted Helen. "And—"

"So what was I going to say?" Pete demanded of Alice.

"Brother to Huey and Louie? Scooby-Dewey-Doo?"

"Exactly! So, he's nice, he's Dewey, he's fill-in-the-blank . . ."

"Very sweet and kind, and seriously good-looking. You asked, Pete. And he has one of the all-time great dogs."

"Then what are you doing here, with us, on a Friday night? Why aren't you playing hide the sausage with the boy and his dog?"

"I'll see him tomorrow." Alice helped herself to more lamb, being sure to snag a big fig. Pete noted that she, like Helen, was a good eater. He approved. "We're going on a hike."

A hike. Is that what men and women did nowadays? It never would've occurred to him. Sure, he hiked, but he had nothing better to do. Certainly, with a woman, there was something better to do.

"Is there anything else you want to know?"

"Yeah," he said. "What's the hitch?"

"Who said there's a hitch?"

"There's always a hitch," Pete said.

"True enough." Alice thought. "He's young. And reminds me of my kid brother—sort of inexperienced."

"You mean he's a virgin?" Pete could not contain the hugest grin.

"You're disgusting! I mean he hasn't done much. He isn't well read—except maybe in theology. He hasn't been out of the States, or even to West Hollywood. He's never seen a drag queen in person or taken a drug, and claims he's never gotten drunk. And frankly, Pete, I don't know if he's a virgin or not."

"Which was the answer to my next question," said Pete.

Helen and Alice, exchanging a look, tried not to smile.

"You could help Dewey expand," said Helen. "Get him out in the world."

"Me? I'm hanging on by my hangnails as it is."

"I'm rather fond of virgins myself," Pete felt compelled to assert.

"Yeah," said Alice, "but you're an old lech."

He flinched and promptly plummeted. What, exactly, did Alice know? Had Helen heard the statutory tale from Mom and passed it on? And did she really think he was old? He *was* old. *And* a lech. He must reek of it.

"Hey, it's a joke," said Alice. "Jesus, Pete, I didn't mean it."

"Yes you did." But he still needed the retraction.

The plum tart was runny and he'd forgotten to make the sorbet! But the chocolate truffles were as good as they could be given the supermarket bittersweet.

They did the dishes together, in short order. Helen drove him home and, before he fled the car, kissed his cheek. All of it proved too much for him. The neck bared by cooking. The praise and chitchat. In bed, his body hummed like an auxiliary generator and the kiss sat on his skin, unassimilable, like a pair of wax lips, all night long.

27

Dewey showed up at the Wren Street house early in the morning along with Merle and a knapsack packed for every eventuality: first-aid kit; water, PowerBars and two nylon ponchos. He'd assumed, correctly, that Alice wouldn't have much gear. She'd spent a restless night partly due to eating too much chocolate and partly to worrying that she no longer owned proper hiking shoes. She was still barefoot when Dewey knocked, and she needn't have worried about footwear because Dewey had already determined that her yard's dereliction was far more urgent than any scenic ramble. The roses, especially; they should be pruned and fed since deadwood and old leaves bred disease. Did she have gloves and clippers?

She took him to the shed where Uncle Walter kept his tools. Nails, screws and sprinkler couplings were sorted into rusty Yuban cans; a pegboard held trowels, shears and saws, all furred with rusty dirt. She opened drawers and found gloves, but the fingers were chewed into bits swirled with mouse droppings. Dewey stepped outside. "I don't like rodents," he said.

They drove to the nursery two doors up from the Fountain, which Alice almost pointed out—*Look, that's my other job!*— but in broad daylight the blond stucco and dark windows had the seedy, evil aspect of mirrored sunglasses. Luckily, Dewey was intent on aphid soap, fertilizer spikes, clippers and elbow-length gloves, and didn't notice the sign. The bill came to over ninety dollars—the gloves alone cost forty—but Dewey, without blinking, pulled out a credit card. Don't you *have* to sleep with a man who spends ninety bucks on your roses?

He was, as Alice might've guessed, methodical. At first she followed him, collecting clippings on a burlap tarp. "You want to go below the V, here," he said. "Find an outside bud, and cut on an angle."

He'd stripped down to a thin ribbed cotton tank that showed his muscled shoulders and arms to very good advantage. Perhaps this was her compensation; in exchange for Nick, she got youth, strength and smooth, clear skin. And trimmed rose-bushes. When she ran her fingers down Dewey's neck, he turned for a kiss and she closed her eyes. Does it really matter who touches you?

Dewey, intent on roses, refused to be distracted for long, so Alice threw a stick up and down the driveway for Merle. When the phone rang, she dashed into the house.

"I thought you were climbing every mountain," said Pete. "Fording every stream."

"Change of plan," Alice said. "Now we're pruning roses. Or he is. I'm just the fawning spectator."

"Well, I called to thank you for your hospitality last night. And to say I left my fine slicer there—a knife? Slightly serrated edge?"

"I saw it this morning," she said. "Do you need it right away?"

"No. Just don't use it to saw cardboard. Or prune roses."

"How about slitting my wrists?" Alice asked, and froze. She'd seen his wrists, even discussed them with Helen. And now this just popped out. She certainly didn't mean anything by it, or hoped she didn't.

But Pete was chuckling. "You're talking the *perfect* tool for the job."

When she finally got Dewey away from the roses, they kissed and rolled around on the living room couch, but when she tried to undress him, he pulled back. "I can't go too fast," he said. "I get so attached. And anyway, I'm starving."

Alice stumbled into the kitchen, so much unconsummated foreplay making her as wobbly and stupid as if she were drunk. She brought out diet Cokes and a plate of last night's leftovers—beet salad, eggplant salad and puff pastry purses filled with spicy quail. Dewey looked it over blankly, took a Coke. "Hey, let's go out for pizza."

Later, as he dropped her off back home, he promised to return tomorrow to finish the pruning and then take Alice to the movies.

"You could just spend the night," Alice said.

"It's Mother's Day, and I have to have breakfast with my family after church. Besides, I already have a bad case of blue balls."

She shut the door and veered through the house. Blue balls? Maybe they were an accepted feature of self-disciplined Christian romance. Still—could he have said anything less sexy?

She woke up the next day feeling fluish and hungover. Her back was killing her. She dragged herself to church and let Pete smirk at her throughout the service.

In her sermon, Helen talked about God, Jesus and the Buddha as mothers. According to Dame Julian of Norwich, she said, God is the bottom-wiper of humankind. For Alice, she added that the Acoma Indians called deer "Mother." "At all times," Helen concluded, "we should all use whatever means we can to regard and treat the world as if we were taking care of a baby."

Dewey was already barbering bushes when Alice arrived home. She changed clothes and gathered a big bouquet, explaining several times that she wanted to see Aunt Kate for Mother's Day. "We should go before the movie."

"Let me finish this hummingbird bush," he said. Or this cape honeysuckle.

"Don't cut back too far," she said. "It's supposed to be an

overgrown yard, not some topiary display." Already her home felt too exposed. "Maybe I'll go see Aunt Kate while you finish."

"But I want to come," he said. "Let me just—"

"Dewey, I want to go *now*. Or we won't make the movie."

"Okay." He started pulling off his gloves. "Why didn't you say so?"

"Who's this?" Aunt Kate said, giving Dewey a stern once-over.

"Nice to meet you, Miss Gordon," he said. "Alice has told me all about you."

"Did she tell you I'm crazy as a Betsey bug?"

"No ma'am."

"I did so," said Alice. "In the car, on the way over—remember?" This was cruel, but Alice couldn't help herself.

Dewey turned pink, and worked his brow. "But we didn't drive."

"Alice dear, you're confusing the boy." Aunt Kate scanned Dewey again. "You mustn't let my niece get the better of you. She's been nothing but mischief since the day she was born."

"Like someone else I know," Alice said. "In this very room."

"Don't be disrespectful, dear." She was still looking at Dewey. "Are you a dentist? You look like a dentist."

"My father's a dentist," he said.

"You do have perfect teeth." Aunt Kate finally turned to Alice. "You know, I already sent in one of your questionnaires, dear. I answered a query in the Society's newsletter and it was sent to me."

"I work for the man who ran that query!"

"Then you're lucky for such an opportunity." She peered back at Dewey. "I had no idea she was interested in William James, did you?"

"I told you why I took the job," Alice said, irritated. "And my boss would love to involve you."

"William worked with a medium for years," Aunt Kate

explained to Dewey. "Leonora Piper. They started visiting her when little Herman died of the whooping cough. First Alice, then William. They wanted to keep in touch with the boy. William found Leonora's work encouraging, if not completely convincing, and he soon became very active researching such phenomena. In fact, he was the first president of the American Society for Psychical Research."

"Dewey knows all that, Aunt Kate," Alice said helplessly.

Aunt Kate fluffed her hair. "William's interest in the spirit world did not help his reputation in scholarly circles. Spiritualism was deemed a fascination of the less-educated classes, and you couldn't dabble in it without raising doubts about your own intellectual integrity. Intellectual snobbery flourished then as now. Spiritualism, suffragism, homeopathy, birth control, free love, Fletcherizing—that endless chewing—were equally suspect. William, however, didn't care what people thought. He investigated fringe phenomena throughout his life, although in the end he said that he knew little more about ghosts than when he started."

"That's really sad," said Dewey.

Aunt Kate glared at him, then turned to her niece. "Would you help me, dear? I would like to change my blouse, but lately buttons are giving me trouble."

"I'll wait in the lobby," Dewey said, and fled.

Aunt Kate took a cornflower-blue silk blouse from the closet and handed it to Alice. "He's not very bright, is he?"

"He's young." Alice unbuttoned the blouse her aunt was wearing. "But sweet."

"I liked the last one, with the bushy hair."

Alice had to think. "Spiro? He was so messed up, though. And mean."

"But very sharp." She slid her arms into the sleeves.

"Spiro could dish it out, but he couldn't take it," said Alice.

"You'd want a man who can do both. This fellow might not be up to your speed, dear. And finding someone who is won't be easy."

"I'm not all that speedy, Aunt Kate. And Dewey might surprise us."

"I'm fond of surprises," she said, "but I've never counted on them."

Dewey was standing next to Dora by the front door. Walking up, Alice dug in her pocket for a quarter. "Here, Dora. I see you met Dewey."

Dora looked at the quarter. "I need this for the bus."

"I know you do," Alice said. "Come on, Dewey."

"Don't go!" Dora grabbed Dewey's wrist. "Push me to my room."

"The movie starts in half an hour," Alice said.

"No!" Dora wailed. "My room!"

"I'll be quick," Dewey said. "It's okay, Dora, I'll take you."

"You wait here," Dora instructed Alice.

She waited five minutes, then asked where Dora's room was, but it was empty. She found Dora and Dewey outside, in the courtyard. "Dewey," she said, "we're going to be late."

"I've got to go, Dora," he said.

"I need twenty-five cents for the bus," said Dora.

"I've given you three quarters," he said, "and now I've got to go."

Dora clutched his arm.

"Dora, let him go right now."

Alice's sternness surprised the old woman, who did as she was told. "Dewey," Alice said with equal sharpness, "come on, let's go."

With a look of shock, he also obeyed. "She's so starved for attention," he said. "I couldn't bear to hurt her feelings."

"She has no short-term memory, in case you didn't notice. You could go back right now and she wouldn't know who you are."

"Still," he said, "what's a few minutes of my time?"

They'd missed only the previews, Dewey's patience and goodwill not costing her a thing. All he'd done was treat a person tenderly, as if he were caring for a baby. He'd probably be an amazing father, but Alice hardly dared articulate the adjacent hope, even to herself. Dewey would marry a gentle and patient person, one who didn't snap at him. And Alice suspected she was not intrinsically good, but selfish, impatient, controlling.

28

The Gnostic scholar spoke to a mere dozen people in the Family Center that Wednesday night. Gnosticism was not a big draw and Alice could see why: it was so arcane. The material world, Gnostics argued, was an abortion resulting from wisdom's intercourse with a demiurge; and that demiurge was none other than the New Testament God, the very one who kept souls enslaved in bodies. As the talk grew more abstract, Alice stopped following; she was watching Jocelyn Nearing, and thinking about Dewey. Kissing Dewey.

Helen, depressed by the small turnout, asked her and Aunt Kate to stay for a cup of tea. Alice had no sooner agreed than Helen prevailed upon Jocelyn, Pete and his mother to join them as well. As they pulled chairs in front of the fireplace, Alice busied herself by setting out a plate of cookies and bringing everyone cups of herbal tea. Pete, in his own mode of social avoidance, stacked chairs in the closet.

By the time she sat down, the conversation was already involved and intense. Aunt Kate, enjoying herself, winked at her.

"I've been wondering, Helen," said Beth, "what your religion consists of, exactly."

"Mine?" Helen gave a short laugh. "Am I that hopelessly vague? I suppose, theologically, I'm in sync with William James. I believe we're part of a greater something—God, the interconnected web of existence, whatever you want to call it. Cultivating a relationship to this greater something constitutes my religion. I believe that this relationship with the other—God, if you will—is transformative, regenerative and essential for a life lived fully." Helen reached for a cookie. "That's the short version."

"But that sounds more psychological than religious," said Beth. "Like a religion bled of specifics."

"So be it," said Helen. "Especially since specifics cause all the trouble. It's insisting on this or that point of orthodoxy or doctrine that has led to wars, inquisitions, burnings at the stake."

"Still, Helen, you've said several times you're considered too religious by members of your congregation. Yet to me you sound downright irreligious, even antireligious."

Helen didn't answer right away—she was chewing—so Jocelyn jumped in. "Helen's *spiritual*," she said. "She's deeply spiritual, but she's not religious, and that's the difference!"

Beth blinked as if a bug had flown by.

Helen swallowed. "Forgive me, Beth, if I seem indifferent, because I'm not. Religion is a matter of life and death to me, I just try to wear it lightly. And Jocelyn, I actually am religious in that I believe the great religions are storehouses of wisdom and practical guidance. And the difference between me and most of my congregation *is* theological. They come to church not to worship God but to be better humans and effect social change—which they do by signing initiatives, or sending checks to Third World relief funds. They get energy through ferocious discussions and in consensus-building, even if the upshot of all the haggling is just new carpeting for the church office."

Helen sat back, as if finished, then leaned forward again. "And I respect their point of view, deeply. But relating to a power greater than yourself generates the energy required to create and to change—and otherwise you'll burn out. I know, I've seen it. But just mention *God* or *spirit* or *higher power* and my secular humanists will balk." She took another cookie and shrugged. "They're humanists. I'm a theist."

Beth smiled blandly. "The New Age church is simply beyond my ken."

"Morton isn't New Age, not at all!" Helen exclaimed. "Excuse me if I get defensive, but that's a sore point with me. Unitarians and Universalists are historically very much a part of America's mainstream Protestant tradition. Unitarianism in particular. We might be post-Christian, but that doesn't make us New Age."

"What's wrong with being New Age?" said Jocelyn.

Logs in the fire shifted. In the background, Pete folded creaky chairs.

29

Alice located the questionnaire in the big box she'd taken from Foster. He'd opened and skimmed each one, flagging anything that snagged his interest. Aunt Kate's answers, at first glance, weren't notable. She'd checked only two of sixty background items (Belief in God, Migraine Headaches), and her description of posthumous Jamesian contact began with a bland disclaimer.

> I have not, strictly speaking, had posthumous contact with William James. Since 1962, however, I have been writing a novel based on his marriage and family life, and have developed a technique of imagination that may interest you.
>
> After my retirement from teaching (June 1992), I found that if I sat still, my mind purged of every thought, I would find myself among the Jameses—William and Alice and their four children in the 1890s. I've smelled the roast on their table, fingered the lace on the mantel, heard William hold forth at the dinner table as Alice compulsively ate the food left on her children's plates. The children schemed and jockeyed for their father's attention, which shone like a blessing, but intermittently and briefly; he was a charming man, but spread too thin. I witnessed his abrupt plunges into fatigue and depression, and saw his secret cache of photographs (portraits of

young women who adored him) in Schlegel's big book on India. I hesitate to call these insights "visions." Rather, I believe the past exists at all times and can be visited through the cultivation of what Emanuel Swedenborg called "inner sight." I should add that William James was my maternal grandfather.

Oh, Swedenborg again. Four years ago, in her most demented, insomniac state, she'd gone on and on about this eighteenth-century Swedish scientist and mystic beloved by Henry James Sr., whose recovery from a two-year "vastation" was precipitated by reading Swedenborg's books.

After writing texts on virtually all the sciences, from mineralogy to physiology, Aunt Kate had explained, Swedenborg set out to locate the human soul. Once he determined that it couldn't be found in the body, he went inward, into his own vast, imaginative mind, and wrote books on what he found there. In the same terse prose style of his scientific tomes, he described heaven and hell with startling specificity—the clothes angels wore, their language and houses; then the dry deserts of hell cut through with streets of vice and excrement-filled brothels.

Swedenborg's inner sight, claimed Aunt Kate, was imagination on its clearest channel, unconscious facts so clearly received, so uncontaminated by emotional distortion, as to align with greater truths. At her maddest, Aunt Kate was convinced that she'd mastered this technique, but after a few months at the Beverly Manor, she seemed to lose interest. Alice was surprised, then, to find Swedenborg mentioned in the questionnaire and wondered if her aunt was as mad as ever, and the stable life at the Manor had merely enabled her to mask it.

She took Aunt Kate's questionnaire to Foster, who reread it at once. "Ah, Swedenborg," he said, glancing up. "Did you know he grew a whole new set of teeth in his eighties?"

"No," Alice snapped, then waited as Foster continued reading.

"If I'd read far enough to know she was his granddaughter," he finally said, "I would've called her on the spot. So when can I meet her? Would the two of you like to come along on my next trip to the medium? Helen said she wants to, and you could bring Dewey. Gustavo always outdoes himself with an audience."

Alice went back upstairs to her chilly office, gazed out at the rain and the mountains lost in the mist, then started another tedious "Gustavo" tape just as Merle bounded into the room, her master fast behind.

Alice, concentrating, waved, but Dewey came up and kissed her, then lifted off the headphones and pulled her into his arms. "I've been dying to see you all day." They kissed more, and he drew her to the floor. His hair was damp, his jacket shed raindrops as the dangling headphones leaked small voices from the other side.

Alice slung a leg over his thigh—off the cold floor—and Merle delivered a rubber pork chop to their faces. "Not now," Dewey said.

They kissed and, despite layers of Gore-Tex, polar fleece, T-shirts and jeans, pressed into each other. Alice found the top button of his khakis, but Dewey stopped her. She rolled away and stared up at the ceiling. "Dewey," she said. "We're only going to make each other sick again."

"I know, I know." He sat up.

She sat up as well, facing him. "Is there some reason you can't have sex?" She touched his knee. "Or don't you want to?"

"Oh, I want to." Dewey grabbed her hands. "But after my last two girlfriends dumped me, my therapist said I should take it real slow." He smoothed Alice's hair, which given the gel and spray she used couldn't have been pleasant; indeed, he gave it a sidelong look. "I just get so attached when I sleep with someone that she said I should get to know the next one first."

"The next one—that would be me, right? So what kind of time frame are we talking?"

"She said at least three months."

"Three months!" Alice burst out laughing and gave Dewey's knee a good-natured shake. "Now there's a rule that's made to be broken!"

His face darkened. "I'd be very disappointed if that happened."

Alice got to her feet. "And I'd be very disappointed if it didn't!"

"Are you joking?" Dewey clambered up beside her. "Sometimes I can't tell if you're joking or not."

"Three months! Dewey, think about it."

He hugged her, spoke into her hair. "I am thinking about it. Constantly. I just don't want to wreck things before they've even started. I want to do it right. I don't know about you, Alice, but I'm in this for the long haul."

She breathed against his clean neck and damp collar, registering her first deep twinge of affection for this man.

Alice herself always had opted for sex over the long haul— assuming sex obviated long hauls. *Something* clearly had obviated her long hauls, and maybe it was premature sex. God knows she'd slept around more or less indiscriminately, had had sexually transmitted diseases and could've been sued for criminal conversation on numerous occasions. Looking into Dewey's sweet, excellent face and clear gray eyes made her feel jaded, sex-hungry, a thief of affections and potential violator of honorable intentions.

Dewey's embrace loosened in stages. He smiled at her. "I have to go to class now." Those perfect teeth.

Gingerly, as if newly fragile, Alice sat back in her chair and pulled on the headphones, Merle curling up on her feet.

Jesús Cristo madre dios. Surely you scientists can detect some meaning in all of this wordage. Put it through your word processors; blend, grind, puree. Gustavo struggles in such miserable conditions, and nobody says one thank-you.

The rain fell steadily. Alice's back began to ache, the mid-to-lower part. She blamed dampness and rolling around on a hard cold floor. The pain latched onto her spine and stayed.

"William had a bad back," said Aunt Kate. At three in the afternoon, they were standing outside the Beverly Manor waiting for Foster, who was bringing Dewey and picking up Helen and taking them all to the medium.

"It always flared up during his most difficult periods, and whenever he faced a big decision. For two years after medical school, he was immobilized. Later, during the two years he equivocated about marriage, he had terrible back pain, and doubted his fitness to be anyone's husband. He didn't want to pass on the 'dorsal insanity.'"

Another fine legacy. "Sounds like a dolphin disease," said Alice.

"Insanity didn't imply mental illness back then as it does now. If you forgot to return library books, or you were chronically late, people said you were *morally* insane . . ." Aunt Kate raised an eyebrow. "Actually, marriage seemed to help William's back. Once he and Alice lived together, he thrived as never before—until he wanted to take another European jaunt. His back trouble was invariably convenient. But marriage, and no doubt sex, were boons to William's spine."

"How come you never married, Aunt Kate, if it's so healthy?"

"'Healthful, dear. And as you now know, the one man I'd have hasn't come up for grabs." Aunt Kate, with a sly half smile, gazed down the street.

"You're not still waiting for him?"

"I haven't given up."

"You've been waiting your entire life for him?"

"Not yet, dear."

"That's so heartbreaking."

Aunt Kate's gaze lit briefly on Alice. "Oh, there are far worse things."

Than waiting all your life for a man? "What, murder and mayhem?"

"How about living with someone nasty and boring? Or someone with terrible personal habits? Or living with anyone who makes constant demands?"

"You had Uncle Walter."

"Walter was easy. I never had to entertain his boss, or tend his ego, or have his suits pressed." She drew her walker in closer. "Walter was born good-natured; his illness, fearful as it was, didn't change that a whit. He was nothing but an asset. I did as I pleased—lived where I wanted, took my trips, had my friends, worked on my book. I saw Colin often enough."

"Excuse me?" said Alice. "You *saw* him?"

"Oh yes. He visits regularly. And we did quite a bit of traveling. We've been all over the world together. India, China, Europe, Brazil."

Alice knew of those trips: every summer, her own visits to Wren Street were timed so as to allow for them. "But you went with a group of teachers!"

"I did say that, didn't I?"

But . . . but . . . Alice's mind stuttered. "How many children did they have?"

"Five. So she wasn't about to relinquish him without a struggle—or without beggaring him. Not that she was a bad woman. She was an excellent mother. They worked it out." Aunt Kate smiled. "And we worked it out."

"They're both still alive?"

"Yes, dear, they live in Phoenix." She shrugged. "I've had the best of him, I'm sure. I never had to wash his dirty socks, as they say."

"But all the waiting and yearning . . . it sounds so bleak."

"My life has been anything but bleak," Aunt Kate said with a certain disdain. "I'm rather pleased with it, all told."

The day was clean, rinsed from the week's rains. The traffic sparkled; the mountains were sharp and clear. Telephone lines ran down the street like stitches. To think that a spinster's fate, complete with a schizophrenic brother and a mostly absent married lover, could please anyone at all!

30

Pete, taking a roundabout route home from the Bread Basket, trundled down Riverside to the stretch locally known as Motel Row, not that there were any motels. The name referred to the fact that people could park overnight in their restyled school bus or home-away-from-home step van or 1964 Alaska camper. Some cars camped there as well, with foil or newspapers taped up inside the windows for privacy. The police didn't bother anyone, provided the vehicles moved at least two blocks away every seventy-two hours; a challenge, unfortunately, for some of them. Today, Pete was particularly impressed by a weathered, cedar-shingled dome on a small Datsun truck: a small masterpiece of *Hobbit*-inspired, psychedelic carpentry.

He was taking this detour because Shirley hadn't come in to claim her food for a week, and it was no skin off Pete's nose to amble a long way home to check on her. Sure enough, he spotted the dark bronze Cadillac, identifiable by Styrofoam wig forms and wads of clothes crammed on the ledge behind the backseat. The front windows were down and Shirley sat sideways across the front seat reading a *Racing Times*.

"Hey there, sweetie head," Shirley said. "To what do I owe this honor?"

"Just passing by. Haven't seen you for a while."

"I'm livin' high on the food chain, lately. Had me some luck at the track. Till today, that is." She moved her long legs off the seat. "Hop in outta that sun. Want me to do you?"

"No thanks," Pete said.

"To you, baby doll, it's free, you know."

"That's okay," he said.

"I mean it. You my main food man. I'd love to toot yo' big ol' horn."

"I'm just glad to see you're still alive and kicking."

"Well, that's a standin' offer. Anytime you perambulating by, you give a tap on the window here." Shirley gave the windshield a fast tattoo with hot pink porcelain nails, then squinted at the nails themselves. "You got an extra ten?" she said. "I'm broke and sure could use a fill."

"I've got a five, is all."

"That's five more'n nothin'."

Pete dug in his pocket, presented a bill.

"I owe you," said Shirley, "and I don't ever forget."

"Come see us at the Basket," Pete said. "You got Mom worried." Relieved, he continued down Riverside, turning right on Fletcher, looping back toward Los Feliz, now passing the Baptist church whose marquee proclaimed *Faith Is Always Rewarded! If It's Not Rewarded, It's Not Faith!*

What did he have faith in—the pitch and slosh of events? The ascension of the soul? Or, for that matter, its descent? He tramped past the box store, the beauty supply, the laundromat. Cars whizzed by. Oncoming pedestrians gave him a wide berth. Walking in such public areas made him feel more acutely the lunatic at large.

"I'm tired of being the mental patient," he'd told Freeman at their last session. "I'm ready to give it up."

"Never!" the doctor cried, lifting his palms as if horrified. "You've spent so much time on the mental patient, put so much work into perfecting him! Don't you dare get rid of him. I want you to keep him in your repertoire and use him at will."

This gave Pete pause. Imagine being crazy at will—crazy like a hat, on and off.

"Of course," Freeman added, "the mental patient doesn't get very many dates."

Dates? Did he say *dates*? "Who said anything about dates?"

"Not you," said Freeman. "But it sure got your attention."

"I don't want to *date*," he muttered.

"Why not?"

Pete bent over his knees, then burst from the chair and did two fast laps from one side of the office to the other. Who would ever date him? Except maybe the fat bearded lady who shopped at the Mayfair. "Because I'm a fucking mental patient," he shouted.

"You're a quick study, Mr. Ross. See how useful mental illness can be? With this persona, you can conveniently avoid every risk in life."

Pete now labored along a short residential stretch of Rowena Avenue where older clapboard and modest mission-style homes had sacrificed front yards and any charm to a wider street. He came to the EZ Loan used-car lot, and the fire station, the cluster of antique stores and thrift shops. *Dating.*

Helen was dating. Alice was dating. Could Pete also be dating?

"Give it some thought," Freeman had said.

During one of his hospitalizations, the men gathered in the ward's common room and read personal ads to each other. They read the women seeking men and, ascertaining that none of them were being sought, checked out the competition. *Youthful professional SWM 62, seeks soul mate, 45 to 65, for traveling, dining and mature love . . . JDM internist, 43, culture hound and avid tennis player ISO svelte, athletic SBF, 18 to 25, for love and marriage.*

Pete, plowing homeward, devised his own ad: *Bus rider, 46, lives with mother, ISO brilliant, self-supporting female for dating. And transportation.*

Passing the chiropractor's office with its purple-and-chartreuse paint job, and the Au Revoir Nail Parlor and the Beverly Manor Rest Home, he was almost to the stoplight when he heard his name called.

Across the busy street, a green Camry had swung to the curb, and Helen's face appeared above the roof. A man sat at the wheel, an older guy, not the svelte, sober boyfriend. "Pete!" Helen called, waving. "Come here for a second!"

Cars flashed between them. Pete, powerless before such a summoning, waited for a clearing, then crossed.

A certain flurry and confusion followed. Momentarily he found himself within the car en route to visit a . . . *spiritualist?* Before they drove a hundred yards, back the way Pete had come, they'd turned into Beverly Manor, where Alice and her frail, dignified old aunt stood under the front awning. Pete was handed Foster's cell phone to call his mother, and stepping from the car, he came face-to-face with Alice.

"What are you doing here?" she said, less than kindly.

What *was* he doing there?

"I nabbed him right off the street!" Helen announced with pride.

Pete dialed the Bread Basket. "Where are we going again?" he asked, but Helen, settling Aunt Kate in the front seat, didn't hear. Then Mom was on the line. He explained as best he could but was greeted with a familiar, chilling silence. "I just wanted to clear it with you," he said, and almost added, *It's not a date.* If anything, it was like a surreal version of a grade school field trip.

"I don't appreciate being put on the spot like this," she said.

What spot? It was a courtesy, telling her where he would be. "I'll be back by five-thirty, or I'll call. There's soup in the fridge, and corn bread. But I should be back before dinner."

"I'm not happy about this, Pete."

Anger, like an enormous sleeping beast, stirred. Pete, this once, let it lie. "I'll see you tonight, Ma."

He was, after all, forty-six years old.

But displeasing Mom frightened him. She was the key to his future. She talked to Anne. She saw Garrett. She was smoothing the way for him, assuring them that the stay-away order could be rescinded without fear of further vandalism or child endangerment. Not for two years had he annoyed, harassed, distressed, molested or disturbed the peace of his victims—his family! He'd had no contact except through his attorney, although Anne had always talked to his mother. Who, in short, had promised to help him see his son again. "But first I have to see for myself that it's the right thing," she'd said. "I won't have my grandson subjected to any more violence."

Not that he'd touched the boy. Just roughed up the house. Sent a barbell through the computer screen. Who knew this translated as child endangerment, a felony. But Pete's record had been clean, so he pleaded guilty to the vandalism, made full restitution, took parenting and anger management classes and, as ordered by the courts, *stayed away*.

"For God's sake, Pete," Alice said, poking his shoulder. "Get in. Or move."

He realized he was blocking the door and climbed inside the car. Alice sat beside him, on the hump, and beside her, too far away, was Helen. Foster nosed the car down to the street.

Alice leaned into the front seat. "Foster, where's Dewey again?"

"A student fell off his bike and needed stitches." Foster looked left and turned right. "Dewey drove him to the emergency room. He said he'll call you later."

"Couldn't anyone else take the guy to the hospital?" she asked.

"You know Dewey," said Foster. "He's got that big heart."

Alice sat back.

Pete rolled down the window and stuck his face into the moving air.

"Shut up, Pete," Alice said.

"Me? What did I say?"

"Just keep it to yourself."

On the freeways to Torrance, Foster explained the protocol of séances. No talking to the medium or to each other. No exchanging looks and glances. Give no clues, no indication of the information's credibility or lack thereof.

At length they headed west into a subdivision built in the fifties for defense industry workers whose jobs had long since evaporated. The modest stucco ranch houses and the neighborhood in general had a bright, bald aspect—ocean light and very few trees. Foster pulled into the driveway of a small, paint-thirsty white house with scalloped yellow trim and a dry crabgrass lawn, its porch too small to accommodate their party of five. They stood blinking in the sun.

A heavy woman with short brown hair and a friendly face opened the door. "This is Patricia, everyone," said Foster. Patricia looked to be in her fifties. "Unfortunately, due to protocol, such is the extent of our introductions."

How do people live in this world? Pete, bringing up the rear, entered a living room all mauve and ice blue, colors found less frequently in nature than in this poly-velvet upholstery and sculpted nylon carpet. Vases of navy-blue silk azaleas, baby-blue roses and peach lilies sat on oak veneer surfaces with one profuse arrangement crowning a many-tiered electric organ. Breathing became more difficult. Too much furniture, not enough room and something—those bowls of flower petals?—perfumed the air like a spill of sweet, dime-store cologne and somehow made his spit taste soapy. Wouldn't a great American philosopher trying to contact the living be damn discouraged to discover himself in this home, where the only book in sight was an oversized Bible in a padded, lace-edged gingham cover?

Patricia led them to a small, snug room off the living room; in houses with matching floor plans, this would be the den, TV or gun room. A round oak table with heavy legs and six chairs sat centered under an elaborate chandelier-cum-ceiling-fan. Blue miniblinds. An altar of sorts had been set up on a sideboard: silk tulips and votive candles under a framed portrait of a blond Jesus in ivory robes—a Protestant Jesus, Pete deduced, as His hands spewed light, not blood.

Patricia stood behind her chair until everyone was seated—Pete finding himself between Alice and Helen—and said, "Help yourself to water." A Tupperware pitcher sat in the center of the table alongside two stacks of disposable plastic cups. "Are we ready?" She rapped the table twice. "Shall we pray?"

Heads bowed.

"May God bless and guide and protect this work," said Patricia.

Pete studied a band of trim below the table's lip, a repeating motif of oak leaves and acorns. Beside him, Alice was withdrawing. She had a way of leaving the room without moving an inch; he'd noticed this at that first dinner at Helen's, when he was so stupid, and again in church during parts of sermons, and also during the sad and sappy stretches of *Bambi* and *The Yearling*.

"May all we do flow from the goodness of God," Patricia sang out, "and celebrate His goodness. In the name of the Father and Jesus Christ, amen."

Someone should open a window or turn on the ceiling fan, Pete thought. The chemical perfume was giving him a headache. And sitting next to Alice was like being perched on the rim of a black hole. He yawned to bring more air into his lungs and his sweat turned cold. Elsewhere in the house a toilet flushed, a door closed.

"Well, well, well, Foster, *mi amigo.*" The man's voice was so loud and abrupt and authoritative that Pete swung around to locate its source. Patricia, her chin lifted, now bore the imperious—or myopic—gaze of a matron glowering through a lorgnette. "I see you have packed the gallery. And such illustrious guests. The whole fam-damn-ily. And associates."

Impressive, thought Pete, how she managed a full-toned male voice.

"Hello, Gustavo." Foster, taking notes on a legal pad, didn't even look up. "What do you mean by fam-damn-ily."

"You know who they are, Foster."

"I do," said Foster. "Do you?"

"Test after test. A man wearies of them, and yearns to be taken at his word. I know well enough who they are, but perhaps they'd like to know who I am. Gustavo Alphonso Octavio

Casimiro Echevarría, formerly of Mexico, *distrito federale*. At your service."

"Thank you, Gustavo," Foster said wearily. "But seeing that everybody has come to meet with Dr. James, would you mind getting him?"

"Why the hurry? The girl and her mother, and the reverend too, surely desire background information on their guide, who is, after all, the crucial link to the illustrious ancestor." The medium turned to Helen. "Am I correct, Reverend?"

"Excuse me, Gustavo," Foster said, writing anew. "Why do you call that woman 'Reverend'?"

The medium examined Helen with obvious distaste. "Am I mistaken? Is not La Grandota a *pastor protestante*? I can smell a cleric anywhere—and in such close quarters, whew! The stench of piety!"

Helen nudged Pete and whispered. "Me! Pious!"

"You are remarkable, Gustavo," Foster said. "Now please use your excellent abilities and help us to meet Dr. James."

"Flattery, flattery. I see through you, Foster, you selfish bore. But I am tired of butting the head. Let me see what I can do."

The medium's eyes rolled up in their sockets, her tongue lolling from her mouth. Pete had seen such tics on the cerebral palsy ward at Woodview, and among the truly brain-damaged. Then Gustavo-as-haughty-matron returned. "Dr. James is not available," he said. "But *un otro hombre* has come to see you."

"We prefer to speak with Dr. James," said Foster.

"How well do I know that? Dr. James, James, James. *Lo siento*, Foster, Dr. James isn't in the mood for family reunions. *Como se dice* . . . intimacy problems?"

There was a silence. Aunt Kate, forgetting or disregarding the rules, spoke to Foster as if to soothe him. "You know, William wouldn't show himself to his wife Alice, either. She went to many mediums after he died, and though he'd promised to contact her, she never got so much as a peep."

"And Madame"—the medium bowed toward her—"allow

me to tell you why. Dr. James is not good with the control. I am living proof of that—although, of course, I'm dead. The sad truth is that Grandpapa does not have a great gift. All mediums want his contact, but every attempt is pure struggle and blunder. I can't say which is worse, his muddy thinking or his inept transmission. Now this fellow today—he transmits loud and clear from deep within the dark valley. You will not miss your Dr. James today."

Patricia rose up from her chair and pushed herself against the table. The towers of plastic cups fell and rolled and dropped to the floor. Lips curling back from her teeth and gums, Patricia jutted her chest like a rooster about to crow. Alice grabbed Pete's arm as the medium's mouth opened in a rictus of pain. With eerie accuracy and perfect pitch, she began to sing in a famous voice.

Are you lonesome tonight? Do you miss me tonight?
Are you sorry we drifted apart?
Does your memory stray to a bright summer day
When I kissed you and called you sweetheart?

Patricia's lips quivered but did not appear to be forming words; the song came intact from her throat. Her eyes were hooded. Her head ticked off the beats between the verses, and again she pulled herself up, thrust out her chest.

Do the chairs in your parlor seem empty and bare?
Do you gaze at your doorstep and picture me there?
Is your heart filled with pain, shall I come back again
Tell me dear, are you lonesome tonight . . .

It was, Pete thought, a stirring performance.

31

Not until she and her aunt were off-loaded at the Beverly Manor did Alice realize that the afternoon's activity, which had taken not even four hours, was over. She'd assumed the visit to the medium would bleed into dinner, but Helen rushed off to a board meeting, Foster drove back to Claremont and Pete, who'd gotten out at the Beverly Manor, walked away. Even her great-aunt abjured any further socializing. "That was absolutely fascinating," she announced at the door to her room. "I adore your friend Foster. And now I'm completely bushed and am going straight down for a nap."

Alice walked home alone. She poked her head into the Fountain on the off chance that Rosalie was working late, but the new bartender was there—a pretty blond guy, just Monty's type—and she didn't stop.

At home, she read old magazines and tried not to worry about Dewey. She wasn't sure how much she loved or even liked him, but there was already a sharp need to see him as often as possible and talk to him every few hours, to make sure he was still interested and hadn't yet discovered any of the things that would neutralize or reverse his affection for her. She fell asleep on the couch, and his call at eight-thirty woke her up. "What's going on?" she asked, cranky from sleep. "Why did you blow me off?"

"What do you mean? I spent the whole day wishing I was with you guys." The student he took to the emergency room, he explained, was a Korean who barely spoke any English, who not only required twenty-odd stitches but also had scratched his eye, and needed to see two specialists, one in Whittier. Dewey had only now gotten home after hours spent in waiting rooms with someone he couldn't even talk to. "Are you coming in tomorrow?" he said. "Will I see you? Don't be mad at me."

Safe, Alice thought. *I'm safe.*

She woke again, hours later, in her bed, filled with a dry dread.

The medium, at this remove, frightened her. Such spastic and grotesque contortions. The performance seemed almost hostile, as if Patricia lured people into her airless private parlor to make hideous faces at them.

I should quit my job, Alice thought. *Too creepy.*

But something else nagged, a more specific, acute point of discomfort. Something Gustavo said. *The girl and her mother . . .*

Finally, somebody had said it out loud.

Alice never felt part of the Lime Cove family, the rowdy, demanding boys, the overwhelmed mother and chronically disappointed father. She imagined Aunt Kate, accidentally pregnant late in life—by a married man who, with five children, wouldn't want another. And who couldn't marry her anyway.

Meanwhile, there was Aunt Kate's niece Mary, with a husband, a big farmhouse, two boys and the yen for a girl. The accidental baby could go to Lime Cove, where there was plenty of room and no resident schizophrenic. The adoption would've been as easy as a title transfer. The family lawyer. A few signatures, a few filings, a small fee. And a caveat: Alice would become the visiting grandniece, who—another caveat—must never be told.

Yet she'd known, on some level, all along.

Alice kicked at her covers. No wonder she'd stalled out. She glared at the dim shapes of furniture in the dark room. No wonder she didn't know who she was or what she should do. At the core of her identity curled a big long lie.

The deer made perfect sense, now: she had clambered up from the unconscious, a coded message. Listen. Pay attention. The Acoma people called deer "Mother"—how much more research did Alice need to do?

Kate would've been forty-four the year Alice was born. Mid-career. Set in her ways. Surely her employer never would have countenanced an unmarried mother on the staff. And Colin Crowley must have told her to give the baby up for adoption. Such a Catholic—five kids!—would never condone an abortion, assuming he even knew about the pregnancy.

No wonder Alice had a thing for married men. As the hart yearns for the water brooks, she'd been yearning for the father she never knew.

In the morning, however, she was no longer so sure. When Dewey phoned, she told him, "Sometimes I wonder if Aunt Kate isn't my real mother."

"Really?" he said. "Why don't you ask her?"

"After that little performance"—Foster tossed a file on his desk—"I've decided to give Patricia a little rest." Alice had stopped by his office before going upstairs. He picked a letter. "I want to try this medium in San Francisco, an automatic writer. And I want to talk to Aunt Kate. She's a treasure trove."

"She'd love that." Alice took three new tapes and went to her office. A pink basket of freesia sat on her desk. Leashed to the basket by ribbon was a plush toy dog, gray with a white chest, a pink tongue.

Alice had never had a boyfriend who gave her flowers or stuffed animals. Or much of anything, for that matter. Kurt gave her the egg that turned into Ana the iguana. The Riverine Ecology guy gave her a pair of rubber boots and a secondhand microscope he'd appropriated from a forgotten storage room. Spiro was too broke and too self-obsessed to give anybody anything. The art teacher gave her some sketches he didn't want, and for good reason. But Nick, he never showed up empty-handed. Always a bottle of premium bourbon. And last December he'd given her a Christmas tree, a six-foot freebie, compliments of his lumberyard, that he'd passed on to her. It wasn't tall enough, he said, for his home's high ceilings, though how could he not have noticed Wren Street's fourteen-footers?

Alice squeezed the little dog, inhaling the crisp green scent of freesia.

32

T hings were happening too quickly. If Pete thought about his life, he was overwhelmed in an instant, so he kept to his routines; walks, gym, Bread Basket, cooking for the girls. And he blamed Freeman, the bully. Every session lately had been a doozy.

"It would seem you have a decision to make," the doctor said after hearing about the trip to the medium and Beth's attendant dismay.

"Duh," said Pete. "To cook or not to cook."

Freeman ignored the adolescent sneer. "That's secondary. You need to decide if you want to strike out on your own just when you're starting over again in a tough profession where you already consider yourself a failure."

"Oh, that."

"*Or* if you want to be one of those fifty-year-old men living with their mothers. You know, the ones bringing the car around, waiting at the pharmacy, eating the early-bird special at the House of Pies . . ."

Pete's heels hit the carpet. "Who told me to move in with Mom? Who set *that* up?"

"First of all, I never told you to do anything. I supported your decision. And secondly, unless I'm mistaken, it has worked out very well."

Pete gaped. "You *want* me to be the middle-aged mama's boy?"

"I'm saying that another decision may be in order."

"But you endorse choice B. And isn't that what I'm already doing?"

"My opinion, even if I had one, doesn't figure into this."

Pete, twisting sideways in his chair, hated the man.

"I can't tell you what to do," Freeman said quietly. "If I'm wrong, you'll blame me; if I'm right, you won't take the credit for making your own good decision. You've got to decide this one on your own, I'm afraid."

Pete spotted them in the Mayfair now: the pudgy, mild-mannered men in cardigans softly dickering with their mothers over the price of grapefruit juice, or scanning shelves of bran cereals as Mom shuffled the coupons.

The Reverend Dr. Helen Harland would never want a mama's boy. She required, indeed deserved, a fully functioning, well-salaried, professionally prominent adult male. Therefore, last Sunday, he'd told Jocelyn yes. No more pussyfooting around. Yes, he'd design the menu and hire a sous-chef, a pastry chef and line cooks, dishwashers too, and set up accounts with purveyors. Yes, he'd be the executive chef, run the back of the house, take the full damn salary and the partnership clause as well.

She'd agreed to Cal-Med chow, a North African/Middle Eastern slant. She'd signed the lease. She had a designer. And Pete.

She'd asked: did he need to go anywhere—Morocco, Lebanon, Sicily? She'd gladly send him. Pete in Africa? Maybe next year. If all went according to plan—which, of course, it never would—the restaurant would open in September. Realistically, it would open in November at the earliest, more likely January.

At any rate, he had lemons curing in salt on top of the refrigerator at home. He was aging butter—*smen*—under the sink. He'd turned the small apartment kitchen into a spice lab. He dried garlic in the oven, thumbed seeds from pounds of mild New Mexico chilies, concocted various dry-spice mixes, took three different tabils—coriander, garlic, caraway and ground

chili—through daily adjustments. Four blends of harissa, ranging from mild to incendiary, melded in the fridge. He put the coffee grinder through its paces, and despite multiple scrubbings, as
she drank her morning coffee, his mother's expression grew
quizzical. "Is that cumin?" Or fennel. Or cayenne.

Pete sat on his meditation cushion, but it was hard to attend
to the breath when ideas flew in at an alarming rate. If you
filmed his stream of thought, there would be a torrent of game
birds amid slick noodles, a dust of spices, a vortex of sauce and
chopped vegetables, lengths of lemongrass soaring like javelins.

He arrived at Wren Street bearing various potions and assorted
groceries for what was now the usual Friday night event.
Tonight the hostess's über-nice new boyfriend was scheduled to
appear. Pete, setting up in the kitchen, asked, "When's Doo-doo
due?"

"He's not coming, Pee-pee."

"Ah." Pete was not-so-secretly glad. He liked their triangu-
lar cabal and saw no need to enlarge it.

"He has a hundred papers to grade," she explained, as if
anybody gave a damn. "And he doesn't like spicy food. Says it's
wasted on him."

"Oh brother," said Pete.

"More for us," said Helen. "C'mon, Alice, let's set the
table."

Pete kneaded the dough for flat bread, bearded and
scrubbed mussels, pan-fried Spanish chorizo with minced shallots and kept an ear cocked toward the dining room door, eaves-
dropping without shame, marveling as ever at the explicitness of
women's conversation. Alice and Dewey were still not having
sex, he learned. She was peeved at him for this and related
infractions: they went hiking in the desert, and he'd given their
only water bottle to a hot fat woman when Alice herself was
thirsty. "And then, last night, we were kissing," she said, "and it
was getting pretty intense—I need another spoon . . . thanks. I

got up to go to the bathroom. I was gone less than a minute, didn't even look in the mirror—a fork over here . . . and when I came back he had the TV on."

"Oh dear," Helen said.

"He said he just wanted to see which *Rockford* was on. He had no idea why I was so upset."

"He does seem young sometimes, even for his age."

Silver was set down with soft chimes. Pete's mouth fell open of its own accord. "He's a fag!" he yelled.

Silence stretched between the rooms, then Alice said with perfect lightness, "Ah, another party heard from."

33

In late May, Dewey came with her to church. Alice had to drive to Claremont to get him because he'd lent his van to a friend whose car was in the shop, and they slipped into the sanctuary just as the organist was launching into the prelude. She hadn't intended to sit anywhere near Pete, but the most obvious places were, not surprisingly, right there. "You're late," he said as she slid in beside him. He looked Dewey up and down. "Trouble getting out of bed?"

"Shhh, for God's sake, Pete."

Dewey took in the congregation and architecture with an alert interest. He squeezed Alice's hand, nervously rubbing her knuckles with his thumb. Once the service began, he paid complete, polite attention—even when a man wearing a beret and pretending to be a beatnik snapped his fingers and announced the annual Morton Coffeehouse party: "Callin' all groovin' hepcats to make this scene / a night of cool poetry and steamin' hot caffeine . . ." At least Pete had the good sense to kick the underside of the pew and hiss like a malfunctioning pressure cooker.

Alice studied the printed order of service. Helen's sermon was "Prophecy, Dreams and Visions: How Spirit Speaks." The first reading was from the Book of Joel:

> And it shall come to pass afterward, that I will pour out
> my spirit upon all flesh; and your sons and your daugh-
> ters shall prophesy, your old men shall dream dreams,
> your young men shall see visions . . .

They stood for the hymn. Alice found herself flanked by good singers—Pete, as ever, and Dewey, who had a strong, clear alto, though some of the words he sang were not in the hymnal. "The Presbyterian version," he whispered.

The second reading was from the great-great-grandpa.

The further limits of our beings plunge, it seems to me, into an altogether other dimension of existence from the sensible and merely understandable world. Name it the mystical region, or the supernatural region, whichever you choose . . . When we commune with [this other dimension], work is actually done upon our finite personality, for we are turned into new [people] and consequences in the way of conduct follow in the natural world . . .

"And so ends our second reading." Helen then called the ushers forward for the offertory.

"Pete," Alice whispered. "You've got to settle down." She patted his knee, and he seized up as if frozen. "Are you all right?"

"Tomorrow," Helen said, "is the fiftieth day after the spring solstice, and the ancient holiday of Pentecost. Pentecost began as a celebration of the year's first barley harvest—farmers took barley cakes to the temple to celebrate another turn of the natural cycles." She held up a disk the color of Rice Krispies. "I couldn't find barley cakes, but I did find a rice cake, which I place here, on the altar, to remind us that our spiritual lives are rooted in the natural world."

Dewey sat rapt, receptive and trusting. Alice could barely believe she was in a church holding hands with a would-be minister. And she took a certain pleasure in imagining how normal the two of them appeared: she in her black rayon slip dress and

Aunt Kate's red cashmere cardigan, Dewey in his khakis and rumpled white oxford cloth shirt.

"Spirit can be described as a kind of informed energy," Helen was saying.

> . . . energy with the quality of mind. Spirit can be sourced at the further limits of our beings, summoned through the junctures where we connect to the web of existence of which we are all a part. Prophecy, visions and dreams are all ways that we access the spirit's wisdom.

Dewey squeezed her hand. *Could this be,* Alice wondered, *what ordinary couples felt like?* That they were doing nothing wrong—mating, with no adultery, no wanton unsafe sex, just exemplary time-honored courtship? *They went to church together. They went on walks. They got to know each other.* Was it possible that she, too, could be an ordinary, marriageable female making her opening bid in the perpetuation of the species? She had yet to meet his family, of course; that, she imagined, came after sex.

And there was the demiurge to her right, twitching, muttering in her ear. "Hung out the bloody sheet yet?"

And several rows up sat Nick's wife.

Meanwhile, Helen was swerving from idea to anecdote.

> Late in his life, my grandfather spent all day reading in the sun. I'd try to get him to talk about his past. "All that's a dream," he said. "Please," I'd say. "Tell me about meeting Grandma." "All that's a dream," he repeated, and this time I heard not dismissal, but a profound, spiritual statement. A dream, after all, is an invisible form of knowledge, known from within.
>
> Sitting in the sun, my grandfather was dreaming his life, inhabiting his own invisible knowledge and truth. As earthly reality loosened its hold on him, the greater,

*invisible reality of the spirit was more and more his
home . . .*

After the service, Alice and Dewey shook Helen's hand and
milled around the pergola under hanks of purple wisteria that
looked like outsized bunches of pale, papery grapes. The day
was unexpectedly warm. Pulling off her sweater, Alice felt someone assist her.

"Wasn't that sermon astonishing?" Jocelyn handed Alice's
sweater to her. "I've never heard anything like it."

"Thanks," she whispered.

"You look so pretty today, Alice. And you must be Dewey,
right?" Jocelyn held out her hand. "I'm Jocelyn. So good to meet
you."

Dewey's mouth was an oval O as they shook, and his
cheeks grew pink in blotches. "I just saw you in *The Tea Master*," he blurted.

"And . . . ?" Jocelyn tilted her head, eyebrows raised.

Dewey cleared his throat. "*You* were wonderful."

"Thanks, Dewey. I guess that's a compliment," she said.
"Now, may I ask you a favor? I'd like to talk to Alice for a
minute. Alone, if you don't mind. If you get us some herb tea,
we'll be done by the time you come back."

He set off without asking what Alice wanted, which was
neither tea nor to be left alone with Jocelyn Nearing.

This is it, she thought, *the great unmasking. The dreaded
I-Know-Who-You-Are speech. The I-Thought-We-Were-Friends
speech.*

"Over there?" Jocelyn pointed to a bench in the church
gardens.

Alice followed her into the warm, damp shade of a tall box-
wood, the perfect spot for a garroting. The two women sat facing the sanctuary, where Helen was still greeting congregants in
the narthex.

"I could think about that sermon for the rest of my life,"
said Jocelyn.

Alice didn't remember the sermon. The pergola itself now seemed a good, distant world, the setting for a warmhearted comedy in which kids tugged at their moms and old ladies clutched their mohair jackets in the sudden moist springtime. Pete stood in the line for coffee, bouncing and scowling, and a few places behind him, Dewey—the friendly, the patient, the good—stooped to listen to a small elderly man. After confronting Alice, would Jocelyn regale the entire congregation? *This phony's been fucking my husband for a year. Dear God . . .* Alice muttered inwardly. *If I live through this, I'll never so much* speak *to another married man.* Her teeth were actually chattering.

Jocelyn nudged Alice. "He's adorable."

"Dewey?" Her voice was trembling.

"Have you been together long?"

"A few months." Probably closer to one.

"God, to be so young and beautiful again." Jocelyn's sigh ended with a throaty laugh. "You are one lucky woman. Now, Alice . . ." She suddenly was matter-of-fact. "Your job with the ghosts is part-time, right?"

"I, uh, make my own hours."

"I don't know if you'd be interested, but my personal assistant left a few months ago and now that I'm starting this restaurant, I could use some help. Helen said you might be available."

Insects buzzed in the bushes in a low electrical hum. A fishy fertilizer smell rose from the flower bed. Alice said, "You want me to work for you?"

"Yeah—make phone calls, answer e-mail, run errands." She smiled, with the crinkle in her lip familiar to anyone who'd ever seen a Jocelyn Nearing movie. "It sounds boring, but I think we'd have fun."

"That's so nice of you," Alice said. "Thanks . . ." She was stumped. "But I don't need more work."

"I'm sure I'd pay more than you're making right now."

The warm air and juicy grass and tender flowers simmered in the sun.

"Think about it." She leaned against Alice. "You look lovely today—and I can see why. Speaking of dreams . . ." A nod to the coffee line. Then Jocelyn turned, gave her a once-over. "You've got a good little figure, Alice. You should wear dresses more often. Women go under the knife for breasts like yours."

As her terror seeped into relief, Alice began behaving as she always did around Jocelyn, almost exactly as Pete behaved. She picked at her dress, her feet kicked at the ground, a tic started her jaw jumping.

"Here." Jocelyn handed her a card, oblivious to the fact that Alice already knew the engraved phone number by heart. "It's so rare to find anybody I'd like to work with. I know we'd have a good time—really. You could start whenever you want, but the sooner the better. This afternoon, in fact." Another cozy lean. "Oh—will you look at that." Dewey, carefully holding three cardboard cups, was coming toward them. "He's just delicious."

Then you can have him, Alice thought. *Take him. He's all yours. It's the least I can do.*

Alice did not relay Jocelyn's admiration to Dewey, who was, to her mind, sufficiently starstruck.

"I can't believe you know Jocelyn Nearing," he said as Alice drove the few blocks to Wren Street. "Why didn't you tell me? She's one of the most beautiful women in America. And when you meet her, she's so friendly. Just a regular person. How long have you known her? And if she really offered you a job, you've got to take it."

"I already have a job," Alice said.

"Foster would understand."

"Foster's not the issue." She pulled into the Wren Street driveway. "Subject closed."

"It's just so amazing that you know Jocelyn Nearing," he said.

"Okay, bub." Alice opened her door into the overgrown pomegranate hedge with its slim new leaves. "You have to understand. This is Hollywood. We see Brad Pitt at the stoplight and Rickie Lee Jones at the diner and Nicolas Cage everywhere"—though truthfully, she hadn't seen Cage once since he'd won his Oscar. "Seeing a movie star is no big deal, Dewey. It's not like seeing God."

"I know, I know. But it's so exciting."

How had she ended up with such a child? Yet Jocelyn called him adorable. A dream. Delicious. But maybe that was all talk. Beautiful women were often generous that way. Jocelyn had also said Alice was lovely, after all, and complimented her weird breasts. Alice had no illusions about her personal appearance. "Well, one thing's for sure," Nick once said, "I wouldn't be marrying you for your looks." At the time she knew what he meant—that he'd already married someone for her looks, and it hadn't panned out—but afterward, when Alice didn't hear from him for weeks, crueler interpretations of the remark came to mind.

They took tumblers of iced sun tea to the backyard. "My next project," Dewey announced. The day's surprising warmth had soaked into the foliage, and you could almost hear the seethe of photosynthesis. All winter, Alice had felt guilty about the rotted limbs on the magnolia and avocado trees, the diseased eugenia hedge, the stack of old firewood turning into compost. But the honeysuckle and rambling Cecil Bruner roses—the Cecils, Uncle Walter used to call them—had gone untrimmed so long that new growth overran and obscured the neglect and formed a kind of private bower. They sat at the rusty white wrought-iron table on flagstone blanketed with blackening leaves.

Dewey drank his tea in several long drafts. "I'll borrow a chain saw next time I come out and get rid of some of those limbs. But you really should get a gardener to take care of this lawn. Just make sure he has a powerful mower." He stood up and walked deep into the yard. "It's so old-fashioned and secret back here." He looked back at her. "Do you have a blanket? Let's get some sun."

Alice brought out a blue candlewick bedspread and more tea. Dewey stripped off his shirt and T-shirt. "It's like a little private park back here," he said. "You should get a birdbath, some stone benches . . ."

They stretched out side by side, propped up on their elbows. Dewey's chest was broad, pale, with a cool tone to the flesh. With all his hiking and biking and basketball he had what some women—women like Jocelyn Nearing, Alice thought—wanted in a male pinup: abs, traps, biceps, washboard stomach, whatever. She herself had never been much interested in male musculature.

Dewey began kissing her with an ardor that was new. When he pushed her dress up past her hips and slid a hand inside her panties, she thought there must be some mistake. "Dewey!" she said, not wanting him to do anything he'd regret. He hummed something and proceeded to tug off those panties and her tights and managed, with surprising swiftness, to shed his own khakis and boxers. As if from some distance—the next yard over, say—Alice understood they were going to have sex. Now that the moment was here, she was vaguely disappointed. *That didn't take long.* She calculated from their first kiss: less than a month? Was that possible? What happened to the three-month plan? Yet she'd been pestering for this; she could hardly object now.

Naked, Dewey was all shapely muscle and pale, smooth skin—another truly beautiful animal, she thought, a gawky stallion. Nick, on the other hand, was a different order of mammal, a mean little fucker. And Alice was too: a female wolverine.

Dewey made love energetically and directly. Whatever sexual awkwardness he'd previously exhibited was now eclipsed by pure, focused drive. On and on, well into the sex act, he had a pure, uncontaminated aspect; he made her think of clean laundry, bottled water, baby powder. *This,* she thought, *must be Christian sex.* Uncomplicated, procreative, missionary-approved, no-edge sex. Healthy—or, rather, healthful—marital-style sex. Nothing like the fraught dark pastime she engaged in with Nick. Dewey sweated and still smelled sweet, like soap and freshly bruised grass, as if he'd never ingested an impure thing. He labored away, happy and vigorous—and why not? He was doing what he was designed for: a top-notch specimen *should* propagate. But his abrupt change of heart had caught her off guard—weren't they discussing *landscaping?*—and Alice had trouble concentrating. Sheer sexual proficiency had never held her interest. Also, how did he know if she was on the pill? How did he know she wasn't a venereal swamp? That's a talk they'd never had. Over his left shoulder, she noted paint curling off the garage clapboard, and then, as he shifted position, she saw that the Cecils had so weighted the gutter along the sleeping-porch roof that it had detached from the eaves.

Dewey's movements increased in speed and urgency as she, in a goodwill effort to participate, shut her eyes and held her breath. As Dewey gasped and spasmed, images passed through her mind: freshly laundered tea towels and the white curve of ultraclean fingernails.

"You're so beautiful," he panted into her neck, once he could speak. "You're every bit as beautiful as Jocelyn Nearing."

That night, after she'd driven him back to Claremont, Alice went to bed and had no sooner fallen asleep than there was a knock on her front door. She scrambled out of bed and ran to answer it. "Hello?" she called. "Hello?" No reply. Then knocking began on her back door. She ran down the hall through the kitchen and drew aside the porch door's little curtain, but nobody was there and the knocking recommenced out front. "Not funny," she yelled, running back to throw open the front door. Nobody was there, either, but a movement out in the street caught her eye.

Wren Street was filled with deer. Dozens of them, hundreds, does and bucks, fawns and yearlings. A river of jostling, trotting deer, with occasional antlers like small, bare trees carried upright in the current.

34

At Wednesday night's service, Helen Harland felt optimistic. She'd had compliments from even her staunchest adversaries for her prophecy and dreams sermon—which, ironically, resembled those she'd initially preached at Morton. Perhaps, by aping Link's style for the last year, she'd weaned them to her own. But her deepest calling, she'd always felt, was to serve as spiritual adviser, and six months ago, she'd despaired of ever being sought after in that capacity. Now she counseled Alice and Jocelyn, and advised Pete on meditation. Seeing the three of them thrive helped divert her from reading too much into every move the church board or committees made. After praying for months for a little detachment, here was the first flush of relief.

And now this: seventy-two people had shown up to hear Foster Allbright, Ph.D., speak on "Survival: A Psychical Researcher's Report on Life After Death." Despite their insistently rational, atheistic stances, a majority of Morton's older members appeared quite interested in the afterlife after all.

"Our beliefs about life after death," Foster began reading from his notes, "stem from one of two points of view: the materialistic on the one hand and the interactionist on the other. Materialists believe the mind is located in the brain, whereas interactionists believe mind exists independently of the brain, and that the brain is essentially a transmitter." He looked up with a small expectant smile, as if to make sure everyone was following his train of thought.

"For the materialist," he continued, "the death of the brain means the death of the self. For the interactionist, the death of the brain means the cessation of transmission. A conscious self still exists and functions. Interactionists therefore allow for life after death, and see evidence for this in out-of-body experiences, near-death experiences, communications from the dead and documented cases of reincarnation."

Foster's shy, mild manner and open-minded skepticism engaged the audience. He gave such entertaining examples of various phenomena—several involving Gustavo, the self-obsessed control whom Helen had heard in person—that even doubters were charmed.

The discussion period was a classic Unitarian Universalist free-for-all. Several older men insisted that there were always rational explanations. "Neurology and brain research have proved that the mind really is inextricably located in the brain," said Nils Ecklund. "Scientists probe the brain and literally touch memories, thoughts and words. The brain forms experience and thought into matter. Thus, the individual self actually *is* matter."

"Why can't the self be like light," Jocelyn Nearing said, "which behaves both like matter and like energy?"

Foster asked if anyone had ever seen a ghost or an apparition, or felt they'd had some contact with the dead. Five or six hands, all somewhat tentative, lifted in response. Aunt Kate spoke up. "I woke up and saw my own father looking quite fit and strong at the foot of my bed. I took note of the time—it was just after two—which turned out to be shortly after his death four hundred miles away. I was flying up to see him the next morning, but he couldn't hold out and instead came to say good-bye to me."

"I don't know if this counts," said Jocelyn, "but I had a friend die suddenly from AIDS, and for three weeks afterwards I dreamt about him all the time. It was as if he felt he'd been rude to die so abruptly and wanted to ease our pain. Finally, in a dream, I said, 'Sam, you don't have to keep coming back like this. Really, it's getting kind of creepy.' And that was the last I saw of him."

Seventy-seven-year-old Della Houseman said, "I died on the operating table and saw a wide grassy field, and across the field, strung out in a row, came my mother and her sisters. But then I had to come back."

Eighty-four-year-old Cassius Tyler said, "I died on the operating table too, and it was like nothing. You know what nothing's like? Well, that's what death was like."

A younger man—in his sixties—spoke with disdain. "These are all prime examples of wishful thinking. It's proven that shock and stress produce chemicals which delude us, protect us from pain."

The discussion period went on for forty-five minutes. Helen put an end to it by inviting people to stay for hot drinks and cookies.

"That was so much fun!" Jocelyn said afterward. "People get so riled up!" She grasped Helen's hand. "And you stay so calm and amused, and make it all seem safe and okay. How do you do that?"

Friday afternoon, Helen agreed to close up for Pete so he could get a head start on dinner. She finished her own paperwork, bolted the front door and printed out the day's journal. Leaving, she dropped it off at Beth's office. "Here," she said. "I'm on my way."

Beth stood at her file cabinet. "Oh, Helen?" she said. Her white blouse was buttoned up. A gold cross swung on a gold chain. Her navy-blue gabardine skirt was calf length, her opaque hose and sensible shoes both the color of Ace bandages. "Do you have a moment?"

Helen stepped further into the small, tidy office, presided over by a carved wooden crucifix. A white-noise machine emitted the sound of waves crashing on a beach.

"So Pete's cooking another dinner tonight." Beth moved behind her desk. "And they're going well, these meals?"

"Oh yes," said Helen. "They're the highlight of my week."

"And his too, I'm sure." She smiled down at her desktop. "Pete's quite attached to you, you know."

"And likewise. I consider him one of my closest friends."

Beth's smile faded. "I'm not sure 'friend' is the term Pete would prefer."

Helen waited out a pulse of guilt. "I've done nothing to encourage him, Beth. Not in that regard. He knows I'm with Lewis."

"I'm sure you've been perfectly appropriate," said Beth. "Still, Pete is especially susceptible to kindness and generosity."

And who isn't?

The wave machine surged and ebbed like a great breath.

"He has you on a pedestal," said Beth. "He adores you."

"You and I both know that such things happen with ministers. Unfortunately. But I truly care for Pete, and I'm a reliable friend. I might have to disappoint him a little bit, but I'm not going to abandon him."

"There may be more at stake than you realize," said Beth. "It's obvious to me that he's pursuing this restaurant project to impress you."

"Really, Beth? Don't you think he just wants to cook—and finally is ready to go back to it?"

Beth leaned forward, fingers on her desktop. "I think he's far from ready to function at such a demanding level. And may never be again."

"Huh. He seems so much clearer and stronger every time I see him."

"Yes, his work here at the Bread Basket has been very cura-tive. It's accomplished what no amount of hospitalization and psychiatry and medication ever has. It's gotten Pete out of him-self and thinking about others." She straightened her desk pad. "He's had a concrete, positive impact on hundreds of people here, and that's given him a self-esteem you can't get anywhere else. Feeding the rich, for example, will not provide that."

The crucifix on the wall was carved with deep angular cuts that accentuated anguish and pain—a Quebecois piece. Helen coveted it. "You're right, Beth," she said. "But Pete was born to cook. He's an artist—and unfortunately, most artists are supported by the rich."

"You're assuming Pete is motivated by his talent. I see him trying to impress the woman he adores."

Helen sat perfectly still. Weren't all motives mixed and suspect? Hadn't she herself been driven to the ministry less by the desire to serve others than by the need to be seen as a spiritual authority—or, for that matter, to be seen as a viable grown-up, period? Whoever got involved with anything, or anybody, for all the right reasons? "But if this new job works out for Pete and I don't," she said, "he'll still be in the right place."

"I couldn't disagree more. Pete is driven by his emotions, and he always crashes. High-pressure restaurant work will destroy him."

The rush of waves again filled the room. Helen dutifully felt a plunging guilt and shame. "What do you want me to do?" she asked.

"Remind Pete where he stands with you—gently, of course, but I don't have to say that."

"I do that on a regular basis," Helen said. "Whenever I sense a . . ." She gestured helplessly. "A flaring of ardor. And I haven't encouraged him, Beth. Pete may resist the truth about me, or deny it, but he *knows* what it is."

"Maybe," said Beth. "But let's remind him again."

Helen went home, directly to her sofa. Surely Reverend Link never went fetal for inadvertently encouraging the affections of an unstable female congregant. Link, in fact, had countless flirtations and probably affairs with who knows how many women in the church, and somehow his sexual insouciance inspired only a jovial, proprietary fondness within his flock,

even—or, rather, especially—among the men, who clearly liked
potency in a male leader. But what kind of a female leader did
they want, other than one they could run roughshod over?

Without ever having met Pete—rather, without ever having
eaten his cooking—Helen might have agreed that community
service was a more ennobling, esteem-building occupation than
being a chef at a fine dining establishment. But she, who never
before cared if dinner was soup from the can or a clay-based
protein shake, now grasped the intelligence and wit of such
work; in his fried squash blossom stuffed with goat cheese and
minced olives she tasted the sun and soil of northern Italy, in his
romesco, a gritty paste of ground nuts, chilies and olive oil, the
essence of southern Spain. The hours spent at Alice's dining
room table were golden blurs, the only stints of pure and profound sensuous pleasure in her presently pinched existence.

35

Pete was soloing in the Wren Street kitchen when she came in. "Where is everyone?" she said.

"I'm here." Pete tapped his chest. "Alice is fetching the child bridegroom."

"All the way to Claremont?"

"He took the train. So she only has to drive downtown at rush hour."

"What's wrong with Dewey's car?"

"Don't ask." He shook a sauté pan. Caramelizing onions rose in a slippery brown wave and folded over themselves. Before seeing Dewey in church last Sunday, Pete had wondered what it was about this too young, too nice Christian boy that had snagged the snappish Alice so snugly; but one look at the actual human specimen and all came clear as air. The kid could make a willing chauffeur out of anyone, of any sexual persuasion.

Helen, Pete began to notice, shifted her position whenever he moved, as if to keep the distance between them constant. He moved to the sink, she fled to the doorway; he returned to the stove, she hustled to the sink. He could have some fun with this, if so inclined. He was not. He'd never seen her this agitated, and it threw him. "Have some vino," he said. "Pinot grigio in the fridge."

She helped herself, inspecting the label as if she even knew grigio from a grappa. He refused a glass himself; he'd have a sip at dinner, at most. Wine in hand, she retreated to the far side of the kitchen. "What's cooking?" she asked.

Lifting a lid, he revealed tiny braising limbs. "Haunch of Thumper," he said. "With papardelle and cavalo nero—this black Tuscan cabbage. But first fava bean and parsley soup—just a demitasseful, with foamed milk. Salt cod with steamed vegetables and aioli. Then the rabbit, followed by an insalata tricolore. Sweet Gorgonzola with honey and walnuts. A small ricotta cheesecake. Hey, so I went a little overboard at the Cheese Chest."

"I've never eaten rabbit," Helen said.

"I'm going bland but grand for the little man."

"That's considerate." She peered out the window into the backyard.

"That's me," said Pete. "Mr. Consideration."

She didn't even smile. In the scant two hours since he'd left her at the Bread Basket, something had ruffled her famous calm. She kept well out of his way yet seemed to want to say something. And he had an idea what that something might be. *I can't keep doing these dinners. My boyfriend doesn't approve.* Pete was no fool. If he were her boyfriend, he wouldn't stand for it. But if Helen had something to say to him, let her work up her own damn nerve; he wouldn't assist in his own dismissal. He rinsed disks of milk-soaked bacalao and set them in a pan with bay leaves and water. He went for wine to add and she scuttled from his path. Did she think he was going to pounce? Or, like an elephant, smash her against the wall until every bone in her body was crushed? He started scrubbing toy-sized yellow crooknecks.

"Did you see Shirley's kinta cloth kaftan?" Helen said out of nowhere. "Gorgeous! How can she be homeless and have such a wardrobe?"

"People give her stuff," said Pete. "And her car's crammed full of clothes."

"So, Pete—do you really want to open this restaurant with Jocelyn?"

He stopped scrubbing, eyed her face. "Some of the time."

"And the rest of the time?"

"I'd rather be snoozing," he said. "I'd rather be sitting in the sun, eating cake, feeding the birds . . ." Also: singing, scratching what itched, fucking the eager, the whole range of basic, underrated pastimes.

"Won't you miss all your cronies at the Bread Basket?"

"Prob'ly," he said, watching her.

"And you're sure you want to give up community service work?"

"You sound like Mom," he said, and perceived the faintest flicker in her eyes. "A-*ha*! The old gal's been at you."

"She has. She's concerned you're taking on too much."

"Maybe I am," he said. "So now, we'll see."

"You don't have to prove anything, you know—not to her or me or anybody else."

"I don't?"

"No," Helen said. "And that's all I have to say."

Pete moved to the stove, checked the lashing ribbons of pasta. He got her drift: to watch his motives, especially as they concerned her. She was right to issue the warning, but otherwise she'd never been more wrong. He had many things to prove, to many people. To Mom, to Freeman, to his probation officer and the custody courts, not to mention his ex-wife Anne, and Garrett Ross, age six.

Helen, having said her piece, stopped retreating every time he moved in her direction. He fed her tastes of cod and rabbit, and by the time the kids showed up, she was almost her usual placid self.

The women went to set the table, abandoning the young Greek god to Pete, who was thus inhibited from sidling up to the doorframe for his weekly earful. Instead he clattered pans; if he couldn't eavesdrop, neither would this comely youth.

Dewey, it seemed, also had something on his mind. He leaned against one counter, then another with ill-acted nonchalance. Finally he spit it out. "Oh, by the way, is Jocelyn coming?"

"Who?" Pete said.

"Jocelyn Nearing. Is she coming tonight?"

"What makes you think that?"

"The other night she said she might. She said she was dying to."

Pete watched steam rise up from the boiling stock.

"So I thought maybe she was coming. That's all."

Pete said, "I don't know squat about it."

At dinner, Dewey's cod went untasted, as did the shiny yellow dollop of aioli, despite Alice's urging that it was like mayonnaise gone to heaven. He ate his vegetables like a good boy, though. The papardelle's sauce was scraped aside and the noodles eaten naked; bacon bits were laboriously located and consumed while the juicy, toothsome rabbit and pricey, ink-dark cabbage stayed intact.

Helen asked Dewey if he'd like to speak at a midweek service—anybody, apparently, merited an invitation. "You could talk on the theology of animals."

Blushing, he accepted, and they set the date.

Pete kept his mouth shut for as long as he could, which was right up through the rabbit course. "So, Dewey," he said then, with such dangerous joviality the gals' eyes snapped open. "Man to man. How do you do it?"

"Do what?"

"Get a girl to drive you all over town."

"Who, Alice? Well, I don't have a car right now."

"Yes you do. *I* don't have a car. You *have* a car. You just lent it out. And I'm wondering, how does that work? Here I am, no car, hoofing it everywhere—and here *you* are, with a car of your own, being chauffeured over hell and gone."

Dewey, abashed, turned to Alice. "I took the train here—"

"And I don't mind driving you," Alice said, then addressed Pete. "I don't mind driving him at all."

"Of course you don't," Pete said. "And that's what I'm wondering about the squire here. How do you get a girl to drive you all over the county—and *enjoy* it—when you have a perfectly good car?"

Dewey frowned at his plate and with his fork moved an edge of dark cabbage off a noodle. "I don't understand your point, exactly."

"Do I have a point?" said Pete. "Let's see." He crimped his forehead in apparent thought. "Are you taking the train back tonight?"

Again Dewey looked to Alice for help. "Uh, probably not."

"You're going to drive him back tonight?" Pete asked Alice.

"No, Pete," Alice said, "probably not—if that's any of your business."

"Ahhhh." Pete's grin grew and grew. "Aren't you the fast one, Dewey. Crashing at the girlfriend's pad so early in the game . . . isn't that a bit precipitous? Have you logged enough hours on the porch swing to take such liberties?"

"Pete," said Alice. "I just have to say, this rabbit is insanely delicious."

He saw then that she was white with fright. He'd gone too far, or was about to; however much he'd like to pester the false, finicky lad to tears, Pete ceased and desisted. "Well, Alice," he said, "that's because the insane cooked it."

36

That Pete guy?" Dewey said, clambering into bed beside her. "He has a thing for you."

"Not for me—it's Helen. He'd give anything to be with Helen."

"Helen? He doesn't stand a chance and he knows it," said Dewey. "He's too weird. And kind of rude."

"Kind of? Pete? He's all bark and . . . actually . . ."—Alice laughed in little sniffs against Dewey's shoulder—". . . all bite." That's one thing she actually liked about Pete: he bit. "Of course, you know who's *really* after Pete?"

Dewey pretended to think. "Nobody?"

"A big somebody," said Alice.

He shrugged.

"Jocelyn Nearing."

"No way," he said. "She'd never . . . And anyway, she's married!"

"Since when did that stop anyone?"

"You're kidding me." Dewey squirmed back to look into Alice's eyes. "Aren't you?"

"She's opening that restaurant with him. And you should hear her. 'Peter's so marvelous, Peter's a genius, Peter's actually *very* good-looking . . .' "

"But that doesn't mean she's after him."

Alice touched his face. "Dew, you're so easy to torture, it's not even fun."

He drew back. "Why would you want to torture me?"

Because, she thought, *because you were the special guest and, refusing even to taste anything else, you ate only bacon bits and noodles and then, after removing every raisin and pine nut from your first piece of cheesecake, had the nerve to ask for seconds.*

It rained all night, and all the next day. Dewey braved the storm in her Toyota and came back with two *Star Trek* videos, an enormous pizza, two six-packs of Coke—diet for Alice—and a chocolate cream pie. He moved the television into the bedroom and they spent the day in bed.

They made love after each video. Alice noticed a watery, milky taste in his kisses that she couldn't quite get over; maybe it had been there all along, and only now, after the initial novelty and urgency had abated, was it bothersome. Here was yet another entrenched, bad pattern: self-destructively looking for reasons not to like a lovely, devoted man.

Sunday morning, the clouds broke apart into fat white curds in a cleansed blue sky. They walked to church on steaming sidewalks. Alice, as usual, started to slide into Pete's pew, but Dewey nudged her firmly forward—an assertiveness that pleased her even as she hoped Pete hadn't seen it. Dewey chose a pew toward the front, and when Jocelyn came in with Thad— the organist was already bashing out the prelude—she slid in beside them. Leaning around Dewey, she waved to Alice and mouthed, "Let's talk."

The prelude stumbled to a close and the service began. Alice fidgeted, *not* wanting to talk about the job again and missing her spy's-eye view from the back of the room. During the offertory, she peeked at her former pewmate, who was characteristically contorted, arm on the back of the empty pew, managing to gaze both upward, as if at some deity, and simultaneously askance.

The children were released for Sunday school, and this time Jocelyn kissed Thad, gave him a little shove but didn't go with him. Then, Helen spoke on the Trinity, a concept, she said, that

Unitarians tended to dismiss without appreciating. She compared the Father, the Son and the Holy Ghost to the id, the ego and the superego, and the conscious, unconscious and collective unconscious, and Buddhism's kayas. She talked about human propensity for triangulation and "the rule of three" in comedy writing, telling a lot of three-example jokes, including the one about the three-legged pig. An especially good sermon, Alice decided, because of the jokes.

Afterward, as they were waiting to file out of their row, Jocelyn turned to Dewey. "Help me, please," she said. "I really want Alice with me."

"I'm doing my best." Rubbing Alice's shoulders out of nervousness, he dug in too hard. When she tried to squirm away, he held her fast.

"Please, Alice," Jocelyn said, "I've got about fifty permits to get and a thousand phone calls to make. I really need you."

"I would, but I'm already committed."

Dewey shook her shoulders, as if to coax out a different answer. "It's just Foster," he said, then addressed Jocelyn. "I know her boss. He'd understand. I'll talk to him if she won't."

"Dewey, for God's sake." Alice twisted free.

Dewey smiled at Jocelyn. "I'll wear her down, I promise."

As they walked home, he kept at her. "Why don't you do it? You'd make good money and meet all kinds of interesting people."

"I do that now," Alice said.

"Yeah, dead people."

"Why, Dewey, was that sarcasm?" She pinched him lightly under the ribs. "I met you—remember?"

He slung his arm around her and drew her close. "I just don't want you to pass up such an amazing opportunity."

"I want to pass it up. And I don't consider it amazing."

"You don't?"

She did consider it amazing that Jocelyn had singled her

out. By now, she was sure, Nick had heard all about little blond-haired Alice at church, and he might or might not have made the connection. She had no control over that, but still had a few principles; she might engage in low-level stalking, but she'd never take a job with Nick's wife. "Restaurants and movie stars don't interest me as much as they do you," she told Dewey. "And Jocelyn Nearing makes me uncomfortable."

"But she's so nice," he said.

They turned up Wren Street on sidewalks saturated and puddled, some water reflecting the blue sky and white clouds while that in the shade revealed pale pink, waterlogged earthworms.

Dewey stopped abruptly at the corner. "There's something you're not telling me."

His perceptiveness jolted her. "No, Dewey." Fear iced her voice. "There's something you're not hearing."

Finally, Monday night, Alice was home alone. She went through her mail, clipped her toenails, poured herself a glass of that haunting white wine Pete had brought, prepared herself a plate of leftover rabbit and pasta, then phoned Helen. "Boy, do I need some time to myself," she said. "Dewey can be a little needy."

"A little?"

"I know," Alice said. "And you know what else is bugging me? Did I ever tell you about the mobile in his dorm room?" A present from a former girlfriend, it was made of six red construction paper hearts hung by fishing line to pieces of clothes hangers. On each of the six hearts, Alice told Helen, one word had been written in silver ink:

DEWEY   CYNTHIA

MERLE   JESUS

GOD   LOVE

"It creeps me out," she said.

"Why, because an ex-girlfriend gave it to him and he still has it up?"

"*That* never even occurred to me! I just can't believe he put it up in the first place. It's so *babyish*, and sentimental, like—I don't know—Ken and Barbie go on a double date with God and Jesus. What kind of God is that?"

Helen laughed in a gratifying burst. "I love that your objections are theological!" she said. "So, let's take this one step further. If you can't hack the Hallmark-variety God, what concept of God can you live with?"

Nothing came to mind, or nothing other than a vague, tumbling darkness. "I'll have to get back to you on that."

She could not sleep. *There's something you're not telling me . . .* So, okay. *Actually, Dewey, I've been in love with Jocelyn's husband for a year.*

What else was there?

When it started to grow light, she dressed and grabbed her keys, drove down the quiet streets and parked in the Beverly Manor's lot. Aunt Kate was working at her desk. "Dear. You're out and about early."

She was coherent, present! Thank God for small favors. Alice positioned herself to where she could see her great-aunt's face. "I have a question for you, Aunt Kate."

"Another?" She seemed encouraged by the prospect. "Do tell."

Now that she had her aunt's full attention, Alice's certainty faltered. "The man you told me about—your boyfriend? What was his name?"

"Colin, dear. Colin Crowley. Why do you ask?"

Because he's my father? In daylight, the possibility suddenly seemed remote. "Where do I fit in with all of this? I need to know."

Aunt Kate's chin made a small, precise tuck. "Come here, dear." She held out a hand. "What is it you're asking?"

"I've been wondering . . . if you're my biological mother."
There.

Aunt Kate's hand was large—she had a piano stretch of ten
notes—with soft, thin, increasingly transparent skin. "You flat-
ter me." She drew Alice closer. "I wish you *were* my daughter.
I do have a mother's love for you. And if I had a daughter, I'd
want her to be exactly like you." Gently she brushed Alice's
cheek. "So sweet. But no, Alice, you are the third child of Mary
and what's his name, the Jewish fellow? Hold on." She closed
her eyes, then slowly shook her head. "When you get older, dear,
memory is *not* your friend."

As a favor to Rosalie, who was having oral surgery, Alice agreed
to work two day shifts at the Fountain for the first time in over a
month. In that familiar humid air scented by chlorine and spilled
drinks, she found herself watching for Nick with a habitual vigi-
lance. The door opened and she stopped whatever she was doing
to see who it was. The phone rang and she picked it up—"Fountain," she said—and each time, in that brief instant before the
caller spoke, came a sickening free fall of fear.

Rosalie stopped by the day after her oral surgery; bored
with sitting at home in the Rowena Arms, she'd taken a walk to
get out of the house. She had a drink at the bar—"Just a light
one, hon. I'm on all these painkillers"—and they chatted. "Any
word from the Voice?" she asked.

"No, and I don't expect any." Alice shrugged. "I'm seeing
somebody else now." A young, sweet guy, she explained. Someone kind to her, and steady.

"It's about time," Rosalie said. "That other stuff went on
way too long."

Alice wasn't so sure the other stuff wasn't still going on: it
seemed to have an unseen, ongoing life of its own, like an under-
ground river. She still dreamt about Nick, his dark, creased face,
the crinkling of his eyes in laughter, the smell of sawdust in his
clothes, the persuasiveness of his hands, his beautiful deep voice.

In these dreams, she could never quite get to him, or if she did, he pretended not to know her.

In the slow early afternoon after Rosalie left, with only two regulars huddled at the bar, Alice imagined being forced to choose between Nick Lawton and Dewey Hupfeld. The correct choice, of course, was obvious. Under any circumstances. Deciding that, even hypothetically, made her feel thin and bright, like a sheet of blank white paper hung out in the sun.

There was no mention of Dewey coming to dinner the next Friday night; in fact, he tried to talk Alice into absenting herself. "Let's go camping," he said. "Let's drive to Lone Pine Friday night and go bouldering in the morning."

"*Bouldering?*"

"There's a field of large boulders we can climb without ropes. It's fun."

"Not this week," she said. "Pete has to practice cooking, and Helen's in the dumps, so we're trying to cheer her up."

Indeed, that Friday Helen's gloom was palpable; her tendency to slump more pronounced. When downcast or upset, she traded ministerial magnificence for awkward largeness. She spoke of a long, rancorous budget meeting the night before. "I gave up my raise so the money could go toward the midweek services, but they gave it to Worship and Celebration for summer services. Thanks, Pete." She took a glass of wine. "When I'm not even there."

She and Alice were keeping Pete company while he steamed couscous for chicken stewed with green olives and his first batch of preserved lemons.

"I kept chanting a mantra under my breath," Helen said. "*This has nothing to do with me. This has nothing to do with me.* And I can't take it personally. They don't even know what they're doing, not really. But I was wondering . . . " She turned to Pete. "Is it true you can get recipes for fertilizer bombs off the Internet?"

Pete whooped.

"The Unitarian bomber," said Alice. "Catchy."

They moved to the dining room and ate room-temperature salads: tiny lentils with oranges and raisins; multicolored peppers flecked with parsley. They piled fluffy yellow couscous on their plates, then the braised chicken dotted with briny green olives and chunks of salty lemon.

Helen swung her fork. "This food cheers a gal right up."

Alice said, "Talk about transcendent."

"Amen," said Helen.

That got Pete twitching and blushing like a schoolgirl.

"Can I ask you both a favor?" said Helen. "In two weeks, I have a visiting minister coming to Morton, and I'll need an unbiased report."

"Why?" Pete said. "Where are you going?"

"I decided that if things turned out badly at last night's meeting, I'd take my remaining vacation time and go on that cruise with Lewis. I leave this Sunday, after the congregational meeting, for ten days."

Pete shot back in his chair, scooped up plates as if they were playing cards and carried them into the kitchen, where he scraped them roughly and piled them in the sink.

"Careful with the china in there," Alice called. Then, softer, to Helen, "Somebody's not too happy about this cruise of yours."

"He'll just have to deal with it." Helen picked up her wine. "If I don't go, I won't have a boyfriend anymore."

Alice went into the kitchen. Pete, filling the sink with water, stirred the plates and silverware with a submerged clatter. "Hey," she said. "Do I have the perfect mantra for you. Repeat after me. *I hate myself, I hate myself, I hate myself.*"

37

To Pete's mind, Helen's sermon on surrender was brilliant, her best yet.

You can't just surrender. You have to surrender to something, and have a sense of what that something is. Preferably, it's something greater and larger and more encompassing than yourself, something dynamic rather than fixed, something that enlarges rather than constricts, something that energizes the spirit and doesn't deplete it.

The yearly congregational meeting to vote on the budget took place after the service, with enough time in between for people to grab a cup of coffee and straggle back into the sanctuary. Xeroxed copies of the budget were passed around and the church president asked for comments. Old Cassius Tyler asked why two hundred and fifty dollars was allocated to repaint the parking lot when he knew some Mexicans who'd do it for fifty. Helen spoke briefly. "I'm disappointed this year's goal wasn't reached. But this budget nevertheless represents many hours' work by many committed members . . ."

With only a handful of the usual dissenters, the budget was adopted.

Then Helen was gone. Off with sober lover boy, the one who let days go by without checking on her, whose lack of ardency was an insult, while he, Pete, would've done *anything*, even go sane, for the woman.

He moped around the Bread Basket. Mornings, after Mom went off to work, he dropped the venetian blinds and watched television for hours at a stretch. Soap operas. The cooking channel. He even skipped the comic occasion of Dewey's midweek talk on the theology of animals.

Mom's report—"A little dry," she said—gave only a glimmer of satisfaction.

On Friday Freeman said, "What gives?"

Pete hated to admit the content and depth of his delusion. "The minister, you see," he said. "She's off with the boyfriend. On a cruise."

"Ouch," said Freeman.

"I always knew he existed," said Pete. "I still hoped I had a chance."

"And do you?"

"No. She's made that clear any number of times." He slumped. "I'd get the message, then go right on hoping for the impossible."

"You've been going after the impossible?"

"Seems so."

"This is easier than I thought," Freeman said with enraging brightness. "So why not go after something that's possible?"

The first Friday night in six weeks passed without Pete cooking. On Saturday he went to the gym and bench-pressed two-twenty, a miracle. On Sunday the visiting minister came to Morton—a gay minister there to tell them how to welcome homosexuals into the church—and Pete did not attend. He spent the hour of worship in Griffith Park, where homosexuals welcomed each other in the shrubbery. He'd lumbered up the bridle path, sweating and talking to himself, a fat—well, not as fat as before— ambulatory package of anguish. Bicycles whizzed by as his heart flopped haphazardly around his chest. He wandered past the merry-go-round through the old zoo, where the cages still stood after forty years' abandonment like a weird playground, partly overgrown with honeysuckle, passionflower, wild cucumber, the bars still intact, the doors removed, the concrete lairs sumptuously grafittoed and used for gang revels. Maybe he'd go native, find some park-dwelling squaw with mud-caked hair and take up residency in a large mammal cage, where he'd pace and glower and beg trail mix and dripping Popsicles from passersby.

He climbed the hills on moist, eroded dirt roads, then up ravines ringing with the clean smell of wet granite. Heart pounding, Pete emerged atop a ridge from which he could see the city in all four directions and, in a pale coppery fuzz to the west, the Pacific Ocean. While he'd encountered nobody on his way up, these high, bald ridges were swarming with joggers, lovers, dog walkers, families, tourists and teenage packs, all of whom had trickled up various paths through the scrub and emerged squinting and breathing hard to cluster at the viewpoints. Pete himself rested in the picnic area on Mount Hollywood—originally called Mount Griffith until the honoree plugged his wife—where a small blond terrier stood patiently on a concrete table as his owner, a plump older woman, fed him bites of her sandwich. A small plane rumbled overhead. Crows squawked and coughed from snags. A hawk wheeled in silence, coring out a deep cone of blue sky. Far to the east, snowcapped Mount Baldy sat like a stone Buddha.

Pete basked in the sun. Somewhere to the northwest, Anne and Garrett lived at their secret address where, he imagined, a deliberate, impeccable normality reigned; Anne had a talent for perfection which he admired but could not live with. On the far side of the mountains was Lancaster—a beautiful word whose connotations included heat, aridity and Carrie Dupray. And due west, in the shining soup, Helen drifted with her mate.

Descending, he selected trails at whim, coming out in a neighborhood of huge homes where handbills for missing cats and lapdogs plastered every lamppost—hope against hope that the pets had not become snacks for the coyotes.

Hope, when you thought about it, was a lousy, vile, traitorous emotion. A flimsy web of wishful nonsense spun in desperation to hold reality at bay.

Pete crossed Los Feliz Boulevard and wandered east, seemingly at random, until he found himself on Wren Street, with its gentle incline, gracious shade trees and old-fashioned Doric streetlamps that somehow resembled the crowns of kings. Alice Black's vast, overgrown yard was full of flowers: all manner of roses spiked with tall orange and yellow gladioli, banks of purple iris with daffodils, red and blue anemones. Pete was halfway up the driveway when Dewey's overbred, underworked working dog ran out barking. Too late, Pete saw Alice on the porch beside Baby Dewey himself, who whistled, leapt down the steps and in a few swift strides caught the dog by her collar.

Pete had neither dog nor girlfriend. Nor did he own an athlete's lanky body, beauty and grace. He felt, at this moment, very old indeed.

"Pete!" Alice called. "To what do we owe this honor?"

The chime of pleasure in her words was unmistakable. If he were a bird, his feathers would've fluffed. "Just walking by," he said.

"You weren't in church today," said Alice. "I looked for you."

"So how was the fag?"

Dewey, still holding the dog, glanced sharply at Alice.

"Oh, it was basic Gender Tolerance 101," Alice said. "But he was pretty good, don't you think, Dew?"

"Really good," he said. "A great speaker."

"Want a cup of coffee, Pete?" Alice held up a mug. His Costa Rican coffee, no doubt, which he'd left behind after the last dinner. "I just made some," she said—urged, in fact. "It's fresh."

He said okay, if mainly to rankle Dewey. Alice vanished into the house, leaving him alone with the youngster, who let go of the dog and stood as if guarding the steps. "She won't hurt you," the boy said of his speckled beast.

Merle sniffed at Pete's shoes and ankles and he somehow resisted the impulse to stamp his foot. He didn't hate dogs, but Dewey's pet neither inspired nor required his affection. "How's it going, Dew?" See? He could be a regular guy.

"Good," Dewey said.

"So you really dug the fag?"

"I'm sorry?"

Alice returned with a cup of coffee.

"The fag preacher . . . " Pete said loudly. "You really dug him?"

"That's not a word I'd use," said Dewey.

"What's wrong with it?" said Pete. "A fag is a fag. So?"

Alice said, "You have to understand, Dewey. The fag stuff's a running joke."

"I don't know the joke, and I don't consider it a very nice way to talk about people."

"Oh, that's right," Pete said. "Forgive me, I forgot I'm talking to the viceroy of nice. The knight of nice."

"Pete," Alice said. "It's all right."

"What's all right? Nothing's all right. Why am I the only one to say so?"

Dewey squared his shoulders, his self-righteousness rising like mercury in a thermometer. Pete found this stirring. "You're so nice, Doo-doo, you give away water to a fat stranger while your girlfriend gets dehydrated—but you got to be nice. You're so nice you stand Alice up to take some moron to the emergency room—never mind that ten or fifty other people were willing to do it, never mind that even your little Jesus college must have an ambulance service on hand. Never mind disappointing Alice. You get to be the hero. I've got your number, Meister Nice."

Alice had one hand clapped over her mouth.

"I listen," Pete said to her. "I hear everything you and Helen say. Things you don't even know you're saying." He toed the ground and remembered more; really, his recall in this matter was downright remarkable. "You have to chat up an Alzheimer's patient instead of taking Alice to the movies. Oh, and for hours at a stretch you don't pay her any attention because you've got to prune her rosebushes so everyone can SEE how nice you are." Pete was feeling better by the second. "You'd rather watch *Rockford* than neck—I mean, talk about a fag. Not to mention that you're hanging around Alice to suck up to a movie star. Ever notice, Alice, that he only comes around when there's a chance he'll see Miss Nearing? Oh boy, if you were any *nicer*, people around you would have black eyes and concussions."

"That's enough," Dewey said. "I think you'd better leave."

"I'll leave. *Avec plaisir.*" Even Pete's French was coming back to him! "And Alice . . ." He handed her his cup. "You could do better with the coffee. Don't be so stingy with the beans, and don't boil the water to death."

She took his cup and met his eye with a brief, instantly suppressed surge of amusement. "Bye, Pete," she whispered.

He left the yard with a new spring to his step. He definitely felt more chipper. He walked to the river, betook himself to Sherwood Forest and found Freddy sweeping the sitting area with a broom made of cattail reeds bound with shreds of plastic sacking. "How 'bout a V8?" Freddy said.

They dragged the rickety lawn chairs down to the lip of the concrete bank and drank boxed juice as the day stretched out long and longer, like a story without a point. Into the hours swam baby ducks, trailing their mothers. White egrets stood on one skinny leg as if on single jointed black sticks. Red crawfish caught the sun and glowed like brake lights. Kids on bikes raced crazily, expertly, on the bumpy inclined banks. Pete and Freddy sat and drummed fingers on chair arms, threw sticks and scratched ears as the adolescent husky pups presented themselves. Schools of swallows performed aerobatics overhead. The river, in no particular hurry, flowed to the sea.

38

I told you he's after you," said Dewey.

Alice took their cups into the kitchen. She had no idea how Pete knew so much about Dewey. She herself hadn't studied Dewey closely enough to draw such conclusions about his character. Yet Pete's accusations sounded accurate, and made her feel championed, and oddly ebullient. She wanted to put her head under something muffling, a pillow or a thick quilt, and laugh as loudly and as rudely as she could. Instead she found Merle's leash and proposed a walk.

"If I make you so miserable," said Dewey as they started down the drive, "why didn't you say something instead of complaining behind my back?"

"You don't make me miserable, Dewey," she said. "Please—that was just Pete being Pete. You can't take it so personally."

He was quiet for a block, then turned to her. "Am I that awful?"

"Let me think," she said, cocking her head.

"If that's supposed to be funny, it's not."

"Oh, Dewey, I think you're wonderful," Alice said. "You're incredibly sweet and dear and . . . *kind*. You've got a perfect body, the world's best dog and—"

"Can you stop joking just once?"

She gave his arm a shake. "I wasn't joking. About any of that."

"I get the feeling you're never quite telling me the truth."

He let Merle pull him to a crape myrtle tree. "I'm not sure if you even know what the truth is. Like who's your real mother—have you even asked? And what color *is* your hair?"

"My hair is dishwater brown, silly. And my mother is my mother. I did ask. And who cares anyway?"

"I do, obviously. Don't you want me to know who you are?"

"Of course." Although nobody need know everything.

They walked in silence the half mile to Atwater Village, with its sycamore-lined streets and small, tidy houses. Dewey pulled her close, rubbed her back and left his arm around her.

She kissed his chest. "I'm sorry, baby," she said. "I'm sorry Pete was such a bear. Uh-oh. Oh no . . ."

A sable-colored boxer had appeared from between two houses and was making a beeline for Merle. Alice stepped forward protectively, but two more dogs arrived out of nowhere, a yellow Lab and brindled pit-bull mix. The three converged on Merle with a hysterical amount of barking, a boiling of fur, as Dewey tried to drag her away. Amid the hackles and whapping tails, Alice caught gleams of pleasure and good nature in the dogs' eyes, a throaty exuberance in their barks. "It's okay," she called. "They're friendly!" She began patting flanks and heads. The dogs looked up, gave her hand a few quick licks, but were mainly interested in Merle. "They're good dogs, out for a romp," she said. "Aren't you," she asked as they bowed and barked to make Merle play, but Dewey held her fast. Abruptly, as if the give-up signal passed among them, the dogs ran off.

"I can't believe people let their dogs run loose like that," Dewey said.

"I liked those dogs. They were having fun," Alice said. "Come on, let's go to the river." She led him down the street and through a gap in the chain-link fence. Down the steep bank, dark water sparkled and jingled like change in a pocket. A man in dirty clothes lay facedown by the water's edge.

"You should never walk here by yourself," Dewey said.

"I don't." She hadn't been to the river since tangling with

that skinny drunk the morning after the deer. That day, it seemed she'd entered a darker world, where weird winos greeted her as an intimate and rescue came in the large, slovenly form of Pete. And if Dewey found Pete intimidating now, he should've seen him so much fatter and crazier back then.

"What's so funny?" Dewey said. "Why are you smiling?"

"Was I smiling?" Alice said, and laughed out loud. "I just love this river," she said. "It makes me so happy."

Dewey gave her a helpless, hurt look. "But it's so ugly. Why would anyone cement over a river?"

"It kept changing course and flooding," Alice said, starting down the bank. "Come on. Let Merle off the leash."

"I don't want her in that water."

"Oh, don't be so overprotective."

He winced but began picking his way down. Alice, waiting, watched five ducklings paddle valiantly behind their mom. Then, a glint of copper caught her eye and she moved closer. Just offshore, under inches of moving water, sat someone's offering: on a trembling bed of rice and beans sat four potatoes, two green apples and two oranges. Scattered throughout were foil-wrapped candies—turquoise, fuchsia, that copper—and golden butterscotch orbs, all lit by the sun and glowing like jewels in the leather-brown stream. For the first time in Alice's life, some kind of prayer, some admission to the universe, seemed in order.

"Hey." Dewey pointed upstream. "There's your pack of dogs."

In the deepest, swiftest part of the river, the sable, blond and brindled trio rode the currents, paws pumping high, big smiles on their faces.

Happiness, pure and gratuitous, surged through her. Setting fingers on her lips, she whistled—and her brothers had taught her how to whistle loud.

"No! Please!" Dewey cried, too late.

The dogs veered toward them, clambered into the rocky shallows and hit the banks running. They shook themselves mid-run with sparkling airborne shimmies.

"Hi, you guys, hi, hi." Alice patted their spiky wet heads. "Did you have a good swim? Are you all cool now?" They squirmed and wagged, left damp imprints and the algae smell of river on her jeans. Laughing, she turned to Dewey, who'd retreated halfway up the bank with Merle drawn in close.

She shaded her eyes. He was suffering, she saw, from her untoward enthusiasms, her disloyalty and foolish pleasure in the unleashed dogs and the ruined river, not to mention Pete's character analysis. In the lumpy concrete between them, Alice perceived an impassable divide. "Oh, Dewey," she said, with deep sad joy, "things just aren't working out for us, are they?"

He looked upriver and slowly shook his head. "I knew it," he said. "I knew we shouldn't have rushed into sex."

39

Shortly after the hygienically white, two-year-old, fifty-passenger *Phalarope* set off from San Pedro, passengers were summoned to the dining room for lunch. Helen and Lewis were seated with two other couples in their mid-forties. One couple was from Pasadena, the other from Seattle. Helen explained that she and Lewis lived apart—"thanks to our work situations."

"What kind of work do you do?" asked Nancy, the Seattle wife, a slim matron who wore her hair in a sleek brown bob.

"Actually," Helen said, "would you mind if I don't say?"

"Oh!" Nancy drew back. "Of course not. I didn't mean to pry."

"You aren't prying," said Helen. "But it's a job that makes people assume things about me, and on vacation I'd love to leave all that behind . . ."

"Yes, yes, of course."

The couples, all somewhat abashed, concentrated on Caesar salads sprinkled with tiny pink shrimp.

"Well," Helen added, "I didn't mean to kill the whole darn conversation."

Nancy's husband—Ted—was handsome and fit, lean as a runner. Placing a hand on his wife's arm, he looked around the table. "I have an idea. Let's none of us say what we do for a living. And on the last day, we can guess."

This was agreed upon with relief and enthusiasm. The Pasadena husband, Paul, suggested they place bets as well. A fifteen-dollar pot was collected—five dollars from each couple—and given to Nancy to hold for the best guesser.

This legislated secrecy quickly added a dimension of humor and sport to the group's interactions. "When I was in surgery the other day," Ted might say at breakfast, then clap his hand over his mouth; later, "I was taking a deposition last week" would be followed by the same coy gesture.

Helen could now speak of Morton to nobody, Lewis having long since shut the door on that subject. Keeping Morton to herself, however humorously, required the suppression of so many other facts of her life that she found herself effectively silenced. She, who at every conference and retreat, training session and orientation seminar, had immediately embarked on at least one if not three new friendships, for once engaged with nobody. Into this void flooded the details of shipboard life and the weird niche of the continent in which they found themselves: the Sea of Cortés.

Helen submitted to the day's planned programs, climbing into pongas—the local wooden fishing skiffs—or the larger rubber zodiacs and *putt-putt*ing to tiny dry little islands with cactus forests and, often, the names of saints, San Francisco, San Tomás, Santa María. These were actual desert islands, as portrayed in cartoons and presupposed in parlor games that asked what famous person, five books, three CDs or foodstuffs you'd most like to be stranded with. Clumps of dry land in the sea, they looked like spoon-dropped biscuits.

On closer inspection, the sand beaches were alive with small stingrays, trails were hedged in teddy-bear cholla and cluttered with scorpions that looked like miniature desiccated lobsters. Life under extreme conditions grew so very peculiar and defensive! Helen was so busy watching her step that she didn't once wish for Beethoven piano sonatas, or William James's *Varieties*, or Simone Weil's *Collected Works*.

June was hot in Baja, the temperature hitting ninety by ten o'clock. She kept a mask and snorkel around her neck and swam as often as she could. Dolphins were almost constant companions, and she loved feeling the faint clicks of their echolocation against her skin. Lewis usually stayed on the ship to read. Late in the afternoons, as evening fell, they sat on the deck and watched the pelicans fly in ever-shifting squadrons, the raffish birds never colliding, then one or another suddenly plummeting into the water with a big messy splash.

Lewis said his mind was roaring. "You'd think I'd get quiet and still, but I'm thinking all the time. Sure this isn't the Sea of Cortex?"

Helen attended the nightly lectures alone. Lewis found them too depressing, all that talk of the sea's intricate, fragile ecology and the insults it suffered—overfishing, invasive tourism, oil spills, dredging.

As the days passed, thoughts of her struggles and disappointments back home slowed, abated, dried up. Surrounded by turquoise water and the pale relentless sky, Helen found that her job receded, diminished until Morton sat like a toy in her consciousness, the church in a plastic train set.

The day the *Phalarope* turned toward home, she went out in a zodiac with half a dozen others to Isla San Miguel, another dirt cupcake on the horizon. The water, sparkling in wavelets, lightly slapped the rubber boat's black bumpers. Half an hour out, the naturalist spotted a spouting fin whale and maneuvered the skiff into its path. Helen and several others quickly slipped on their snorkels and dove into the warm sea.

At first she saw only a shadow or darker current moving under the surface, but gradually a profile formed around a head that was nothing, really, like a head, but much more like the streamlined nose of a speedboat. The whale approached at an angle, and Helen assumed it would detect her and change course out of shyness if nothing else. The whale, however, saw her and seemed determined to maintain its course, regardless. Helen made a brief, clumsy attempt to swim away, but the futility of her movement defeated her. Swim out of a whale's range?

So she hung below the blinding surface, treading water, breathing through her snorkel, helpless. First came the flattened head with its endless smile, and next bulged the small eye, fist-sized, liquid and convex. Helen, had she reached out, might have touched it. Then there was skin, a battered-looking expanse with the pale dull glow of unpolished marble and clusters of barnacles that looked like small dead mountain ranges. Helen registered these details with a stunned, detached precision. What, exactly, had she expected a fifty-ton mammal to look like—a large fish? Stonehenge was closer to the mark. Her continued attention was no longer inspired by enthusiasm or curiosity, or the vain, ridiculous desire to connect with this enormous creature. Now, at its mercy, she watched in terror to gauge her own small fate. A sole, lazy flap of flukes produced a quick, enveloping rush.

She accepted help back into the zodiac. Unlike the other swimmers, she was in no sense exhilarated; she could not say, like Nancy, that she'd felt "privileged and honored" in the whale's presence. *Scorched, struck down* and *obliterated* were the words that entered her mind. She took to her cabin without dinner and could not sleep, read or accept the consolation of Lewis's embrace. Even the idea of prayer struck her as distasteful, so much so that she couldn't imagine ever wanting to pray again—not from lack of faith, but rather from too close a brush with its source. Curled against the wall on her bunk, Helen understood why God did not make full-frontal appearances to humans. A single whale was too much to bear.

The next day, they went ashore at Cabo San Lucas, where she called home to retrieve her messages. There were only four—eerily few, given her eight-day absence. "Just thought I'd call and let you know your visiting preacher was great," Alice said. "Smart and funny, and actually pretty touching." The visiting preacher himself was less heartening: "That's one tough crowd. Sure they're not Baptists, or some sourpuss sect of Scotch Presbyterians?" Then, Alice again: "Hope you're having a great time. I just have to tell someone—Dewey and I split up . . . I'm okay, just in a state of shock."

On the last morning, the three couples sat down together to

guess one another's occupations, writing their hunches on boat stationery. Seattle Ted and the Pasadena wife, Ellen, tied for first place with three correct guesses. Everybody said Lewis was either a writer or a college teacher, and he was both, though nobody suspected that his full-time job was at a halfway house for alcoholics. And nobody scored a single point off Helen— variously thought to be a therapist, a social worker, a school principal. "You can't be a minister!" said Nancy. "You're too much fun. You drink. You swear. You two aren't even married!"

Under cover of the table's laughter, Helen turned to Lewis and whispered, "Not to mention that I despise my church."

She arrived home late on a hot Friday afternoon. After the teak-paneled *Phalarope*, the parsonage seemed stale, dusty and depressingly shabby; she lived out of cardboard boxes, for God's sake. Helen opened windows and checked her messages. Only one, again from Alice: "Aren't you home yet?"

Next door, the church was equally quiet and dingy. She let herself into the main office, thinking the secretary might've fielded calls and there'd be a sheaf of pink messages in her box. But no, only two: a member calling to see if Morton had enough folding chairs for Saturday's wedding, and a note from Frank Rosen of ministerial relations: *We should talk.*

She phoned Frank from her office. "Talk about what?"

"Oh, Helen," he said, "Well, I'm afraid your visiting speaker caused a stir."

"That's what he was supposed to do."

"This stir may not be what you had in mind. Worship and Celebration are upset; they feel you should've consulted them." This committee of four women was responsible for the Sunday services in Helen's absences.

"What upset them? That the minister was a homosexual?"

"Not at all," Frank said. "But he had an agenda, and to anyone coming to Morton for the first time, it would seem that his agenda was our agenda."

"How many visitors did we have last Sunday?"

"That's not the point. Church members felt misrepresented, and uncomfortable."

"Homophobia's a very uncomfortable issue," said Helen.

"What homophobia? Such name-calling, Helen, is insupportable. Nobody here is afraid of homosexuals. We all have homosexual friends and family members, Helen. Nobody wants them discriminated against. But they can't come in and take over, either."

"Ahh," she said. "I see."

"I'm not sure you do," said Frank. "We're aware, you know, of what's happening in our denomination—how many churches have gone that way. It's one thing for gay people to join the church as members, but to come in as ministers and dominate church policy with their issues—"

"I appreciate your frankness, Frank, but I need to go now. Call a meeting with whomever. Just let me know when, and I'll be there."

"Heads up, though, Helen. You'll probably hear more about this."

She depressed the button, then dialed Alice's number. "Do you have any plans for tonight?"

"Hey—welcome home," said Alice. "What shall we do?"

"Let's see." Helen pushed aside the red velvet curtains. Link's roses were covered with shriveled brown blooms. "Do you know where to buy heroin?"

"Oh no," said Alice. "Did you have a terrible time?"

"Not till I got home. Maybe kabobs in Glendale is a better idea."

"I was sort of liking the heroin idea," Alice said. "But kabobs are fine."

"Shall we ask Pete?" Helen waited, then wondered if the line had gone dead. "Are you there, Alice? We don't have to invite him."

"It's all right," Alice finally said. "But don't tell him I broke up with Dewey. I don't want to hear what he has to say about it."

"I understand. But are you okay? Are you depressed?"

"Not a bit!" said Alice. "I miss Merle, but from the moment Dewey drove away, it's like I've been let out of a cage. I tried, Helen. I tried to be a good, average girlfriend and do all the normal things normal couples do. But to tell the truth, I was never so bored in my entire life!"

Early on a Saturday night, Hari's Kabobs was already packed, so Helen, Pete and Alice waited in the designated area by the takeout window. As ever, waiting with Pete was not relaxing, contagiously so. Within minutes, half the people around them were rocking, picking at this or that, and/or rising from the bench and plastic chairs to wander in tight circles. Alice twirled her short hair and kicked at the ground.

Helen, observing this, felt unaccountably happy. "You don't know how glad I am," she said, "to be with the two of you."

The waiter led them to a table under a ficus tree in whose limbs hung two canaries in a cage. After they ordered, the busboy brought a stack of lavash, which looked like a thick-leaved book, and a plate of hot pink pickled turnips, green olives, orange carrot sticks.

"Look at these colors," said Pete.

"Pretty!" Helen took a carrot. "So what's new with the restaurant?"

Pete selected a slice of pink turnip. "Met with what's his name—Mr. Jocelyn—the husband, to look over the design plans."

"Is he an architect?" Helen asked. "I forget what Jocelyn said he did."

"Builds sets," said Pete. "But he's built everything at one time or another."

"What's he like?"

Pete shrugged. "Doesn't say much. But he has good ideas—

and luckily she's got the dough to do 'em." He pushed the plate of vegetables across the table. "Eat a turnip, Alice. Don't turn up your nose, that's just beet juice on 'em and you like beets. Delicious!" To prove it, he bit into another slice.

"So is he some slick Hollywood type?" Helen said.

"Not even close. He's from Bakersfield or somewhere. Kinda cowpokey. You know, manly and mum." He nudged the vegetables closer to Alice. "Just try one," he said. "You might like it."

She delicately lifted a turnip slice. "So is he Jocelyn's partner in this whole restaurant deal?" she said.

"Who—the husband?" Pete said. "He'll oversee the construction, if that's what you mean."

"I guess," said Alice.

The waiter brought hummus and an oily orange eggplant dip.

"I was wondering the same thing," Helen said. "Are they partners, or is he just doing the design work?" *A shared project,* she thought, *might be the very thing to rekindle that marriage— or shake it loose from its moorings.*

"I have no idea." Pete dragged a flap of lavash through the hummus. "All I know is that she's holding out for you, Alice. Won't even think of hiring another assistant."

"I've told her no a hundred times," Alice said. "What do I have to do—announce it in skywriting?"

Pete made a face at her.

Overhead, the canaries twittered and trilled. *It's far easier here,* Helen thought, *with these people than it was for any five minutes on that boat with Lewis. Easier, and a lot more fun.*

Their dinners arrived on enormous oval plates: kabobs with mountains of saffron-stained rice and charred whole tomatoes and peppers. Alice had ordered chicken; Helen mahimahi.

"Look at this." Pete tipped his plate to display five small, thick lamb chops snuggled together with quartered onions in between. "If this isn't the cutest darn thing I have ever seen."

That night, Helen phoned Lewis at eleven-thirty, waking him up. "Something's going on at Morton," she said. "I don't want to sound paranoid, but it's strangely silent. I sense troops a-massing. I need some kind of strategy."

"Here's one," he said. "Get a good night's sleep and call me tomorrow."

"I was wondering if maybe you'd come down."

"Now?"

"Why not?" said Helen.

"I can't. I'm in bed, Helen. And I'm whupped. Jesus, can't we please talk about this tomorrow?"

She bit her wrist for several seconds, then moved it away from her mouth. "I imagine we'll have to talk sometime."

"What do you mean by that?"

"At some point, we'll have to hash it out. But for now, let's call it quits."

He groaned. "Do we have to do this right now?"

"We can do it whenever you like. At your convenience."

"I am *not* the enemy," Lewis said.

"You aren't much of a friend, either."

Lewis called back in an hour, but by then Helen was resolved. She'd commit herself to Morton and wage the necessary wars to make it hers—an effort Lewis would never support. He'd only encourage her to disengage, to believe her life's work lay elsewhere, but he was wrong. Now she could retrench.

In the morning, Father's Day, Helen preached to a scant thirty-two people—Pete, Jocelyn, and Alice among them—and in the week following a sullen calm reigned. Not one call from Lewis, probably a good thing. The Worship and Celebration committee declined to meet with her; they were too busy, they said, planning the summer programming. The old emeritus himself, Reverend Link, had promised to deliver the first sermon of the summer—his first appearance in the pulpit since he retired three years ago—and Helen did not object.

Helen had to cancel what would've been the last midweek service when the speaker, her old friend Jean Trimble, called with a terrible head cold. She offered to come the next week, but Helen was dubious. "The church year will be officially over, so we'd probably only have a handful of the stalwart. I hate to have you drive all the way down from Santa Barbara for that."

Jean had known Helen since she was studying for her first degree in early childhood development twenty years ago and had seen her through all her career changes. "I don't like this flatness in your voice," Jean said. "Let's have a party with whoever shows up and celebrate the end of your awful year."

40

At a time when she knew for certain Dewey would not be in their office, Alice drove to Claremont, cleared out her things and left the expensive clippers and elbow-length rose-pruning gloves with a short note on his desk. *You might need these, A.* After telling Foster that she'd now be working from home, she loaded up on tapes and questionnaires and left.

Two weeks later, she drove out again to give Foster the transcriptions and pick up another batch of tapes—and also the first pages, Xeroxed, from Foster's new medium, the automatic writer.

"She's good," he told her. "This is the sort of communication we've been waiting for. Let me know what you think."

Alice glanced at the small handwriting, which filled the pages from edge to edge with downward slanting lines; it looked like knitting, or one of those lunatic manifestos Scotch-taped to telephone poles in the park. "So how's our friend upstairs?" she asked.

"Dewey?" His face worked for a moment. "Better than he has any right to be."

Alice was struck with a deep fondness for this man. "You mean his keening over me has subsided to low moans?"

Foster chuckled. "Actually—and I don't know if I should tell you this . . ."

"Spill," said Alice.

"Well, he got back together with his old girlfriend."

"Cynthia? That blonde who ran him off?"

"Yup. Once she heard he was running around with an exotic older woman, and famous chefs and movie stars in Hollywood, her interest in Dewey rekindled with a vengeance."

Alice thought this over. "I'm glad," she said. "Happy to have been of service."

The first page of the automatic writing took Alice two hours to decipher.

The view is broader here, the span of biological life ever so less significant. Only with great effort does one recall the poignancy and sting of life's paltry struggles. Of those we left behind we think: they shall join us soon enough.

It requires enormous effort to send word back. Even those who leave life determined to do so perceive that the cellular bondage, however miserable, is brief—an insect bite, a crow's caw, a snowflake's tumble from cloud to earth.

Twinges of regret, often quite vibratory, pass through our realm for the painful sequesterment of souls in the physical life. We can recall how convincing the senses were, how deep the fear of their loss. We remember how baffling and horrific it was not to know that death is the sweet return.

Some of us wish to extend this comfort, but the effort required is herculean. Imagine hurling stones into a thundercrack—the approach is scorching, the action unclear and the results rarely those desired. Most often, the projected stone falls on deaf ears or is dismissed as a dream, a phantasm, a by-product of fancy or indigestion.

I maintain, however, that the technique can be refined . . .

She stopped typing to put on a dress for the midweek service, some psychotherapist speaking about joy. Since this was the last Wednesday before summer break, Helen said there'd be a party.

The therapist, like Helen, was in her forties. Jean Trimble had long curly brown hair, lively eyes—also like Helen—and large white teeth. Her deep tan somehow suggested the practice of nudism. She wore a long crinkled cotton skirt with sandals and had gold bands on several fingers and toes.

Joy, she said, was rarely free-floating. It was tethered to sorrow, which rarely existed where joy had never dwelt; and vice versa. Joy and sorrow were the balancing weights in the dance of human emotions. Joy without sorrow was mania, Jean said, and sorrow without the memory of joy was depression. "So let's all remember a few recent joys. Just bring them to mind. Don't worry. You won't have to share them."

Oh, watching Merle leap, Alice supposed, was a joy. And eating Pete's b'stillas. And those three dogs swimming in the Los Angeles River. Not to mention the quiet joy of walking into the Wren Street yard the day Dewey left: the joy of coming home. The shrink was right, an ache pulsed in each of these memories.

"Joy isn't an individually owned feeling," Jean continued, "Each drop of it adds light and loveliness to the world. Now I'd like you to recall a time when you felt joy for someone else's good fortune."

When my sisters-in-law had their babies, Alice thought. *When Helen preached a dizzying sermon. When Pete cooked a genius meal.*

"Even our enemies' joy should be welcomed. I'd like you to remember a time when somebody you don't like had an occasion for joy. A situation, maybe, where you lost out to them. When you didn't get the job or promotion or the lover of your dreams—and someone else did."

The audience, like Alice herself, was beginning to fidget. She could practically see arguments forming in thought bubbles above some of the older folks. Pete, of course, was swinging his big foot and rearing back as if on the brink of incoherent exhortation. The gay couple, Phil and Todd, were conferring with each other. Jocelyn, however, sat like an icon of serenity, apparently reliving her rivals' and enemies' triumphs with perfect equanimity.

Alice imagined Jocelyn felt joy when Nick came back to her those two times after he left. And maybe when she saw his so-fabulous restaurant design. And maybe Dewey felt joy when Cynthia reopened her arms to him. "When we see joy as something we can participate in, despite its source or its subject, our envy and sense of deprivation diminishes and true joy takes its place . . ." Jean paused, smiled. "And that's it. There's only so much to say about a matter of such pure experience. To that end, I brought some music so we can engage in my favorite joy-producing activity: waltzing."

Waltzing. Oh great. Like the lecture hadn't been corny enough. "Remember," Jean said. "Those of you who choose not to dance, or are unable, can still participate. Joy doesn't belong to the dancers alone."

Alice shivered: Why did so many of these evenings degenerate into hokiness? And why didn't Pete bark, or growl, or snigger instead of rising dutifully to move chairs and clear the dance floor?

Jean Trimble strewed cracker crumbs on the linoleum, then asked an older man to dance. When Jocelyn tapped Pete's shoulder, he didn't recoil at all, just finished stacking a chair and escorted her to the dance floor. Todd nabbed Helen while his partner remained seated. Alice, helping Aunt Kate to the side-lines, spotted an old geezer coming her way. "No thanks," she said, and he promptly moved on to the small pink-haired woman standing beside her. "I'd love to," she said—pointedly, Alice thought. Seven or eight couples were out on the floor, which was about all the room could hold for something as sprawling as a waltz.

Years ago, Aunt Kate had said, "Walter, we've got to teach this girl how to dance," and gave Alice lessons in the box step and the waltz. Aunt Kate counted as Alice danced with Uncle Walter, who was so fine-boned, fragile and distracted that it was like dancing with spiderwebs. Finally, he'd stopped in the middle of a Strauss waltz and, stepping back, crossed his arms. "There is no step for zero," he said. "And that is the failure of the dance." Alice's own dancing had never progressed much further. She had managed, when properly intoxicated, to move rhythmically to rock and roll, disguising her ineptitude as willful humor and irony, as if she knew perfectly well how to dance but chose to be silly. A few years ago, her former friend Rachel had announced with great authority that you could tell the way a person made love by how he or she danced—exactly the wrong thing to say to someone so self-conscious and inept at it. Alice hadn't danced since.

Helen waltzed with a gusto and bounce, as if the waltz were another folk dance. Two older couples moved with ease, clearly having danced together often. Jocelyn and Pete also had a quiet swiftness. Given their ordinary street clothes—she in a pink linen shirt and gray capris, Pete in jeans and huge white running shoes—their movements were fluid yet contained, even stately. Jocelyn was smiling broadly, with obvious delight—or joy, as the case may be. Who knew they'd dance so beautifully together?

Jocelyn caught her watching, and the famous smile expanded, the famous lips whispered something to Pete, who in turn swung around to see Alice, too. He raised an eyebrow and swung off.

Alice understood then that wallflowers, however voluntary and contented, supplied the sorrow of the waltz.

"This is just marvelous," said Aunt Kate. "You must dance all you can, Alice, while you can."

"I hate dancing."

"You and William both. Too much in your own heads. I've come to think that neurasthenia is nothing but an inability to let go of one's tyrannical introspection for even so much as a millisecond."

When the waltz ended and the dancers stepped apart, Pete sauntered up as Alice knew he would. "C'mon, Miss Black," he said, and held out his hand.

"Oh no," she said. "That's okay. You don't have to. No, ask Helen."

"Up." He waggled his hand with ominous impatience.

"I'm not a very good dancer," she said, standing.

"You will be, if you dance with me."

At least she couldn't tip over, given his ballast.

Taking a firm hold of her, he set off in a pace deliberate and slow. Waltz 101, the remedial course. They rotated through the room in three-quarter time. ONE two three, ONE two three. Her neck rigid, she looked high, afraid to see other dancers lest she head right into them. Corners of the ceiling wheeled by, and acoustic tile with lakelike water stains the color of tea. "I hate this," she wailed softly. Pete applied pressure at her waist, a clear signal to pay attention and to relax. Her other hand was in his warm, meaty mitt. Since he was steering, she merely had to keep going. "Oh dear, oh dear," she said. Yet so far, no misstep, no mashed toes. "This is too hard, Pete," she cried. "I can't keep up."

He took her back through the room in wide, smooth arcs. He was, she realized, like the stutterer who ceased to stutter when singing: on the dance floor, Pete ceased his tics and flinching and turned into a regular smoothie. Alice dared to lower her chin. Shoulders, backs and elbows swept by, and faces, some lost in concentration, others lit with pleasure. Helen, in passing, widened her blazing eyes. "Will this piece ever end?" Alice inquired into Pete's ear. This was like being fastened to a languidly spinning, bottom-heavy top. Or to a revolving planet with profound, centrifugal pull. Jupiter, perhaps.

Who knew Pete had grace, let alone grace enough for two?

The waltz went on forever. Pete brought them through the dancers unscathed, and again set out into the whirling midst. Alice gave up objecting. When the music did crescendo and cease, the dancers stepped apart and Alice located Aunt Kate, who was smiling dreamily. But before she could head over there, another waltz began and Pete stepped into it, taking her along. "No!" she said. "I can't. Please . . ." But he was ineluctable, and it was easier to follow than to make a scene. What had Helen said about surrender? You needed to do it to *something*, preferably something larger than yourself.

The overhead fluorescents were turned off then, leaving only the candles and a floor lamp burning. Over Pete's shoulder, candle flames smeared into streaks. Alice's eyes adjusted, and in the radiant dimness faces bobbed into view as if from some warmly remembered past. She swung past Beth's impassive, faintly disapproving face, and the unfocused pleasure on Aunt Kate's.

Her hips seemed to unlock, and she moved more easily. Pete relaxed his grip, giving her room if she wanted it. Unintentionally, she stepped in even closer; there was so much of Pete, though, that she couldn't get too close without pressing into him, which she did—at which point he reclasped her, and held her there. Oddly, this caused her no alarm. Under her hand, Pete's back had the breadth and tautness of an overpacked suitcase, and there was the wide, shallow trough of his spine. Something like laughter was gathering in her chest. She couldn't misstep. Was there such a thing as physical conversion? Where the body gives in and the mind is left behind? She felt her lips stretching into a smile, *Dammit all.* "Enough, already," she said, though when the music slowed into a final, elegiac reprise, regret surged in a dull gray tide. "Thank God," she said as the music stopped. "Finally."

Pete's hands withdrew. A draft funneled in between them. "I need to cool off," he said, and cocked his head at the open door. She followed him out to an arbored patio overlooking a slope of shrubbery. On the side of the building, a low-wattage bulb hosted a sphere of bouncing moths. Pete blotted his face with a clean white handkerchief, stopping to glance with alarm at his other hand, his left, which rested on the railing.

It would seem that Alice's own smallish paw, like some bat or critter freshly sprung from the bushes, had perched on his wrist.

I must like him, she thought.

Behind them, the music started up again, a polka this time.

Pete's lips twitched. The renegade hand now closed around his wrist and tugged, to no discernible effect.

Oh.

Her miscalculation hit with scorching embarrassment. Of *course* Pete didn't mean anything by his dancing. Their mutual ease was neither personal nor specific; clearly he danced that way with everyone. How sad—pathetic, really—that she'd assume otherwise.

Even as she thought this, Pete came toward her, his lips twitching, his brown eyes filling with sweetness.

They were kissing when Beth's voice rang out onto the patio. "Pete?" she called. "Are you there?" Turning together, they saw her shadow, an obelisk stretching from the doorway onto the concrete.

He held Alice firmly. "I'm fine, Ma," he said. "I'll be there in a minute."

"Pete," she said sharply.

"Go back inside, Ma," he said.

The obelisk wavered for a long moment, then withdrew.

"So what's this fellow's name again?" Aunt Kate said as they drove back to the Beverly Manor.

"What fellow?"

"Your dance partner, dear. Don't be coy."

"Pete."

"And what can you tell me about Pete?"

She could feel Aunt Kate looking at her. "He's a nut."

"A nut *and* . . . ?"

"A cook, I guess. He's a friend of Helen's."

"And more than a friend of yours?"

"Look! He's a real live nut. I mean, he's tried to kill himself a bunch of times. He sees a psychiatrist. He's been in mental hospitals."

Aunt Kate spoke sternly. "Now dear, there's nothing wrong

with being in a mental hospital. There's a theory that part of William's two lost years, 1872 to 1874, were spent at McLean's in Somerville. In fact, I hear a local man is writing a novel based on William's time there."

"Yes, but Pete still lives with his mother!"

"So? William didn't leave home for good until he married Alice at thirty-six, and even then he took *his* aunt with him."

Alice said nothing, but could see the small, thin smile on Aunt Kate's lips.

41

He was awake all night long, his whole effort directed at staying quiet, taking long deep breaths, trying not to panic.

Kissing Miss Black was never what he'd had in mind.

In the morning, he drank a cup of coffee. Mom moved about the kitchen, barely looking at him. "I hope you know what you're doing," she said.

He said, "I'm taking a walk."

He headed down Los Feliz and by Riverside Drive he was already sweating. Motel Row, this morning, consisted of several older RVs and step vans, a station wagon with curtained windows and several aged campers mounted on pickups. The smell of coffee and frying bacon drifted through a rig's screen door. Generators and small air conditioners wheezed and clattered.

The windows of Shirley's bronze Cadillac were covered by newspaper held in place by the electric windows. Pete gave a quick rap on the passenger-side glass, then another rap. A corner of newsprint lifted and Shirley's face, young in sleep, peered up at him briefly before disappearing. Pete waited, rocking on his heels. It was a too-bright, milky day, the marine layer burning off, the temperature leaping.

The Caddy's door opened and all six feet two of Shirley unfolded onto the sidewalk in a black miniskirt and a black T-shirt. "Sugar!" she said. "Don't tell me you lonesome?" She rubbed her red-bristled chin. "Caught me 'fore I even shaved."

"Does this thing run?" Pete nodded to her bedroom.

"Took Burgie to Gardena yesterday. Went eighty-five easy. Took two quarts of oil, though." Shirley looked at him carefully. "Where you wanna go?"

"Lancaster," said Pete.

"Lancaster? Ain't hot enough here for you?" She surveyed the Cadillac. "You got gas money?"

"Hundred bucks or so," said Pete. "And credit cards."

"Hey, then. Le's fly."

They fueled up at the Beacon station, where Shirley shaved and Pete sprang for a case of motor oil. The trunk was crammed with Shirley's wardrobe, the backseat with more clothes and wig forms. Cadillacs, thank God, had the legroom, since Pete ended up with the box of oil under his feet.

They trailed a plume of blue-white smoke, the air conditioner rattled and occasionally coughed out a hit of cooler air, fumes filled the car, but the ride was smooth. They took the freeway up toward the mountains, then followed the 210 east to the Angeles Crest Highway. Pete thought of something. "Hey, Shirl, can we find a phone before we head over the Crest?"

They got off on Foothill Boulevard and Shirley pulled up to a bank of phones near a Shell station. "You got twenty for me, baby?" Pete handed her a bill. "You make yo' call, I be right back," she said, and pulled away.

On the answering machine, Freeman's voice was careful and modulated. *This is Dr. Freeman; you can leave a message for me after the tone. Please leave your number, even if you know I have it. If this is a real emergency you can page me by pressing star and entering your number, then pressing the pound sign. Hang up and I'll get back to you as soon as I can.* Pete did not leave a number. He did not press star.

"Dr. Freeman, I know you may never talk to me again," he said, "although I sincerely hope you do. I'm heading out for a day, maybe two. I don't need an ambulance." He scanned the street for the Cadillac. "Call it a test flight." He set the receiver carefully in its cradle and started pacing the sidewalk.

I hope you know what you're doing, Mom had said. Pete

hoped so too. At the moment, he was on his way to Lancaster, if only to see what happened. Or didn't happen. To see what he would and would not do, so far from Mom's corrective care. If he were a fly fisherman, Pete reasoned, he'd probably be in waders midstream; if a monk, on silent retreat. But he was Pete, and being Pete meant a road trip with Shirley. Unless his sidekick reappeared, however, such reasoning was moot.

He considered walking in the direction she'd gone. A sweating behemoth lingering on street corners was sure to draw attention in this suburban enclave of wealthy white Republicans—though he wasn't breaking probation unless he left the county. For that matter, wasn't Lancaster in L.A. County? Ditching Mom was naughty, off his program, but not an arrestable offense.

Nor, so far as he knew, was kissing Miss Black.

Just then Shirley swung up neatly to the curb. "Provisions, sweethead," she said, revealing gigantic coffees from Starbucks and a pound box of See's candies. "Bordeaux creams. Milk *and* dark chocolate." Also, she had changed into beige capris and a close-fitting black wig with severe bangs.

The old Cadillac pulled up the San Gabriel Mountains like a team of powerful horses, its huge engine noisy as a thresher. Pete eyed the temperature gauge. The Crest went up five thousand feet in a few miles, but the needle stayed in the cool zone.

Shirley drove with surprising skill and restraint, accelerating on the curves, rarely braking, maintaining an even speed. "My daddy learnt me to drive on this road," she said. "I'll have me a Bordeaux cream, now, the light kind."

Shirley seemed such a product of her own creation that it never occurred to Pete that she had parents. "You grew up around here?"

"Altadena, by Jet Propulsion Laboratory. My mama still live there."

"You ever see her?"

"Every Sunday for supper."

"In drag?"

"I'se always in drag, babyhead."

"What does your mother think of that?"

"She don't care how I dress. She jus' wish I find a job in phone sales, you know, get off the street, that's all she care about. But then I lose my disability. She say I can live with her, but a girl likes her freedom, know what I mean?"

"I do indeed." Pete selected a bittersweet Bordeaux cream. Although he generally preferred a higher grade of chocolate, he had to admit these candies hit the perfect balance of sweetness and salt.

At this altitude, the sky was a pure, hollow blue. The narrow blacktop hugged chaparral-covered hills, the stinkweed dark, oily green, the sage blue-gray, the dried wild buckwheat a deep russet. The rangy, thin-trunked oaks were more like bushes than trees. Old California looked like this. *California Yesterday:* that was Pete's fourth-grade textbook. He could still remember the Indian in his loincloth on the cover raking something with a stick.

"Your dad still alive?"

"Nope," said Shirley. "The good die young. Keeled over, not yet forty."

Like Pete's dad!

"How old are you, anyway?" he asked.

"Why, baby, you know better than to ask a girl that question," Shirley said. "I'se forty-six."

His age! The same age, almost, as Helen Harland. Pete tried to take this in.

"So what you want in Lancaster?"

"I don't know. Look around. Maybe see someone." Pete hadn't articulated a plan even to himself. "Or maybe not."

Shirley, following Pete's directions, exited east down a wide boulevard bordered by cinderblock walls beyond which sat family homes, three to five bedrooms apiece. Olive Tree Estates, Juniper Hills, Poppyfield Park, Jacaranda Ranch, realms of first mortgages and rampant repossessions.

The Fuselage, a pink stucco building with a real military scrap fuselage protruding over the entry, was coming up on the right.

"You thirsty?" Pete said.

Shirley waggled her paper coffee cup. "Still got an inch or so to go."

"I was thinking—pull in here—a taste of something stronger? I'm buying."

She eyed the bar. "I like soldiers as much as the next gal, but they ain't always likin' Shirley."

"It's dark in there," Pete said, "and nobody's under seventy."

"So why you wanna go in?"

Pete shrugged. "Drinks are strong. They leave you alone." His father took him here, years ago. They'd come up to check out some land, and for a brief escape from Mom; boys' day off, his father called it. Today, Shirley was as close to a male friend as he had on hand. And sooner or later, he needed to know if he could hold hard liquor.

"I'll go in," Shirley said, "but you drinkin' on yo' own."

"What does that mean? Don't you drink?"

"Nope."

"Never?"

"By the grace of God and the fellowship of Alcoholics Anonymous," Shirley intoned, "I have not found it necessary to take a drink for sixteen years."

"Oh brother," said Pete. "Are you kidding?"

"That's why my life so blessed. That's why we drivin' in style. I works for my good luck. Don't drink, don't drug, don't molest nobody who don't want me to. Still got a small problem with the ponies, though. But . . ." She gave a languid, benevolent wave. "Let's go in, have you a highball." She checked the mirror. "But don't let nobody come at me. How I look?"

"Fine," Pete said. "But forget it."

"Forget what?"

"I'm not going in there to drink alone, for Christ's sake."

"Why not?"

"I don't want to."

Now Shirley shrugged. "Don't mean to spoil your fun, sugar."

"Let's go. Turn left up there, then."

He tried to think of their next destination as Shirley steered down another wide, multilane road, this one rife with body shops and anonymous small industries. A gigantic bone-handled pistol mounted above Guns Inc. caught his eye. The town seemed full of emblematic architectonics, as if nobody could read.

"Stop here," he said.

Shirley, easing the car to the curb, frowned at the storefront. "Guns scare me, sugar."

"You don't have to come in."

"I ain't waitin' in no car. Not in no hundred fuckin' degrees."

Pete held the store door for her. Could he hang in close proximity to certain, instant death and not be tempted? Why not find out now, before the restaurant opened, before he centrally located himself in various people's lives?

"Why lookit." Shirley went to a row of ladies' purses hung by their shoulder straps from a low beam. She singled out a pale pink leather bag with a small side opening—a hidden pocket for a petite, lady-sized gun. Shirley bunched the bag so the pocket opened like obscene lips. "Wanna stick yo' big ol' gun in there, baby?"

"Jesus, Shirl," said Pete.

"May I help you?" said the man behind the counter. Older, bigger, chubbier than Pete, the salesman had a remarkably level, snow-white flat top. His blue knit polo shirt said *Guns Inc.* over the left tit. A small, snugly holstered gun rode his hip.

"I'm looking for a handgun," said Pete.

"Got your certificate?"

Pete looked at him blankly.

"Got your certificate saying you know how to handle a gun?"

Pete kept looking at him.

"State law. You a peace officer?"

"No."

"We can waive it if you're a peace officer."

"Where would I get a certificate?"

"There's classes. Over by the front door, on the bulletin board, you'll see flyers for different classes in the area."

"No way you can waive that?"

"You military?"

"No."

"Nope. You don't need a certificate for antiques. Or black-powder guns."

"Do you have any antiques?"

"Over here." The man led Pete to a glass case displaying little handguns with ornately carved handles.

"You got ammunition for these?"

"Sure do." For the first time, the man seemed to notice Shirley, who was examining the taxidermy mounted overhead: an elk with wide, varnished horns, a yellowed mountain sheep, a dust-dulled pheasant. The gun dealer made a small noise, part growl, part purr.

"Can I see that one?" Pete asked. It was a pistol from 1939, army issue. Heavy and cool in his hand, it had a long, pitted barrel. Four hundred and sixty-five dollars. "You take credit cards?"

"Sure do," said the man. "But you still gotta leave it here ten days."

"What?" said Pete.

"Yeah. New laws. Gives us time to do the background checks, make sure we're not selling to felons or the mentally unbalanced."

"Ten days? What about for shotguns?"

"Don't sell shotguns."

"Oh man," Pete said. "Well, then, never mind."

The man placed the pistol back on its felt and motioned him close. Pete leaned over a bit, expecting either a gun-buying tip or a scolding. Not so softly, the man said, "I always wanted me a big tall Amazon like that."

Shirley trained her eye on him as if he were another poor example of taxidermy. "Sugar," she said, "I don't like men with guns. I'se what you call a pacifist."

Pete threw himself into the front seat.

"What now?" said Shirley.

"I don't care. Drop me off anywhere. You don't have to stick around." It was noon; by now the Bread Basket would be open, Thursday's volunteers would have noticed his absence—and also that the operation was running smoothly without him. He'd all but removed himself already so his transition to Jocelyn's restaurant wouldn't cause any problems.

"I ain't drivin' back over them mountains by myself," Shirley said. "And what you want a gun for, anyway? You ain't gonna shoot nobody, are you? Ain't gonna shoot yo'self, now?"

"Apparently not. But I've got some things to figure out, and I don't know how long it's going to take me." He needed to regain his equilibrium. Take his own pulse. Let the dust settle. Maybe check the temperature of one Carrie Dupray.

"Take yo' time, babyhead. I likes it here."

"Great," Pete said with maximum dismay. He hadn't figured on entertaining anybody; but did he expect that with a wave of his hand, Shirley would just vanish? "Fine. So what do you want to do?"

"Me? I want to find us a motel with a swimmin' pool. Then I want to check out the dog races."

42

The double room at the Desert Inn held two queen-sized beds with quilted spreads in a swirling purple floral print and a Magic Fingers option—four quarters to activate. "Swanky," Shirley said. "I'm gonna take me a shower."

Pete sat on a bed, ate Bordeaux creams, looked up Dupray in the Lancaster white pages and wrote down the number on the pad by the phone. He drew a long box around the seven digits and scalloped the edges.

"Dope motherfuckin' water pressure," Shirley called from the bathroom.

Pete drew another box around the first box and filled it with cross-hatching, then edged that with sawteeth.

Shirley stepped out in a black swimsuit with very large, dented bra cups and a pink-and-white polka-dot scarf tied around her waist like a sarong. "I got this little number jes' yesterday. Forgives all a girl's shortcomings, don't it?" She lifted the sarong to reveal the telltale bulge. "Sure you ain't got time fo' a dip?"

"Thanks, but no," said Pete.

Carrie would be eighteen now. Legal. A graduating high school senior in this land of gangs and porn rings and methamphetamine factories. But Carrie would flourish, as cheerful, naughty and willful as ever—unstoppable, in fact, and oblivious to Pete's or anybody else's misery and equivocations.

Squinting, he read on the phone how to dial an outside line. Punch 9 first. Each local call cost seventy-five cents. What a rip-off. Hadn't he seen a pay phone by the office? He stretched out on the bed. In a minute, maybe, he'd go and see.

Shirley woke him up. "They ain't no dog races, but a guy at the pool says they playin' ball over the JetHawks stadium." She was on the other bed and touching up her nails. "Like it?" She scissored fingers at Pete. "Orchid blush."

Pete drove—licenseless, ergo illegally—so Shirley could let her nails dry.

The stadium sat on a patch of desert floor like a weird detention facility, with another Lancastrian monument at the entrance: a thirty-foot JetHawk, a big-beaked, grinning concrete raptor with jet engines on its back.

Shirley lingered in the car, applying her lipstick. "You think I'm passin'? I ain't trustin' that military don't ask, don't tell bullshit."

"You look fine to me," said Pete. "And if there's trouble, we leave, right?"

Shirley rolled her lips together and checked the results.

She had her benign, even winning side, but Pete had seen her go off at the Bread Basket in loud, abusive tirades and, once, in a fit of fairly violent slapping. She had a rap sheet several pages in length, mostly for pandering, but also for disturbing the peace. The JetHawks stadium, Pete thought, might not be the best venue for a transvestite with the chronic itch to slap.

"We'll leave, then," Pete said, "at the first sign of trouble."

"You call it, sweethead."

They walked through heat shimmering off the parking lot, the loudspeaker blaring the Grateful Dead's "Mama Tried." They bought tickets from a woman in a glassed-in booth who had flowers painted on her face and a peace button on her collar. The Association were singing "Cherish" as Pete and Shirley handed their tickets to young girls whose faces were also painted, and who returned each stub with a pink daisy.

Pete hesitated over the flower. "What's this?"

"It's Hippie Night tonight," said the girl. "You know, flower power, peace, love and rock 'n' roll?"

So Pete took his flower and followed Shirley through the tunnel into the stadium, where bell-bottoms abounded, as did beads and halter tops, leather sandals, fringe and incense. Men in long-haired wigs were not unusual.

"Why, ain't this my lucky day," said Shirley.

They found their seats, excellent ones, right behind the catcher, but at the top of the first inning Shirley wanted to roam. Pete roamed with her, to keep an eye on things. "Mr. Tambourine Man" rasped from the speakers, followed by Janis Joplin singing "Ball and Chain"—the tapes were a collage, Pete realized, nothing played in its entirety. Every few minutes, the announcer's voice broke into the song to announce a hippie dance contest after the fourth inning. Contestants were needed.

Pete was in no mood for more dancing. That had gotten him into enough trouble as it was. Was he the only person alive to whom a kiss seemed momentous? And what if that's all it was, just a kiss or two, a bit of sport for Alice Black?

Shirley soon had several flowers in her hair, and a big beehive of blue cotton candy she tore into with her orchid pink nails. On the railings, spectators had arranged small stuffed toys—plush dogs and cats and dinosaurs, even the techno-hybrid skyhawks—as if to afford these objects a better view. Pete and Shirley came to the area where, at any other stadium, the box seats would be; here, though, wily entrepreneurs had set up booths. One booth sold CB radios. Another offered information on careers in law enforcement for retired military personnel. A plump woman in a long skirt and beads had a massage table and an old-fashioned sidewalk sign: 15 MINUTE NECK AND SHOULDER MASSAGE, $15. Making no pretense of watching the game, she motioned them over and applied free daubs of patchouli oil to their wrists. Shirley bumped Pete's hip. "Hey, sugar, le's get you a relaxin' massage."

"I don't want a massage," he said, stepping back. "You go ahead, though."

"Ain't no stranger touchin' me . . ." said Shirley, "'less they a payin' customer." She bumped Pete's hip again, and whispered, "Get me a booth, cocksuckin' five bucks a minute, I'd put this girl right outta business."

No doubt.

In the next booth, a barber sat in his own chair. "Come on, sweetcake." Shirley ruffled Pete's mop. "You *do* needs a haircut."

The barber chair provided an excellent view of first base. It was late in the late afternoon, a day or two away from the longest day of the year. The sun hovered over distant black hills, the light was thickening, the wind picking up. When the barber shook open the purple plastic sheet, it snapped noisily, then swelled like a sail. The Modesto team left the field. The scoreboard was decorated with a jaunty model of the stealth bomber. "Puff (The Magic Dragon)" blared, then "Marrakesh Express" and a partial "Layla," in between calls for dance contestants.

The barber was a handsome older man with salt-and-pepper hair. "This damn wind," he said. "I moved over to this side of the park, and it followed me." He sprayed Pete's hair with water, combed it, sprayed again. He sprayed after every few snips, the water evaporating instantly. At some point, Pete realized that Shirley wasn't beside him anymore. When he tried to look around, the barber held his head in place. "You sure have a lot of hair," the man said. The Modesto team ran onto the field and, a quarter hour later, ran off. The haircut was taking forever. The announcer called the dance contestants onto the field. Jimi Hendrix blasted through the speakers. As water misted over his face, Pete spotted Shirley between home plate and first base. She'd knotted a yellow shirt around her waist and put on a pair of jeans and knee-high boots. Whipping scarves as she danced, she was more disco-stripper-drag-queen than flower child, but hey, what can a girl do with only a moment's notice and whatever's stuffed in the back seat of a Cadillac Fleetwood Blow-'em? Shirley whipped her scarves, did the swim and received one of five prizes, a stuffed, beak-dominated three-foot JetHawk with turbines on its back.

Tufts of hair flew past the corners of Pete's eyes as the barber muttered curses and sprayed more water on his head. When it came down to it, only one thing interested Pete: Did Alice Black want to kiss him again?

The fifth inning began. On the sidelines, Shirley was dancing wildly with the pep squad. Hot desert air blew on the nape of Pete's neck.

III   THE ZOO

43

During a lull in interviewing line cooks, Pete sat down in a gray flannel booth to read the letter:

The cold has eased off and there's been only a little rain every day, which everyone assures me is more typical for October. Yesterday Sister Mary Theresa and I walked the cliffs at Ballycotton where we ran into none other than Angela Lansbury. She has a house in the area, and looked very healthy, very rosy cheeks.

Mom had been in Ireland for three months, since late July. Still, each time he heard from her—hell, each time he *thought* of her—Pete needed to move, to do something, to get out into fresh air, to somehow outstrip the discomfort the very subject of Mom engendered. He thought of it as "that old familiar feeling," and Freeman cheerfully dubbed it "that white-hot core of anger," which formerly, in its most potent doses, had made Pete desire to be dead.

He'd awoken on a hot weekday morning last July to find her seated in the living room, her gray leatherette handbag perched on her knees, her few other possessions—small clock radio, overhead crucifix, cervical support pillow—already removed to the Dodge sedan at the curb. Pete, assuming she was headed back to the convent, was instantly sick at heart. But no. She was moving to the mother house of a five-hundred-year-old convent in the town of Castlemartyr, County Cork.

The very name! Castlemartyr.

She didn't know how long she'd be gone. This was an exchange program—Irish sisters to California, California sisters to Ireland—like some perverse hostage swap. Some exchanges were permanent, others not. At any rate, he was on his own. "Which is obviously what you want."

"Ma—what makes you say that?"

"You've got your fancy new job. Your little girlfriend."

"I've barely got my toes in the water!" Construction on the restaurant had only begun. He and Alice still hadn't yet spent a night together. They'd been waiting for Mom to have a convent sleepover—not flee the country. "Nothing's for sure, Ma. I don't know what's going to work."

"Our arrangement was never meant to be permanent."

"But you did agree to stay through the end of the lease in November, didn't you? And help with the custody stuff."

"Aren't you making enough to cover the rent?"

"That's not the point," Pete said. Why was she so cold? What had he done except take a job—and start dating?

She flew to Ireland *the very next day*.

"Excellent!" was Freeman's response, when Pete relayed the news. "She's stayed perfectly in character. You can't fire me, I quit!"

"Meaning what? She said she'd stay till I was self-sufficient. *And* seeing Garrett again."

"Yes?" said Freeman. "And your point is?"

"She didn't. It's like once I actually started to get back on my—"

"Exactly," said Dr. Freeman.

"In a few months, maybe, it wouldn't have felt like such a *blow*."

"Mr. Ross, it takes both parties to effect a graceful, mature, conscious separation. For whatever reason, your mother lacks that ability."

"I thought bonding was our problem."

Freeman shrugged. "Healthy bonds make for healthy separations."

Pete considered this. "Then I really *am* fucked."

"Why do you say that?" Freeman smiled—a rare and, to Pete, somewhat sinister proposition. "You held up your end. All told, you've kept your balance, except for that little field trip to—where was it? Bakersfield?"

"Lancaster. I needed to do that. Even you said it was—"

"Absolutely. You're doing fine. And someone, I suspect, had a problem with that. Someone who saw her job coming to an end."

The next applicant approached Pete's booth. Early twenties, small-eyed, shaved head, a cooking school graduate—one more of the passionate kitchen hoodlums he'd been interviewing for days. Pale from long nights spent in windowless kitchens and after-hour partying, cranky from reversed circadian rhythms and crystal meth, these kids manned lines throughout the city, moving from venue to venue mostly to break the monotony of standing in one tight spot and doing the same dozen movements, hour after hour, night after night. "Did you bring a résumé?"

The kid yanked up a T-shirt sleeve, revealing a triceps tattoo:

Café Pinot
Patina
2424 Pico
Valentino
Primi

Hired. The new restaurant, Pete thought, would go well on the kid's arm.

. . .

Jocelyn had named the place La Plage, which, being in Holly-wood, wasn't close enough to the beach for the name to be descriptive. In fact, it was a joke, or Jocelyn's attempt at one: when her French friends came to California, she said, they always wanted to go to *la plage*. "So now, I'll just take them to my restaurant!" She'd originally planned to call it Thaddeus, after her son, a name more in keeping with what Pete would name a restaurant. But Thad himself vetoed the idea; he wasn't flattered, and didn't want his name on anything that was absorbing so much of his mother's attention.

Pete had some concern about any name whose meaning could be changed with one letter, and Alice agreed that La Plage was a mistake. Henceforth, the two of them referred to it, among themselves, as the Plague. Over the last month, crazed with preparations for the opening, even Jocelyn called it that.

As Pete had predicted, September and October slipped by and the grand opening was now slated for November 20. And on December 1, he was moving in with Alice.

Pete had two more interviews, then took the subway and a bus to Griffith Park, where he set off down a bridle path toward the zoo. The sycamores' leaves were crumpled, brown and crisp, the hillsides tinder-dry, primed for rain or fire by weeks of Indian summer. At the golf cart shed, he spotted Alice coming toward him. When they were still yards apart, he caught a whiff of her as well.

"I know, I know." She extended an arm to keep him at bay. She'd been working at the Los Angeles Zoo for two months, since August. A friend of hers from Fresno State, Cara, was an animal keeper there, and had asked Alice to be her assistant. Pete had never seen his work-surly girlfriend so thrilled by a job prospect, though for the time being, the pay was nonexistent.

Apparently such jobs were rare because the work was so sought after, and the employee pool so suspect—every goon in the world (except Pete, that is) wanted to work with wild animals—a prospective assistant had to volunteer for at least six months, and even then no salaried position was guaranteed. Alice had accepted the challenge cheerfully. "If I'm around most days, and show good sense, and let the supervisors and keepers get to know me, Cara says I'll have an edge when they start hiring." In the meantime, she still transcribed tapes for Foster.

The other downside was the smell, or at least it would've been had Pete actually minded it. Hacking up big tubs full of fish for the penguins was the novice zoo volunteer's unavoidable fate. Also, Alice was always spraying down the animals' habitats, the high-powered hoses blasting urine and excrement off the concrete and sending much of it into a misty suspension which seeped through the tightest weaves. (This was such an acknowledged fact that keepers were not allowed in the zoo's public areas during business hours.) Alice left her coveralls and mucky boots in a locker at work but still needed a shower afterward, and even then . . .

Pete would never have trouble finding her in the dark.

Today she was especially aromatic. "No way," she said when he tried to cozy up. "Penguin-diet day."

He pushed past the restraining hand and kissed her forehead. Her hair, now chin-length and straight, was a hennaed brown—and oh so pungent! (Funny what a person can almost come to like.) A little penguin-diet stink—what was that?

Last July, the day his mother bolted for Ireland, Pete, swamped by the primal foulness of abandonment, had tried to cancel his plans with Alice for that evening. He was not fit company, he said; "I'll see you tomorrow or so."

"Pete, don't," Alice said. "Come over."

"I can't. I'm really going through it."

"So, go through it here," she said. "Not alone."

"It's not a pretty picture. I shouldn't involve anyone else."

"Either you get over here or I'm coming over there."

He went to Wren Street. Alice had kissed his head, and cooked him a passable omelette, and taken him to her bed, and let him talk. He hadn't wanted their first full night together to be a wallow in his oldest, deepest personal hell, the wastes of his mother's indifference and his attendant self-loathing. "It feels like I have to die," he said, meaning exactly that: the discarded infant starves to death. He now knew better than to perform the obligatory self-harm, though his damnable feelings didn't.

That's what had happened with his marriage, too, he told Alice. A dramatic reenactment of the old, chronic events, albeit with a whole new cast of characters. "I didn't even need Mom. I created the whole sick drama by myself," he said. He'd pushed his wife into leaving, then went on his suicidal tear.

He described the attempts. The overdoses, the car crash, the slashed wrists. Once he started talking, he couldn't seem to stop the whole vomitous outpouring: violence, jail, court, probation, loss of custody, the stay-away order, hospitalizations.

Alice held on tight, weeping for what he'd gone through.

So today, kissing a girl who absolutely reeked? No big deal.

Later that night, Alice whapped his chest with the side of her arm, waking him up. "Pete, look!" she'd whispered sharply.

"What?"

She didn't answer.

"Look at what?" He rolled over to see her face and she was fast asleep. The glowing red digital time, he noted, was 3:48 A.M.

The VA hospital phoned at eight in the morning. Uncle Walter had passed away in the night.

"That's so funny," she said after hanging up. "I woke up thinking about Uncle Walter. Poor old guy." She sat at the kitchen table. Pete stood by, wondering if he should mention her dream or vision, whatever it was, and decided not to. Despite her gig with Foster, Alice hadn't warmed to the paranormal, and even disparaged her own considerable talents. She always knew how many phone messages were waiting, and almost always who'd called; Pete tested her. Although she didn't balance her checkbook, she could state her bank balance to the dollar. And when they went out to dinner, he always made her guess the bill—fast, no calculation allowed—before he saw the figure himself, and she was usually within cents. "Just a number in my head," she said, "but it creeps me out. It only started since the deer." So Pete stood silently beside her as she sat with the fact of her great-uncle's death.

Finally she grabbed his shirt. "I have to call my folks," she said, "and tell Aunt Kate. Will you walk over there with me? Do you have time?"

"Sure." Pete didn't have to be at the restaurant until two. "Pete Ross, at your service." He made toast and strong coffee, then tucked in his shirt and walked with Alice through the cool, pale, too dry morning to the Beverly Manor.

Aunt Kate was reading in bed. "Hello, dear. Is that big fellow with you?" She craned to see past. "Hi there," she sang to Pete. "I had a bad night. I couldn't sleep and then, in the wee hours, Walter paid a visit. He walked in and sat on the foot of my bed, a vision of good health."

"Well, Aunt Kate—"

"He's dead. I know. My father did the same thing when he passed on. You rarely see a person that clearly if they're not just loosed from their body. And I've read about it in Gurney's book, *Phantasms of the Living*—or is it *Phantasms of the Dying*? I can never remember—does phantasm pertain to the percipient or the perceived?" She placed her open book facedown. "It doesn't matter. I was pleased to see Walter's etheric body so robust; it must be a relief for him to be free of his material form, it failed him so completely." Bright tears spilled down her cheeks. "I'd like there to be a funeral."

"I'll ask Helen," Alice said.

"I thought she moved away," said Aunt Kate.

"Not very far."

Helen was living at an interfaith retreat center in Santa Barbara, earning room, board and a small salary as the events coordinator. She'd been there since August, when, during a retreat with fellow UU ministers, Morton voted to release her from her contract. The director of the retreat center, whom Helen had befriended, said, "If your church doesn't want you, we sure do." After tending to the details of her dismissal, Helen moved to a cottage on the retreat grounds.

Pete wasn't completely clear why Morton gave her the old heave-ho, something about how the midweek services created a schism; and the fag minister hadn't been a big hit, though of course nobody wanted to talk about that. The majority of the congregation, it seemed, simply yearned for sleepier, pre-Hellenic times, when their leader left them to themselves. When she first applied for the job, Pete suspected, they must have been charmed by her energy and enthusiasm, her almost hypnotic pastoral solicitude; but once she was among them, they couldn't keep up. Too many mission statements, too many back-to-back, piled-on spiritual concepts, too many exhortations to do good works. Helen wore them out—as, he saw now, she would've worn him out, had things turned out differently.

In the end, she wasn't technically fired; rather, something called a "negotiated settlement" provided a no-fault mutual acknowledgment of a bad fit. Theoretically, this wouldn't tarnish her career within the denomination—should she wish to pursue one. Apparently, she did not.

Helen arrived at Wren Street the night before Uncle Walter's service. Pete cooked dinner just like in the old days—less than six months ago, but now seemingly from other lifetimes altogether. He made *gorma sabze*, the Persian lamb stew with greens, kidney beans and dried limes—the recipe courtesy of Ivo Meberian, the rug dealer, from whom Jocelyn had bought rugs for La Plage in a series of protracted negotiations much relished by both sides. During one transaction, Ivo had brought over a pot of this stew, and Pete had never tasted anything like it. That sharp, concentrated lime, the rich lamb, plump melting beans.

As the women set the table, he cubed feta cheese with

olives, drizzled olive oil, crumbled brittle Greek oregano and eavesdropped, as ever, without shame, by the doorway.

"Things good with . . . our mutual friend?" Helen asked.

"Oh yeah. All we do is chatter. Tug on each other. Eat."

Pete froze to catch Helen's response but heard only the clink and gentle thump of silverware and plates.

"He's moving in December first—did I tell you?" Alice said. "When the lease is up at his place. He's here all the time, anyway."

"You do look good, Alice. Healthy."

"Fat you mean. I've gained all the weight Pete's lost." And then Alice laughed, a pure, happy noise.

Helen told them at dinner that she'd decided to leave the ministry and become a Jungian analyst. "Forget church administration," she said. "I want to work one-on-one as a spiritual adviser."

Pete couldn't resist. "Won't you miss the community service work?"

"Community service work?" Helen roared. "At Morton I *was* community service. I was it! Nope, from here on out it's individuals, one at a time! By the scruff of the neck!" She was already in conversation with a small university in Santa Barbara that trained analysts. Meanwhile, she had her job at the retreat center. "Every few days there's a different group, each with its strictures and rituals. In one week, we had Baha'is, neopagans and recovering Moonies. This week it's Jewish feminists and Zen meditators!" She laughed her hearty laugh. "It's like an ongoing, intensive version of my poor old midweek services."

"The variety show of religious experience," said Alice.

Pete, thinking this such a clever comment, fluffed his girlfriend's hair.

"I miss those midweeks," he blurted, and almost added, *They saved my ass.* But he'd be hard pressed to explain how those dank chilly evenings with cranky old people, sputtering candles and an endless stream of hokum trickling from the podium could have accomplished such a feat.

44

Alice happily would have spent all her time at the zoo, except that it would have cast her among the more obsessed and lunatic of the volunteers. *But I am just another wild animal nut*, she wanted to say—if only to get it out there, for once and for all. And whoever could've guessed that this was her calling?

Cara had—her old sidekick from Cal State Fresno, where they'd been roommates and biology lab partners until Cara moved into zoology. They'd shared a house, an iguana, an African gray parrot, a German shepherd and many cats. After college they lost touch in stages, as Cara went on to graduate school and internships, Alice to crappy lab jobs and distracting boyfriends. But Cara had tracked her down and persisted in calling until Alice picked up the phone, and they were working together again, an old pleasure renewed.

Cara took care of two rhinos and helped out with the elephants. Alice was assigned to a baby East Indian rhino that was small as a cow, a female with long winsome black eyelashes. Alice fed and hosed her and scratched her up around the ears, which was exactly like scratching a huge leather shoe.

She also cut browse in the park and was on hand to work with other keepers, who constantly asked her to spray down habitats. She helped in the food barn, chopped the dreaded penguin diet, filled tubs with elk or monkey chow, assembled meals-to-order from fruits, vegetables, pellets and hay. During the Indian summer heat waves, she even made Popsicles for the animals. For the polar bears, arctic seals and walruses she froze fish, apples and lettuce in twenty-gallon tubs of water. For the lions she froze two-gallon buckets of cow blood.

"You have a born instinct," Cara told her, "and excellent judgment." Who had ever said such things to Alice? Then again, when had it ever been true before? She hardly noticed that she wasn't getting paid.

"Please don't tell me William James worked in a zoo," Alice said in describing her new job to Aunt Kate.

"No, but he was head of the zoological society and ran the zoological museum when he first worked at Harvard. He had wanted, at one time, to be a naturalist, and went to South America with that pompous, wrongheaded Agassiz to gather specimens and ship them back to Cambridge, all to disprove Darwin's theories. I never knew quite what to make of that trip. I suspect William wanted to get out of his parents' sepulchral house—and away from the Civil War."

When Jocelyn heard about Alice's job, she phoned. "What do those animals have that I don't? And if you say animal magnetism, I'll kill you."

Alice hadn't been surprised to hear her voice; they spoke almost daily, if only to pass the phone to Pete. Nor did she take the remonstrance to heart; Jocelyn had hired an assistant back at the end of June, a former maître d' and restaurant manager named Cliff, a gay Louisianan who pretended to have a big crush on Pete. Whenever Cliff phoned for Pete at the Wren Street house, he'd say to Alice, "Hah, baby doll, is our Tiny they-ah?"

No, Alice spoke to Jocelyn often, but otherwise avoided her. Why compound the existing deceptions? Some encounters, of course, were inevitable. The first time Alice picked up Pete at La Plage, Jocelyn insisted on conducting a tour. After that, when Alice went to get him, he'd be waiting outside and sometimes Jocelyn was with him, just to say hello, or to scold her for not coming around. Twice, Nick's black truck was in the parking lot. Seeing it made Alice so queasy and mute with fear that Pete asked both times if she was getting sick.

He cooked a series of dinners for investors to which Alice was routinely invited. She begged off, first with cramps, then with work, but finally confided to Pete that being around Jocelyn and all those rich people made her nervous. He understood, they made him nervous too; he'd mostly be in the kitchen anyway, and except for Jocelyn, Alice wouldn't know anybody.

That, alas, wasn't true; Nick was at each of those dinners.

Alice hadn't seen or heard from Nick since the night last spring when he'd given back his key to the Wren Street house. Hang-up calls came for months, but they had ceased around the same time Alice got together with Dewey—who knew if there was a connection. Alice obviously had no clue as to what, if anything, Nick knew about her presence in the margins of his life.

Now the grand opening of La Plage loomed—a large private party for investors and purveyors, family and friends. This Alice couldn't get out of, so she'd made sure to help Pete with the invitations. Cara, Foster, Helen and Aunt Kate had all RSVP'd.

She would run into Nick sooner or later. At the opening, at least, the encounter wouldn't come as a shock—at least not to her. Alice bought a new dress made of stretchy, copper-colored velvet that matched her hennaed hair. Nick, however surprised to see her, would be civil and cool, and treat her like a stranger as he did in her dreams.

Pete wanted to buy Jocelyn a small congratulatory present for the opening, a crystal paperweight or a silver frame for the first menu, and Alice had agreed to drive him to Beverly Hills, to a store that sold such useless items. On Thursday, two days before the pending bash, she came home from work early. She stank as usual—the ammoniac tincture of urine and carnivore shit—but paused en route to the shower over a food magazine on the kitchen table that Pete had left open to a photograph of a red-and-yellow fishing boat on the blue-black Mediterranean.

She looked up at a light tap on the back door and watched the slow rotation of the glass knob, but the person who entered was not Pete.

"Nick," she said.

With a nod, he came inside, turning his back to close the door, then standing before her like a gentleman with his hat in his hand. Only he had no hat. Alice's fingers acquired a strange electrical buzz. The white tabletop stretched between them. Nick addressed her with a long, dark look. She noted its intended force, but did not feel it.

His beard was whiter—almost all white, in fact—and made him look older. He'd lost weight, too, and was haggard in the face. "You going to offer me a drink?" he said.

Alice opened the refrigerator. "There's wine in here somewhere." She smelled her rankness—boy, did she ever need a shower.

"When did you start drinking wine?"

She looked back over her shoulder. "You don't want any?"

"There's nothing stronger?"

"I'll see." She went into the dining room and crouched at the hutch, listening to herself panting. Yesterday, carrying a crated lemur from the medical center to its habitat, she'd heard the same sound of plain, unabashed fear. But she'd always felt this way around Nick.

She found the bottle of brandy she'd drunk from the night the deer came into the house. Pete had used some for cooking, and there was still half a bottle, but she didn't want Nick to have any. She reached past the sticky liqueurs dating from Aunt Kate's residency and grabbed a half-full quart of vodka. Nick preferred amber liquors, but this would have to do.

"God, I've missed that pouring hand." He took the drink and toasted her.

He *had* been fond of her, she realized. She *had* amused him.

"Did anyone ever tell you you've got the best pour in town?"

"You." Alice backed away, self-conscious about her smell.

He wore blue jeans and an acid-green cotton T-shirt that matched his eyes under a soft, coffee-brown leather jacket. Expensive, fancified farmer clothes. "Not going to join me?"

"No," she said. "I'm about to go out."

Half the vodka went in two gulps. He exhaled loudly, then smiled at her. "You look really good, Allie. Healthy."

"Thanks," she said in a whisper. "How are you doing?"

Nick tilted his glass. "Drinking too much. But that'll stop soon enough."

Alice thought she heard a car. Maybe Pete got a ride from the restaurant. She listened for a slammed door, a footfall. "This isn't a good time for me," she said. "I'm expecting someone."

"Pete?"

A general weakness washed through her. So he knew.

"You went and found yourself a mighty fine cook." Nick leaned against the tiled counter. "And it's just what the doctor ordered. You're beautiful."

The white enamel trembled between them, and the open magazine showing the bright boat and dark sea.

Alice whispered, "This is such a bad time . . ."

"Let me just say something, then I'll leave."

Of course he wanted to say something. God knows she deserved a talking-to. She'd been out of control. Obsessed. A stalker. She'd spied on his wife, sneaked onto the periphery of his life and set up camp. Made herself the girlfriend to his wife's business partner. Did she think this could go forever undiscovered, forever unremarked?

"I know you're with Pete, but I can't get this one idea out of my mind. It dogs me. I wake up with it. I go to sleep with it. I think—I hope—that once I've told you about it, once you know . . ." Nick squinted into his drink, then up at her.

"Okay," she said, and wished he'd hurry up.

"Sometimes it's just one image—a door opening. Sometimes it's more like a story, like I'll be in my truck, maybe alone, maybe with Thad. It's summer. We're up around Porterville. The hay's cut, the hills are gold. July, late June—hot."

"This is something that happened?"

"No, baby. Not yet."

Now she thought she did hear the front door open. "Nick." She held up a hand, but heard nothing further. "Sorry, go on."

He studied her face in silence.

"Please," she said. "I'm just nervous about Pete coming."

Frowning, Nick gazed at the floor, but his low voice started up again. "It's one of those afternoons. You know, thunderheads. Green air. Bugs screeching."

She knew those days, all right. She grew up in them. You didn't know whether to go inside or outside. The dogs, not knowing either, whined and whined.

Now, she felt like whining. Did he have to stretch it out like this?

"We're driving toward the mountains, along a river; the Tule or the Kaweah. Ground squirrels everywhere. Trees are showing the back side of leaves—it's about to rain. You can smell it . . ." Nick drank, and when he spoke again, his voice was lower still, and softer. "When we get to the foothills, the road gets smaller and smaller till it's just this weedy dirt drive curving through the oaks toward the river."

Alice practically had to hold her breath to hear him.

"There's a white wooden farmhouse with a deep porch and big shade trees. A couple of good-for-nothing dogs get up to greet us. And the screen door opens. A woman comes out of the house." He looked up into Alice's face. "You, Alice. It's always you. The door opens. You come out."

She held on to the back of a kitchen chair. *So I wasn't the only one who'd concocted scenarios.* A surge came, of triumph, vindication: *It wasn't all in my head.*

His low, fuzzy voice started in again, and she felt it in her muscles. "I'm asking, Alice, if you still have feelings for me . . ."

After the months of silence and rejection, now this. The disjuncture was too great for any immediate clarity. She might have gone to him, embraced him, gathered him up, been gathered, sinking into him, and doing so promised such enormous relief; but she stank. And she was embarrassed for him, a little. His daydream seemed so *Little House on the Prairie*, so set-dressed and sentimental. Really, it was just a variation on the I-Need-a-Good-Woman-to-Come-Home-To speech she'd heard, less artfully told, perhaps a dozen times. She used to want the part, desperately.

Imagine being that woman, tucked in some rural hideaway, waiting for her men to come home. As if she'd ever give up the zoo. Or Pete.

Nick waited, his eyes downcast.

Didn't he know this was all a dream? They'd had some connection, and all that bittersweet yearning; they'd been together in a way that briefly comforted, but then caused pain—such gratuitous pain.

Yet she wasn't ready to say the half dozen words that would send him away for good.

Nick roused himself, as if reading her mind. "You don't have to answer me now. Think it over." He started around the table, and Alice again drew back, but he wanted only the vodka beside her on the counter.

She watched as he filled his glass. "You told me to get on with my life, Nick," she said. "And I did."

"I had to take that chance. I had to give my marriage one last push. Or I wouldn't know what I know now. Even Jocelyn admits it's over this time."

"This time?"

"I moved out." He set the bottle on the counter. "I'm at the Red Lion in Glendale, with the Peterbilt reps and snap-on tool salesmen. I've got a suite on the eighth floor, great view of Burbank. Maybe you'll come see me there." He slammed the vodka, blew out sharply. "Jocelyn knows all about you, by the way—about us."

Guilt flashed through and around her, a harsh, nasty light.

"I'm sorry, baby," Nick said. "But there comes a time at the end of a marriage when the truth comes out. When it's a relief to finally speak it. That's how you know you've reached the very end."

"How is she?" Alice whispered. When he didn't answer, she raised her voice. "Is Jocelyn all right?"

"No-ho, baby." He shook his head. "She is not all right. She took it hard. She really likes you. A lot. *That* was a problem." He gave a mirthless laugh. "She doesn't care much for me, not right now."

"Well, Pete doesn't know a thing." She shoved the chair against the table. "I kept my mouth shut. Like you told me to." She turned, then, and walked out of the kitchen, through the breakfast nook and dining room, across the living room to the front door. Inasmuch as she had any intention, it was to leave the house and yard and neighborhood and keep going into the hills, into the landscape, as if she could grind herself into scrub and rock and dirt.

In the front doorway there was a darkening, and then Pete grabbed her shoulders. "What's wrong?" He shook her, almost roughly, to make her look at him. "Did someone else die?"

She pressed her forehead into his chest. He was already trembling, his panic torched by her obvious distress. "No, nobody died."

Nick must have followed her, because Pete then said, with surprise, "Nick?"

They were all three in the hall, Alice in the middle.

"What's going on?" said Pete. His voice—like the hands on her shoulders—quaked.

He should be calm, Alice thought, *calm and firm and in command, if only this once.*

"I was just leaving," Nick said.

And Alice, her eyes shut, pressed her body against Pete's to let him pass.

45

Really, whenever Pete thought about it, which was at least five hundred times a day, he almost had to admire Nick Lawton's timing and the near comprehensiveness of the destruction.

Jealousy howled at full bore, of course, but every bit as sickening was the depth of his own ignorance regarding another person, and therefore of every other person. He saw now that he'd never known anybody, not really, ever, which in a fundamental sense cast him eternally and unbearably alone.

That day, after Nick had left the house, Alice said, "I thought we'd die before anybody knew. Nick made me promise not to tell a soul."

That Alice would honor Nick's injunction over his right-to-know made Pete frantic with injustice. He had a right! He worked for Nick's wife. And he'd slept beside Alice for a hundred-plus nights, skin to trusting skin.

"I never dreamed he'd tell *Jocelyn*," Alice said. "Nick's the most secretive person I've ever met. He wouldn't even let me see his teeth!"

This stopped him. "Why wouldn't he let you see his teeth?"

"He has a roan incisor he's shy about." Alice said.

If they weren't at war, they might have laughed and riffed on this.

Pete then asked what to his mind was a logical question. "Are you guys going to live together now?"

"What do you think? What makes you even ask that?" She

was yelling and crying. "If that's what you think, just leave! Go on! Get out!"

He did want to leave, if only to let things settle, to get away and find his bearings. Accordingly, he stood and started walking.

"Where are you going?"

He had no idea, but he couldn't stop.

"Don't do this, Pete. Please don't go."

"I can't think," he said over his shoulder. "I'm too upset."

"If you leave now . . ."

He hadn't stayed to hear the rest of the threat. And if he hadn't heard it, was it still valid?

At any rate, Pete had to be rational. Nick Lawton was a handsome, desirable, manly man. Any woman would want him. Certainly more than she would ever want Pete Ross. Even Alice. *Especially* Alice. Why should *she* settle for damaged goods? Why take the teetering, cowardly fat boy when you can have an apex of American manhood, the cowpoke with bucks, the Marlboro Man with smarts and a six-figure salary? Pete himself had always wanted to be the strong, silent type. Except he couldn't keep silent.

And he'd liked Nick Lawton, the power of the man, the self-sufficiency, the dark gravity. Pete wasn't self-sufficient, or magnetic. Pete was a barely reformed Mama's boy with a dependency on SRIs and an expensive psychiatrist, his morning constitutional and exercise-induced endorphins.

He spent the night at his apartment for the first time in weeks. Sitting perfectly still was a help. He got up once—forced himself to—and phoned La Plage, left a message on Jocelyn's voice mail. "Are you okay? Call, if you want, or I'll see you tomorrow." She did not call. Nobody called.

In the morning he dressed, went into work and waited, his door open.

Jocelyn came in an hour later. "I assume you had no idea," she'd said.

"None," said Pete.

"God help us. And now? Did she go back to him?"

"I don't know," said Pete.

And then they had no choice but to finish preparations for tomorrow's party, rehearse the staff, get ready to act as if they weren't gutshot.

Sometimes Pete thought that in fact Nick's timing had saved them.

An hour before drinks were to be served, Jocelyn came into his office and handed him a wrapped-up box. It was flat and heavy, as if filled with lead handkerchiefs. Taking it, he remembered that he and Alice had been headed, that awful Thursday, to buy Jocelyn a gift as well.

He lifted the lid to find a set of Georg Jensen marrow spoons. Pyramid pattern, of course. Twelve of them. A fuckin' fortune in marrow spoons. Not that Jocelyn had ever seen the matching Wren Street sterling; he'd mentioned it, though, on more than one occasion, and she had paid attention.

"I bought them before we knew," Jocelyn said. "You can exchange them. Or pawn them."

"Never," he said. "They're perfect. Thank you very much."

"You know what's most fucked?" Jocelyn wore an apron over a beautiful full-length, toffee-colored dress. "The revising. It's like I have to go back over everything and see things for what they really were—the late jobs, the times he slammed out of the house and stayed gone most of the night, a hundred incidents I didn't even know I remembered. But they're coming back . . . one at a time."

"I know," Pete said, though his own process seemed far less precise, more like the slow churning of a black, tarry plasm with the occasional nauseating freefall.

Jocelyn's hair was piled on her head. She was beautifully made up for the party, and gaunt with fury. "I thought Alice was just shy—that she was the one person who wasn't going to hit me up to read her screenplay or introduce her to my agent." She paused. "Have you talked to her?"

He ran his fingers down the concave silver scoops. "Not a word."

The La Plage dining room, with its teak walls and warm gray booths and light-diffusing sconces, improved with the addition of people. The design still struck Pete as corporate, a room where suits and pearls were shown to best advantage. A thick greenish wall of glass divided dining room from kitchen. Through the glass you could see the stainless-steel wood-fired rotisserie twirling shanks and trussed birds.

Yesterday, at their usual Friday session, Freeman had coached a stunned, barely speaking Pete in the only things he had to say to guests. "Thank you for coming," "Eat something," "Enjoy yourself."

Pete and Jocelyn opened the doors at six o'clock sharp, greeted everyone, raised their glasses in toasts and made sure the oysters and cod cakes were passed, the champagne and Pellegrino poured.

Helen arrived with an older professorial type whose name Pete didn't catch. "Thank you for coming," he told them. Alice's boss Foster also came and, having not heard the news, asked after her. Pete snagged a glass of champagne and, handing it to Foster, directed him to Helen. "Please, have some food, enjoy yourself." Most terrifying was a cameo by Dr. Freeman himself, who shook Pete's hand, then Jocelyn's, then strolled around, ate hors d'oeuvres and shook Pete's hand again. "Thank you for coming," Pete said, the doctor's departure affording him such relief that for a moment he confused it with happiness.

Two nights later, La Plage opened to the public. A soft opening with no publicity or press releases. A three-day run before Thanksgiving, then a day off, then the weekend. This was Pete's idea, to give his staff a chance to work up their routines. He and Jocelyn came to work at ten in the morning. His office was off the kitchen; hers was upstairs. They talked on the speakerphone and ate lunch together in the dining room, amid many papers.

He spent Thanksgiving at the Bread Basket, where from eleven until four they fed anyone who showed up, about a hundred people in all. The next day, he phoned the management company that handled his apartment and renewed the lease for another six months.

One of the dishwashers had a wife who did housekeeping work, so Pete, who could stand only so much bachelor squalor, hired her on a weekly basis. He'd applied to have his driver's license reinstated, and when the approval came through, the line cook with all the tattoos drove Pete to the DMV, where he passed the written test and had his picture taken. Wt. 227. Downright svelte.

Before going in to work one morning, he walked from his apartment to the car dealerships on Brand Boulevard in Glendale and managed to purchase, with minimum contempt toward the garrulous trash-talking salesman, a brand-new, last-year's-model Toyota truck. White. No radio. Air-conditioning a must. Cash on the barrelhead, compliments of Jocelyn, as he needed to drive to farmer's markets all over the city. Which he then proceeded to do.

La Plage had been open three weeks when the *Times* restaurant critic came in. Two line cooks recognized her from other places they'd worked. Pete had never seen her before, though the former one had been a staunch supporter of Trotwood and Peggotty. This new critic was small and gray-haired; dressed in a Chinese worker's shirt, she wore horn-rimmed glasses and looked more bookish than like any kind of sensualist. Her husband ordered a lovely Alsatian white, and brought two bottles of red of his own. Their choices, Pete saw, were excellent. La Plage was far too young to review, but there would probably be a short write-up based on this early visit.

The food he cooked was superb, Pete knew, although he personally couldn't taste a thing. For weeks now, everything he put in his mouth had the same scorched flavor, occasionally rinsed in the pale, salty taste of tears.

During those first weeks, he began to see Jocelyn differently. Before, she'd been hesitant and careful in her decisions, sometimes to a maddening degree, and then would heedlessly give in to pushy vendors. Pete thought she'd never settle on a logo, or a china pattern, or carpets for the lounge area; she drove poor Ivo half mad, having him hump rug after rug from his Glendale store. But once the restaurant was opened, Jocelyn simply worked. Serving as general manager, she handled the front of the house, the public, the waitstaff, the general upkeep. For someone who'd never run a restaurant before, she had a good sense of priorities and, most of all, knew when she needed help. Luckily, Cliff and the sommelier had substantial management experience. Pete was also impressed by her endless patience and low-key camaraderie with the sleek young hostesses, the awestruck busboys, the gaping line cooks. She took meals with them, endless burgers, bowls of soup and grilled cheese sandwiches. And she spent the hours from 3 to 6 p.m. with her son every day.

Both she and Pete had Helen on their speed dial.

"I still can't tell, exactly, what happened with Alice," he told Helen. "So I have no idea what, exactly, I should do."

"Then sit tight," Helen said. "Let things unfold. Pay attention. Let your own coast clear. You'll know what to do soon enough."

Pete also reported a troubling new development in his meditation—a darkness flickering in the corner of his eyes. At Woodview, detoxing Valium addicts had complained of such dartings in their peripheral vision, and often slapped the air beside their heads. But he wasn't a Valium addict.

"Oh, I know that flickering well," Helen told him. "That's anger. So this is good, very good. You're angry. Which seems completely appropriate."

Pete sat on his meditation pillow and let his thoughts rage and ebb and sneak back, poisonous and seductive. He was building a case against Alice partly because she hadn't called, and partly because even if she did return to him, he despaired of having lost that mad pitch of pure, happy affection they'd capered in all fall. "But what should I do about this anger?" he asked Helen a week or so later.

"Be present for it. Let it pass."

"Is that *all*?"

"Don't you have work to do? A restaurant to run? Left foot, right foot, Pete. You'll get to where you're going."

On a Wednesday in mid-December, Pete went to Encino and sat in a room with his ex-wife and their his-'n'-hers lawyers. The next morning at eight o'clock, he drove to the courthouse in downtown Los Angeles. In the lobby he met Anne, and together they went to the clerk. Anne gave their case number and asked to have it advanced. They were directed to the elevator and rode it to the sixth floor, where they checked in with the bailiff. "We're here to have a stay-away order lifted," she said.

They sat on plastic chairs, Anne in an off-white gabardine suit with a pale blue T-shirt, Pete in khakis and a wrinkled white dress shirt. The district attorney came up and spoke to them. "Do you feel safe?" he asked Anne. "Do you feel you can adequately protect yourself and the child if there's more trouble?" Pete stared into the beige linoleum, at its thin, streaky clouds and darker flecks. Anne answered yes, and yes. "There is still a criminal protective order in effect," the D.A. said. "If things start to escalate, don't wait until there's a crime. Call this number right away." He tapped a sheet of paper, handed it to her and moved on. They proceeded to a bench in the courtroom proper, and Pete concentrated on the grain in the wooden bench in front of them, which reminded him of pews, of Morton. His knees, damn them, were bouncing like pistons. He breathed. Anne touched his arm. The judge had called their names.

That Sunday, he drove to Anne's new ranch-style home in the hills and knocked on the front door. His son answered. Garrett at six was a taller, somehow flintier version of his four-year-old self. He had tawny skin and the quick, dark eyes of his paternal grandfather, Gabrielo Rosales. Anne managed to smile at Pete, and wished both father and son a good time.

Their itinerary, devised in advance, was well-known to both parties: a Claymation movie followed by pizza at Garrett's favorite restaurant. Going to the movie was, Pete realized, a smart idea (Anne's) in that they could sit by each other without having to speak and thus get used to each other's presence. After an hour, Pete began to relax. Then he heard his son's laughter, a surprised chortle at some pratfall on the screen.

Too much, Pete thought. *Too much.* He gasped for air in the dark room, felt dwarfed by twenty-foot cartoon creatures, and yearned for daylight, oxygen and wide-open space. Yet he did not flee. He kept to his seat, in case Garrett laughed again.

After the show, in a red booth at Barone's Family Restaurant, surrounded by families and older couples, Pete said, "You doing okay, Garrett? Anything you want to say? Anything you want to know?"

Garrett toyed with his silverware and rolled up the scalloped edges of his place mat. "Are you better, Dad?" he said. When Pete didn't answer right away, he added, "Mom said you were sick."

Sick. Years of random detail flooded Pete. The strongest image—a tent-and-box city teeming with homeless men, women and children—was a place he'd never actually been. "I'm much better, sweetheart," he said. "And thank you, very much, for asking."

He was making up the kitchen schedule in his office one afternoon. The dining room was set for dinner, dinner prep was in full swing. Jocelyn was with Thad at some play date or music lesson. Pete sorted through Post-its of requests stuck on his door by his employees. One wanted this night off, another wanted more shifts, another needed to leave early on such and such a date. The holidays were complicating everyone's schedule. Someone in the kitchen was whistling "Red River Valley," and there was banging on the back door. He filled in another calendar day, hopefully making everybody happy; the schedule was like an ever-shifting puzzle, with too few pieces or else too many. He was peeling another Post-it off the page when, from behind, someone grabbed his arm, pulling his hand off the diary.

Alice: crying and grabbing, saying his name as if calling him back from a remote, dangerous place.

He rotated in his chair and grasped her wrists. "Hey, hey, hey," he said. She crumpled to her knees and wrapped her arms around his calves, roaring into his thigh. "Aunt Kate had a stroke," she cried. "And now she's dead. And I can't wait anymore, or pretend not to care, or give you room, or whatever the fuck I'm supposed to be doing. I can't. I don't want to. Please come back to me, Pete. *Please.* I can't stand this for another minute."

46

After the grand opening of La Plage took place without her, Alice discovered that she felt unmistakable relief. The truth was out. And now that at least some of it was out, the rest followed, almost in spite of herself.

She told Helen, "I only came to your services to spy on Jocelyn. At first anyway."

"Let me ask you this," Helen said. "Did you get anything else out of them?"

"Of course," said Alice. "Like my whole life."

"Well," Helen said, "it takes what it takes."

To Aunt Kate, she said, "I've been taking pages from your wastebasket and reading them."

They were having Thanksgiving dinner together in the Beverly Manor dining room. Aunt Kate looked up from her plate, startled. "Whatever for?"

"I—we, Mom and I—had the idea to collect them, and publish a book of them, to surprise you with it. But maybe it wouldn't be such a nice surprise."

"A book made up of trash?" said Aunt Kate. "What a horrifying prospect."

"I'm sorry," Alice said. "I felt bad for going behind your back."

"And I feel bad you had to read such rubbish!"

"It's not rubbish! It's wonderful."

"Yes?" Aunt Kate cocked her head, wanting to hear more.

"Really, I loved everything I read." Alice had planned the

conversation only so far, and as of now she was improvising. "I'd like to read the whole book, whatever you have of it, but I don't want to steal it."

Aunt Kate removed her glasses and pinched the bridge of her nose. "Oh dear," she said. "I suppose it's time . . ." She put her glasses back on and poked at a slice of turkey with her fork. "I'll tell you what. I'll read it to you out loud."

I deserve this, thought Alice, *and more.*

The first session lasted over three hours, during which Aunt Kate read half a dozen pages and rambled on about each character and incident—exactly as Alice had feared. Some good came out of it, though. Her aunt was too tired to read again for days, and when ready to resume, she said, "I must pace myself. I can't go for more than an hour." She stuck to this, and for the next few weeks, when Alice came home from the zoo, she showered and went directly to the Beverly Manor. Once, Aunt Kate was too deep in a rewrite to read, and another time she was stuck in the 1880s, grilling Alice about her married life with William. Otherwise Alice stretched out on the bed and listened.

Having embarked on these sessions as penance, she found both the novel and the explanatory digressions bearable and even pleasurable, once a reasonable time limit was established. Certainly it was the most coherent Jamesiana she'd been privy to in recent months. One afternoon, she asked if she could record the readings.

"As if I'm another medium?" said Aunt Kate. "I think not." But the next day she said, "Where's your tape recorder?"

On several occasions, she said, "Alice, dear, this is such a help. You'll never know how much it means to me."

Who knew how little it would take.

Alice arrived on one chilly mid-December evening to find her in bed.

"Read Chapter Five yourself." Aunt Kate pointed to a manuscript draped over the typewriter. "I'm feeling fatigued."

"I'll wait," Alice said, sitting down on the bed. "You can read it to me tomorrow. But we should talk about how you want to publish this. You could hire a freelance editor to go through it—or I'd be happy to do what I can."

"I wouldn't want to saddle you with anything, but I'd love to keep it in the family. You know, after Henry Senior died, William edited a selection of his writing. It proved a very good thing for William to do. He'd disparaged his father's work when the old man was alive—and deservedly so. Henry Senior was not a rigorous or very interesting thinker. He made all kinds of pompous, silly pronouncements, and often contradicted himself. Going through his father's papers, though, William found some things to admire—and he was also in a position to excise Henry Senior's most egregious effusions. Editing your father! An act of love and revenge in equal measure!" She gave her niece a wry, meaningful look. "The end product, however, was William's first book. It broke the publishing barrier for him. It didn't sell at all, of course, but only William expected otherwise. In the editing process, he'd formed a new respect and affection for his father, and naturally expected the book to inspire the same in others. But the truth of the matter, Alice, is that Henry Senior was a blowhard and a bore—and I'm afraid my own work has more in common—"

"Oh, Aunt Kate, you're not anything like—"

"Nevertheless—and this is the point I want to make—the whole editing endeavor proved very beneficial to William: he was able to get his father out of his system and move on to his own destiny." She smiled and wagged her finger at her. "I can only hope, my dear, that my poor book might have such a salutary effect on you!"

She had a stroke that night, and was taken by ambulance to a hospital in Glendale. Alice joined her there and held her hand, waiting out the eternities between each breath. Sometimes her aunt's hands would pull away and scrabble around on the sheets, and her legs would jump, her breathing become raspy and frantic. Alice would call the nurse then, but these episodes passed. Aunt Kate never regained consciousness, and around two in the afternoon, the breath Alice awaited never came.

Helen performed her second funeral at the Wren Street house on the Saturday afternoon before Christmas. Alice's parents came down from Lime Cove for the night, and four second cousins arrived from the Bay Area. Alice's brothers, busy with work and children, sent flowers and regrets. Pete prepared a brunch for the mourners, then left for the restaurant. Saturday was La Plage's busiest night.

Cara had given Alice a week's compassionate leave, but she didn't know what to do with herself and went back to the zoo two days after the funeral. Coming home after that first day, she found a thick envelope from Foster slipped through the mail slot in her front door. "I hesitated, at the funeral, to give you this," he wrote in a cover note. "But then I thought you might find it comforting. I did." It was more of the automatic writer's close-knit pages.

I do not recall the exact moment of passing over. Rather, I found myself viewing the room from a new perspective, and feeling better than I had in a long time.

Alice came in with a pitcher of milk and set it atop the dresser. She came toward me, yet her attention was fastened upon a point below. I could see only the top of her dear gray head. I desired to report on my abrupt recovery, but I was stuck at the strangest altitude, and she would not look up.

Alice commenced to moan dreadfully; I saw then that she held a man in her arms, some frail-limbed, lifeless fellow who, I realized, could only be myself. Henry came inside the room, and from his ashen face, I fully understood that I had crossed over.

I was desperate to convey my perceptions to them, but they paid me no mind. She wept and stroked the lifeless body on the bed. Stately Henry stood there, shaken, at a loss. Whereas I soon could move about at will, and with remarkable ease—I who only days before was carried from the steamer because my feet had swollen to a hideous size. Now, light as a fly, I was inclined to caper and exhult that my dyspnea and aortic distress had so absolutely subsided.

The house filled up; Billy motored up with the Tulley girl, Aleck arrived by train. Harry—oh responsible one—came somewhat later, having met first with the bankers.

My new form, or formlessness as it were, had no appreciable effect on others. They did not see me; indeed, I could pass through them—how loud the heart beats and the juices slosh; the blink of an eye crashes like the felling of a giant sequoia! Only this: on the humid summer night, I incited Peggy to rub her arms for warmth.

In the next few days, I observed my own material remains transmogrified by flames, most of me interred in the family plot in Boston and the rest scattered in the woods at Chocorua, the children digging into the urn with silver spoons and somberly sifting Papa into the crosshatch of pine needles on the forest floor.

Thus does a fellow sink from the foreground to the background, and become mere speckage on the ever-shifting canvas wherein he once figured prominently. If this sounds mournful, it is not; there is a great easing in the passage; indeed one wonders how we rallied so continuously and strenuously, with such heat and heart, to what now appears least significant of all: the this and the that, the here and the there, the now and the then of our paltry lives. All that gratuitous particularity! All relations—the keen affinity of the mountain for the mineral; the tree for its chlorophyll, the husband for his wife— are happily subsumed into seamless, continuous, ever dynamic reconfigurings, each pattern weaving, widening or constricting into the one which succeeds it, with the truth of every moment lying just beyond itself . . .

47

It counts as an honor to cut up a euthanized hippopotamus. Most volunteers would never hear of such proceedings, let alone be allowed to help. But Alice was invited to both attend the death and assist with the dismemberment. "They're trying you out," Cara said. Though she was hardly in the mood to confront the frank realities of physiological existence, any trace of squeamishness—whatever the excuse—was the sort of thing that could wreck her future chances.

Four of them worked through the morning and into the afternoon. Some parts had to be sent to research labs, others to schools, and the bulk was packed into heavy-gauge black garbage bags for manageable disposal. The deceased animal was an old male who hadn't been able to stand for days. For twelve years he'd had the same keeper, who was there for the euthanasia, insisted on it, but afterward her boss told her to go take care of her other hippos. After all, habitats still needed cleaning, the live animals needed feeding; zoo life didn't stop because an old hippo went down.

It was past three by the time they finished up. Alice checked on her baby rhino, fed her a turnip and rubbed her gums until the long black eyelashes lowered in bliss. Then she called Pete and—craving the sheer, sizable fact of him—asked him to meet her. "I smell bad," she cautioned, "like blood." After hanging up, she shed her boots and coveralls, hung them in her locker and scrubbed her arms and face.

Burton, an elderly security guard, was manning the back

gate and she lingered for a moment by his golf cart. "You hurry on home," he said. "Gets dark fast in the park. These days are awfully short."

The shortest of the year.

Then his walkie-talkie crackled, and Alice waved as he drove off. The sun already had slid behind the park's mountainous hump, but an hour would pass before true darkness fell. She set off down the service road between the zoo and golf course, where shadows seeped into the manicured grass and enormous shade trees and oblong sand traps. The sycamores were bare now, their trunks a vivid white, their branches an intricate fractal lace. Mist gathered in the fens.

Down the road, a cream-colored car nosed up the hill, some extravagantly designed relic of the early sixties, a Chrysler Newport Imperial or Continental. Somebody lost, or exploring. There was a sign, OFFICIAL VEHICLES ONLY, at the foot of the road, which was supposed to keep people out even when the gate was open. Kids were driving those old boats these days, and Alice hoped this one didn't contain a group of teenage boys who, when far from parental jurisdiction, were often reflexively cruel. But when the car crested a rise, she saw just a single driver, an older woman, small and intent—so small, in fact, that she could barely see over the steering wheel.

Alice stepped to the side of the road, thinking the car would pass, but it stopped alongside her and the tinted electric window lowered.

"Excuse me," the woman said. Her steel-colored hair was pulled back in a bun, and she wore thick-lensed glasses that magnified her blue eyes. "Is there some sort of zoo office up this road?"

"Not exactly." Alice checked to see if Burton had returned to his station, but his golf cart was nowhere in sight. "What did you need?"

"I'm looking for a zoo person. I need help with an animal."

"I work for the zoo," Alice said. "What kind of an animal?"

"I was just now driving down Bronson Canyon, and I hit a deer."

Alice stepped closer to see if the woman showed any sign of injury, a bump on the head or a cut. "Are you okay?"

"I'm fine. You're very kind to ask. But the deer, I'm afraid, is not."

"Did you kill it, or was it just injured?"

"Oh, I'm afraid I killed it."

Alice walked to the front of the car, but the bumper looked fine. She came back to the driver's window. "Here's what you do. When you get home, look up animal regulation in your phone book. It's listed under city offices. Tell them where you hit the deer, and they'll go pick it up."

"But I have it with me," the woman said.

The backseat was an expanse of spotless beige upholstery.

"In the trunk," she added.

"You have the deer in your trunk?"

"I didn't know what else to do," the woman said.

She was tiny—the hand on the steering wheel child-sized at best, more like a doll's. "How did you get it in there?"

"I had one of those strength surges, I guess. I just did it." The woman gestured toward the rear of her car. It was, in fact, a Continental. "Do you want to see?"

Having already cut up and bagged a hippo, this didn't seem so daunting a task, though Alice couldn't quite believe the deer would prove real. Was it a phantom, she wondered, and this just another "episode" she was having—or had she wandered into the small woman's episode? Then again, maybe she'd hit one of those little goat-sized gazelles that escaped from the zoo years ago and still lived in the park. "Let's have a look," Alice said.

The woman turned off the engine, stepped out and was even smaller than Alice first thought, not even five feet. They walked to the rear of the car and the woman unlocked the trunk, which sprang open heavily, but only about an inch. Alice had to lift it up. And sure enough, there was fur, brown and bristly, and a tangle of legs and hooves, the head at an awkward angle. The one visible eye was bright and shiny. Alice, taking a good, deep look into it, stepped back and yanked the tiny woman with her at the very instant the front legs started slicing the air. For a long moment, the deer performed a kind of frantic, upturned bug dance, accompanied by a shrill and familiar snorting. Then one hoof found the lip of the trunk, and from this single contact point, with much more scrambling than grace, the doe somehow pivoted about, pushed back to leap, but ended up tumbling onto the pavement.

She is *hurt,* Alice thought.

The doe sprang to her feet then and shivered, as if surprised to find all four feet on the ground. She took a step, and another, then set off at a tentative trot. Following the fence downhill, she gained speed and, taking a cart path, swerved into the golf course and pranced prettily across the fairway. A golfer waved his iron at her and she began to run flat out, sailing across sand traps, then over a steel barricade—nothing to it—and up onto the hillside.

Alice and the woman watched until she was out of sight.

The small woman's face, with those magnified eyes, was a portrait of surprise. "I guess I only stunned it," she said.

48

He'd prepped all afternoon, so the exercise and fresh air were balms, and he wouldn't need to get back to work until six or so. Besides, Alice had sounded thoroughly stressed and asked for him. These days, with each other, they were still so halting and gentle.

"I'm going to meet Alice at the zoo," he told Jocelyn, who'd received the news of their rapprochement quietly.

Pete had told her right away, since he felt that she, too, had a right to know, and for that she was grateful. "I'm glad for you," she'd said. "And also, a little bit, for me." Not that she and Nick were going to reconcile. They now communicated only through lawyers.

Rain had finally come several weeks ago, and a green fuzz of sprouting grass carpeted the hills. Taking the long way, over hill and dale, Pete smelled loam and dampness and pine.

Today, La Plage had its first notice in the *Times*, a "First Impression" by the restaurant critic. *Chef Peter Ross is back at his lyric, wide-ranging best, producing inventive dishes with big, clear flavors.* She also remarked that the food was *extremely expensive*, the room *coolly formal*, yet expressed pleasure in being greeted by *Jocelyn Nearing herself*, who, *all told, has created a lovely, impressive new restaurant*.

Pete, too, was impressed. Jocelyn could've easily gone flooey. The morning after the opening, he told her, "You could fall to pieces for a day or two. There's time. I sure wouldn't blame you." He realized, of course, that he was also talking to himself.

"I've been in pieces for years," Jocelyn answered. "Over stupid things. I've used up my torn-to-pieces-hood."

Pete took the bridle trail down toward the merry-go-round, through the mentholated air of a eucalyptus grove. Water trickled in the streambeds, and the muddy, leaf-choked banks were a slick, rich brown. He thought about his mother in her rain-marinated convent and no longer felt instant panic, only the dull ache of anger and a first hint of pity. "She's always been tightly wrapped," Freeman had recently said, as if this were a matter of fact. "The whole time I've known her and, I'm sure, for years before that. I'd bet she was an uptight, unhappy little girl." What a novel idea: Mom unhappy even before Pete came along.

She had yet to write a single word to Alice. Whereas Jocelyn, of all people, had sent a card: *I was so sad to hear about Aunt Kate.*

He was pleased, walking to meet her, that they were together again, sleeping side by side. Things were quieter this time between them, more serious. The heady play had stopped, and that was okay. For the time being, Pete didn't mind the solemnity.

So he had a girlfriend again, one who'd spent the day chopping up a hippopotamus. Not many men have such luck.

Movement on the hill called him back into the fragrant, cool, darkening day. A deer was springing over bushes in high, lovely arcs like so many short bursts of flight. He stopped to watch until the deer topped the ridge and disappeared down the other side.

Pete patted his pocket for a pen, to no avail.

He'd just have to remember, then, to put venison on the menu.

Acknowledgments

While some of the persons mentioned in this book are historical figures, all of the main players are purely imagined and any resemblance to someone living is wholly coincidental. The novel's setting is loosely based on an existing neighborhood, but I have distorted it at will with imaginary elements and unrealistic distances. The story itself is a fiction.

William James has been the subject of countless books and studies, many of which were helpful to the writing of *Jamesland*. In particular: *Genuine Reality: A Life of William James*, by Linda Simon; *William James Remembered*, edited by Linda Simon; *William James: The Center of His Vision*, by Daniel W. Bjork; *The James Family*, by F. O. Matthiessen; *The Jameses*, by R. W. B. Lewis; *Alice James: A Biography*, by Jean Strouse; and *The Book of James (William James, That Is)*, by Susy Smith.

I am also indebted to *Griffith Park: A Centennial History*, by Mike Eberts, and *Survival? Body, Mind and Death in the Light of Psychic Experience*, by David Lorimer.

A number of people generously lent their expertise and experience to this book. The Reverend Brandy Lovely, Kathy Klohr, and the Reverend Nicole Reilley spoke to me frankly about ministry; Margy Rochlin about aging actresses. Bernadette Murphy introduced me to Lancaster, Pam Ore to the work at zoos. Tracy Sullivan provided legal technicalities, Kate Schmidt the details of physical training. Russ Rymer and George Sumner supplied anecdote and wit.

I owe much to the book's exacting first readers: Mary Corey, Susan Faludi, Vanessa Place, Mona Simpson, and Lily Tuck.

Many thanks to Amber Qureshi and Abby Weintraub at Knopf.

ACKNOWLEDGMENTS

A generous award from the Mrs. Giles Whiting Foundation was deeply encouraging and appreciated.

As ever, my boundless gratitude goes to Maxine Groffsky and Gary Fisketjon.

ALSO BY MICHELLE HUNEVEN

"Huneven has fashioned a sexy, moving, and (mostly) unsentimental novel about romantic folly that takes place in the most improbable of settings: a drunk farm. . . . Imagine Magic Mountain *for alkies."* —Esquire

ROUND ROCK

Combining the rueful slapstick of Richard Russo, the affectionate gaze of John Irving, and the insight, warmth, and grit of Pam Houston, Michelle Huneven has written a wise, generous, and captivating novel. The setting is Rito, California, where water is known to run uphill and human lives go gloriously awry. Rito is where Red Ray, a wildly self-destructive drunk, finally got sober and built his Round Rock, a halfway house where other shipwrecked persons could do the same.

Among Red's charges is Lewis Fletcher, a man as burnt out on alcohol as he is on graduate school. Both Lewis and Red are drawn to Libby Law, whose wayward husband abandoned her in Rito like "a litter of kittens." As these and other credibly nicked and dented specimens of humanity struggle for love and self-acceptance, Michelle Huneven constructs a work of believable complexity, irresistible charm, and unblinking truthfulness, overall a laugh-out-loud comedy for the heartbroken.

Fiction/Literature/0-679-77616-8

VINTAGE CONTEMPORARIES
Available at your local bookstore, or call toll-free to order:
1-800-793-2665 (credit cards only)